# JUST A TASTE

---

CRYSTAL KASWELL

# Copyright

This is a work of fiction. Similarities to real people, places, or events are entirely coincidental.

JUST A TASTE
Copyright © 2019 Crystal Kaswell.
Written by Crystal Kaswell.
Cover by Najla Qamber Designs

Contains portions of Sing Your Heart Out © 2015, quoted with permission.

*for Pete*
*thanks for the career*
*XO*

## Also by Crystal Kaswell

### *Sinful Serenade*
*Sing Your Heart Out* - Miles
*Strum Your Heart Out* - Drew
*Rock Your Heart Out* - Tom
*Play Your Heart Out* - Pete
*Sinful Ever After* – series sequel

### *Dangerous Noise*
*Dangerous Kiss* - Ethan
*Dangerous Crush* – Kit
*Dangerous Rock* – Joel
*Dangerous Fling* – Mal
*Dangerous Encore* - series sequel

### *Inked Hearts*
*Tempting* - Brendon
*Hooking Up* - Walker
*Pretend You're Mine* - Ryan
*Hating You, Loving You* - Dean
*Breaking the Rules* - Hunter
*Losing It* - Wes
*Accidental Husband* - Griffin
*The Baby Bargain* - Chase

### *Inked Love*

*The Best Friend Bargain* - Forest — coming in 2019

### *Standalones*

*Broken* - Trent & Delilah

*Come Undone* - A Love Triangle

### *Dirty Rich*

*Dirty Deal* - Blake

*Dirty Boss* - Nick

Sign up for the Crystal Kaswell mailing list

## About This Book

I have everything I should want. Only the thrill is gone. My days are grey.

Until I meet Meg. The inexperienced college student is a breath of fresh air. Sassy, sexy, completely unimpressed by me. She hates my cocky grin. She huffs at my one-liners. And when she asks if I have some place better to put my mouth...

I make her an offer. Her place, my place, any place, as long as I can make her groan all night long. I'm as surprised as she is when she says yes. Who would have guessed that booksmart, guarded, gorgeous as all hell Meg would want me to be her first?

We keep it simple. Three rules to protect both of us.

No feelings, no secrets, no falling in love.

But some things are easier said than done.

From the author: *Just a Taste* is a smoking hot enemies to friends with benefits to lovers romance with all the heat, humor, and heart you crave. Come see why readers say "no one writes broken bad boys like Crystal Kaswell." Please note this book is a retelling of *Sing Your Heart Out* from Miles Webb's POV.

## Chapter One

MILES

The music journalist has a straight face.

If anything, he's overly earnest.

He holds his pen to his notebook as if he's about to record every word that flows from my lips.

As if we're not on camera.

As if he works for the *New York Times* and not for some MTV knockoff video blog.

Fuck, I don't care where the man works.

I can't take another bullshit question.

I barely manage a smile. "Lyrics *come* to me."

He tilts his head to one side, not at all catching the double meaning.

It's not my finest work, but I've had an ass full of this bullshit.

The guy clears his throat. "There are no love songs on the album. How do you think your fans feel about that?"

"Love isn't my thing."

"But you must have your fans' interests in mind…"

I look to the camera with a smile and run my hand

through my wavy hair. "I put what I feel on paper, then Drew, Pete, and Tom help me turn those words into sound. That's what our fans want."

"Would you write a love song?"

Damn, he's green. It's difficult keeping a straight face here. "I don't plan out what I'm going to write."

"But on the first Sinful Serenade E.P.—"

"Those songs weren't about love."

Confusion spreads over his face. I don't blame him. I'm a bad interviewee at the moment.

From his spot on the sidelines, Tom glares. Though our drummer isn't really a sidelines kind of guy. Tom laps up fame. He's as well-known as I am, and I'm the face of the band.

All right, Tom, message received.

Attention offstage is the price I pay for attention onstage. It comes with doing vocals.

It didn't use to bother me. Not when I…

Well, I don't have time to get into that.

I shoot the camera a panty-melting look. "I write a song when there's something stuck in my head that won't get out."

The guy finally gets it. He leans back with a smile. "How does it feel, your video hitting number one?"

"Feels like a lot of women are dying to see me naked."

"And your song sticking in the Top 40 for weeks?"

"Feels like a lot of women want to hear me moan."

The guy nods. "This album has been getting great reviews. How do you feel, everyone claiming that Sinful Serenade is the next big thing?"

Can this guy start a question with something other than how do you feel?

I didn't sign up for therapy. I've been through enough of that for one lifetime.

Fuck, this is bullshit. But I have a job to do here. At least this is true. "We want to make music, period. We're always going to be there, playing, whether the crowd is ten people or ten thousand."

The guy nods, happy with the footage. "Thank you so much for coming in, Miles. It's been great talking to you."

He's not selling that story. I shake his hand anyway.

The director calls cut. I shift off my stool and move away from the bright lights pointed at my eyes.

There isn't much room in this tiny studio. The director and the journalist are on one side of the room, checking the footage on their digital video camera.

Tom is standing in the other, shooting me the evil eye. His dirty blond hair falls over his green eyes as he shakes his head. "Fuck, Miles. I thought you made my life difficult."

"I showed up, didn't I?"

He looks toward the director, then his gaze comes back to me. "Women hear you groaning about all that pain in your soul, and they fall in love with the idea of fixing the broken bad boy."

"And?"

"Give them more to use. They'll fucking enjoy it."

"I'm not talking about that."

He shoots me an obviously not that look.

"I'm not bullshitting our fans."

"Yeah, it's bullshit? You don't write those miserable songs because there's too much pain in your soul?" He mimes tearing his heart out of his chest. "You don't stay up at night, staring out the tour bus window, wondering if some girl will ever see into your soul?"

"Not when I have you, Sticks." I press my first two fingers together. "You and I are like this. You see every bit of pain in my soul."

He rolls his eyes. "Fuck off, asshole."

"You started it."

"And I'm the immature one?"

I nod.

He stares back at me. "You want to be successful or not?"

"What do you call this?"

Tom huffs. "A start." He runs a hand through his sandy hair. "You've got money. Good for you. Unless you're gonna spread it around, lay off the sanctimonious bullshit. Me, Pete, and Drew have to eat."

Tom hasn't wanted for anything but fame, fans, and adoration in a long, long time.

He's the one being an asshole.

Not that I expect anything else.

I shoot him my sweetest smile. "I'll play up the broken bad boy thing if you skip sex for a month."

He laughs. "You go first."

He doesn't stand a chance. He's already thinking about inviting the makeup girl over. Hard to blame him. She's hot. Red hair. Nice tits. A tight dress that shows off her cute ass.

But the way she's looking at us—*Ooooh, another rock star to fill my quota.* It's more bullshit.

Sudden fame is supposed to be fun.

Women throwing themselves at my feet is supposed to be fun.

But I didn't get into writing songs for more bullshit.

The hair stylist, a short brunette in an equally tight dress, waves hello. Her pink lips curl into a smile.

Her eyes fix on mine.

They plead *fuck me*.

Okay. If she doesn't ask about songs, I'll fuck her.

## Just a Taste

Whatever it takes to turn off my fucking head.

---

I GET BACK TO OUR PLACE IN THE HOLLYWOOD HILLS a few hours later. Tom is home. No doubt he's still with the makeup girl. The man enjoys his one-night stands.

He enjoys everything he does. He's especially giddy about his newfound fame. It's all he's ever wanted: to feel important and adored. And the money—we are cleaning up. But then, I already have more than I'll ever need.

I shower then settle in my room. There's something nagging at my gut.

Usually, that means I'm about to figure out the start of a song. Today, nothing comes.

This is a recipe for picture-perfect inspiration. Windows wide open to blue skies. Clean, empty room. Guitar riff down the hall.

I close my eyes and push my thoughts out of my head. As much as Tom annoys me, the drummer is right. Women want to fall in love with the broken bad boy. My past speaks for itself.

If I came forward with all that shit, I'd have women eating out of the palm of my hand.

We'd get tons of press.

Be twice as popular.

But there's no fucking way.

It's funny. I don't want anyone to know about my past. But it's there on the album. And on the one before that. Every single one of our songs is about some ugly feeling I pulled from my gut.

My past is there for anyone who wants to look.

But no one does.

They sing the catchy chorus. They compliment the song. They make it into what they want it to mean. And that's fine.

That's my job.

But just once, I wish someone would understand me.

My shoulders shrug of their own accord. I have everything I want. I'm not getting hung up on the minor details.

I close my eyes and channel that feeling in my gut.

Slowly, I coax the words into my pen.

I've got three lines down when my door opens.

Drew takes a quick look on my bed, deems it worthy of his ass, and takes a seat. He's got his guitar in his lap.

His dark eyes meet mine. He says nothing. Just nods.

His fingers move over the fretboard as he plays a riff. Then he's moving into a chord progression, the start of one. It's not quite there, but it's got potential.

"We don't need to write another song for six months, easy," I say.

He motions to the pad of paper sitting on my desk.

Fair point. I take another look at the lyrics. They might work with this. "Play it again."

He does.

It sounds just as good the second time.

The third time, I hum along to work out the melody of the verse.

Drew doesn't offer commentary on the lyrics or the melody. He's all guitar, all the time. As long as he gets solos in a handful of songs, he's happy.

Well, happy is relative. Drew isn't exactly a happy-go-lucky guy.

"What about a major-to-minor there?" I offer.

He shoots me an *are you really giving me advice look*, but he does try it. Then he tries something else.

Then something else.

That's it.

We both know it.

I nod.

He starts from the top.

This time, I make notes of the cadence as I hum through the song. Usually, I'm strictly lyrics then music. But that doesn't exactly endear me to the other guys in the band.

We go through it again. Again. Again.

Until there's a knock on the door.

"You two are going to hurt my feelings." Pete is standing in the doorframe. His black hair is the same shade as his shirt, jeans, and sneakers.

The hair is his natural shade, but the eyeliner?

I have to hand it to the guy. He has a look and he pulls it off.

"Get your emo ass in here if you want to play," I say.

"You've been checking out my ass?" He winks. "Don't let Cindy know. She gets jealous."

I guess that means they're on. Lately, the two of them breakup and get back together every other week.

Drew attempts to hide the frustration creeping onto his face, but he fails miserably.

As much as I love starting shit, I know better than to press this issue. Pete is madly in love with his high school sweetheart. Drew is adamantly against relationships of any kind—his certainly failed spectacularly enough.

I'm not about to tell our bassist he's a poor sucker for believing in love. He knows my feelings on the subject. It blows up in his face often enough that he must feel it too.

Love destroys everything beautiful.

When it destroys him, I'll be there, ready to write another fucking song.

It's the only way I'm capable of helping.

"Your girl gonna get jealous if you go to your brother's party?" I tease.

"Which one? Tom throws a party every other night," Pete says.

"This weekend," I say.

Pete shrugs.

I look to Drew. "You bringing your friend… what's her name? With the nice tits?" I remember Drew's friend Kara vividly, but the guitarist is suffering from some delusion that the two of them will be flirty friends forever.

She's cute, smart, sweet. She won't have trouble finding someone to warm her bed. If it's not him…

He's going to be one miserable motherfucker if he has to watch her with someone else.

Drew glares. "Say that again, see what happens."

Fuck, he makes this too easy. Riling up Drew is fun. And it's for his own good. "She's hot. If you don't get some of that…" I shrug my shoulders as if to say *I will*.

I won't.

But someone will.

He spent our entire tour texting her nonstop, but he can't admit he's into her.

Pete shoots me a *grow up* look.

I shrug back. *What's it hurt?*

"You should clear your bed for her," I say.

"You should fuck off," Drew says.

"I'm hearing that a lot today," I say.

Pete chuckles. "I wonder why."

I ignore their attitude. My eyes meet Drew's. I arch an eyebrow. "Is she coming?"

He glares. "With a friend. Don't think about touching either of them."

I won't, but it's fun pretending. "What if the friend is begging me to fulfill all her fantasies?"

"You want to work on this or not?" Drew asks.

I let it go.

I wait for Pete to grab his bass, then I settle in to my seat. This, us making music, is where we belong.

This is the only place where there's no bullshit.

## Chapter Two

MILES

**F**uck, I'm getting old.

There's a raucous party downstairs and there are only two thoughts going through my head.

One is *that's too fucking loud*.

The other...

Not going there.

I've been struggling with these lyrics all week. I'm not going to figure them out today.

Might as well make someone come. I need out of my head.

I slide my notebook into a drawer, clear my bed, head downstairs.

Tom really outdid himself. This party is in full swing. The music is pounding. Everywhere I look, people are getting hot and heavy.

Everywhere except the table in the corner. That's top-shelf shit and it's going fast.

Someone brushes up against me. A woman. It's not an accident. I don't have to look at her to know that. I can tell from the way her hand curls around my forearm.

"Oh my God. Are you really Miles Webb?" She moves closer. "I'm a huge fan."

"Thanks." I pull my eyes away from the booze to look at her. She's a cute blonde with her fake tits on full display.

Her tongue slides over her Barbie pink lips. She looks up at me like I'm a trophy she needs on her mantle. "Is this really your place?"

"Yeah." I try to meet her gaze, but she's already off somewhere. Thinking about the guy she thinks I am. The one who cracks jokes in interviews. Who winks at the camera. Who pours his pain into his lyrics.

Which guy does she want?

Does she even care?

"I just saw that article in Rolling Stone. Did you really—" she starts going off about some story I told a reporter.

I'm not sure how true it was, how well I remembered. I was way too trashed.

And now—

Fuck, she's still looking at me like I'm a *hot rock star* box she has to check.

A year ago, I wouldn't have given a fuck. I'd have whisked her to my room, thrown her on the bed, found as much thrill in checking the *hot blonde groupie* box as she will in—

Whoever she thinks I am.

Right now.

I'm already over it. But fuck, that table in the corner is calling my name...

Better this than that.

I slide my arm around her waist and nod to the stairs. "You want to go upstairs?"

Her eyes light up. Her jaw drops. She can't believe I'm asking. "Is it really true you have a Kurt Cobain poster in your bedroom?"

## Just a Taste

Why the fuck does she want to know that now? I push my objections to the back of my head. "You can find out."

Her eyes get wider. She nods with enthusiasm. Nearly tears off my arm.

She starts saying something about how much she thinks about me. The times she's thought about me. The things she'd done as she thinks about me.

It should be flattering—a hot chick fucking herself to me should be exciting.

But it's not. It's bullshit. She doesn't think about *me*. She thinks about a guy in a music video.

I scan the room. For something to make this more interesting. I should make her day. Invite Tom to watch. But he's lost in the fray.

Drew too. Not that he'd ever accept that invitation.

Pete's always down to watch when he and his girlfriend are in the off phase of their on/off drama shit.

But shit, they're on right now.

And he's off someplace.

Which means it's just me and her.

Just our bodies.

I lead her into my room.

Onto my bed.

Out of her clothes.

She tugs my t-shirt over my head. Pulls my jeans and boxers to my feet. Then she's dropping to her knees.

I let my thoughts drift away long enough for it to feel good.

I slip on a condom, throw her onto the bed, get behind her.

But the way she's grunting already, without me even touching her—

Fuck, this is bullshit.

My body is responding, but my head is off some other place, and it's not coming back.

I'm tempted to call this off now, but I'm not going to be a selfish fuck.

I press my eyelids together and stop trying to push my thoughts away. It's almost fucking working when the door opens.

That must be the no-longer-MIA bassist.

Only it's not.

It's a woman. She's staring.

Staring and blushing.

My bedmate shrieks. She scrambles off the bed and pulls a sheet over her chest.

The newcomer stares.

"Miles," she whines. "You fucker! I told you I don't do threesomes."

It's too bad. The desire in this woman's brown eyes is intriguing as all hell.

A hundred bucks says she'll stick around if I ask this woman to watch.

Fuck, I'm considering it.

But the way she's staring… she looks more dumbstruck than anything.

I raise a brow. "You mind?"

She barely manages to take her eyes off my cock for long enough to offer an apologetic smile.

"I'm sorry." She presses her lips together. "Excuse me. I thought this was the bathroom."

Sure, she did. It's a bad excuse, but if I'm going to have bullshit sex, I might as well do something fun. The clueless fan being punished by the big, bad rock star…

Could be interesting.

I nod to the hall. "Next door on the left."

Her gaze goes back to my cock. Again, she blushes.

Again, she barely manages to pull her eyes away from my hard-on.

---

Twenty minutes later, I'm washed up and back to mingling. The Steele brothers are nowhere to be seen, but Drew's on the couch. With his friend.

The two of them are drunk off their asses, but given the way she's cozying up next to him—well, I hope he took my advice about clearing his bed.

A redhead in a tight dress and high heels paws at my arm. She shoots me that *please fulfill my rock star fantasies* look.

I used to get off on that kind of adoration, but it doesn't do shit for me anymore.

I play my part. I make a joke. I offer her a charming smile. But I'm not here.

My gaze shifts over the room.

There she is, the "shy" girl from upstairs.

She's cute—chestnut hair, brown eyes, long legs. Fuck that's a short skirt. And she's wearing sneakers. Those legs are all her.

She looks as out of place as I feel. Not just her casual shoes, but the tortured expression on her face.

Her eyes meet mine and her cheeks turn red.

She's picturing me naked.

And goddamn is it showing in the flush spreading over her chest.

I'm not about to let her get away with that *Oops, I can't believe I walked in on your tryst* thing.

She forces her gaze to the floor, then makes her way through the crowd, to the kitchen.

I excuse myself and follow her.

"You're not big on respecting people's privacy, huh?" I ask.

She turns and gives me a long, slow once-over. This time, she manages to keep her gaze off my crotch.

She clears her throat as she makes eye contact. "No, I'm not big on alcohol. I can't find anything else to drink."

Sounds like Tom.

Sounds like bullshit too, but on the off chance it's not...

I make a point of brushing the back of my hand against her shoulders as I pull open the fridge.

Her eyelids press together.

She takes her tongue between her teeth.

She wants me.

Badly.

I drop my voice to something low and seductive. "Help yourself."

"Thanks."

She grabs a water bottle and holds it to her chest. Her eyes stay glued to mine. They're going wide. She's working something out.

Realizing something.

It spreads all over her face.

Then it stops.

She stops.

She's just staring at me.

What the hell? "You okay?"

She nods. "I don't walk in on casual sex very often."

Uh-huh. No way in hell am I buying that story.

But there is something about her expression.

She seems innocent.

Like it really was an accident.

"I was looking for the bathroom." She takes a step backward. "Excuse me. I should go."

Huh? Fangirls don't usually run away when they finally have the attention of their celebrity crush.

But there's no fucking way that story is true.

Something isn't adding up here.

I have to figure this out. I offer her a smile. It's as sincere as I get lately. "You're not going to let me formally introduce myself?"

"Okay." She pulls her hand from her side. "I'm Meg Smart."

"Miles Webb." I take her hand and shake. Fuck, she's nervous. Her palm is clammy and her brown eyes are filled with apprehension. "I'm surprised we haven't met before."

"I don't go to parties."

"Guess that makes this my lucky day."

There's something about the earnest expression in her eyes.

I almost believe that shit upstairs was an honest mistake.

One more question and I'll know.

"Why'd you decide to come tonight?" I ask.

Again, she blushes. This time, she manages to hold my gaze. "My friend convinced me I wouldn't hate it."

Shit, I do believe her.

That means no clueless fangirl roleplay.

But this—the way she's looking at me like an actual human being who she desperately wants to fuck—is way better.

"What's the verdict?" I ask.

"I still don't like parties." Her chest heaves as she inhales. She exhales with purpose. Her eyes go to the floor, then they're back on mine. "Why'd you come tonight?"

She blushes at the word come.

I point upstairs. "That was my bedroom you burst into."

That blush deepens.

Damn, she's shy.

I better take this slow.

I move a little closer. "I don't blame you for looking. I'd do the same."

She nods. Presses her lips together.

Her eyes dart around the room but her body stays turned toward mine.

Then her eyes are back on mine. She stares at me like she's staring into my soul. "You... You're, um... you're in the band? The one throwing the party?"

Fuck.

So much for that.

"Yeah. Sinful Serenade. I'm the vocalist."

Damn, the way she's looking at me...

It's innocent and depraved at once.

She clears her throat and takes a step backward. "I'm looking for my friend." Her eyes meet mine. "Kara."

Fuck, Meg is Drew's friend's friend.

Which means she's one of the only two women here I shouldn't flirt with.

Of course, that only makes her more appealing.

I'm still not good at avoiding shit that's bad for me.

"She's tight with some guy in your band," Meg says. "They go way back."

I nod. "Yeah. Drew had a lot to say about her during our last tour."

Meg presses her lips together. "I should really find her. And go home." She takes a step toward the party. "I have to study. You know how it is. Or maybe not, being a rock star and all. But I have a test tomorrow." She nods an awkward goodbye and takes another step away.

"Meg."

"Yeah?" She spins on her heels. Her eyes meet mine. Her eyes scream I'm thinking about you naked.

I motion to the couch where Drew and Kara are cuddling. "Your friend isn't in a state to drive."

And Drew isn't in a state to do shit about that.

How is it I'm the responsible one in this situation?

I follow Meg to the couch.

Kara nearly jumps off the cushion to throw her arms around Meg.

Drew stares at Kara, his dark eyes wide and full of I want her out of that dress wonder.

"Are you having fun?" Kara hugs Meg. "Please, tell me you aren't completely miserable."

Meg relaxes into her friend's arms. Though relax is relative. She's still tense and awkward. "Only partially."

Kara laughs. "That's a start."

Drew shoots me a look that says *don't get any fucking ideas about her*.

But that's a lost cause.

I already have lots of ideas about this girl.

She's too cute and innocent to resist.

"I'm ready to go home," Meg says. "I can call a cab."

"No." Kara shakes her head. "I can drive."

Not like this she can't.

I let them get the whole No, I'll drive; no, you're drunk too out of the way, then I step in.

"I can drive you two home," I say.

Drew glares.

I stare back at him. "You'd do the same."

He nods and settles back into his seat. He shoots me that Touch her and you die look again.

Please.

I'm not about to touch the woman my best friend is lusting after.

But Meg...

Well, I don't take orders from anyone. Certainly not from Drew.

I turn to Kara. "Your keys?"

She pulls them from her purse. "It's a manual."

I smirk. "That's fine. I know how to handle my stick."

## Chapter Three

MILES

By the time we're on the freeway, Drew's friend is asleep in the back seat.

Meg crosses and uncrosses her legs. Her palms skim her short skirt. Her soft thighs.

Fuck, the girl is all legs. And I'm desperate to have them wrapped around my hips.

To have her splayed out under me, clawing at my chest, groaning my name like it's her favorite word.

Like she's *there* with *me*.

Which is stupid. She already has some idea of me. But, hey, try telling my cock that.

I never used to have this kind of stamina. I held my own sure, but I wasn't ready to go an hour after fucking a groupie.

I guess that's my head.

Once again, I'm trying to command my body. To force it to feel nothing but pleasure. To force the physical to overtake the ache in my head.

"Kara lives in Brentwood," Meg says. "You can take the 101 to the ten to the—"

"I know."

Her eyes flit to mine for a split second. It's enough to turn her cheeks bright red. "You drive a lot?"

"Lived here awhile." Since my mom died. But fuck knows I'm not thinking about that. It's a quick trip to *drown my thoughts by any means necessary*.

And I'm pretty sure Meg isn't actually aiming for some *leggy virgin and big bad rock star* role play.

Too bad.

I'd love to peel that skirt to her waist, run my hand over her ass, think up all sorts of ways to punish her.

Spankings to start.

Then—

There are too many possibilities.

"The Wilshire exit," she says. "It comes up quick after the—"

"Yeah."

"Right."

"Should be twenty minutes." It's not enough time. Or maybe it's too much. I'm not exactly good at keeping my pants zipped.

I'm safe.

I'm not hurting anyone.

Hell, I'm fulfilling all these fangirl's fantasies. Giving them a story for all their friends.

I see them trading gossip.

Posting replays on Reddit, Facebook, Twitter, whatever.

Some *Rolling Stone TMZ* cross-over piece of shit magazine ran an exposé on my conquests. They tried to get some good dirt, some women talking about what a selfish cad I am, but they didn't stick the landing.

Yeah, I sounded like a slut. A slut with skilled hands and a "gorgeous cock."

Seriously.

A woman said that.

Don't get me wrong. I have a love/hate relationship with the fucker. But I'm not sure I'd use the word gorgeous.

Maybe demanding.

A demanding motherfucker.

Right now, he's begging me to ask about the cute brunette.

She was staring. But now she's acting like she can't stand me.

What gives?

"Anything you want to discuss?" I lower my voice to a teasing tone. Maybe she didn't walk in on me on purpose. But she was looking. She was thinking about it.

She clears her throat, but it does nothing to stop her blush. "I'm not sure what you mean."

"You are."

Her eyes flit to the window. She watches as we pass a row of buildings downtown. The dim lights of the city blur together. The one time LA looks beautiful. "Kara is my closest friend." The implication is there. *I'm not going to make that complicated.* "I don't know how close you and Drew are, or how long you'll be in Los Angeles, but I figure you and I are mutual friends..." Her voice trails off, like she's trying to convince herself of something.

She's close enough to right.

Fuck knows Drew is going to spend all his free time with Kara and her massive tits.

"How about we agree to never discuss this again?" Her voice skips. Like she can't bring herself to expand on *this*. Like she can barely even think *holy fuck, I walked in on him naked, and the image is still burned into my brain.*

"I can't agree to that."

"Why not?"

It's not what she wants, for one. She's overselling her

objection. What's the Shakespeare line Damon was always quoting? *The lady doth protest too much.*

"You're too cute when you blush." I try to reel it back. For my uncle's sake. So he doesn't start rolling over in his grave.

"Let's pretend it never happened."

"If it bothers you that much." If she's really not into me, I'm not going to press it. Sure, there's something really fucking appealing about her disinterest. It's the most refreshing thing I've felt in forever. Another sign I'm a mess, but I'm way past the point of caring. "It's not a big deal."

She presses her lips together.

All right, I'm throwing this out there. "Nothing you haven't done before."

She nods, but nerves still drip into her voice. "Of course."

My smile is involuntary.

"I've had boyfriends."

I arch a brow *so?*

"We did all sorts of stuff."

God, she's calling it *stuff*. Could she be more adorable? "There's no shame in being a virgin."

"I know." Her expression gets shy. "But I'm not."

Uh-huh.

"It's really none of your business."

"Then why are you trying to convince me?"

"I'm not. I just… want to set the record straight."

"Uh-huh."

"Yeah." She nods.

"About all the stuff you do?"

"What do you call it?" Need drops into her voice. Then she shrugs and shakes it off.

"I don't know. Stuff is kinda growing on me."

She stifles a laugh.

"Hand stuff, mouth stuff, cock stuff."

She tries to repeat the phrase. Struggles though it. "What is... cock stuff?"

"You tell me."

"I, uh..."

"Do a lot of stuff?"

"Not a lot. Just, uh... I have. Before."

"Okay."

She half-smiles. "I have."

"I believe you."

Her eyes meet mine. She stares at me, trying to figure me out. "No, you don't."

No, I don't. But I'm not going to press her on it if she's that desperate to drop the subject. "If you don't care, why are you trying to convince me?"

"Well, uh..."

All right, let me help her here. "What's your favorite sexual position?"

She opens her mouth like she has a response, but nothing comes. Her eyes flame. With fire. This need to prove me wrong.

I love it.

"Maybe you don't know the name. But you want to describe it," I say.

"Well, uh... Missionary."

Maybe. She seems like the type who wants to feel every inch of someone's skin against hers.

Who wants to look her partner in the eyes.

Who wants to kiss as she fucks.

To be *there*. And not closing her eyes, recalling a music video.

"Second favorite?" I ask.

She leans forward, ready to launch an answer.

Doesn't.

Her lips press together. Her eyes flare with irritation.

At me.

For being a dick.

I deserve it. And, somehow, I want it. I love that I irritate her. That she isn't trying to hide it. That she isn't trying to impress me.

That she's staring at me like she's *still* picturing me naked.

Picturing us together.

"I can show you a few good ones." Shit, Drew is going to kill me. But, at the moment, I can't say I care.

She sucks in a deep breath. "Excuse me?"

My eyes meet hers. "You do want to fuck me."

It spreads all over her face. *Yes, of course, right now.* "I…"

"You've been picturing me naked all night."

"I saw you naked. I couldn't help it."

I flip my blinker. Move out of the merging lane. We're on the ten now. One freeway to go. Fifteen minutes.

Then however long it takes to get to her place. Wherever it is.

She gives me that long once-over. Her lips part. Her fingers dig into her thighs.

"You're thinking about it," I say.

"I'm not." Her eyes stay on my jeans.

"I'm better than whatever you're imagining."

Her gaze shifts to my waist. My chest. "Did you even know that girl's name?"

"Yeah." At some point.

"What was it?"

Sarah. Sandy? Steph? Yeah, that's it. "Stephanie." Maybe. Not that it matters. "It's just sex. You'd know if you—"

"It's none of your business."

"Suit yourself." I shrug.

She crosses her legs. Turns to the window.

She's pissed. Because she's embarrassed by her lack of experience?

Or because I'm stepping over the line?

She shifts her position. Folds one leg over the other. Crosses both. Places both on the floor.

Leans forward to turn on the stereo.

It's set to radio. To KROQ, the local rock station. They're playing our latest all the time.

Making us a million times more famous.

There—

The car fills with the sound of my groan. It's a good take. A great performance.

But it still makes me cringe. There's too much in this song. Too much of me.

It's bad enough people hear it on their own.

Sitting here, while understanding spreads over her face, while she stares at me like she can't believe I wrote this song.

Like she wants to know the guy who wrote that song. And not the guy in the car with her, who's an unrepentant asshole.

Like she's can't believe I was ever struggling this much to hold it together.

I want to believe that too. I want to be this guy, the one who doesn't give a fuck about anything or anyone except what he needs.

I want to make her come until she can't stop. Then never talk to her again.

One night. One exchange. Nothing but a few hours of pleasure for both of us.

Why does it have to be more complicated than that?

She changes the station to KEarth. Oldies.

"You're cute when you're nervous." I need to focus on her. On anything besides the shit going through my head.

"You have a problem with oldies?" she asks.

Yeah, they were Damon's favorite. It hurts too much to hear them. It hurts too much to hear my own fucking groan.

It hurts too much to breathe.

He's everywhere. In everything.

People say it gets better, that it goes away, but they're wrong. It doesn't.

"That's why you changed the station? Just wanted to hear *Build Me Up, Buttercup?*" I want to give her a medal for stopping the sound of my heart pouring into the car. But I'm not about to admit that.

"No, I was hoping for *Happy Together*."

God dammit, she's too cute for words. I can't help but smile. My eyes go to hers. "You want your first time to be good?"

"I'm not a virgin."

Maybe she's not. Either way, I'm offering to fuck her. "I'm happy to oblige." That's it. One offer. If she says she's not interested, I leave. Call someone else.

"I don't need your pity sex."

Pity? Is she out of her mind? "There'd be no pity about it. I want to fuck you too."

"There's no too. I don't want to... I don't date."

"It's just sex. I might let you buy me breakfast in the morning, but it's not a date."

Her eyes go wide. Interest spreads all over her face. She stammers, looking for words, failing to find them.

Meg turns the radio up. Leans back in her seat. Looks out the window.

It is a beautiful night. The sky is a clear, deep blue. There are even a few stars.

Meg stays quiet until I pull off the freeway. She directs me to her friends' place, helps her friend out of the car, up the stairs.

They linger at her apartment door. Talking about something.

They're too far away. I can't tell if it's a serious conversation. Or if it's the usual good night.

Are women as depraved as men?

Is her friend whispering something about she can't wait to feel Drew's cock inside her? How she wants him to come on her massive tits?

Somehow, I doubt it.

Fuck, that will piss him off like nothing else. I compose a message in my head.

*Your friend's tits looked amazing in that dress. You think she has them out for a reason? You think she'd want them around my cock?*

*I bet someone's going to come on them.*

*If it's not you...*

He might actually hit me for that.

A *thud* pulls me back to the moment.

Meg is on the ground, on her hands and knees. She leans back, rubs her skinned knee with her hands.

Shit.

I need to pay more attention.

I get out of the car. "Hey." I move closer slowly, so I don't scare her.

She looks up at me, equal parts confused and relieved.

"You mind?" I kneel next to her.

"It's fine. I can clean up at home."

"You're bleeding."

She nods *okay*.

I look closer. I'm not exactly an ER surgeon, but I've cleaned up after enough fights to know first aid.

My fingers skim her calf. The outside of her knee. The top of her thigh.

Her eyelids flutter closed.

She sucks a breath through her teeth. But I can't tell if it's pain or arousal.

Either way—

She needs closer attention. "This is a bad scrape. You have a first aid kit?"

Her brow scrunches with concentration. "I can handle it."

I shake my head. There's no way I'm sending her home injured. "I bruised plenty of knuckles in my day. I'm bandaging that. Either we do it at your apartment, or we go to a twenty-four-hour pharmacy."

She nods. "My place."

I lead her to the car. Open the door for her.

She looks at me funny, like she doesn't buy me as a gentleman, but she still gets in. Mumbles a thank you.

I slide into my seat. Turn the car on. Ask for her address.

It's close.

A five-minute drive this time of night.

She rolls down the window, closes her eyes, soaks in the feeling of fresh air.

A sigh of relief falls off her lips.

It's exactly how I feel.

This girl is a breath of fresh air. Maybe that's a sign I should walk away.

Too bad I'm not going to listen to it.

Chapter Four

MEGARA

Clothes cover the already limited floor space of my tiny studio. The desk is littered with papers and notecards. The kitchenette is no better.

Damn, it looks like a slob lives here. I've been lax about cleaning, about taking care of myself, about everything really. Ever since Rosie... it's hard to do anything.

I never want anything.

Only I want Miles.

I want him on my bed.

Want us out of these stupid clothes.

And not just the guy who sings *In Pieces*. Not just the wounded poet who understands every place I hurt.

This guy.

The tall, broad, blue-eyed flirt who shrugs off sex with two women in the same night.

The guy I *saw* fucking someone else.

But God what I saw—

Is it always that attractive? Are all guys that sexy when they're hard and ready to go? Or was it him?

The strong shoulders, the broad chest, the defined abs, the tattoos.

And his cock—

I swallow hard.

He's here to clean my wound, not fuck me senseless.

It still makes no sense—why would someone like Miles want someone like me?

I take a deep breath, trying to shake it off. Figures, I want something bad for me. It's fitting really. If I'm not careful, I'll fall down the same rabbit hole that destroyed my sister.

I kick a pair of underwear out of view and take a seat on the bed.

Miles is close.

There are only two feet between the bed and the wall. There's nowhere else for him to be. The reasonable explanation does nothing to calm my racing heart.

Miles scans the walls, taking in the movie posters breathing life into the otherwise drab room—the *Star Wars* original trilogy, *Jurassic Park*, *The Matrix*, *Dark City*, and *The Terminator*.

His lips curl into a smile. It's honest. More honest than he seems. "I like your décor."

I try to reach for some response, something that will convince him—and myself—that I'm not interested, but nothing comes.

I don't need his help.

I can tell him to go. Open my mouth and say *you know what, I've actually got this. I work in an ER. I've seen worse wounds. Cleaned worse wounds. This is barely a scrape.*

*Just a pretense to get you here, really.*

Instead, I sit when he nods to the bed. I want him here. I want him in my room.

I want to accept his offer. Say *yes, please, let's go right now.*

*As long as it makes this hurt less. Even for five minutes. Ten. An hour. How long does it usually last, anyway?*

But I can't. I'm too scared. I'm not brave the way Rosie was. Not that it did her any good.

His voice is low. Matter-of-fact. The guy who sings me to sleep, not the one who teases me for accidental voyeurism. "First aid kit?"

I point him to the bathroom.

He disappears for a moment. Returns with a bottle of rubbing alcohol, a bag of cotton balls, and a wide bandage. I don't remember buying any of this. Must have been Rosie's.

I guess she doesn't need them anymore.

"You don't have any antibacterial cream?" he asks.

"Only have the kit."

"Get the cream for next time." He uncaps the rubbing alcohol, presses the cotton ball over it, and tilts the bottle. His eyes find mine. "This will sting."

Miles drops to his knees, kneeling in front of me like he's about to pull off my panties and plant his face between my thighs.

The beautiful mental image dies the moment he presses the cotton ball to my skin. Ow. Ow. Ow. It doesn't just sting. It burns like hell.

"Fuck," I mutter.

"Here." He presses his lips together and blows cool air over the wound.

It lessens the sting but it sets the rest of my body on fire. He pats my skin dry and applies a bandage. There. Fixed. We're done.

Only he's still here, still planted between my legs.

He looks up at me. His fingertips trail along the inside of my calf as he pulls his hands back to his sides. "Better?"

"I could have handled that." I press my knees together.

I want him. I can't deal with that. I need to tell him to leave. "But yes. Thanks."

"My pleasure."

He's still here. I'm still in my bed. It would be easy to remind him of his offer.

Maybe I can be casual and aloof too. Maybe sex is the secret to not feeling like my heart weights a thousand pounds.

Or maybe I'll go down the same path my sister did.

I clear my throat. "It's getting late. I should go to bed." I don't add *by myself*. Or *with you*.

It hangs in the air, the possibility.

We're in limbo.

He sees it too, but he doesn't say anything. He just nods and sits next to me. His jean-clad thigh pressed against my bare skin. "You have a phone?"

My hands share none of my caution. They dig into my purse and offer him my cell.

He taps the screen for a moment and hands it back. There he is, in my phone, Miles Webb. I have his number, his email, his address even.

He stares at me like he's thinking about how easy it would be to pin me to the bed and pull my panties to my knees.

Or maybe I'm projecting.

His lips curl into a smile. "Let me know if you need anything."

"What would I need?"

"To satisfy your curiosity."

Time to put an end to this flirtation. I clear my throat and throw my shoulders back. I can do confidence too. "Listen, Miles. I'm sure you're a great guy in a lot of ways."

"You think I'm an asshole."

No, that would be easy. But I can see the guy who sings

*In Pieces*, this side of him. I try to push it aside. To remember my point. "I'm sure I'll see you again, what with our mutual best friends."

"True." His voice is calm, totally unfazed.

"But I'd appreciate it if you'd stop flirting with me."

He nods a yes. "If you stop staring at me like you're thinking about what you want to do to me."

I know what I want to do to him. I want to tell him to go screw himself. I fire up an insult and turn to face Miles. But when our eyes connect, my mouth goes sticky.

My body goes into overdrive.

It wants every part of him.

Now.

He chuckles. "That look, right now, you're thinking about fucking me."

I try to object, but I can't. It's vivid. It's the most beautiful thing I've felt in months. The only good thing I've felt in months.

"I don't want to make you uncomfortable. If you're not interested, stop undressing me with your eyes, and I'll stop flirting."

Are people really this direct and confident? It's unnerving.

An electric current courses through my body, settling between my legs.

What would his hands feel like farther up my thighs? Under my skirt? Under my panties? My body is begging me to find out.

"I won't stare." I press my palms together, but I'm not at all convincing. I'm staring right now. "I'll work on it."

He pushes himself to his feet. "I really hope you don't."

*I'm not interested.* I open my mouth to say the words. Nothing. I am interested. I'm unbearably interested.

Shit. I have to say something... "Have a safe ride home."

His lips curl into a cocky smile. "Sweet dreams."

He nods goodbye on his way out the door.

Damn, that was close.

I collapse on the bed. My heart is pounding against my chest. My lungs are totally void of oxygen.

Miles Webb, the gorgeous rock star, singer of the band poised to be the next big thing, wants me. He could have any buxom actress or model he wants, and he wants me. Flat-chested, gawky, wallflower me.

## Chapter Five

MILES

Tom shoots me a dirty look as I walk in the door. It's his usual *I can't believe you aren't taking this seriously* look.

As if being five minutes late to practice is the equivalent of missing a show because I'm getting high in the bathroom.

He wants more. Good for him. If I was a better person, I'd be sympathetic to his need to fill the hole in his heart.

But I'm not a better person. And he's an obnoxious motherfucker.

Even when he's right.

"Nice of you to show up." He falls onto his stool, crossing his arms with a huff.

I shoot Pete a *what the fuck* look.

The bassist shrugs. *What do you expect? Tom is Tom.* He would know. He's been living with the guy since he was a kid.

"Is he even ready?" I motion to Drew, who's sitting in the corner, ignoring us in favor of tuning his guitar.

Pete shoots me that *what the fuck is wrong with you* look. He shakes his head. "You trying to start shit?"

"I'm not that easy to bait," Tom says.

Pete nods *you are*.

Drew continues ignoring us.

Tom stares at him like he thinks the frustration in his grey-green eyes will somehow force Drew to work faster.

When it doesn't, the drummer turns to me. Looks up at me like he can't be bothered to even contemplate why I'm so difficult.

"Yeah?" I crack my knuckles. I used to play rhythm, but now I only break out my guitar if I'm working on a song.

Not that I've worked on any of my own shit lately.

That's supposed to be *it*. The thing that clears my head. That spins my thoughts into silk. That turns the world into a place that makes sense.

Lately, it doesn't happen. I sit down to write and nothing.

I can throw together a few cliché phrases. At this point, I revel in it. I take any songwriting gig I can find. Anything to force my thoughts into some sort of order.

People call pop songs trash. Disposable confections designed to dull the brain.

To a certain extent, they are.

But it takes a lot of skill to craft a novel flavor of cotton candy. It's not easy turning four chords and *baby, I love you/why don't you love me* into something people hum for three weeks straight.

"Are you even here?" Tom pushes off his stool. He stretches his arms over his head, letting out a bored yawn. "I have places to be."

"You finally convince a woman to go for a second round?" I ask.

Pete's dark eyes fill with disappointment. *Why do you always pick fights?*

He doesn't have to say it. I know him too well. He knows me too well. At this point... fuck, between all the times I've invited him to watch and the very loud phone sex he has with his girlfriend when they're on—

It would be too much information if it wasn't so hot.

He's dirtier than a *Penthouse* forum letter. And the few times they've been so *excited* they didn't wait until they had privacy—

It's free porn. I'm not gonna complain just 'cause I have to sleep next to the guy on the road.

I try to go there, to recall his girlfriend's perky tits, but my head goes straight to Meg.

The long legs.

The *I need to fuck you* look in her dark eyes.

The *God, you're irritating* groan.

How does she groan when she comes? Has she ever come with another person?

Fuck, to be the first person to watch her eyes roll back in her head—

The first name on her lips—

"Are you okay?" Pete's deep voice is sincere. He's actually capable of sincerity. It still terrifies me.

"Fine." I need a grip. I'm making things more than they are. So what if she's a leggy virgin with an adorable glare? There are plenty of leggy virgins out there.

It doesn't matter that she looks as miserable as I feel.

Or that she's as desperate to be out of her head.

It's already too much, too personal, too intimate.

"Where'd you go last night?" There's accusation in Tom's voice.

I hate it. I hate it more because I deserve it. "Malibu."

"Needed a better view to contemplate all the pain in your soul?" Tom's voice is almost teasing.

"Something like that," I say.

"What happened with Drew's friend?" he asks.

"He doesn't have a black eye," Pete says. "Couldn't be that bad."

Tom taps the guitarist.

Drew slides his headphones off his ears. "Yeah?"

"You ready to go?" Tom asks.

"You done with the gossip?" Drew asks.

Pete chuckles *yeah right*.

"How's your friend?" Tom asks.

"With the perfect tits," I bait Drew.

He takes it. As always. Glares. Lets out a low growl. Shakes it off. "She said Miles was a gentleman."

"Hard to believe," Tom says.

"I always make sure a woman comes first," I say.

Tom laughs. "That line is old."

"Only cause you overuse it," I say.

"What happened with the friend?" Tom asks.

"You saw me leave?" I ask.

"I hear things," Tom says.

I shoot Pete a look.

He shrugs *what do you expect?*

I should know better. His loyalty will always be to his foster brother.

"Offered to take her virginity," I say.

Tom raises a brow *are you for real?* When I don't reply, he shrugs, and picks up his sticks. "Can we get on with this. I have a meeting."

"What are we selling this time?" I ask.

Tom rolls his eyes. "If you hate money so much, sell your uncle's place and move into a van."

It's a good point.

Fuck him for saying it. Fuck him more for it being true.

---

I POUR MYSELF INTO EVERY LINE OF EVERY SONG. AT this point, I know the notes. I can sing this shit in my sleep, no matter how high or low I go. But the emotion?

I have to find it every time. It always feels good, in the moment.

After—

I get through *In Pieces* no problem. But when Tom calls for a break, and I step away from the mic stand, head toward the coffee shop where we break—

Fuck, how am I going to get through three months of this?

I reach for something to distract me. It's a bad idea texting the cute virgin. But, at the moment, I don't give a fuck.

*Miles: How about a picture of your wound?*

I slide my cell into my back pocket. Don my sunglasses. Move into line.

The barista looks at me like she's desperate for an autograph. Then I give my name as *Damon* and she steps back, sure she mixed things up, fades into normal *you're a cute guy* customer service.

I find a seat in the corner. The guy across from me gives me that *do I know you from someplace* once-over.

I turn enough I'm out of his eyeline. I'm still not used to being famous. I don't know that I'll ever be used to it.

My phone buzzes with a response.

*Meg: Something tells me sending you pictures is a bad idea.*

*Miles: Suit yourself. I was going to send you something very nice in return.*

*Meg: Nice how?*

Not what she's thinking. Though, if she asks…
*Miles: A picture for a picture.*
I really hope she asks.

---

Somehow, I make it through our break, through the rest of practice, my drive back to our place in the hills. I try to stay as much as I can.

Every time I spend the night at my uncle's house, the rest of the band looks at me like I'm about to crack.

Even when they keep their concern to themselves, it's written all over their faces.

*Where did he go? Was he trying to score? Did he drown his sorrows in a bottle? Is he high as a kite right now? Why else would he go MIA?*

Living here, in this mansion the label rented for us, is like an extended summer break. We spend the morning sleeping in, working out, making breakfast. Then it's lazy afternoons by the pool. Or watching movies. Or visiting an interested woman.

The same at night.

The only break is practice—three times a week—or other band shit. There's always something.

A show to test a b-side.

A meeting with our dick of a manager.

A photo shoot for a magazine.

Too much time to get into trouble.

For a while, I read. I make dinner. I catch the last half of the Romero flick Tom and Pete are watching on the couch.

Eventually, I head to the backyard, roll my jeans to my knees, dip my feet in the pool. It was hot as hell this afternoon, but the temperature is finally cool. Cool enough I'd think twice about skinny dipping.

Not if I had a cute girl begging me to take my jeans off. Say Meg—

Fuck, why does my head keep going back to her? I'm not getting stuck on anyone.

Even if she's the first person who's looked at me like a human being in forever.

For a while, the highlights bouncing off the water steal my attention. Then my phone buzzes with another text.

*Meg: Don't complain if you think it's gross.*

Her skinned knee. It's bruised and just starting to scab. Gnarly. Familiar.

Fucking adorable.

Not the wound. Her sending this picture to me like she wants me to kiss her boo-boo.

Or maybe I'm reading into shit.

Maybe all she wants is a picture of my dick.

That would be better. For both of us. Hell, I should whip it out right now.

Convince her to fuck me or push her away forever.

I don't.

I make a fist. Hold my hand to the light the best I can.

*Click. Zoom.*

My scarred knuckles aren't as raw as her skinned knee, but they've been with me a lot longer. Hell, I could barely play guitar for a long time. Punched too many assholes.

*Meg: That's not what I thought you'd send.*

*Miles: Imagining some place a little lower and a lot more exciting?*

Fuck, I can see her blushing. Is she working up the courage to ask? Or convincing herself to tell me to fuck off?

It was hard reading her last night.

Like this, without those big brown eyes to guide me? It's impossible.

*Meg: No, I wouldn't expect you to send a picture like that unless I asked.*

*Miles: Accurate.*

*Meg: I'm not going to ask.*

*Miles: Good. You have to earn that.*

*Meg: Really?*

*Miles: Yeah.*

*Meg: You wouldn't? If I asked?*

*Miles: Depends on how you asked?*

*Meg: How should I ask?*

On her knees, pawing at my jeans.

*Meg: I'm not asking. I have to study.*

*Miles: And you can't handle a distraction of that magnitude.*

*Meg: Magnitude?*

*Miles: You saw.*

*Meg: It was dark. I couldn't see that well.*

*Miles: Really? 'Cause I seem to recall you staring for a solid thirty seconds.*

I check the time on my cell. Too early to sleep. Too late to go out.

About time for a booty call. But it doesn't seem like that's what she's after.

*Miles: It's almost eleven.*

*Meg: Just got off work at the ER. I really should study.*

*Miles: You work in an ER?*

*Meg: Yeah. Why do you ask?*

*Miles: Your reaction times are a little slow.*

*Meg: Rude!*

*Miles: Or were you just that interested?*

She's quiet for a minute. No doubt working past a blush. Or a desire to call me an asshole.

*Meg: I don't do much in the ER. I'm a scribe. Means I write down Drs' orders, put information in the computer, that kind of thing. Don't need fast reaction times.*

*Miles: Uh-huh.*

*Meg: I have to go. I have a lot of homework to finish before bed. Good night.*

*Miles: Sweet dreams.*

For a while, my cell goes silent. I head to my room. Strip to my boxers. Pretend I might fall asleep.

Eventually, she replies.

*Meg: Did you mean what you said in the car? About sleeping with me.*

My cock answers for me. It rouses to attention. Screams for her soft thighs.

*Miles: Is that an invitation?*

*Meg: Just a hypothetical question.*

*Miles: Hypothetically, I can be at your apartment in twenty minutes flat.*

*Meg: Would you really come right now? It's the middle of the night.*

*Miles: That's the usual time for a booty call.*

It needs to be that simple.

Simple is good.

Simple is the only way no one gets hurt.

*Meg: Never mind. I should go to bed. Forget I said anything.*

*Miles: I'll be your first.*

*Meg: I didn't say I was a virgin.*

*Miles: You are.*

*Meg: And you know that how?*

*Miles: It's cute you're so defensive about it.*

*Meg: It's not cute.*

*Miles: Why not admit it?*

*Meg: What's it matter to you? Trying to hit a quota of "virginities taken"?*

*Miles: Don't have a fetish for it. But I would like to fuck you, Meg. I'd want to fuck you if you'd been with a million guys.*

*Meg: Really?*

*Miles: Yeah. As it is, I want to be your first.*

*Meg: Oh.*

*Miles: I'll make sure you enjoy yourself. That it doesn't hurt. That you come. That's what I want.*

*Meg: Oh.*

*Miles: This is where you tell me if it's what you want.*

*Meg: It's complicated.*

No, it's simple. I ease her into it, make her come, make her come again, kiss her good night. Period, the end.

That's all it has to be.

All it's going to be.

## Chapter Six

MEGARA

All week, my phone is silent. There isn't a peep from Miles. No new texts when I wake up. No new texts when I check my phone at lunch. None during my study break between class and work. None when I get home from a shift at the ER.

His last text sits there, that smooth, confident offer to take my virginity. Like it's no big deal.

To him, it isn't a big deal.

It's not like I've been waiting. It's just that not dating makes it difficult to have sex.

I don't want a boyfriend. I really don't. But I don't want to be a notch on someone's bedpost either.

Miles is a slut. There's nothing wrong with him being a slut, but I don't want to lose my virginity to a guy who goes through three women a week. Not if he's going to forget my name the way he forgot that other girl's name.

The ball is in my court. I keep it there. Miles and I are friends by association. That's all.

Late Thursday night, I get home particularly

exhausted. I don't have the energy for homework. I collapse in bed and turn on the radio instead.

KROQ does its usual Nirvana, Smashing Pumpkins, 90s and 00s rock thing. Then it's his song, *In Pieces*. It still tears me apart. It still presses every single bruise.

> Three weeks now.
> Can't sleep.
> Gaping hole in my chest
> shows no signs of recovery.
>
> That word, a joke, you laugh.
> "Running away again, kid?"
> A minute here
> and then you're gone.

I close my eyes, willing my thoughts to go anywhere but that awful memory.

It doesn't work.

I'm in that hospital room, watching doctors try to save my sister. I can see her blue lips, feel her cold hands. They're freezing, no grip, no signs of life at all.

> Lights out.
> Can't sleep.
> Heavy head,
> but no one else can see.
> (No one ever did).
> A lost cause still,
> worse than before.
> No signs of recovery.

She's dying. I watch her die again and again. The same stupid dream I have every night. The reason why I can't allow myself a single minute of free time. Because my thoughts go back to her and all the ways I failed her.

An opiate overdose.

I had no idea.

How could I have no idea?

> That word, a joke you laugh
> Running away again, kid?
> A minute here
> And then you're gone
>
> Four weeks now
> That hole, that dread
> I can barely breathe
> Anywhere but here
> Anything but this
> I want to take your lead

She's gone. It's been three months. Just like the song goes, the gaping hole in my chest shows no sign of recovery. I can't sleep. I can't breathe.

How is it possible that Miles went through something like this and came out calm and unaffected?

I try to study but I can't focus. The question eats at my mind. How is it possible that Miles, the cocky player, is the same guy as Miles, the wounded poet?

Why does it feel like he can see every stitch in my heart?

I shouldn't ask. I should leave it alone.

But I have to know.

I don't think. I pull out my cell and text him.

## Chapter Seven

MILES

My phone buzzes with a new text. It's not Tom—he's across the room. We're at some sweet sixteen party for a Disney star.

Apparently, I worked on one of her songs. I owe it to her to attend. Hell, I don't even mind. With a crowd this age, most of the adults try to pretend like we're civilized people.

Sure, there's booze in the kitchen and there's someone getting high outside. Yeah, I just saw two teenagers sneak upstairs. But if I squint, it's a normal high school party.

When I let my gaze focus, it's clear this shit is fucked up. A dozen suits talking to teenage girls. Some are professional. Others are flirting.

Offering them fame for sex.

A record deal for a blow job.

It's fucked up. Even if it's the best chance some of these women are going to have.

If they were *women*, I wouldn't mind so much. Fuck knows I'm not in a place to judge. Look at all the shit I've given up for fame.

But these are girls. Teenagers.

I try to shake it off as I check my phone.

It's not Drew or Pete. It's Meg.

I can't look. She makes my stomach twist. She fucks up my head. It's hard enough keeping it straight here.

I slip my cell into my pocket. Scan the room for some way to occupy my head.

Shit. There's Aiden. Flirting with a cute girl. And I do mean girl. She barely looks sixteen. If that.

No way. Aiden isn't the kind of guy who cares if a woman is "technically an adult." Asshole doesn't even hold up his end of the *fuck me for fame* bargain. And that's the least of his transgressions.

"Hey." I interrupt them. "Didn't know you'd be here."

He shoots me a vaguely irritated look. Then the girl's eyes light up and she claps her hands together *oh my God is that Miles Webb* and Aiden is all smiles. "Sweetie, have you met Miles?" He says it as casually as possible. Like we're drinking buddies.

I guess we were once.

I'm the reason he's still our manager. That he's still working for this fucking company.

Yeah, his uncle owns the label. And said uncle is completely unwilling to listen to "rumors." But if we hadn't—

Fuck, I can't change that. But I can do this.

"Ohmygod, I'm such a big fan." Her words blur together. She extends her hand. Shakes with enough force my t-shirt ripples. "I love that one song. Where you're in the video in all white. Oh my God, it's so hot. My sister is always sending me pics. She's ob-sessed with you. Not that I… oh my God, it's just a great song."

"Thanks." I let my hand fall to my side.

"Did you write it?" she asks.

I nod *yeah*. "The lyrics. The band writes all the music together."

"Really? Are they here?" She scans the room, her eyes wide, her chest heaving.

"Am I not your favorite?" I tease.

"Well, um… I think it's so sweet… how Pete has a girlfriend. It's just… you don't see that a lot. His school sweetheart. I know. Wanting him is like wanting them to break up. But it's like I just want them to make it, you know?"

"I do." In theory.

"Is he here?" She jumps forward. Wraps her arms around my wrist. "Please tell me he's here."

"Sorry." I shake my head.

Aiden reaches for her. "I can arrange a meeting. He might want to—"

I cut him off. "You can meet his brother."

"Ohmygodreally!" she shrieks. "I'm going to die. He's so cute."

"What about me?" I tease.

"I know… you're all so cute." Her cheeks flush. "Where is he?"

I pull her away from Aiden.

He mutters something about how they'll pick this up later. But that's not happening. Not as long as I'm here.

I find Tom, flirting with a cute starlet, and introduce the teen. He plays his part. Flirts just enough she beams. Not enough she thinks he's interesting.

When I nod to Aiden, Tom gets it immediately. Makes sure she finds someone else who will keep an eye on her.

I want to tell her to run the fuck away. This shit isn't worth it. Even if she's one of the few people who makes it, she isn't going to fill that hole inside her.

But I can't crush the kid.

All I can do is keep that fucker away from her.

I swear to God, one day I'll get the asshole fired. For now, he's bulletproof. For now, his uncle is keeping him safe.

But, honestly, even if Aiden were a random asshole, I doubt people would care about his indiscretions.

As long as he makes money, he's good for the company. And there are only two things anyone here cares about— money and image.

---

It's still there.

The text on my cell.

My urge to respond to her.

*Meg: Can I ask you something?*

It's a simple question. Not even a question. A request for a question.

And I'm desperate to say *hell yes, ask me anything, I want to pour my heart out*.

Fuck.

I need her to stop talking to me. She fucks with my head. I didn't want *anyone* at the party.

Sure, seeing Aiden's bullshit didn't exactly set the mood. And the crowd was a little younger. And most of the women were looking at me like I was a trophy.

But there were plenty of women my age.

Plenty who were desperate to fuck me.

I tell myself to turn my cell off, but my fingers disobey me.

*Miles: Shoot.*

*Meg: Do you write the lyrics for Sinful Serenade?*

*Miles: All but one song.*

*Meg: In Pieces?*
*Miles: Nope. That one is 100% Miles Webb.*
*Meg: Really?*
*Miles: You getting at something?*

My stomach twists.

I shouldn't care what she's going to say. I shouldn't care how she looks at me. That she wants to know if I'm the guy that writes those songs.

Sure, I don't know how to be that guy when I don't have a pen in my hand.

Sure, Damon wouldn't be proud of any of the shit I do *except* for those songs?

But that doesn't fucking matter.

I'm here. I'm alive. I'm honoring the last promise I ever made to him.

If he wants more—

*Meg: It's hard to imagine you going through something like that.*

Fuck, he doesn't want anything anymore.

He's gone. He's always going to be gone. It doesn't matter what I do to honor his memory.

I can win a thousand Grammys, or swear off sex for a decade, or donate a billion dollars to charity.

He'll still be gone.

It's still going to hurt.

I turn my cell over. Try to think about anything else.

He's a whisper in my thoughts. Shaking his head *if you run, you're gonna be running forever.*

My phone buzzes again.

I swear, that must be Tom. There's no way this girl is following up that text.

*Meg: I only mean, because you're so casual about everything.*

I have to give it to her. She's really doubling down.

I should agree. Tell her she's right. I'm casual. I'm empty. I don't feel a fucking thing.

I'm the asshole who fucks three women a week. Who forgets their names the next morning. Who baits my friends until they snap.

That's what she needs to hear.

That's who I want to be. That guy who doesn't feel all this shit.

It would be so much easier. I want it to be easier.

*Miles: What do you know about how casual I am?*

*Meg: You're casual about sex.*

*Miles: And?*

*Meg: You're aloof and unaffected.*

*Miles: Says who?*

I suck in a shallow breath. *Put the phone down, asshole. Stop convincing her she's right. Stop convincing her you're more.*

*You're gonna convince yourself.*

Fuck that.

*Meg: The guy that wrote that song. He's affected. He's tortured. He hurts deep down inside.*

*Miles: And I don't?*

I can't stop my fucking fingers.

*Meg: It doesn't seem like it.*

*Miles: Are you this rude to all your friends or only me?*

*Meg: We're not really friends.*

*Miles: Apparently not.*

It's not supposed to hurt, her thinking this little of me. I shouldn't care about her opinion. About anyones.

Sorry, Damon. I know I'm supposed to stop running. But, I didn't promise that.

I've stuck to my promise. I fucking hate it, but I'm doing it.

*Meg: I'm sorry. I shouldn't have said that.*

*Miles: I've heard worse.*

*Meg: I didn't mean any offense. I swear.*

I shrug my shoulders. I. Don't. Care.

Her. Opinion. Doesn't. Matter.
None of this matters.
It's done.
I'm done.
Maybe I'll still fuck her, but that's it.

## Chapter Eight

MILES

I dream about all the depraved ways I want to punish the good girl. Wake up with easy shoulders and a settled stomach.

For once, we have a busy day. Back-to-back appointments. A bunch of shit about our image, our sound, our next album.

I love to give Tom hell for caring so much about fame and money, but it is necessary. And better him than me.

These are torture.

We finish, grab dinner at a place near the studio.

Drew waits until we're back at the house to say it. "Kara and I are gonna catch the midnight showing of *Jurassic Park* at the Nuart."

Pete shoots me a look. *Don't bait him.*

I don't take his advice. "Then her place after."

"Seriously, dude, it's old," Tom says. "He's not gonna fuck her. He doesn't have the balls."

"It's called friendship. You could try it if you weren't so annoying." Drew turns to me. "Meg is coming."

"I'm invited?" That's... surprising. Maybe he's over the whole *don't touch my friend* thing.

"Kara thinks she's into you." His voice stays matter-of-fact. "She thinks you're a dick too."

"Girls like that," Tom says.

Pete shrugs *they do*.

"Glad you're leaning into the whole broken bad boy thing," Tom says.

This time, Pete shoots his brother the *don't look*. When Tom rolls his eyes, the bassist shrugs. "You both need to grow up." He shakes his head *assholes* and heads to his room.

"I bet you wish you said that," I say to Tom.

"I'm not the one holding on to high school." Tom shrugs. He's not nearly so... removed. When he objects to something, he makes it known. But even he knows better than to insult his brother's girl.

It's not so much that Pete's girlfriend is flawed in some way. More that he's more and more miserable every time they fight and breakup.

And he's more a shell of himself every time they kiss and makeup.

Maybe I should understand—I know a lot about going back to something that hurts me—but I don't get it. How can love be worth that kind of pain?

Drew shakes his head. "Meg wants to fuck you. But don't fuck with her. Seriously, Miles. I like Kara."

"You *like* her?" I ask.

"Again, this concept of friendship—I understand how you struggle," he says.

"She is hot," Tom says. "If you're not interested—"

"You want to die?" Drew asks.

Tom just laughs *it's too easy*.

It really is. "You think she's into threesomes?" Fuck knows Tom and I shared a lot of women back in the day.

"You think I couldn't take both of you?" Drew asks.

He probably could, honestly. He has enough fight in him. "I'll be good."

"Don't lie to yourself," Drew says. "Just don't break her heart."

"I'm not gonna—"

"Not on purpose," he says. "But—"

"I know."

"Make sure she gets it," he says.

"They never do," Tom says.

"That's why you need to make sure." He shoots me a serious look. It's a plea.

"I won't." I do understand friendship. And even though he's the moodiest guy in the universe, Drew is my friend. I'm not gonna fuck shit up for him.

I'm not trying to hurt anyone.

It's just going to be sex.

Me making her come.

So I can stop thinking about her. Period. End of story.

---

Fuck, she looks good.

Her white tank top shows off her shoulders. And that skirt—

Perfect for making her come. In the dark theater. Or back at her place.

Or pressed up against the wall in the alley outside.

Anywhere. As long as she's screaming my name.

She clears her throat. Blushes the world's most adorable blush. "Hi."

I nod *hey* back. I'm keeping this sex. All sex. Sure, I'll make her laugh. But I'm not talking about the guy who wrote *In Pieces*. I don't know where he is and I like it that way.

"Thanks."

Drew does nothing to hide how much he wants to fuck Kara. Not that I can blame him. She's wearing a dress that shows off her curvy figure.

I nudge him *watch it*. If he's going to insist on this whole *we're just friends* thing, he should probably keep his eyes off her tits.

Meg barely notices them. Her eyes drift over me slowly. Shoulders, waist, hips. Then back to the tattoo on my chest.

She's obsessed with the thing. Because she can't quite make it out? Or because she thinks it's the key to my heart?

Maybe because she wants to touch me, period, the end.

I'm not sure which I want.

Drew barely manages to pull his eyes away from Kara. He nods hello to Meg. "Hope you don't mind us crashing your girls' night out."

"Who could resist the chance to watch *Jurassic Park* on the big screen?" Meg beams. Fucking beams. For the first time, she seems like she's where she wants to be.

The joy in her eyes—

I like it way more than I should.

Thank fuck her shirt slips. My thoughts go to exactly where they need to go.

Her blush deepens. "Should we get tickets? It's almost midnight."

Kara pulls something from her purse. "Already got 'em."

Perfect. "Meg and I can grab seats. You guys get drinks." I need to make her blush again. Drew isn't going to like my methods.

"Sure." She moves into the theater.

It's a small space. One screen. About a hundred seats. Maybe a hundred fifty.

I press my palm to her lower back. Lead her into the space. A seat in the middle. So I won't touch her.

Not yet. Not here.

Her eyelids flutter closed. A sigh falls off her lips.

She takes an aisle seat. I take the one next to her. Turn toward her. Just enough to invite her to respond.

*This* is what I'm thinking.

Our bodies. Her groaning my name as she comes. Her cunt pulsing around my cock.

Nothing else.

Meg turns toward me. Her eyes fix on my jeans. Travel up my body slowly.

I try to keep my eyes on hers, but it's hard with her skirt riding up her long legs. "You keep looking at me like you're thinking about throwing me on your bed."

"I do not," she teases.

"You do too."

She shakes her head. It sends her dark hair over her eyes, cheeks, shoulders.

Over her adorable blush.

I brush a strand behind her ear.

She looks up at me, utterly intoxicated.

"Any thoughts you'd like to share?" I ask.

She pulls back. "This movie, it's all about how men shouldn't fuck with female creatures. It should be a warning to you."

Fuck, she's too cute. "True."

"You like *Jurassic Park*?"

"Why? Did you also not imagine the guy who wrote *In Pieces* as liking *Jurassic Park*?" Shit, where did that come from? I need to lay off the heavy shit. Keep it about sex.

"I didn't consider it."

"Guy who's been through that kind of pain. He'd want something dark, *Alien*," I say "Maybe *Terminator Two*."

She laughs so hard her tits shake. Joy overtakes her. Lights up her eyes, curls her lip corners upward, softens her grip.

It's a gorgeous laugh. And it's such a sharp contrast. This girl is walking around in knots.

Easing some of that—

It shouldn't soothe something in me, but it does.

I try to find some way to convince both of us it's meaningless, but Drew interrupts.

He steps over us, taking the seat next to me. "Kara's in the bathroom." He shoots me this knowing look. *Don't fuck this up*. But he can't keep up the stern expression. He's too worried. He's too into his friend. "Meg, find me if Miles is giving you trouble. I'll take care of it."

"Next you're supposed to threaten violence," I tease him. "So we all know you're tough."

"You think I won't punch you in the face?" Drew asks.

"You have before." It's a funny story. "It was over a riff. I called it derivative and Drew snapped." All right, maybe it's one of those *you had to be there* situations.

"Fuck you. That was an amazing lick." Drew shakes his head, mostly teasing.

"Not gonna change my mind no matter how many times you hit me." I chuckle.

He grins as he flips me off. The guy is in a good mood around his friend. Or maybe I'm being less obnoxious than usual. "Damn, forgot about my favorite part of this movie, when the T-rex eats the piece of shit lawyer."

"I was going to be a lawyer," I say. "Drew is pretty subtle sometimes. He can be hard to understand."

Drew shakes his head. Shoots me this look I haven't

seen in a while. *I trust you to not fuck this up. Don't abuse that trust.*

It should encourage me, but it shakes too much loose.

Not going there.

Checking out the cute virgin's blush. The heave of her chest. The long legs.

I want to make her come because she's adorable.

And sexy as hell.

Not because I want more of her.

That would be fucking ridiculous.

## Chapter Nine

MILES

I make sure Drew gets the chance to escort his friend home. Which leaves me and Meg alone.

It's a cool night, but I'm already on fire. She's so fucking cute, shifting her weight between her legs, looking at me like she's picturing me naked.

"Your place is close," I say.

She nods *yeah*. "You could walk me home."

Fuck yes. "Sure."

She motions *this way*.

I follow her through the moonlit neighborhood. West LA is nothing like the Orange County suburb where I grew up. The rows of houses are dark. No streetlights keeping kids safe all night.

She slows until I'm next to her then keeps time with me. She's tall. Her legs are nearly as long as mine.

Fuck, those legs—

I let my gaze flit over her again. "You have the same idea I do?"

"I doubt that." She laughs.

I don't. "Your friend and mine?"

She arches a brow.

"He needs to get laid. And he's looking at her the way a dog looks at a bone."

"They're just friends." She says it without any conviction.

"Doubt it."

"Why?"

"You didn't notice them eye-fucking?"

"No, I did. Just… She says they're just friends. I don't have any reason to doubt her." She turns at the intersection. Onto Sawtelle.

Her place is close.

Really fucking close.

My heartbeat picks up. My body is eager. Too eager. I haven't fucked anyone all week. I haven't done that in—

I don't even know.

Still. No matter how badly her body is screaming *take him now*, I have to ease her into this.

I have to go slow.

"I like your skirt," I say.

"Thanks."

"You wear it for me?"

"In your dreams."

Fuck, she's too cute. "Oh, no, I had a dream about you already, and it was a lot more fun."

Her cheeks flush. "You did not."

"I did. In fact—" I lean close enough to brush my fingers against the back of her hand. Just enough to test her reaction. To see if she wants this too.

She leans into the gesture.

Sighs as I run my finger over her thumb.

"You were wearing something a lot like that skirt," I say.

She swallows hard.

"Only without any panties."

She struggles through a breath. "I don't believe you."

"I didn't save my sticky sheets."

"You didn't… You're just flirting."

"No. We're past that point." All right, no more games. No more bullshit. Just our bodies connecting. I brush her hair behind her ear. "You want me, and I want you. There's no reason to hide that."

She tilts her head to one side, offering her neck to me.

I stay slow. Run my fingers over her shoulder. Just enough to brush the straps of her tank top. Just enough to make her think about me stripping her naked.

"Okay." She looks up at me, equal parts needy and nervous. "What does that mean?"

"It's up to you. I'm not going to push you to do anything you don't want to do."

"Oh."

"If you're not ready, I'll walk you home. That's it."

"And if I am ready?"

"Then I'll make sure you come so hard you forget your name."

Chapter Ten
---

MILES

She stays close in the elevator. The walk down her hall. As she pulls her keys from her purse.

This is it. Her place.

Either she invites me in or—

I don't fucking know. Usually, I don't care whether or not a woman rejects me.

I don't invest enough to care.

But with this girl...

It's different.

I move closer. Run my fingers over her cheek. It's not like me. I don't go for gestures this intimate. This *boyfriend*. But it feels right. "Did you make your decision?"

She takes a deep, slow breath.

She's still scared. Because it's new or because she doesn't trust me. I don't know.

Either way, I need to set her at ease.

I let my fingers skim her neck "Turn around."

She does. Her eyes find mine. They fill with this pure, deep need.

She wants me. All of me.

It's exactly what I need.

And, fuck, she's so sexy blushed and panting.

I force myself to move slow as I bring my hand to her lower back. I pull her body into mine one inch at a time.

Her pelvis, her stomach, her chest.

Her lips.

I kiss her hard. Deep. With everything I have.

Kissing isn't my thing, but I want her lips on mine. Want her groaning against my mouth.

Her body melts into mine.

Her hand goes to my hair. She tugs at it, holding my head against hers, pulling me closer.

I pin her to the door.

She gasps as my cock brushes her cunt.

All this fabric in the way, but I can feel her heat all the same.

I release her. Take a small step backward. So I won't pounce on her before she invites me in.

Her brown eyes fix on me. "I want to do this, but not if I'm going to be some girl whose name you can't remember."

"I don't do relationships." The words are familiar, but they feel foreign on my tongue. It's like I can hear Damon shaking his head, asking me what I'm running from.

"Me either. But… I don't want to be another notch in your bedpost."

Maybe this is enough. To quiet that voice that I'm disappointing him. Hey, it's not like I'm lying to her. I'm offering her *a* relationship. Maybe it's not the love of a lifetime, but it's honest. "We're friends, right?"

"Something like that."

"Sinful Serenade is gonna be in Los Angeles for the rest of the year. It might be nice having something consistent."

"So I'm convenient?"

"No. You're sexy. And different." My eyes flit over her body. "Most girls trip over themselves trying to impress me. You don't."

"That's all it takes to win you over?"

Some of it. There's something else too. Something I can't explain. "We could be fuck buddies."

"Monogamous?"

Yeah. I nod.

"But you sleep with a different girl every night."

"Only most nights." That doesn't matter. Right now, it barely appeals. I close the distance between us. Shift my hips, pinning her to the door. "I don't play games, Meg. If you're not interested, tell me."

"No, I am. But I…" Her eyes go to the floor. "I haven't ever done it before."

I know, but now's not the time to point it out. "We can take it slow."

"No. I want to do it."

Fuck, she's too cute. "You're eager."

"You're hard."

"Accurate." Way too hard to go slow. But I've resisted worse temptations. "Let me lead. I'll walk you through this."

"Okay." She takes a deep breath, unlocks the door, invites me in.

Her room is cleaned up. Her bed is made. Like she was expecting company. Planning for this.

She moves to the sink, fills two glasses, brings one to me.

No offer of a drink.

Huh.

She takes a long sip. Swallows hard. "I have terms. I'm sure you do too."

I'm not sure she's going to like them. "Shoot."

"I want total honesty. No secrets. No lies. No deception at all."

"I don't want you getting the wrong idea here. This isn't going to turn into some boyfriend/girlfriend relationship."

"Good. I don't want a boyfriend. During the week, I barely have time to study. And…" Her voice trails off. Her gaze gets fuzzy. Like she's drifting off some place ugly. "I don't want that kind of connection to someone."

I set my glass on her dresser. Move closer. Close enough to read her better. "You seem like a nice girl."

"No, I don't."

Yeah, but who likes nice? "Okay. You're a little defensive, and it's awfully rude that you assumed I never hurt." I run my fingertips over her chin. "I like you. But you're never going to be my confidant. You're never going to be the shoulder I cry on." I need to make this clear. To both of us.

"Do you cry?" It's half teasing, half curious.

"Honesty, right?"

"From both of us."

"Haven't cried in a while. You?"

"Can't say the same."

Fuck, all that pain of hers is right there. On the surface. How does she deal with it? "I'm not a monster. I don't want to hurt you."

"You won't. Not if you're honest."

I don't know. She's reeling from something. I want to fuck her senseless. But I can't add to that. I can't let her believe in something that isn't there. Maybe she thinks I'm a shallow asshole, but she's asking about *In Pieces*.

She's not sure.

She believes there's more.

Some part of her wants to know that guy.

Some part of her wants the tortured musician who sings her to sleep.

That isn't happening. "See, these conditions, they worry me. Make me think you're after more than just a good time."

"Now you're the one being presumptuous."

"Fair point." Maybe she gets it. That I'm a shallow asshole. That I'm not the salve for her wounds. "Okay, I'll agree to total honesty. But I have my own condition. The second you develop feelings for me, this is over."

"What if you develop feelings for me? What if you fall in love with me?" She tugs at her skirt. "Isn't that possible?"

Honestly, I wish it was. I wish love was as beautiful as pop songs made it out to be. "No."

"Whatever." Her nostrils flare. Her brow knits with frustration. "I'll tell you if I develop feelings for you."

"You're cute when you're flustered."

"Fuck off. You're not cute when you're acting like nothing has ever mattered to you."

How the fuck can she tell?

No. She's just trying to fuck with me.

She got lucky pressing the right bruise. She doesn't know. No one knows.

I clear my throat. "It's a compliment."

"Not to me."

"This, us being on the same page, matters to me."

"Me too."

"We're fuck buddies and we don't lie to each other." I take her glass. Set it on the counter. "And you'll tell me if you develop feelings for me."

She nods with understanding.

I offer my palm.

She takes it. Shakes. Stares up at me like she can't wait to devour me.

## Chapter Eleven

MILES

Fuck, I'm on fire.

The leggy virgin is my fuck buddy.

She's inviting me to be her first.

No. It's more than that now. She isn't some idea I have of a woman who will save me—a smoking hot geek girl who wants to fuck all night and talk Star Wars all day.

She's Meg. The defensive, biting, guarded woman who wants to keep me out of her heart as much as I want to keep her out of mine.

God, I must be fucked up if that's my criteria for a friend with benefits, but I can't say I care.

I'm done worshiping my misery.

Even if it's the cause of my success.

I meet Meg's gaze. Her brown eyes are still filled with nerves, but there's a hunger to her expression.

She needs this as badly as I do.

But she's new and scared.

I need to be careful with her.

I need to make sure we both savor every moment of it.

I move closer. Until my body is pressed against hers. Until I can feel all the heat of her against me.

Her breath catches in her throat as my crotch connects with hers.

I'm still hard. Our conversation wasn't nearly enough to cool me down. I'm not sure anything could cool me down right now.

I stare into her eyes as I trace the neckline of her tank top. "Had enough of conversation?"

She nods.

"Me too." I push her straps off her shoulders then roll her top over her black bra. Fuck, she has nice tits. "Been thinking about this all week."

Surprise streaks her expression. "You have?"

"Yeah." What is it about this girl? Why can't she see the affect she has on me? My body is already raring to go.

I trace the outline of her bra as slowly as I can manage.

It's torture, not touching her properly, but the way her breath catches in her throat is worth it.

I make my touch harder. Harder. Until a soft groan falls off her lips. "First time I've gone a week without sex in a long time."

"Because of me?"

"Yeah." My voice drops to something low and seductive. It's too much like my usual routine. I need to do away with all that bullshit. Even if I'm desperate to make this an experience she won't forget. "Wouldn't be right fucking some other girl if I was thinking of you."

Her brown eyes go wide. Then her eyelids press together. Her head falls to one side. Her dark hair goes with it. It falls over her eyes, nose, lips. Like she's lost in passion.

I need more of that.

No. I need all of that.

Right now, this isn't the rock star and the virgin.

Right now, it's Miles and Meg.

No pretenses. No bullshit. Nothing but our bodies.

Fuck, I haven't felt like that in…

It's been too fucking long.

I slip my thumb into her bra. Drag it over her nipple.

She lets out a sharp gasp. An I need this gasp. A this is exactly where we both belong gasp.

There aren't many places where I feel at home.

Behind my guitar. On stage.

And here.

When sex is real, there's nothing better.

I toy with her with my thumb. Soft, slow circles. Then harder ones. Then hard enough her teeth sink into her bottom lip.

A groan falls off her lips.

Her fingers dig into my shoulders.

She looks up at me with a nod. Inviting me to take over. To take her. To show her every bit of pleasure in the world.

Right now, that's the only thing that matters.

I unhook her bra and roll it off her shoulders.

Fuck. "Your tits are amazing."

Her cheeks flush. She still doesn't believe how much I want her. How much I want this. Is it some insecurity on her part or some assholeness on mine? I can't deny the latter, but, fuck, this is no place for pretenses.

Her eyelids flicker open. Her brown eyes fix on mine for a second, then her lids are closed again.

I'm not going to convince her of anything with words.

I need to do this with my body.

I need to force her out of her head.

I bring one hand to her hip and pull her body into

mine. Cup her breast with my palm. Tease her nipple with my thumb.

Her back arches. Her crotch rubs against mine. Her lips part with a groan.

She leans into my touch.

I tease her nipple until she's clawing at my chest, then I move to her other breast and toy with it just as mercilessly.

I back her into the bed. Go to push her onto it.

But something is off.

She's tensing up.

I brush her hair behind her ear. Bring my lips to her ear. "You're nervous."

She shakes her head. "It's nothing."

It's something. But it's normal too. "I'll go slow." I brush my lips against her neck. "Trust me. I've got you."

Slowly, she nods.

She does trust me. It fills me someplace I'm usually empty. It's been a long, long time since anyone has had any faith in me. And trust?

I burned those bridges to the ground a long time ago.

Fuck, it feels so good, the way she's looking at me.

I bring my hands to her hips and push her onto the bed.

Her breath catches.

Her palms go to her sides.

Slowly, I lower myself to my knees between her legs.

She watches with rapt attention as I nudge her knees apart.

Her tongue slides over her lips.

She nods. It's something between I trust you and hurry the fuck up.

I want to.

But I need to savor this.

Fuck, how I need to savor this.

## Just a Taste

Slowly, I take her nipple into my mouth.

She tastes good. And the way she's tugging at my hair…

This is exactly what I need.

I toy with her until I can't take her groans anymore then I kiss my way to her lips.

I need more.

All of this.

My hands go to her thighs.

My tongue plunges into her mouth.

I kiss her hard as I slip my hand under her skirt.

She sinks into the bed.

Slides her hand under my t-shirt.

She takes her time exploring my torso.

Her fingertips are just right against my skin. But it's more than the heat of her touch. There's something about the way she's dragging her hand over my skin.

Like she's desperate for every inch of me.

It's intimate in a way I don't recognize.

It's more than I can take.

This isn't supposed to be sweet.

Tender maybe, but not sweet.

I push it away as I rub her over her panties. I can get this back to sex. I can keep this about our bodies.

Her moans vibrate down my throat.

Her nails dig into my skin.

Her touch gets hungry. Needy.

Perfect.

Slowly, I peel her panties to her knees.

I watch anticipation spread over her face as I bring my hands to her chest. I toy with her nipples until she's panting, then I drag my hands down her torso, undo her skirt, push it and her panties to her knees.

She stares up at me, hunger filling her brown eyes.

She's naked under me and I'm looking at her eyes.

This isn't good.

And it isn't happening.

I'm not getting attached. Period.

I'm staring because I want to watch her come. That's it.

Her teeth sink into her lip as I bring my hand to her inner thigh.

Her breath hitches as I bring it higher, higher, higher…

She gasps as I tease her clit.

Fuck, she feels good.

And she's already wet.

She's already desperate for me.

I stare down at her, gauging her reaction. The apprehension from earlier is gone. She's not nervous anymore.

She's in her body.

She needs me more than she needs anything.

I'm more than happy to deliver.

I tease her with one finger. "Damn, you're wet."

She responds with a groan.

I slide a finger inside her. She tenses. Tugs at my hair. Bites her tongue.

"Close your eyes," I whisper.

She does.

"Just breathe."

She nods.

Slowly, her taut muscles relax.

I push my finger deeper.

Pleasure fills her expression.

Deeper.

Her shoulders tense.

I slow my pace until that discomfort fades.

My lips find hers.

I kiss her hard as I drive my fingers into her.

She kisses back like she needs more.

## Just a Taste

Like she knows exactly what she wants.

I'm about to give it to her when this awful sound cuts through the air.

My phone.

The ringtone set for Tom.

Damn, the asshole really knows how to fuck with me.

I reach for my cell to turn the damn thing off. "Ignore it." Tom fucks with me enough. He's not ruining this.

But Meg isn't here.

She's tensing up again.

I push off her. "You okay?"

She shakes her head. "The phone. You should get it."

What the hell? She wants me to answer the call? "You're about to come and you'd prefer I use my hands to answer the phone?"

Her nod is shy. Hesitant. "Do you doubt your ability to get me back here?"

"No, but I'm going to scream if I'm not inside you soon."

Her nails curl into her palms. She stares at me like she's going to devour me.

But she still nods to the cell.

It makes no sense.

I push off the bed with a heavy sigh. Sure enough, there's Tom's contact on my screen. It's like he knows I'm about to defile Drew's girl's best friend and he's trying to stop me. "Yeah?"

"You need to get back here." Tom spouts off something about our manager being at our place in Hollywood. Being drunk and indignant, threatening to kick us out of the house the label is so kindly paying for if I don't show him the song I've been working on ASAP.

I guess, this time, my hate goes to our insufferable manager and not to the bossy drummer.

It does sound like Aiden.

Especially when I kept him from fucking a teenager. I'm sure he's pissed and looking for retribution.

There's no way around it. Nothing I can do but play his stupid mind games.

The guy has the power to destroy us. Even if I could live with it—that's questionable—I can't do that to my friends. Sanctimonious asshole that he is, Tom is right.

I'm the one with enough money for a lifetime. They're the ones who will struggle to pay the rent after the cash runs out.

"Give me an hour," I say.

"You need to be here yesterday," Tom replies.

Fine. As much as Tom gets on my last nerves, he's my friend. I'm not gonna force him to deal with this alone. "I can't teleport. It will be at least half an hour."

"Good." The phone clicks as he ends the call.

I leave my cell on the kitchen counter. Run my hand through my hair.

Not how I want to end tonight. I look back to Meg. "It's nothing you need to worry about. Just some drama at the Hollywood place."

"And you'll be there in half an hour?"

"Around that."

"You really think we're going to… in thirty minutes?"

Fuck no. I shake my head. "That's not enough time to do this right."

"Oh." She pulls her arms over her chest. "I guess you're leaving then."

Yeah. But maybe that's for the best. I need to untangle my head. To make sure I don't get attached. Still—"I'd really hate to leave without making you come."

"Oh." She squeezes her thighs together. Slides back against the bed. Her fingers curl into her sheets.

That trust we had before is gone.

I stare back at her. Offer my best apologetic expression. Apologies are not my strong suit, but this is all I've got.

Her expression softens.

She nods. Forces a smile. "You have a serious time crunch there."

That, I do. I take a seat on the bed. Place my body next to hers.

No more talking this time.

No more thinking.

Nothing but my hands on her skin.

And her groans in my ears.

I brush my lips against her neck.

Drag my fingertips over her nipples.

I copy her posture, sit up with my back against the headboard, my legs flat on the bed.

My hands go to her hips.

I pull her body onto mine.

She sinks into my skin.

Her crotch brushes mine.

Her eyes find mine.

I stare up at her like she's everything I want.

Maybe she is.

But this is it.

My hand curls around her neck. I pull her into a deep kiss.

Slip my other hand between her legs.

This is sex.

Me bringing her pleasure.

Period.

The end.

My tongue slips into her mouth as my thumb slides over her clit.

She begs for more with her kiss.

But I take my time.
Rub her softly.
Then harder.
Harder.
There.
She breaks our kiss to groan.
Her nails dig into my shoulders.
I keep that same pace, that same pressure.
It's exactly what she needs.
She moans.
Kisses back like she's trying to consume me.
Fuck, her lips feel good against mine.
She tastes good.
And the way she groans like I'm everything she needs…
I rub her with that same pressure.
I take her all the way to the edge.
Her nails dig into my skin.
Her tongue slides around mine.
Her hand tugs at my hair.
Then she's there, pulsing around me, groaning my name.
I don't give her a chance to rest. I can't. This feels too fucking good.
I stroke her harder. Harder.
Until she's wound up again.
She sucks on my tongue. Arches into me. Presses her thighs against my wrist.
Then she's there.
She pulls back to groan my name.
She growls it loud enough to wake the neighbors.
Pleasure spreads over her expression as she falls onto her back.
She looks up at me with a hazy smile.

Fuck, that feels good too.

Too good.

I lean down to press my lips to hers. "My cock isn't going to forgive me for leaving."

"I'm not sure I will either."

"I'll make it up to you." I slide off the bed. My head is already full of thoughts of driving inside her. Waiting a week to do it… it's going to be the sweetest torture. "Sleep tight." I grab my stuff and move toward the door.

"You too. Once you get home, I mean."

I nod a goodbye.

Then I leave.

But my thoughts stay on her the entire ride home.

When I get back, Aiden is already asleep on the couch.

God, this is all such bullshit.

I head to my room, collapse on my bed, and I think of Meg.

But I keep it every bit as dirty as it should be.

'Cause that's all it is.

That's all it can ever be.

## Chapter Twelve

MEGARA

"Sweetie, *Futurama* movies do not count as movies," Kara says. "I'll let you have it because I love you, but you have to know it's total bullshit."

"You're such a stickler."

"You're the one who came up with the idea of taking turns. I don't give a damn. We can watch sci-fi every week. Anything except *Battlestar Galactica*."

My phone buzzes. I try to ignore it. It's difficult. I haven't heard a word from Miles since he left my house late enough it was technically Saturday morning.

It's been more than twenty-four hours.

I tap my fingers against my cell's screen. "It's not the show's fault everyone called you Starbuck in high school."

She watches my tapping and raises a brow. "You gonna check your phone?"

"It's probably nothing."

"Uh-huh." She shakes her head and moves to the kitchen. "Frosted Flakes or Cocoa Puffs?"

"Both."

Kara and I have a weekly routine. Sunday brunch. It's

supposed to be for homework, but mostly we watch movies, eat cereal straight from the box, and drink medically unsound amounts of caffeine.

Last year, our weekly meetings were the only time I wasn't studying. I was so focused on that stupid MCAT. It was the only thing I paid attention to. It's why I didn't notice Rosie's slip into addiction. It's why I let it slide when she told me she was fine, even though that uneasy feeling in my gut screamed that she was lying.

My phone buzzes again.

I know it's Miles. He and Kara are the only two people who text me.

But I don't want to be desperate to turn my phone over. I don't want his reaction to have the power to leave me in knots.

I don't want my body to be so… hungry for his.

But, God, the memory of his hands on my skin, his lips on my hips, his groans in my ear—

My cheeks flush.

My sex clenches.

My hands work on their own. They unlock my cell. Go straight to his text.

*Miles: Any soreness?*
*Meg: No. I'm good.*
*Miles: Only good?*
*Meg: Only good. I'm studying.*

Sort of.

Kara plops next to me. She hands me a can of green tea and a bowl of puffed corn coated in sugar and cocoa powder.

I pop open my can and take a long sip.

She taps my shoulder. "Is that who I think it is?"

"We're just talking."

"That is one hundred percent grade-A bullshit." Her laugh is easy. "You should come up with a better lie."

"Maybe."

"Any details?"

"Uh… not yet."

"And you're… sure he's a good idea?" She stares at me, challenging me to tell the truth.

"No. But he's—"

"So hot."

I nod *yeah*. "And really… it's like my body is on fire when he's around. But in a good way."

"And you feel like you're going to die if you don't touch him?"

"Yeah."

"Did you… touch him?"

"A little." I press my cell to my chest. "Is it like that for you? With Drew?"

"It's different." She doesn't add *we're friends. I can't touch him. No matter how much I want to*. Even though we both know it's there. "You know he's a slut."

"Drew?"

"Miles."

Yeah, I caught him with a stranger. He could barely remember her name. It should scare me more than it does. "I know."

"And you're just…"

"Having fun."

She raises a brow *really*.

I nod *really*.

"Be careful, okay?"

"I will."

"Are you gonna keep texting him?"

I motion *a little*.

"I'm going to put in something I like."

"Okay."

"Something with subtitles."

"Go for it." I turn back to my phone.

*Miles: We have a show next week. Why don't you come? Then you can come and come and come.*

*Miles: That was three. But three is the bare minimum.*

I turn my phone over and slide it into my pocket. "There's a Sinful Serenade show next weekend?"

Kara taps the remote, starting play on some independent film with stark scenery and a minimalist soundtrack. She raises an eyebrow like she's challenging me to explain. "Friday. Starts while you're at work, but I can wait."

I shake my head. "I'll take the bus."

"You can't take the bus to Hollywood that late. No way in hell. I'll pick you up."

"You'll miss—"

"It's decided," she says. "And you'll text me if you decide to leave with someone?"

"I promise."

―――

My shift at the ER ends at ten on the dot. By 10:05 p.m., I'm in Kara's car, in one of her bodycon dresses, applying makeup with an unsteady hand. Black eyeliner, dark lipstick, plenty of blush. One of the upsides of having dramatic features is that I can pull off a lot of makeup.

I run a comb through my messy hair. It doesn't help. Better to return it to a work-appropriate ponytail.

At least the dress is nice. A little short for my long legs, and I certainly don't fill it out well, but it looks better than I'd expect given the ten inches I have on Kara. Or the four cup sizes she has on me.

I scroll past our flirty texts about nothing to get to Miles's promise.

*Miles: We have a show next week. Why don't you come? Then you can come and come and come.*

*Miles: That was three. But three is the bare minimum.*

I'm not dreaming. This is really happening.

Kara parks three blocks from the venue at an expired meter. She smiles. "Here goes nothing."

I take a deep breath, pulling in all the confidence I can manage. The walk to the venue nearly undoes me. These aren't even heels. They're wedges, short wedges, but I can barely move in them.

Kara gives our names to the bouncer. We're on the list. I've never been on a list before. I've never been anywhere that needed a list.

I try to channel Miles's cool aloofness but I fail. I'm teetering. My dress is too tight. Do people really go clubbing for fun? I feel hopelessly out of place.

Until I hear his voice.

It's a low moan, not actual words, but I'm still positive that Miles is the guy who is singing. Which means Sinful Serenade is in the middle of a song.

Sound echoes around the high ceilings. It gets louder the farther we get into the club. A guitar screams. Drums pound. The bass-line throbs. The energy from the music flows into the room.

There must be three or four hundred people squeezed into a space meant for far, far less. Mostly girls, mostly screaming their lungs out.

Everything is dark, almost black, save the bright white stage lights.

Miles stands on the front of the stage, his fingers wrapped around a microphone, his eyes closed as if he's feeling the song so deeply he can't bear to keep them open.

All of my attention is on Miles. His voice is beautiful. Not just beautiful. It's breathy, and throaty, and wounded as all hell. Every word comes out with a thousand pounds of emotional force behind it. It's like his voice is seeping through my skin and bones, all the way into my soul. It's like I can feel whatever it is that made him write this song.

It hurts. Not as badly as *In Pieces*, but enough.

The songs ends. There's no break. Sinful Serenade transitions right into the next number. This one is faster, harder, louder. It's more upbeat, but there's still an undercurrent of hurt in Miles's voice. I catch a few of the lyrics. They're beautiful wisps of poetry.

Right now, he's not cocky, arrogant, or aloof. His heart is in his words. The ache in his soul is in his words.

My chest is heavy. I'm hurting with him.

I close my eyes and lose myself in his voice. There's so much sound around us—the screaming, the guitar, the bass, the drums—but all I can hear is Miles. It's like he's singing to me.

The song ends. I open my eyes, startled by the quick return to reality. The room feels darker and brighter at once. Miles feels closer and farther away.

The singer smiles at the crowd with that same cocky expression on his face. He waves and blows a kiss. A dozen girls squeal, sure his adoration is meant for them.

He looks back at his bandmates. Can't say that I'm paying much attention to the other guys. They seem to be in some kind of blissful, meditative state. They're all so effortlessly cool.

Miles looks back at the crowd. "I'd like to dedicate this next song to a very special girl. I'm not sure that she thinks much of me, but, Meg, I wrote this song, too."

The drummer brings his sticks down hard on his drum kit. "Only the lyrics, Romeo."

Miles sends the drummer a sweet smile then blows him a kiss. Must be some kind of inside joke. The drummer shakes his head, stands, and pulls off his shirt.

The screams are so loud I can't even think. The crowd likes him sans shirt. They like it a lot.

Hard to blame them. He's an attractive man—wavy dirty blond hair, sculpted torso, a tattoo with thick black lines on his chest and snaking down his arm.

Next to me, Kara laughs. She's eying Drew like she hopes the stripping will start some kind of chain reaction. I don't call her on it.

Miles tugs at the bottom of his t-shirt, teasing the crowd to a chorus of cheers. He walks over to the equally handsome dark-haired bassist and hands him the mic.

It's unfair, having four attractive men in such close proximity. There isn't a woman alive who could resist all four of them.

Miles's eyes go back to the crowd. If I didn't know better, I'd swear he's looking at me. I'd swear he's doing this solely for my benefit.

He pulls it higher, higher, higher. And then it's off his head and on the ground.

There's barely an inch of fat on his body. He has a six-pack. And those v-lines. They make it difficult to think. The color tattoos that decorate his chest and arms keep my brain in a *damn, he's hot* loop.

Miles drags his hands over his sculpted chest like he can't bear how sexy he is.

The cheers are deafening. Mr. Miles Webb is certainly the object of lust. Hard to blame the girls staring at him with their eyes wide and their jaws dropped. No doubt, there will be a dozen pairs of panties on stage by the end of the song.

He could have any woman he wants, and he wants me.

He made me come.

He's going to make me come again. Three times. He promised three times.

Miles takes the microphone back. "Is it hot in here, or is it just me?"

The crowd screams.

"So, it's just me?" He winks at the crowd. He points to the guitarist then to the bassist. "Only two songs to go. Think we can get the string jockeys shirtless by the end of the show?"

There's another set of cheers. Every guy in the band has his fans.

Miles smiles that same smug smile. He throws up four fingers and uses them to count down.

The song starts. It's one of their singles. It plays on KROQ but not nearly as often as *In Pieces* does. It has a slick guitar riff, a throbbing beat, and, of course, a perfect vocal melody.

Kara squeezes my hand. I can't bring myself to look away from Miles to catch her expression. No doubt, she's ecstatic, too. I squeeze back. I shift my hips to the music. I scream. Just another fan. Just another girl who wants that sexy boy on stage she'll never have.

Only, I can have him.

I have had him.

The song transitions into the next. The last song, according to Miles's earlier claim. There is something final about it. It's like everyone is playing harder. Miles goes all out with his vocals. He's not in smug mode, not flirting with the crowd. He's there, in the music, in the moment that made him write this song.

It's captivating, sexy, and terrifying at once. There's more to Miles than bad boy rock star. There must be, or he wouldn't be so lost in his words.

The song ends to a chorus of screams and cheers. The Sinful guys wave goodbye. Miles takes a bow. The drummer blows kisses. He even holds his hand up to his ear to make the call me motion. They walk off stage, and a roadie collects their discarded t-shirts.

Kara pulls me away from the main crowd. She gives our names to the bouncer guarding the backstage area. He lets us pass.

The small space is crowded with gear. There are other musician types here—must be the opening act—but most of them are busy soaking in groupie adoration. One of them is sucking face against the wall. And, oh, God, he's getting a hand job.

I guess they don't call it *sex*, drugs, and rock-and-roll for nothing.

There's a door marked Sinful Serenade. It's a lot less busy than the rest of the backstage area. Drew is sitting on the couch alone. The light-haired drummer is surrounded by a cloud of fans. His attention turns to us.

He nods to Drew then to Kara. "Kara, right?"

"You're not sleeping with my friends." Drew waves the guy off. "So why don't you get Aiden to put another one of our songs in a commercial while I'm occupied?"

The drummer offers his hand. "I'm Tom."

"Meg." I shake.

"Nice to meet you. And to see you again, Kara." He nods a goodbye. "Sometimes, I think I'm the only person in the band who cares about making money." Tom shakes his head with outrage and returns to his cloud of fans.

"Want a drink?" Drew asks. His gaze fixes on something behind me. "Maybe a shirt."

I turn. It's Miles, standing there in his tight jeans, still sans shirt. He shakes his head, but he still grabs a t-shirt off the couch and pulls it on.

Miles throws Drew a cocky wink. There's no challenge or animosity to it, just mutual understanding. They're teasing each other.

Drew goes to grab Kara's wrist but she pulls it into her chest. He looks at her a little funny. She shrugs like it's nothing.

"Come on, Kendrick. You'll miss the good tequila."

She nods. "Meg, you want something?"

I shake my head. "No thanks."

She follows Drew to a table in the back, leaving me alone with Miles. Or as good as alone.

He runs his fingertips over my exposed shoulders. I'm hot instantly. It feels good being near him. It will feel better without the audience, without the space between us, without the clothes.

"I like your dress," he says.

"Thanks."

"And the heels, too. Tall girls are usually afraid of them."

My mouth refuses to form words.

"Bet they give you extra leverage when you're pressed against a wall."

A blush spreads across my cheeks. I open my mouth to speak, but it's still not happening.

Dammit, he's effortless again. And I'm nervous and bumbling again.

This is too much, too fast. I need to collect my thoughts. I take a step backward. "Excuse me. I changed my mind about that drink."

The bar in the corner is mostly booze in every color. There are mixers. Only one interests me. Grapefruit juice. Truly the most under-appreciated fruit in the world—tart, sweet, and sour all at once. I pour myself a large glass and take a sip. It's not fresh squeezed, but it's not bad.

I want Miles. I'm sure of that.

But there are other feelings stirring in my gut. Something besides desire. Something I might not be able to handle.

By the time I'm done with my juice, the room is packed. People bump into me, nod hellos, introduce themselves in breathy voices meant to imply I'm another girl here to hand out blow jobs to anyone with the ability to play a musical instrument.

I slip out of the room. The backstage area is equally slammed. It's a real party scene—people drinking from red cups, flirting, kissing, sharing stories, and laughing at the top of their lungs. I find the closest door and push through it. Air. I need air. And I need to not be here.

The alley-slash-parking lot is an asphalt wasteland. There are a few loners leaning against the wall smoking cigarettes. I copy their position, breathing deep to suck in as much air as possible. Instead, I get a lungful of smoke.

Forget that. I move to the corner of the parking lot.

A girl in a mini-dress and stilettos waves at me. "We don't bite, hun."

She giggles and motions for me to come closer. I do.

There are half a dozen people milling around a parked car.

One of them, a skinny guy in a suit, is tapping white powder out of a baggie onto the back of his cell phone. He drags a credit card across it and rakes it into straight lines.

They're doing cocaine.

My heart races. I can't be around this. That's how it starts. How it started for Rosie. First, it was her jerk boyfriend dragging her to parties where everyone was desperate to be up or down. Then she was trying drugs— Rosie never was the type to back down from a dare.

Then she was gone.

It happened so fast. Just playing along, being one of the cool girls at the party, and then she's gone. Overdosed. Dead.

The skinny guy leans over, bringing his nose to the back of the phone. And just like in a fucking movie, he snorts the line.

He snorts the other line, sits up, and rubs his nose. Then he's back at it, raking another line and passing it around the table.

My phone buzzes in my purse. I ignore it. I have to watch these people, to see what they're doing, to see why this had so much power over my sister.

They laugh. They stare at each other with the deepest anticipation, like they can't wait to be in the middle of bliss. Another person snorts. The skinny guy taps out another two lines. Snort.

I can't move. I'm a deer and I'm staring straight into the headlights.

There's a sound behind me. Someone else is out here now. Maybe a smoker desperate for an even stronger high.

"Meg."

It's Miles.

His voice booms. "What the fuck do you think you're doing?"

## Chapter Thirteen

MEGARA

He takes steps toward me, but I'm still stuck in the headlights. Who the hell are these people, and why did my sister throw her life away for this?

He's behind me. I can feel his body, hear his breath. His fingers wrap around my wrist so tightly I lose sensation in my fingers.

"Excuse us." He pulls me away from the people, all the way to the sidewalk across the street. "Do you do coke?"

It's dark here. The headlights are finally gone. "No."

"Then what were you doing waiting your turn?"

I have no response.

His grip tightens around my wrist. "You do drugs?"

I dig my heel into the concrete. "That's none of your business."

"We're friends. Makes it my business."

I grit my teeth. "You made it clear we're not confidants."

He takes my hand and tugs me away from the scene. "Look me in the eyes and answer me. Do you do drugs?"

My gaze goes anywhere but his eyes. "No. I don't do

drugs." The sky is dark enough that I can see stars. So many stars. "I don't even like being around drugs."

"I'll take you home." He pulls me toward the sidewalk.

I'm the wet blanket again, the girl who can't handle the party, the girl who belongs at home.

I pull my hand free. "That's not necessary."

His voice gets serious. "You look like you saw a ghost."

Those people might as well be ghosts. How long until one of them is lying in a hospital bed, heartbeat fading to zero?

I take a deep breath. "It's nothing."

"No lies. That's our deal."

"I just remembered something awful." I hug my purse against my chest, something to keep the warmth in my body. "I'm not going to talk about it."

He shifts. His expression softens. His eyes brighten like he's trying to lift the mood. "You want to give me some hint what's wrong?"

"Not particularly."

"The sooner you tell me, the sooner we leave, and the sooner you get to fuck me."

My cheeks flush red again. "You're—"

"Don't say dreaming, because we both know what my dreams are like." He leans closer, holding my stare like he's daring me to explain.

I need to not be talking about this or thinking about this. And there's no way I'll be thinking about it if we really do sleep together.

So, fine, I'll tell him as much as it takes to change the subject. "There was someone in my life who went down a bad path with drugs. It still hurts but I'm not going to talk about it."

"Oh." His voice is soft. There's a hint of vulnerability in his eyes. "I'll take you home."

"You have to promise to drop this subject."

"It's dropped." He leads me around the corner. We walk in silence for a few blocks then Miles stops.

In front of a motorcycle.

He pulls two helmets from a compartment and hands one to me. Then he slings a motorcycle jacket around my shoulders. "This might make your thighs a little sore."

I climb on after him and hold on for dear life.

## Chapter Fourteen

MEGARA

My knuckles are white. My wrists are numb. Every muscle in my body is tense from the vice grip I have around Miles's waist.

The man drives like a Goddamn maniac.

I pull the helmet off my head and shove it into his hands. As usual, he's effortlessly cool and I'm trembling. Only known the guy for weeks, and we already have a pattern that gives him all the cards and leaves me with none.

He locks his bike, looking me over like he's trying to read my mind. He shrugs his leather jacket off his shoulders. "You'll want one before you know it."

"Fat chance." I dig my purse out of the bike's tiny trunk. "You've saved the damsel. You don't have to stay." I turn and step toward the door. Who does he think he is, judging my past? My choices? Trying to protect me after telling me he'll never have feelings for me?

"Meg."

"What?"

"You're wearing my jacket."

Ugh. I am wearing his extra jacket—it's early fall in Los Angeles, but the air is cold when it's whizzing by at eighty miles per hour.

I return the garment without another word.

My stomach is in knots. I want him in my room, in my bed, but not if he's going to treat me like the pathetic girl who can't handle her shit.

Those people... Their eyes were empty. I can't get it out of my head. I need it out of my head. I need to think about something else now.

Miles can deliver on that. Does anything else really matter?

I motion for him to follow and I make my way through the lobby. His calm steps remind me that he is still effortless. I am still clumsy and out of my comfort zone.

I press the button for the elevator. My hands are anything but steady. I press them into my thighs and take deep breaths.

Miles leans closer. His voice is steady, reassuring. "I hope the bike didn't wear out your thighs."

A blush threatens to form on my cheeks. I bite my lip. I can be cool too. I can be calm too. "It didn't."

"Good."

The elevator doors open, and we step inside. Miles hits the button for my floor. He says nothing.

*Ding.* We're at my floor. Miles moves steadily, his hand pressed gently against my lower back. His touch rekindles the fire inside me.

I don't want to banter or fight. I don't want to talk at all.

I want him naked in my bed. Now.

Deep breath. I can do this. I unlock my door and slide it open.

"Is that an invitation?" He drags his fingertips over my back. "I'd really hate to leave without making you come."

The mouth on this guy! He doesn't lack for confidence. "Come in."

He laughs at my choice of words but, for this time I feel like he's laughing with me, not at me.

Some of the nerves in my stomach settle. This, having sex for the first time, is a big deal. But I can handle it.

Shit. I promised Kara I'd text her if I left. I stop at my door and dig through my purse.

Miles looks at me quizzically. "Someone else you'd rather talk to?"

I shake my head. "Kara. It's a girl thing."

He slides his hands over the hem of my dress. That hand is so, so close to exactly where it needs to be.

I find my phone and tap out a text to Kara.

*Meg: Went home early. Everything is fine. See you Sunday.*

Miles plucks my phone from my hand and slides it into his pocket. He presses his body against mine, pinning me to the wall.

I close my eyes and soak in the weight of his body. God, he feels so good. We're almost there.

When his lips connect with mine, every bit of ugliness fades. My awful memories fade. The outside world fades. Every moment that isn't this one fades.

The kiss breaks. My body is buzzing. I'm desperate, but I can't let it show. I channel Miles's aloof confidence. I'm cool, calm, collected. No problem.

His eyes pass over me again. "You look amazing in that dress."

"I know."

"You're supposed to compliment me after that."

"I know that, too."

He sits next to me. His lips curl into a smile. "You've got to butter me up a little if you want me naked."

Damn, the man is a mind reader. Or maybe he's used to women wanting him naked. Doesn't matter. Right now, I need him naked.

I press my thigh into his. "You have tattoos, right?"

"Several."

"And you got them just so you'd have a reason to take off your shirt."

"You caught me." He laughs. "You sure you weren't drinking at the show?"

I run my fingers over the hem of his t-shirt. "Positive."

He moves my hand gently and pulls his t-shirt over his head. Damn. He's even more attractive up close. His chest and shoulders are strong. I run my fingers over his sculpted abs and trace those v-lines at the top of his hips. They're like an arrow pointing to a prize.

A prize I need desperately.

But I don't want to rush. This feels good. It's the only thing that feels good. I'm going to savor it.

His tattoos are just as sexy as his muscles. Somehow, the ink makes him hotter. It's like his songs—his soul is on his skin for anyone to see. It's obvious and mysterious at once.

What does it mean, the Chinese-style dragon adorning his shoulder and bicep? The rose and thorns on his chest? The words above the flower: be brave, live?

I wish I was brave enough to draw my soul on my skin. To offer up my pain in a song for the whole world to see.

I trace the words with my fingers. "When did you get that one?"

"About a year ago."

"No women's names?"

"Love is temporary. Ink is forever."

I look back into his eyes. "You won't fall in love, or you won't fall in love with me?"

"I won't fall in love."

"How can you be so sure?"

"I am."

"But how?"

"Because I know."

I press my hand against his stomach to remind myself why I invited him in. "That's not an answer."

"I'll make you a deal. You accept my answer and—"

"You can believe whatever you want." Even if it doesn't make sense. The Miles in that song, the Miles who tattoos a mantra on his chest—that Miles is committed, passionate, vulnerable.

The one sitting next to me... If I didn't know better, I'd be sure that nothing had ever hurt him.

Miles ignores my objection. "If I ever do fall in love, I'll add her name to my collection."

"Whatever makes you happy."

He digs his hand through my hair. "This makes me happy."

A blush spreads across my cheeks. He's in control again, and I'm the prey again. I need to do something to affect him, too.

I brush my hand against the waist of his jeans.

"Doing some more investigative work there?" he asks.

I nod.

His breath gets heavy. "What are you hoping to find?"

I tilt my head so my lips are inches from his. "The reason why you're so arrogant."

"You already saw me naked."

"It was too dark. I didn't get a good look."

I cup the bulge in his jeans. Words flee my brain at an

alarming rate. My body takes over. It knows one thing: it needs to touch him.

I rub him over his jeans.

His kiss starts slowly. He sucks on my lips. Then he's scraping his teeth against them. He tastes amazing, like salt, sweat, and Miles.

I shift my body on top of his, straddling him. His thighs are between mine. His crotch is against mine. I can feel him through his jeans. He's hard. And he's warm. And damn do I want these stupid clothes out of the way so I can feel him properly.

Anticipation spreads through my thighs and pelvis. I sink into his body, grinding my crotch against his. My nerves slip away. There's no room for nerves in my brain. There's no room for anything but the overwhelming desire to touch Miles and have him touch me.

It feels so fucking good, being in this moment, thinking about nothing but this moment.

His voice is heavy. "I've been dying to get my hands under that dress all night."

He needs this too. It relaxes me, makes me forget he holds all the cards.

Miles pulls the straps off my shoulders, exposing my breasts. No bra tonight. I don't need a bra in a dress that hugs me as tightly as this one does.

His eyes go wide. His pupils dilate. "Damn." The pad of his thumb brushes against my nipple. "Better than I remembered."

I swallow hard. He was thinking about me when he was alone?

"What do you remember?" I ask.

"The taste of your skin." He pulls me closer and presses his tongue against my nipple.

Damn, that feels good. I dig my fingers into his shoulders. He groans against my skin as he teases my nipple with his tongue.

I barely manage to form words. "Is that all you remember?"

He swirls his tongue around my nipple. Sensation overwhelms me. Every flick of his tongue sends pleasure straight to my core. He can take as long as he wants to respond if he keeps doing this.

Hell, he can give up words forever if he keeps doing this.

His teeth scrape against my nipple. I gasp reflexively. It hurts just enough to feel amazing.

He pulls his mouth away and replaces it with his fingers. "And that sound you make."

"You like it?"

"No. I love hearing you groan. Want to hear it every fucking day."

He pinches my nipple, just hard enough that it barely hurts. Desire shoots through me. I groan. His pupils dilate. His lips press together. He does love it.

I love it.

Finally, we can really agree on something.

This is far too much thinking.

I need to stop thinking.

I grind against Miles. He groans as he brings his mouth back to my chest. He sucks on my nipple. Soft then hard then soft again.

My body floods with pleasure. He's too good at this.

I reach for the button of his jeans. "You're wearing too many clothes."

He pulls my dress up and over my stomach and chest. I lift my arms so he can pull it all the way off. To turn it into a pile on the floor.

He grabs my hips and shifts our position so he's on top

of me. So his hips are pressing into mine, and his cock is against my clit. Except for the stupid fabric between us.

He smiles. I'm not sure if it's smug or playful or confident. All three maybe. Right now, I feel at ease. Like he's not pushing or prodding me. Like he wants me comfortable, wants my pleasure. After all, he thinks about my breasts and the sounds I make when he touches me.

He wants me to feel good. Sexually. But that's something.

That's a lot.

Miles drags his lips over my neck. He shifts to his side, unzips, and slides off his jeans. It's all effortless. He's smooth, in control. I must seem like a desperate mess.

This is almost happening.

We're going to have sex.

He's going to be inside me.

Miles slides his fingers over my stomach. "You're nervous again."

I shake my head, but I can feel the trembling in my hands. I have almost no experience, and Miles is clearly some kind of sex god.

He's staring at me, his eyes filled with sincerity. He really is concerned about me.

"You are," he says.

Still, I shake my head.

His lips curl into a smile. "It's cute that you don't want to admit it."

I don't want to be cute. I want to be sexy. I want to be making him as needy as I feel.

Confidence. I can do that. I drag my fingers over his torso. "Don't you have a better use for your mouth?"

"Oh." His voice gets low. "You mean this." He trails his lips against my chest, stopping to draw circles around my nipple with his tongue.

"Yes. That." Pleasure surges through me.

His hand slides between my thighs. "You don't have to hide how badly you want this. I mean, it's cute and all—"

"I'm not cute."

"Try adorable."

"Didn't we discuss the appropriate uses for your mouth?"

He nods and presses his lips into mine. It's a hard kiss, possessive even. "How's that?"

I struggle through a breath. That is amazing. "It's a start."

He smiles, takes my hand, and places it on the waistband of his boxers.

I pull the damn things to his knees. No piercings, but he's big.

I wrap my fingers around him. He places his hand over mine, guiding me.

I stroke him harder.

Faster.

His lips find mine. It's fast and hard and messy. I kiss him back, sucking on his tongue, scraping my teeth against his lips.

He groans into my mouth.

He wants me. Miles, the sex god, wants me.

My heartbeat picks up. We're really doing this.

I watch him fish a condom from the pocket of his jeans. My palms get sweaty. Nerves rise up in my stomach. What if it hurts? What if I'm not good enough?

Miles places his body next to mine. He drags his hand up my leg and strokes my inner thigh. "Relax. You won't do it wrong."

I nod a yes.

He pulls my panties off and presses his lips to my neck.

I groan as his fingers skim my clit.

He scrapes his teeth against my neck. His voice is low, hungry. "Don't hold back. Your groan is sexy as fuck."

I have no control over my vocalizations. Taking in this experience is about all I can handle.

He sucks on my skin as he moves his fingers closer. Closer. They slide over my sex.

It feels good but it makes me even more nervous. We're close to doing this. Nerves fade away as he rubs me. I take a deep breath and look into his gorgeous blue eyes.

His expression is heavy with need, but it's attentive too. Somehow, I trust him to guide me through this.

I let my eyelids press together and I sink into the bed. Slowly, he slides a finger inside me. He warms me up then it's two fingers. Three. I gasp.

That's intense. It hurts. I dig my nails into his shoulders.

"More?" he asks.

I nod.

He takes his time speeding up, going deeper. The discomfort fades to pleasure. Then it's a lot of pleasure.

Then his thumb is on my clit, stroking me. I groan as my sex clenches. That feels amazing. And the pleasure is building so quickly. With a few more strokes I'm at the edge. About to come.

Then I'm there. All the tension in my sex builds to a fever pitch then it's unwinding, spilling through me. I scream his name as I come.

It takes a moment to catch my breath. I blink my eyes open and stare into Miles's. He's still attentive, but he looks even needier. Like he's desperate to be inside me.

I want that.

I press my hand into his chest. "I want to do this. I'm ready."

## Just a Taste

He groans something that resembles a yes as he unwraps the condom and slides it on.

No more waiting.

This is happening.

He grabs my hip, pressing me against the bed, shifting my position so his cock brushes against my clit. I thrust my hips forward, and his tip strains against me.

Every nerve in my body is turned on, and they're all screaming the same thing. I need him inside me. Now.

I shift my hips to push him a little bit deeper. Deeper.

It's intense. There's pain but there's pleasure too. I dig my nails into his back until there's more pleasure than anything else.

I shift my hips to push him deeper. I can feel how my sex stretches to take him.

Miles goes slow. His eyes are on mine, watching my reactions. There's no sign of that arrogant, aloof guy. He's here, in this moment, committed to my pleasure.

He goes deeper. Deeper. It hurts but I don't want him to stop.

I tug at his hair. "Don't stop."

I kiss him like the ship is going down.

His hands curl around my back. Our bodies press together. It's intimate, the way he's holding me, the way he's kissing me, the way he's sliding inside me.

Then he's there. I'm full. It still hurts, but the pleasure far outweighs the pain.

My body takes over. I rock my hips to match his steady rhythm. It's slow. A good slow. A hell of an intense slow.

Pressure builds inside me. It's such sweet, perfect pressure.

I close my eyes and surrender to the feeling of Miles inside me.

I groan as loudly as I can. Something to let him know

how much he's affecting me, how fucking good he's making me feel.

After a few more thrusts, I'm there. My sex clenches. Tighter and tighter. So tight I can barely take it.

Then I'm coming. I groan his name as an orgasm washes over me. It's different than before. More intense. Deeper.

Miles grabs my wrists and pulls my hands over my head. Then his lips are on mine. He thrusts into me so hard it hurts.

He groans into my mouth. It feels good in a different way, knowing he's close, feeling his pleasure.

His posture changes. His eyes close. His breath gets heavy.

I have to bite my lip to contain myself. It's still intense. It still hurts. But I don't want him to stop. There's something about hearing his groans and feeling his muscles tense.

It's hot as hell.

I want to feel him come.

His teeth sink into my neck. That, too, hurts just enough to feel good.

A few more thrusts and he's there, groaning against my skin as he comes.

He holds me for a moment. Our bodies are pressed together. It's intimate in a different want, overwhelming in a different way.

I take deep breaths, trying to process the experience. I had sex with Miles. Lost my virginity to him.

It's real. Adult. Dangerous.

He presses his lips to mine then untangles our bodies and takes care of the condom.

I sink into the bed. I had sex with Miles. It really happened.

## Just a Taste

The weight on the bed shifts as he brings his body next to mine. He slides his arms around me and pulls me close.

This still feels intimate.

There are no pretenses. I can't remember the last time I spent this long with my guard down.

His lips press against my neck and I lose track of conscious thought.

It's not really safe, his arms, but it feels like it. It's comfortable.

A few more minutes and I'll figure this out. A few more minutes and I'll get into my pajamas. Just a few minutes…

## Chapter Fifteen

MILES

This is a regular thing.

I need rules about staying the night.

Like *don't fucking do it, under any circumstances, I don't care how much she says she gets it, that will give her the wrong idea.*

That's my usual rule.

It's a good one. Keeps people from getting hurt. Meg may not think much of me—well, not when I'm dressed. She's right about some things.

The others—

Well, I'm the one trying to convince her of them. I can't exactly fault the girl for buying into my casual *I don't give a fuck about anything but making you come* act.

Don't get me wrong. Making her come is already at the top of my priority list. It's easier than writing a song. As satisfying as getting on stage.

And less drama too. No lectures from Tom. No anger from Drew. None of those *do you live to disappoint me* looks from Pete.

I always thought it was bullshit, when people would say

that disappointment is worse than anger. Up until the first time I saw disappointment in Damon's eyes.

Now...

What would he say about this situation?

Something about honesty. Not running from my feelings. Facing the shit that scares me.

My fingers go to the tattoo on my chest. The one I got for him. He didn't like tattoos. He would have hated it. Which would have made him love it more.

Fuck, I miss him.

I close my eyes. Will myself to fall back asleep. To feel something beyond this dull sense of dread in my gut.

It's ridiculous. I spent last night playing then taking a gorgeous woman's virginity.

I should be on top of the world.

Everything falls into my lap. Tom is right. I have it easy. I have it so fucking easy.

But everything feels so fucking hard.

It's too bright in here. Already morning. Late in the morning.

Sure, we don't have rules about staying the night. I can change that. Add something about leaving first thing. Before she wakes up and sees me in her bed and thinks it means something.

Sure, she thinks I'm an asshole. But it's not like she'd be the first woman who fell for a guy she thought was an asshole.

Didn't stop my mom. And look how that worked out for her.

Ugh.

It's too fucking bright. I stand. Pull the curtains tighter. It doesn't help. They're too sheer.

They're sad, plain things. Whatever came with the apartment, I'm guessing. They look like something that

## Just a Taste

would grace the decor of a bureaucratic office in a dystopian hellscape.

Not the curtains that help Meg sleep. That let in the light of the sun. Or the stars. Or the busy street below.

She's near so much life here. It's not like my place in Malibu.

It's not like the place in the hills. Yeah, that one is big, rowdy, brimming with energy and people. But it's bullshit so much of the time. Someone trying to win favor. Someone Tom is trying to win over.

Speaking of—

I check my cell. A few missed texts from him. Checking in, at first. Then more frantic.

*Tom: Where the fuck did you go?*

*Tom: There's a chick here who's begging to see you naked.*

*Tom: She's too hot for you. Even with you being famous.*

*Tom: All right, if you're not up for the task, I'll comfort her.*

*Tom: Seriously, where the fuck are you? It better be some random woman. If you miss our thing tonight, Drew is gonna kill you. But he's gonna have to get in line.*

I know he writes because he's worried. Deep down. In some part of his soul buried under a sign flashing *money*.

But I still can't bring myself to cut him slack. It's not like he admits he cares.

Sure, that wouldn't go any better for him, but—

I'm not a fucking child. I don't need him babysitting me.

I shoot back a *see you then*, check my calendar to see what the fuck it is we're doing tonight (private gig for some billionaire's daughter), move into the bathroom.

Grab the extra toothbrush sitting on the counter. Maybe I'm underestimating Meg. She went to the trouble of laying all this shit out.

Making me feel welcome in a way that screams *don't*

*stay too long.* Or maybe my thoughts are cloudy again. There *is* something about her. Something messing with my head.

I finish with the toothbrush. Piss. Wash my hands. Step into the shower.

Her toiletries are spare too. Not cheap, necessarily. Just ordinary. Like she picked out the first thing she saw.

But maybe she just likes this strawberry body wash. Maybe she needs this specific brand of grey shampoo or her hair is a mess. Women are particular about their hair.

I know that much.

The hot water feels good. Like it's washing away all the ugly shit in my head. This is a nice space. With the sun streaming through the window, bouncing off the white tile, it's bright. Airy. Inviting.

I rinse my hair. Soap. Shampoo. Condition.

There's a sound in the other room. She's waking up. Thinking *he needs to go* or *do I have to feed him breakfast* or maybe *God, I hope he takes me to breakfast.*

I shouldn't assume she's interested in more time with me. Sure, she asks me those weird questions. And she looks at me like she's staring into my soul. And the way she traced Damon's mantra, like she understood something deep inside me, something I needed her to know—

Maybe I'm the one getting the wrong idea.

Maybe I'm the one who wants to buy her breakfast.

Fuck, I have to buy her breakfast. I can't take the girl's virginity and leave her hungry. I have some manners.

She moves closer. Knocks on the door.

"Come in," I yell.

She does. She's wearing my t-shirt. It annoys me when other women do that, but it's cute on her. It drapes over her slim frame in a way that screams *put your hands under this.*

She nods *hi*, moves to the sink, wets her toothbrush.

And she stares at me.

At my shoulders, chest, stomach, cock.

She doesn't try to hide it. She just stares like I'm the greatest thing she's ever seen.

Fuck, I'm already getting hard.

"You don't have to make it so obvious you want me," I say.

"It's not obvious."

"You can." I stare back. Take in her long legs. Her dark eyes. Her cute ass.

She nods *sure*. Tries to focus on brushing her teeth. Fails.

I know I need to have some manners and buy her breakfast.

But there's no reason why I can't make her come first. Hell, if anything, that's true hospitality.

"I know you want me, Meg, but you don't have to come in here half-naked," I say.

"I want nothing but caffeine."

"Really?" I make a show of reaching my arms over my head.

Her jaw drops. "I, uh… believe what you want."

"You fell asleep last night."

Her cheeks flush. "You wore me out."

My chest warms. Pride isn't an emotion I feel often. Not since Damon died. But right now I'm bursting with it. "Come here." I motion with my hands, just to make a point. "I still owe you one."

"What?"

"Three orgasms." I make the same *come here* motion. "A promise is a promise. Though I'm thinking I'll go for four."

"Total or right now?"

"Only one way to find out."

Her blush deepens.

Fuck, she's too cute. It's going to make this go too fast. "Do me a favor and grab one of those condoms." I motion to the medicine cabinet. I stocked it last night.

Her eyes go wide at the size of the box—it is a lot of condoms—but she still grabs one. She turns to me. Pulls my t-shirt over her head.

I help her into the small space.

Her body brushes mine. Then it's her forehead against mine. She's tall for a girl. Only an inch or two shorter than I am.

There's something right about it. Something I can't contemplate at the moment.

I don't know what that means.

But I know I need to feel her cunt pulsing around me.

I pull the shower door closed. Press her against the sturdy tile wall.

It's slick. Slippery. She has to wrap her arms around me.

I bring my hands to her ass. Hold her in place as I press my body against hers.

She shudders as my cock brushes her pelvis.

Her eyelids flutter together.

I lean down enough to bring my lips to hers. She kisses back with every bit of need in the world.

She hates my guts, yeah.

But she loves the feeling of our bodies joining.

As much as I do.

I shift my hips, pinning her tighter.

She kisses me harder.

Fuck. I have to pull back to catch my breath.

She looks up at me like she's about to consume me.

"You sore?" I brush her hair behind her ear.

"A little. But I still want to go."

My lips curl into a smile.

"What?"

"You're so fucking sexy." I run my fingers down her neck and shoulders until she's panting.

"Thank you."

Fuck, that's such a Meg reaction. It kills me, how adorable she is. Makes me hard enough to cut glass. "This is a small shower. Might be a little tricky."

"Show me." Her voice drips with this perfect mix of enthusiasm and defiance. It's *hell yes, I will do that and it won't be nearly as hard as you say. I'm a pro.*

"Turn around."

She does. It puts her shoulders under the showerhead. Water drips off her back. Over her ass.

She looks even more delicious like this.

I place my body behind hers, so I can feel the warmth of her back. She's slick from the shower, but that only makes her feel closer.

More right.

I wrap one arm around her. Bring my fingers to her collarbone.

She shudders as I trace the line.

I let my hand drift lower. Over her chest, between her breasts, down her stomach.

Her shoulders tense.

"Relax." I nip at her ear. "We're just getting started."

"Make me."

"Is that a challenge?"

"Yeah?"

"I like the way you think." I hold her body against mine with one hand. Bring the other to her leg. The inside of her knee.

A lazy circle. Then another.

Higher and higher—

Softer and softer—

Until she's shaking so hard she's about to slip.

I hold her tighter. Bring my lips to her neck. Kiss her harder.

She groans as my fingers skim her clit.

I keep that same soft stroke again and again.

Until she's clawing at the tile wall.

She's there. Brimming with bliss.

Right now, in this moment, I'm her entire universe. I like it more than I should.

But I don't give a fuck about the implications.

Only about making her come.

I suck on her neck as I stroke her harder. To the right. The left.

Up.

Down.

Right.

There. Her breath hitches as I find just the right spot. Just the right pressure. It's different in the water. Softer and harder too.

I scrape my teeth against her skin.

Her groan gets louder.

I keep that same pressure, same pace. I toy with her neck as I push her closer and closer.

Her body melts into mine.

She reaches back, scraping her nails against my thighs, holding my body against hers.

I keep my pace.

Stroke her just how she needs me.

There.

Her breath hitches as she comes on my hand. She arches her back against me, grinding her ass against my cock as she groans my name.

I give her a moment to catch her breath, then I go

right to where she needs me. Stroke her until she's groaning my name like a curse.

When she catches her breath, she looks at me with those big, brown eyes. Like she can't believe I exist. That this exists.

I kiss her hard.

Then I stroke her a little harder.

"Fuck." She pulls away. Throws her neck back.

I hold her body against mine as I stroke her to orgasm.

She comes again. Faster this time. And harder too. She claws at the tile like it's the only way to contain her pleasure.

I let the feeling of her satisfaction soak in for a moment. Then I tear the wrapper, roll the condom on my cock, bring one hand to her hip. "Time to go for four."

She responds by grinding against my cock.

Fuck, it's hard to believe she didn't do this before last night. She's a fast learner. "How's your balance?"

"Could be better." Her back sinks into my chest. "I'm distracted." Her voice is playful.

Like she can stay here, in this perfect space, forever.

If only.

"I'll make it fast." I press my lips to her shoulder.

She places her hands on the tile. Thrusts her ass in the air.

I pull her into position.

It is slippery in here. And I'm already wound tight. This is going to be too fast.

I want to savor her all fucking day.

But that's out of the question. This is going to have to be enough.

I slide into her slowly.

She groans as I fill her.

Her head falls to one side. Her wet hair goes with it. Whips her shoulders and chest.

I hold her steady as I drive into her. Slowly at first. Then faster. Deeper.

Until I need the support as much as she does.

Fuck.

She rocks her hips to meet me. She's too early. Not quite at the rhythm, but it's still driving me out of my fucking mind.

I dig my fingers into her hips. Guide her so we're moving together. So she's pushing me deeper with every thrust.

My eyes close.

Her groans run together. They fill the shower. Mix with the water in the strangest, most beautiful music.

We move like that until she ignores my instructions. Starts going faster, harder, deeper.

If she keeps that up—

I slip my hand between her legs.

She gasps as my thumb brushes her clit. Then it's one of those perfect low, deep groans.

I stroke her exactly where she needs me.

She comes fast, rocking me deeper, groaning louder, clawing at the slick walls. Her legs shake. Then give out.

I just barely catch her. I'm too lost in bliss.

"Come here." I pull out. Wrap my arms around her. Turn the shower off.

She nods, in a post-orgasm haze, and melts into my arms. I lift her. Hold her close as I carry her into the bedroom then lay her down on the bed.

She looks up at me with those big, brown eyes.

Right now, she isn't trying to figure out who I am deep inside. Or what I want. Or whether or not she hates me.

Right now, she knows exactly who I am and what I want.

Right now, I'm exactly who she needs and what she wants.

I shift onto the bed.

She spreads her legs. Looks up at me so I know it's an invitation.

I bring my hands to her hips. Bring her body into mine.

Fuck. She feels good.

Her eyes close. Pleasure spills over her face. And something else too. This satisfaction.

After all that, she must be spent.

I *do* need to make this fast.

My body sinks into hers as I thrust into her.

She pulls me closer with her thighs. For a second, she blinks, looks at me like I'm everything she wants.

Then her eyes close and her expression gets hazy.

I let go. Move harder. Deeper.

Until I'm exactly—

Fuck.

I come fast.

She digs her nails into my back, pulling me closer, spurring me on.

It's intense. More intense than it's been in a long fucking time.

I thrust through my orgasm then I untangle our bodies. Take care of the condom. Return to the bed.

She looks up at me with that same hazy smile.

"Better than caffeine?" I tease her.

"Better."

My chest bursts with that same pride. I should hold on to it on the ride home. I should leave now.

If I stay—

No, it's just good manners. Can't fuck the girl and leave her hungry. That's rude.

"You still want the caffeine?" I roll onto my elbow. Try to keep my gaze on her long body. It defies me. Goes right to her brown eyes. "I'll buy you breakfast."

"I should really study." She says it with almost no conviction.

"Meg, I expect better from you." I run my finger over her collarbone. "You can't use me for sex then send me home without feeding me."

"Would you even let me buy you breakfast?"

"Of course not." I can't help but smile. "It's on me."

## Chapter Sixteen

MILES

Meg shoots me a *really* look as I open the door for her. She raises a brow when I pull out her chair.

She sits.

I sit across from her.

The easiness of the morning isn't quite gone. But it's different.

Maybe it's the motorcycle—it *is* a lot, but, hey, I offered to walk someplace closer.

Or maybe she's as miserable when she's dressed as I am.

Is she miserable?

Right now, it's hard to tell. She has some of the ease. Some of that satisfaction.

But there's something else missing. Something weighing on her.

Maybe I'm reading into things. Maybe it's me. Or her idea of me. The one I'm encouraging.

Can't blame the girl for buying into my bullshit.

Only…

Does she?

"Am I supposed to buy you as a gentleman?" She picks up the menu with a soft smile. She's teasing.

Maybe I am reading into things. Maybe she's easy and I'm uncomfortable.

I'm not really sure what this is. Good manners, yeah, but something else too.

I don't usually take women to breakfast. I don't usually spend the night.

Yeah, yeah, I'm a cad, a dog, an asshole. Whatever. Sometimes you have to be cruel to be kind.

I learned that the hard way.

"Am I not?" I take my menu. Scan it quickly. I'm not really into food the way some people are. I like it fine. Like to try new things, to fill my stomach, to tell myself something about nourishment. But I'm not like Tom with his lust for novelty. Or Drew with his need to enjoy the good Mexican food in Los Angeles, whenever possible. Or Pete with his desire to experience expensive tastes.

Tom would say I'm a spoiled rich boy. Unaware of how lucky I am. Throwing it all away.

I guess I can't argue.

"You're a polite young man?" she asks.

Right now, I don't give a fuck what we eat. But it matters to me, sharing a meal with her. Making sure she's fed. And more than that, making sure she eats something she enjoys.

It's not just bringing her pleasure.

Or taking care of her needs.

Something more confusing.

"Of course. I'm the nicest guy anyone's ever met," I say.

Her laugh dissolves the tension in her shoulders. "I'm guessing most people would disagree."

"Probably."

"But I already got in your pants."

"Don't tell me you don't want to do it again."

Her cheeks flame red. She mimes zipping her lips. Looks down at the menu. "So this… we're getting breakfast."

"Yeah."

"After…"

"Fucking."

Her blush deepens. "After you spent the night."

"I prefer *fucking*, but sure."

"Does that…" She looks up at me, asking me to finish her sentence.

I do. "We're friends."

"Just friends?"

"Friends with benefits."

She nods *okay*. "So this is…"

"Not a date."

"Just two friends who—"

"Fuck—"

"Having breakfast after… fucking." She barely gets out the last word. But she does. Her eyes go wide, like she's surprised she managed to say it.

It's fucking adorable.

And hot as hell.

I'm not sure how she does that, but I really fucking like it.

"I guess we should ask all those questions," I say. "Where you get to know each other."

"Why do you think I want to know you?" Her voice is teasing. "Maybe I just want…" She motions to my crotch.

"Damn, Meg, I can't believe you'd use me so transparently."

"I know. I'm terrible."

"Truly."

"And now I'm stuck making conversation with a guy who has—"

Far better uses for my mouth. But I'll hold off on the heavy flirting until we're someplace private. I don't trust myself with her. "Nothing interesting to say?"

"I guess we'll see." Her smile is soft. Inviting.

"I guess we can start with the usual. What do you do?"

She nods, accepting the premise. "I go to UCLA, premed. I work as an ER scribe from six to ten Monday through Friday. It's a lot of grunt work but it's great experience. And you?"

"I went to Stanford. Poly-sci."

Disbelief streaks her expression. "That right?"

I shouldn't blame her for buying into my bullshit. I really shouldn't. If anything, I should be impressed with myself.

Only I'm not.

I don't want her to believe that shit.

I shrug my shoulders. "You don't believe I went to Stanford?"

"No, I do. You seem like the type."

"Like…"

"Smarter than you look."

"How do I look?"

"You know how you look." She runs her fingers over the menu. "What do you do now?"

"I work in the entertainment industry."

"Is that the line you normally use?"

Sometimes. It's nice being a normal person when I have the chance. "Most women either know who I am or they don't care."

"Are you that famous?"

"Depends on how recently we dropped a music video,

how well it's doing. We have a handful of diehard fans but we're not famous enough that everybody knows our names. It's been different since *In Pieces*. More people stop me on the street. It was our first hit. Our only top 100 song so far."

"Have you made a lot of money?"

Fuck, she is too cute. I laugh. "I like that you asked that. Most people would think it's impolite."

She tries out an effortless shrug. Gets part of the way there.

She's not an effortless person. But I like that about her. I like that she tries.

It's sweet.

"We made a good amount. We're poised to make a great amount. But we're not there yet." My eyes go to the window. "Money isn't an issue for me. I inherited a lot. I could quit the band tomorrow, never work again, and still be okay."

"That is a lot."

Yeah, but I'd give anything to not be in this position. I'd much rather Damon still be here. Still be shaking his head and muttering *if you run, you're going to run forever.* "It's a shitty way to become a millionaire."

Recognition streaks her expression.

She knows what it's like to lose someone.

She must. Why else would she be asking about *In Pieces*, trying to get the key to my heart?

Does she think I'm a salve? That I somehow have the answers?

She couldn't be more wrong. I don't have a single fucking answer. I don't have shit.

She shifts back in her chair, her expression more and more awkward by the second.

She doesn't want to go there either. Good.

"Where are you from?" I ask.

Relief spreads over her face. "Orange County."

"My uncle lived in Irvine for a while. It's not terrible. A little—"

"Sterile? Void of personality? Full of people who care about the color of their neighbor's house more than anything else?"

"You one of those people who complain about going beyond 'the orange curtain.'" People from Los Angeles, or people who've lived here a long time, have a lot to say about the county fifty miles south. I can't blame them, exactly. There's a lot of shit wrong with Orange County.

But it's like someone insulting Tom. Sure, he's a know it all asshole, but he's my fucking family. I'm the one who calls him a know it all asshole.

"Who says that?" Her nose scrunches with distaste.

"You don't think—"

"It's different, sure, but it's not like Los Angeles is this place where people are never superficial. It's just... worse there, somehow."

"I take it you're saving for a condo at the Irvine Spectrum."

"Oh my God, are people really buying those condos?"

It is absurd, buying a condo at the nexus of two freeways, where the only thing to see is a shopping center the size of a small town. "You mean you don't think I should invest?"

Her laugh gets easier. "Are condos a good investment?"

"Depends who you ask." My eyes meet hers. "Your parents still live there?"

Her expression darkens again, but she shakes it off. "I don't like to talk about my family."

I get that. "Where are you going to medical school?"

Her voice gets defensive. "I don't want to talk about it."

"I was inside you an hour ago, but your med school applications are too personal to discuss?" I mean it to come out teasing, but it doesn't. I want her to tell me. I can't stand that she isn't telling me.

Fuck.

"Excuse me." I stand. Move to the bathroom. Piss. Wash my hands. Then my face.

This isn't how this goes. We're just having fun. I'm not trying to get into her heart.

She's not getting into mine.

If she's defensive, all the better. That will make it harder to hurt her.

And I really don't want to hurt her.

I take a few deep breaths. Repeat Damon's mantra.

I hate that fucking mantra.

Hate when it works.

After another ten, I return to the main room. The server is dropping off her coffee. I order my own. Settle into my seat.

What is it she wants?

I need to figure it out. So I know what to offer her.

No, that's not quite right. I don't want to fake shit anymore. I want to be honest.

I can't remember the last time that happened, but I do.

She shoots me an apologetic look. "I shouldn't be so defensive, but I... I've never done anything like this before."

That's fair. "It's simple, really. We have fun."

She stirs milk and sugar into her coffee. "Nothing is that simple."

"This is. We have amazing sex, we talk, we eat, we go to shows and make out backstage. When it stops being fun, we part ways."

"If you're adamantly anti-commitment, why do you want a fuck buddy?" she asks.

It's a good question. There are a lot of things I can say, but only one of them matters. "I like you."

"It's that simple?"

I want it to be that simple. "Why do you want a fuck buddy? Can't make it to twenty-one without fucking unless you're avoiding it."

"You're that hot." Her shoulders ease. Her smile spreads. "So hot I lost my mind."

"Besides that."

"I need the distraction."

"You're going to wound me talking like that."

"Uh-huh." She takes a long sip of her coffee. Lets out a sigh of pure pleasure. "I'm applying to Harvard, Johns Hopkins, and Columbia."

"You want to be on the East Coast?"

She nods.

Far from her family. Well, from the place she grew up. I don't know where her family is now. Maybe they moved to New York.

Maybe she has tons of cousins in Jersey.

I shouldn't assume.

Besides, it's none of my business.

Thank fuck, the server arrives with my coffee. I'm no snob—I'll drink a lot of coffee—but I do need the caffeine.

Yeah, it's a cliché, but it really fucking helps.

I nod a thanks, order my breakfast, wait for the waiter to leave. "I'm going to add another term to our arrangement. Anything we do together—I'm paying."

"I can pay for myself."

"I'm sure you can, but I insist."

She stares at me for a minute. Finally nods. "Okay."

Good. It's what makes sense. What's fair. She's a college

student who works as a scribe. I looked it up. They make nothing. And her apartment must be a fortune.

I'm sure her parents have money. If she grew up in the parts of Orange County that scream of fakeness and sterility. But still…

I want to take care of her that way.

It's just manners.

That's all.

"Fine."

She sips her coffee. Lets out another sigh of deep, pure pleasure. Then she settles into the conversation. Talks about the process of applying for med school.

It sounds a lot like law school. A lot of studying, a lot of preparation, a lot of essays about love of medicine.

It sounds fucking hard.

Then she asks about me. About how I got here.

There's a lot to say. I focus on the practicalities. Getting into a fight with Tom in high school. Playing in a jam band with him and Pete. Meeting Drew in college.

Pulling the four of us together to make shit work.

Honestly, Tom did most of that. He does make shit happen.

Now, we're officially three years old with two albums. A good one. And a great one. But then I don't go around pointing out the flaws in my early work. I fucking hate it when musicians do that.

Yeah, I get it. After two albums I know a lot more about writing songs. But those early ones were a part of me too.

They have something to them… this rawness and excitement.

Fuck, I miss that.

Sometimes, I'm not sure it really exists. Maybe it was all the shit I was using.

Maybe there's nothing exciting in the world.

Only...

I swallow hard. I'm not saying that about her. It's ridiculous. It's just... good, talking to another person.

That's all.

She's interested. She knows nothing about music, but she loves it. So I explain a little.

She nods, attentive, even when it goes over her head.

It's easy.

After breakfast, we walk over to Abbot Kinney. I buy her another drink—this time she wants an iced green tea. Tease her about how she needs to commit to one type of caffeine.

We window shop.

She stops in front of a trendy boutique. Stares at a Star Wars t-shirt.

"Want me to buy you that?"

"I don't need any help looking like a nerd."

"You don't realize the effect you have on guys, do you?"

"I don't have any effect on guys."

I slide my hand around her hip. "You have this irresistible innocence. I'm surprised there aren't creeps trying to corrupt you twenty-four seven."

"I already have you."

"I can't be around twenty-four seven."

"Why not?" She moves into the shop. Turns her head away from me but points her body toward me. She wants me closer. She just can't say it. "What do you do when you're not torturing women with your sexy voice?"

I brush her hair behind her ear. Run my fingers along her neck until she just barely purrs. "You think my voice is sexy?"

"You know it is." She pretends she's interested in the overpriced sweaters on display.

I take an orange one from her hands. Refold it. Return it to its place. "I go to shows. Play video games with Drew or Pete. Try to tolerate Tom's bossiness."

"And when you're alone?"

"I run. I think. I read."

"You read?"

"You this rude to all your friends or only the ones who make you come?" I tease.

"The latter." She just barely smiles. She likes teasing me.

I like teasing her.

I like it too much.

I like her way too much.

## Chapter Seventeen

MILES

As usual, Tom gives me shit about my arrival time. I'm early, but, hey, what does that matter when I'm the last to arrive?

I shrug him off. Focus on my performance. On falling asleep without thinking about Meg.

I fail, sure, but I do manage to make my thoughts really fucking dirty.

It's a quiet week. I take care of some shit, watch *Night of the Living Dead* with Tom and Pete, spend breaks in practice texting Meg.

Tom gives me more shit for that, but I do get the drill by now.

Whatever I do, the drummer gives me shit.

When I get my test results, I send them straight to Meg. I'm pretty sure Damon would be proud of me, for once.

All this fucking around and I'm always safe.

How I made it through the last two years without catching something, I don't know.

But I did.

And now I'm—

Fuck, I'm getting hard just thinking about it.

She texts back fast.

*Meg: Oh.*

*Miles: Oh?*

*Meg: Yeah. Oh. Good with oh.*

*Miles: I'm not going to assume you're on birth control.*

See Damon, I'm a fucking gentleman. This girl—what I want from her—terrifies me, but I'm not running. I'm holding my ground.

I can get that right.

I can get one fucking thing right.

*Meg: I'm on the pill. It seemed like a good idea when I went to college.*

*Miles: I'll bring condoms. It's up to you.*

*Meg: Okay. I'll think about it.*

*Miles: I want to take you somewhere Friday. What time do you get off work?*

*Meg: Ten.*

*Miles: Send the address and I'm there.*

## Chapter Eighteen

MEGARA

After work Friday, I change in one of the handicapped bathrooms. This is the sexiest outfit I own—low cut chiffon blouse, tight black skirt, black wedges—but I don't feel like it fits. Eyeliner and red lipstick do little to help matters.

It's strange. I felt sexy when I was with him. I felt totally irresistible. But right now, I feel awkward and stiff.

The sexy outfit is only making matters worse.

Oh well. I'm not planning to spend much time in my clothes. Damn, I'd like to skip straight to me and Miles in bed together. It made sense. It felt good. I want to feel that good again.

I make my way through the ER.

A nurse winks at me. "About time you went out. You're too young to work so hard."

I nod a polite good night and go on my way. The older nurses are always teasing me about wasting my youth. They don't understand that bars and parties aren't fun for me. They make me think about Rosie losing herself. I don't want to explain that to them.

But I do want to explain it to Miles. I want him to understand. My heartbeat picks up. It's scary, how much I want him to understand.

The ER is quiet for a Friday night. The waiting room is sparse. The counter is empty except for a man with a bandage over his nose. He got into a fight.

He looks familiar.

He's shorter than I am. His hair is light. He's wearing one of those button-up shirts. The same that Rosie's boyfriend always wore.

No.

No, no, no.

That is Rosie's boyfriend. Jared.

What the hell is he doing here? He lives on the other side of town, closer to a dozen different hospitals.

He should be in jail by now. Or dead from an overdose. Not standing in the ER with a broken nose.

My breath picks up. My heart pounds against my chest. I turn so my back is to him. I can't risk him recognizing me. If he offers his condolences, I'll break another one of his bones.

He's hurt. Thank God. I shouldn't smirk—future doctors should never smirk over people's injuries—but it feels good to see him bruised. He deserves every bit of pain in the world. If it weren't for him, Rosie would still be alive.

"I've never seen that look before." It's Miles. He's three feet away, spread out on one of the ugly grey chairs. His expression is knowing. And accepting.

"It's nothing."

He stands and moves close enough to whisper. "You may as well tell me. You know I'll drag it out of you."

"Maybe I'm smirking because we're going to have sex."

"I know what that looks like, and it involves a lot more blushing and squeezing your knees together."

So I am that obvious. Doesn't matter. Someone broke Jared's nose. At least I know he deserved it.

Miles laughs. "Should I be jealous?"

"What?"

"You're staring at that guy." He motions to Jared. "Is he your ex-boyfriend or something?"

"Or something."

"What—he broke your heart, and you paid one of your friends to break his nose?"

"You really think it's broken?"

Miles nods. "Likely." His fingers brush against my wrist. "Did he cheat on you or something?"

"Or something."

He leans closer, lowering his voice to a whisper. "Want me to kick his ass?"

"Would you really?"

"For you, yeah." His smile is genuine. Proud even.

I like it more than I should. I like it a lot. "That's okay. Someone already did." I should feel horrible about wishing this pain on Jared, but I don't.

Miles laughs and slides his hand around my waist. "Meg Smart. I never thought I'd see the day."

I clear my throat and adopt my most mature stance. "There is no day. Now, where are we going?"

"You're glad someone kicked that guy's ass."

"He deserves it."

Miles's eyes connect with mine. Joy spreads over his face. "Do you trust me?"

"That depends on what we're talking about."

"This guy hurt you. Right?"

"You could say that."

Miles pulls me toward the wall so we're out of the way. "I'm going to do something to hurt him back."

I should feel sick at the suggestion, but I don't. This asshole stole my sister's life from her.

He needs to hurt. He needs to bleed.

I nod. "Okay."

Jared is still filling out paperwork. I haven't seen him since before Rosie died. He didn't come to the funeral. At the time, it pissed me off, but now I'm glad. I would have killed him if I saw him that day.

I want to kill him now.

The two-faced asshole was so fucking polite to me. He acted like a gentleman, like he was a prince and he'd treat her like a princess. I guess his idea of royalty involves massive opiate indulgence.

He needs to pay for what he did.

He needs to hurt.

Miles grabs my arm hard. "Go wait outside. Now."

No. I need to tell Jared he's the scum of the Earth.

"You're not getting in trouble on my watch," Miles says.

"I won't get in trouble," I say.

Miles lowers his voice. "You wouldn't be able to hurt him if you tried. You're not that kind of person."

My face screws. What the hell does Miles know about what kind of person I am?

"Trust me." He leans closer. "Hitting him isn't going to make you feel better."

"I want to watch."

"Wait outside or it's not happening."

"Fine." As long as Jared hurts. As long as he pays for what he did to my sister.

I go outside and sit on one of the benches in front of the building. Cool air sends goose bumps over my arms and legs. This outfit is not appropriate for the fall evening air.

Time slows. My excitement twists to panic. What if Miles really does hurt the guy? What if he's doing something illegal? What if he's going to get into real trouble?

I try to calm down, but deep breaths aren't working. I like Miles. We *are* friends. I don't want anything bad happening to him.

There are footsteps behind me. Miles. He sits on the bench next to me and drops something on my lap.

A wallet. Jared's wallet.

"What am I supposed to do with this?" I ask.

"Return it to the lost and found."

"But... what? Why?"

Miles smirks. "I have his address and credit card number now."

"And?"

"And he's going to send himself a few dozen custom t-shirts about what an awful asshole he is."

The stiffness in my neck relaxes. It's a prank. An illegal prank but only a prank. It's not like Miles is going to wait outside the guy's house with a baseball bat.

Miles will be okay. He won't get hurt.

He leans close enough to whisper. "Unless you want to do something that will really hurt him."

My breath collects in my throat. "Like what?"

"The possibilities are endless. All sorts of accidents no one could ever trace back to us." Miles plays with the hem of my skirt. "It depends how much he hurt you."

"More than anyone else ever has."

"What happened?"

I try to find the words, to find some way to explain, but my throat is too dry. It's impossible. I can't say it. I can't say *Rosie is gone. He's the reason Rosie is gone. He's the reason my sister*

*OD'd. The reason the world is a dark, ugly place.* "I... it's a long story."

He slides the wallet into his pocket. "You must have loved him a lot to hate him so much."

Anger rises up inside of me. The thought sickens me. My hands curl into fists. "No."

Miles shakes his head. He doesn't believe me. He thinks I'm hung up on the asshole who destroyed my sister. Miles probably thinks that I'm in love with Jared, that he's the reason I don't want a relationship.

"I never loved him. I barely know him. He was my sister's boyfriend and he... he ruined her life."

"Call her. Let her decide what to do with him."

My heart sinks. Everything is heavy. I open my mouth to speak but no words come out. "I... I can't. She died a few months ago."

"Oh, fuck." He turns to me, his eyes wide with concern.

This isn't part of our deal. He's not supposed to be concerned, and I'm not supposed to let him take care of me.

"What happened?" His voice is so soft. It's the sweet Miles, the one who wrote all those songs.

I shake my head. I can't discuss this. I can't even say it out loud.

His voice gets softer. He runs his fingers through my hair. "What happened, Meg?"

"She..." It's hard to breathe. There. Inhale. Exhale. "She overdosed."

"An accident?"

"Yeah." I press my fingers together. This is too close, too personal. I need to get up, to get out of here, to be anywhere else. Jared doesn't matter. He's nothing. Just another loser who will dig his own grave.

## Just a Taste

"I'm sorry," he whispers.

His arms wrap around me. He pulls me into a tight hug. It's intimate. Too intimate. He's seeing inside me, seeing all the things I try to keep hidden.

I can't take it. But I can't move. I can't do anything to lean into Miles's touch.

He pulls me tighter. I slide my hands under his leather jacket and press them against his lower back, over the soft fabric of his t-shirt.

He's warm. He's here. But he's not mine. We'll never have that kind of relationship.

I take a deep breath. "Just put the wallet in the lost and found, okay? I want to go home."

"Okay. Where is that?"

"Give it to me. I'll do it."

Miles pulls the wallet from his pocket and hands it to me. I stare at the sky. There are big, grey clouds covering the moon. The stars are tiny and dull, like they can't bother to shine tonight.

"Meg." His voice is so soft.

"I'm fine." My throat is sore. My eyes sting with tears. I blink them away. I can't cry here.

"I'll take you home."

"No." I wipe my eyes with the back of my hand. "I'm going to say I found this out here. And then we're going out."

If I go home, I'll drown in how awful this feels. I have to do something else. Anything else.

I march into the waiting room, drop off the wallet, and march back to Miles.

He's standing there, his eyes wide with affection. It's like he's desperate to do anything to make this hurt less.

His voice is a whisper. "Come here."

I stay put. This isn't what we're doing. I've already said too much. He's already seen too much, too deep inside me.

"Can we go?" I ask.

He shakes his head and wraps his arms around me. It's a tight hug. I want to push him off, to bang on his chest until he releases me.

But I can't. His body feels too good. I need the comfort too badly.

I take another ragged breath. I dig my fingers into the slick fabric of his leather jacket.

I can't cry in front of Miles. Not even if this is some other version of Miles, the one who hurts deep inside, who writes songs about the unspeakable agony of losing everything that matters.

"It's okay." His cheek brushes against mine. "I know how much it hurts."

I want to ask him how. I want to ask who he lost. I want to comfort him too. But I can't speak. I can't move.

I can't do anything but soak in the feeling of his arms against me.

This isn't what we're doing. We're casual. Not confidants.

After a few more breaths, I'm calm enough to release him. I pull back, slowly shaking him off. Cold hits me. It's brutal and sudden, like I'm shedding my favorite coat to step into a snowstorm.

His eyes stay glued to mine. "You look miserable."

I shake my head. "I'm fine."

His eyes turn to the street. "Don't make me call you on our 'no lies' clause."

"Can we please get out of here?"

He says nothing.

I need to turn the mood, to change him back to the other Miles. At least I know what that Miles wants. I make my voice light. "I'll go crazy if I have to make conversation with you for one more minute."

He smirks but he doesn't laugh. He's not quite back to snappy, sarcastic Miles. Not yet.

And I'm not back to acerbic Meg either. My defenses are down.

It's terrifying.

Miles wraps his hand around my wrist and leads me to his car. Or the car he borrowed from one of his bandmates.

I settle into the passenger seat. My skirt rides up my thighs, but it does nothing to entice Miles to touch me.

He pushes the ignition button. "You're not as good at pretending you're okay as you think you are."

"I don't want to talk about it."

"I'm not going to fuck you out of your misery." His lips curl into a smile. "I know. In my dreams, right?"

I nod.

"All this dreaming. I must be pretty fucking desperate." He brushes my knee. "Listen, Meg—"

"If the next words out of your mouth aren't something about how irresistible I am, you can save your breath."

"You're painfully irresistible." He trails his fingertips up my thigh. "I was thinking about fucking you the entire drive here." His eyes find mine. "Almost crashed this damn car."

Yes. Now. That makes sense. That feels good.

This hurts. It hurts so fucking badly.

Miles's voice gets low. Breathy. "I was planning on driving you to Malibu and fucking you in the back seat."

"The passenger seat isn't good enough?"

He smirks. "Only for round two." His hand slides over my thigh, back to my knee. "But I'm not going to be your human distraction." He puts the car in gear. "Don't sulk over it."

"You're the one who invited me out."

"We're out. If you want to spend the night pouting over not getting in my pants, I'll drive you home."

I pull the seatbelt over my chest. "What's the alternative?"

"I take you to Malibu. We have a conversation under the stars."

"I'm not really in the mood to talk."

He laughs. "You don't say."

I take a deep breath. I *am* irritable. I can't stand how mixed up I feel around Miles, how close I am to clinging to him and crying my heart out.

It's dangerous. Falling for him is the first step to falling apart. He's a drug. Different than the heroin that took hold of my sister's life but just as deadly.

I should go home. I should cry myself to sleep.

But I can't. I need someone.

I need him.

"I'm not cranky. I'm just hungry," I say. "Can we stop for something to eat?"

"Your wish is my command."

## Chapter Nineteen

MILES

After a quiet trip to an overpriced organic grocery store (of course, she gets sashimi), we move into the car.

Head to Pacific Coast Highway.

We travel in silence. I try to focus on the road. She hugs her bag so tightly her knuckles turn white.

I ignore it for as long as I can.

Which isn't very long.

This is bad news. No, it's worse. It's news that changes everything. That rearranged the nature of our agreement.

We aren't on even ground. We aren't two people who desperately want to fuck each other.

She's a girl aching over her sister's drug overdose and I—

I'm the exact opposite of what she needs.

Fuck.

I should have ignored her smart mouth. The hurt in her eyes. The way she's always looking at me like she believes there's more.

She paws at her skirt. It does nothing to cover those long legs. God, those legs.

I can pull over the car, snap my fingers, and get those legs wrapped around me. I can be so deep in her she doesn't remember her fucking name.

She sure as hell won't be stuck in some awful memory about her sister and the asshole who fucked things up.

I have his address. He's gonna pay for hurting her. Only a matter of figuring out a way to do it without Meg knowing.

I already took the girl's virginity. I can't turn her into a criminal on top of that.

Or under it.

Fuck. I can't stop thinking about getting inside her. That top is damn sheer. I can see the outline of her bra. Like it's begging me to rip it off.

Yeah, my cock got me into this mess. But hard to blame it for keeping me in this mess when it's going so unsatisfied.

It's not gonna forgive me for this.

She turns up the radio. It's way too loud, especially for such an overplayed oldie.

I turn it down. "You know, when I mentioned conversation, I was assuming you'd also make an effort."

"Conversation isn't my strong suit."

"I can tell."

"Or yours."

God, the mouth on her. Makes it hard to do anything but drag her to the back seat. "We both know my strong suit. What's yours?"

It's dark and the car doesn't handle nearly as well as my bike. Have to pay attention if I want to avoid the two of us drowning in the Pacific Ocean.

"Spades," she says.

## Just a Taste

I melt. She's so fucking cute. "How the hell do you come up with spades?"

"Well, it's obviously not hearts."

"And not comedy."

She flips me off.

I fight a groan. She's making this so hard. "You're good at driving me out of my mind."

"In what way?"

"You mean besides how fucking crazy I go thinking about touching you again?" Dammit. I need to keep those thoughts to myself if I want this to go well.

Her cheeks go red. She sighs like she's thirty seconds from coming. But she shakes it off.

She folds her arms and glares at me in irritation. "Don't tease me if you're going to stick to that ridiculous no sex tonight declaration."

"Not that you care?"

The devil on my shoulder echoes in my brain. *You're not helping her by taking sex off the table. You'd be better off taking her to a table and fucking her till she screams.*

"Whatever," she says.

I slam the brakes to stop at a red light. The beach is a few blocks away. She's still pouting over not getting in my pants.

I should say yes.

Fuck her.

Use her as a distraction. Let her use me as a distraction.

If she were another girl, one I didn't give a fuck about, I'd consider it. My cock would be a lot happier.

But she's not another girl.

I can't stand the thought of using her.

Or her using me.

I don't know what the fuck I'm doing. But it's not that.

"It's flattering," I say. "That it upsets you so much."

There's a smart-ass look on her face, but she doesn't say anything. It really does upset her.

God, I know how this hurts. She must be desperate to feel anything else.

I *should* fuck her. It's the kind thing to do. I should give her every chance to run away from her pain, the way I run away from mine.

That's fair.

But I'm not fair. Or kind.

I park the car. There's a blanket in the trunk. It has a better use, but it works fine for a picnic. I lead Meg to the beach and lay the blanket over the sand.

Big waves tonight. A full moon too.

She looks at me curiously.

"I figured you'd rather not eat in the car," I say.

"Thanks."

"Are you cold?"

She's obvious about staring at my chest. "Only if you're about to offer me your shirt."

"Leather jacket's in the back seat."

Her eyes drift to the sand. She shakes her head, plops on the ground, and focuses all her attention on her dinner.

She's a messy eater. It's so fucking endearing.

I sit next to her, sucking on a strawberry. She's lonely. She's hurt.

She needs a nice guy who will take care of her. She doesn't need me as a fuck buddy.

Only, I want to hold her, to comfort her, to do whatever it takes to make her feel better.

Her brown eyes are filled with hurt. That deep hurt that never fucking ends.

"I know you don't want a boyfriend," I say.

She stares back at me, defiant and strong. "And you don't want to be a boyfriend."

Yeah. So why do I feel so compelled to hold her and ask her what's wrong? "We are friends. You can talk to me."

Her gaze drifts back to her dinner. "I'm not interested."

There's a feeling in my gut I don't like. "Pretty sure I should take offense to that."

She stabs her sashimi. "Then take offense. But it's not something I want to talk about." She chews and swallows. "You said, 'I won't be the shoulder you cry on.' Well, you're not going to be the shoulder I cry on, either."

I should be relieved that she doesn't want to count on me, but I'm not.

I hate it.

I hate her hurting.

Fuck.

I drag my fingers over her palm. "You're drowning in something. You don't have to tell me what it is, but I'm not going to watch without throwing a life vest."

She pulls her arms over her chest. "Thank you for the sentiment. But I'm fine. My sister died three months ago. I still miss her sometimes, but it's nothing out of the ordinary."

Bullshit. "She was a drug addict, wasn't she?"

Her voice gets loud and defensive. "That's not any of your business."

"If it affects our relationship, it is."

"What relationship is that? We've had sex and breakfast." She takes a deep breath, staring into my eyes with fierce determination. "My sister, Rosie, started doing drugs behind my back. It went on for about a year. She lied the whole time, and I looked the other way, because I didn't want to believe it was possible. I was studying for the

MCAT, and I didn't have any spare energy to worry about her."

Even she doesn't believe that. I keep my eyes fixed on hers. "Why are you trying to convince me you're over it?"

"I'm not."

"You'll never be over it. Not really."

"Whoever you are, can you bring back the Miles I met last month?"

I wish I could. I wish I was that guy. Where the fuck is he? "Even that guy would notice how upset you are."

"Fine. I'm upset. You did your friend duty and asked what was wrong. I did my friend duty and gave you the details. Can we close the book on this conversation?"

"No."

She plays with the blanket. "Is there a reason why you're cross-examining me?"

I move closer. Until I can feel how warm she is. "It's the decent thing to do."

"You never struck me as a decent guy." She stares at me like she's daring me to take offense.

I'm not that easy to bait. "You're lucky I don't offend easily."

"I can try harder to offend."

I take her hand. Some of the hurt in her eyes is replaced with determination. She's defensive as hell.

It shouldn't hurt that she isn't talking to me.

I weigh my options. I can't tell her here. If she freaks and runs off, she'll be stranded on a dark street ten miles out of town. I can't fuck her with this hanging over her head.

I have to do something to make her feel better. Something she won't hate me for tomorrow.

"It's not something I talk about," she says. "It's not personal."

That look in her eyes is determined. Like she's desperate not to reveal anything. I respect that. And I understand it.

I can't make tonight about us. It's about her.

I lie back on the blanket and stare at the stars. "Fine. But I'm still not having sex with you tonight."

## Chapter Twenty

MILES

Meg falls asleep under the stars.

I pick her up, carry her to the car, drive to Damon's place.

She tugs at my t-shirt as I put her to bed. Looks up at me, those brown eyes full of need. "Stay."

She must be tired. She's usually more guarded. Usually more ready to tell me to fuck off.

"Go to sleep." I press my lips to her forehead. It's an impulse. It feels right. Which is wrong. But, right now, I don't care.

Her fingers curl around my neck. "Please."

Everything inside me screams *stay in her bed. Hold her all night. Make her come.*

It's torture pulling away. A torture I've never felt before.

Shades of that fucking phone call. But different too.

That, I couldn't change.

This—

It's all on me.

I saw her. I wanted her. I didn't care that she was bad news. That this whole thing was a bad idea. For both of us.

And now, I'm here, lying in my teenage bedroom, staring at the Nirvana poster on the wall, begging Kurt Cobain for insight.

If anyone knows better, it's me.

The guy was a miserable drug addict who took his own life.

He doesn't have insight.

Anything he has to offer is in his songs. That's what people want from him. That's the only reason why people are curious about him.

He poured his misery into his music. So people thought they knew him. Then when he kicked the bucket—

It only made him seem deeper, more interesting, more tortured.

It's funny. When I put this poster up at fourteen, I still saw the guy as a role model. As an ambition.

Now, he's a warning sign.

I can't look at the poster without hearing Tom's voice. *You want to join the twenty-seven club too? You want to be a line item on Entertainment Fucking Tonight? Not important enough for the main feature. Just gossip for a few days, until the next story breaks. Rock Star Overdosed at Twenty-Six. Found dead in his Malibu Mansion. Survived by his band, because he was too big an asshole for anyone else to care.*

A wife and kid didn't save Kurt Cobain.

This girl isn't going to save me.

---

Sleep has always been a struggle for me. At the moment, it's impossible. I toss and turn. Catch a few hours of unconsciousness.

Give up around sunrise.

I fix coffee, hang at the pool, watch the sky turn blue. It's beautiful. The picture of inspiration.

Not at all helpful.

Nothing makes this easier. Not the enormous house, the gorgeous vista, the words spinning around my head.

There's something there. The start of a song.

I let the words dance for a while. Until they settle into familiar steps. Then I find a pen and notebook in the kitchen. Close my eyes. Let my thoughts drift onto the pages.

I don't think when I write. Not when I write one of *my songs*.

It just happens. My subconscious takes over.

It spells out exactly what I need to hear. Even when I don't want to hear it.

Especially, when I don't want to hear it.

There.

A verse.

A chorus.

It's rough, but it's the start of something. It's too much the start of something. Too obviously about this, about her.

About how little I can handle her.

I can't. I can't let her in. I can't invite myself into her heart.

There's nothing to consider. The decision is made. It's over. It's happening.

So what if I have the bones of a song?

If I'm finally in touch with that guy, the one who's capable of facing his pain, of standing and letting it wash over him instead of running like a fucking coward.

It's not a good thing.

It's just not.

I turn my notebook over. Toss the pen to the other side of the table. Try to focus on the view.

The ocean, the sky, the neighbor's ten-million-dollar mansion, and the other one, on the other side.

I'm pretty sure that guy is an A-list actor. An Oscar winner. And the other one is some suit. A guy in finance or tech or some other industry I don't understand.

An entertainment lawyer down the street.

A washed-up sitcom star.

A family with family money.

Everyone in the neighborhood gets it. Ten million dollars should buy you a certain level of privacy. Parties are fine, as long as they're contained to your mansion. Make enough noise the neighbors hear and they'll call the cops.

Who come racing.

What other crime is there in Malibu? It's bored rich people with massive mansions.

Not that I mind. Parties were fun when I was using. Now, they might as well be a flashing *Temptation* sign. It's boring as hell talking to drunk and high people.

Hearing empty praise does nothing to entertain me.

Which leaves finding someone to take home.

Now that Meg and I—

No, I'm ending this. I don't care how much my heart is screaming *no*. I'm not doing that to her.

Maybe I'm running away.

Maybe I'm doing the right thing.

Either way, I'm not hurting her worse. That has to count for something.

And, tonight, after I make sure she gets home okay. After I text her friend so she has some consolation. After I break the news to Drew—

It feels so far away. So impossible. I try to imagine hitting a party with Tom, finding a pretty girl to hold my attention, fucking her until she's clawing at my chest.

The images refuse to form. It's all wrong. It's not her. It needs to be her.

I don't want some random woman groaning *Miles, harder, harder.*

I want Meg.

I want her brown eyes filled with pleasure.

I want her short nails digging into my back.

I want my name rolling off her smart mouth.

Not just because she has those long legs and that sweet groan.

Because she sees me. Because she shows me her. Because her sister overdosed and she's the only person who knows how badly this hurts.

How tenuous this is.

It's not fair to her. It's a dick move. It's better to end things now.

Better for both of us.

I sure as fuck can't handle her looking for the key to my soul.

Even if my heart is screaming *keep her around, whatever it takes*.

Footsteps rouse my attention. I stand. Stretch. Attempt to find clarity in my yawn.

Things are plenty clear.

I need to do the right thing here.

It's simple. It's just fucking hard.

I release my arms. Shrug my shoulders. Take a steady breath.

The words are there, on my tongue. *Let me drive you home. Then we'll talk. This has to end.*

But as I turn, and find her gaze, the words disappear.

The hurt in her eyes disappears as she looks me up and down. Her expression gets hungry. Needy.

Like she'll die if she doesn't have me.

Like she'll die if she doesn't erase her thoughts right now.

Maybe I'm wrong. Maybe this is what she needs too.

Or maybe I'm listening to my cock instead of my head.

She moves through the sliding glass door. Steps onto the concrete. Holds her hand over her head to block out the sun.

She looks at me the way she did last night. Like I'm a life raft and an anchor around her throat.

Both feel true.

How the fuck is that possible?

I reach for a response. Something to set the record. But my body won't allow it. "Good morning." I move toward her. "You must have slept well."

She looks up at me with the world's most demanding expression.

"It's almost noon."

"You should have woken me."

I thought about it. "You swore at me when I put you to bed."

"Asked you why you invited me out for sex then took me to a strange house to sleep?"

"Something like that." I can't help but smile. "You're cute when you swear."

Her cheeks flush. "Thank you."

Fuck, I want to make her blush again. I want to push her buttons. All of them. Love, hate, lust, need, anger, comfort. I want to make her feel everything.

I want to be capable of that.

The way she is.

Right now—

No, it's impossible. I need to do the right thing. Whatever that is. "Are you okay?" It's not much, but it's a start.

"You wrote that song. You know what it's like to lose everything that matters to you."

Yeah. I nod.

"Are you okay?"

"Fair point."

She looks at me, waiting for me to expand. To open up my heart and spill every juicy detail.

If I could I would. Really.

But I can't. I'm not capable.

That guy—the Miles who spins his thoughts into songs—is already gone. The only sign of him is the words scribbled on paper.

"Do you want to talk about it?" she asks.

I hold my poker face. "I don't talk about that with anyone."

She shrinks back, wounded. Nods with understanding.

Maybe she does get it. Maybe this doesn't have to end.

She hurts. I hurt. We hurt less when we fuck. We part. Keep our hurt to ourselves.

It's a good plan.

So why does it feel so wrong?

"Do you have anything with caffeine?" she asks.

I motion to the coffee maker inside. "It's a few hours old."

Her brow knits with frustration. Softens as she realizes something. Something about me. About us.

Whatever it is, she doesn't share it.

I shrug it off. Lead her to the kitchen. It's not like I'm going to send the girl home hungry and uncaffeinated.

The drink softens her expression. And her defenses. Everything inside her—all that shit from last night—rises to the surface.

It's all over her face.

It's right *there*.

How does she live like that, with all her pain so close?

It can't be the right thing, cutting her off, making her face that alone. It feels wrong. No matter how much I reason with myself *you can't keep this up unless you tell her.*

And there's no way I'm telling her.

That's just—

It's out of the question.

"You're more obvious than you think you are, Meg." Even if I am ending it. I'm not doing it with her this miserable. I move closer. Close enough to brush my hand against her lower back.

For a second, all that hurt on her face disappears. Her expression turns to pure need.

She tries to push it away. Focuses on her coffee. Makes her glances faster. More furtive.

She wants to touch me. To fuck me. But she's holding out.

Making me wait.

As revenge for last night.

Or because she isn't ready.

Or because she's the one considering dumping me.

I don't know. I want to know. I want to be that place where this makes sense. Where we make sense.

There isn't much I understand these days.

But her body?

I know how to make her purr. I need more. I need to know every fucking inch of her.

I need to take care of her.

It's ridiculous. I'm incapable. Beyond incapable.

But I can do this.

I can at least feed the girl breakfast.

I open the fridge, pull out a carton of eggs. It's not the finest meal in the world, but it's something. "Scrambled eggs okay?"

"That's fine."

I grab a bowl. Start mixing.

She takes a seat at the kitchen island. Looks around the kitchen like she can't believe I live here. That anyone lives here.

It's hard to blame her. I come here to get away sometimes. But, every time I leave, the hole in my heart gets a little deeper. I feel the loss of Damon more.

His voice gets louder. But further away too.

It's more obvious I'll never see him again. That it will never stop hurting. That I'll keep disappointing him, again and again.

What would he say, right now?

Would he tell me to run to her? Or run away? Which one is running away from my pain?

*Be brave, live.*

It's what he always said.

The ideal I continue to fail to uphold.

I contemplate the matter as I fix breakfast. Scoop eggs onto plates. Refill my coffee.

Meg nods *thanks* as I set the plate in front of her. She drowns it in hot sauce. Eats quickly. Sets her fork down.

She gives me this look, like she's waiting for me, waiting for something. "Thanks for breakfast."

I don't know what it is. What she wants. I don't know why I care so much. "You still hungry?"

Her expression says *yes*, but she shakes her head. "I have food at home." Her eyes drift to my mouth, shoulders, chest. She focuses on that tattoo—Damon's mantra—for a moment, then she makes her way down my body.

I stand. Give her the chance to stare.

She relishes in it.

The frustration in her eyes fade. She is hungry. For me. For us. For this.

Maybe it doesn't have to get complicated.

Maybe this is the right thing. Running to this girl who needs comfort, who can lead by example, instead of running away from this tiny hint of intimacy.

Is it too fucked up, keeping this from her?

I don't know.

I'm quickly losing interest. The way she stares—fuck, I'm already on fire. I'm already forgetting my head.

Good intentions—

Where the fuck are those?

I have *fantastic* fucking intentions. Her screaming my name. Coming on my hands, my face, my cock.

Doesn't matter as long as she's *there* with me. As long as she's *mine*.

Not in a possessive way. Not in an *I want you to call after* or an *I love you* way.

In an *I can't stand how badly I need your body against mine* way.

I find strawberries in the fridge, rinse them, toss them onto a clean plate.

She looks at me with those hungry eyes. Her lips part. Her tongue slides over them.

Because she wants me.

Or because she wants the fruit.

I don't know. I don't even care about anything other than keeping that look in her eyes.

I'm not hurting her.

That's out of the question.

Leaving now, leaving her hungry and wanting—that's hurting her. This is just two people making sense of an ugly world in the best possible way.

I place the plate in front of her. "Do you want to go home?"

Her eyes flit to the plate, then back to my lips.

If she says yes, I'll take her home. I'll spell this out. I'm not giving her comfort she doesn't want.

But if she says no, if she wants to stay, if she wants to turn the ugly world into someplace beautiful as much as I do—

I don't know why I said no last night, but I'm saying yes now. Somehow, it's different.

Something is different.

I swear, it's not just my cock getting greedy and demanding. It's not just my heart thudding against my chest.

It's something in her eyes. Some understanding.

She just barely shakes her head. No, she doesn't want to go home.

Good. "It's up to you, Meg. If you want to go, I'll drive you home. But I'd really hate if you left before I was done with you."

## Chapter Twenty-One

MILES

"Done how?" Her chest heaves. Her lips part. It's on the tip of her tongue.

I say it for her. "Last time I went for four, but I do like to break records."

Her blush spreads to her chest. She moves closer. Picks up a strawberry. Places it between her lips. Sucks on it like she's desperate for every ounce of it.

It's too fucking sexy.

And adorable too.

She has this need to prove herself. There's something about it. I want to help her prove it. To watch her prove it.

I want to push her into proving it. "You're nervous."

Her eyes flare with the slightest hint of irritation.

"It's cute."

She swallows the berry. Bites into another. It irritates her so much, that I find her adorable.

But why?

It drives me out of my fucking mind.

I already want to tear her clothes off. Fuck her senseless. It's ridiculous how much I want it.

More than I've ever wanted anyone.

More than I've wanted anything besides a high in a long, long time.

"That's one opinion on the matter." She sucks on the tip of a strawberry, daring me to push her.

I pick up a berry. Bring it to my lips. Suck on it like it's her perky nipple.

Her eyes go wide. Her cheeks flush. Her chest heaves.

The frustration fades.

The pretense drops.

It's just me and her.

I set the plate down. Move closer. Close enough to undo the top button of her top. "You were begging me last night."

"Not begging."

I press my lips to her neck. Let my fingers trail over her next button.

Her chest heaves. She turns her head, offering her neck to me, beckoning me to touch her.

"You were desperate," I breathe.

Her nails dig into her thighs. "No…"

"It took everything I had to turn you down." I scrape my teeth against her neck. Softly. Then hard. Just as hard as she likes.

She groans in response.

I bring my hand to her chest. Trace the outline of her bra. Teasing her.

Teasing myself.

Fuck, having her here, like this, desperate for me—

It's the best thing in the world.

The only thing that makes sense.

"Why did you?" she asks, like she's trying to break my trance, like she's trying to bring reality into this.

But I'm the one who brought reality here.

## Just a Taste

I'm the one who needs to explain.

"I don't want you thinking about anything else when I touch you." I slip my hand into her bra. Run my fingers over her nipples. I'm not playing fair. But I don't give a fuck.

"I won't. I couldn't." She gasps as I run my thumb over her nipple. "I don't even know what day it is."

Me either. I undo the rest of her buttons. Push her blouse off her shoulders. Pull her body against mine.

She groans as my hard-on brushes her ass.

"I need to hear you come again."

"Okay," she breathes.

"Fuck, you're so cute."

"No." She shakes her head, sending her hair in every direction.

"Would you prefer sexy as hell?"

"Yes." Her eyes flutter closed.

I sink my teeth into her neck. Softly. Then harder. Hard enough she lets out the world's most perfect groan.

"Miles…"

"This will be easier on the couch."

She nods *yes*. Tosses her shirt and bra aside.

Then it's her skirt.

I push her panties off her hips. Then I pull her body against mine. She's naked and I'm clothed—just barely, I'm only in my boxers, but I am clothed.

I'm sure it means something. Maybe something about how I'm an asshole who's manipulating her. Or how I can't share some part of myself.

None of that sinks into my brain.

Her skin against mine.

This tiny bit of fabric between us.

Me playing her like a fucking instrument. Knowing exactly how to make her sing—

It's amazing.

She shifts her hips, rubbing against my hard-on as she kisses me hard. All this need pours from her to me.

She needs me too.

Needs this too.

I can't remember what the fuck I'm trying to do here. But there's no way I can do anything but give her what she needs.

I scoop her into my arms. Bring her to the couch. I lay her down. Slide onto the couch. Bring my body over hers.

She looks up at me as she wraps her legs around me and pulls my body into hers.

Fuck, she's so sexy like this.

I run my hand down her neck, chest, stomach, hips.

Her back arches. Her eyelids press together. She groans as she bucks her hips, rubbing her cunt against my cock.

Fuck, that feels too good.

I need to make her come first.

If she does that again, I'm going to forget all my manners.

I kiss her hard. Just once. To feel all her need. To feel everything she's willing to give.

Then I drag my lips down her body. Her neck, collarbone, breasts. I toy with her nipple until she's panting.

Then it's the soft scrape of my teeth.

Harder.

Harder—

Hard enough she groans *please give me more.*

And I do. I torture her until she's tugging at my hair. Until she's begging for more.

Then I move to her other breast, torture her some more.

Her breath hitches as I press my lips to her stomach. Her pelvis. Her inner thigh.

Then she jerks. Nervous. Scared.

"I'm going to eat you out." I press my lips to her thigh. "Have you ever done that before?"

She shakes her head. "But don't go easy on me."

"I couldn't." I want her too badly. I need her too desperately.

I slide my hand up her body. Toy with her breast until her nerves fade. Until her groans run together.

Slowly, I bring my lips to her inner thigh.

Higher and higher—

There—

She shakes as I bring my mouth to her cunt.

"Miles—" She digs her hands into my hair, already begging for more.

My body takes over. I lick her up and down, testing her reactions, finding exactly where she purrs.

There.

I focus on that spot. Go harder. Faster. Just high enough—

She comes fast. She tugs at my hair, groans my name again and again, squeezes her thighs against my cheeks.

It's so fucking beautiful. The most beautiful thing I've seen in forever.

I give her a moment of respite, then I bring my mouth to her. This time, I take my time tasting her, toying with her, flicking my tongue against her clit, scraping my teeth against her lips.

She melts into the couch.

She digs her heel into my back.

She reaches for me. Scrapes her nails against my back. Her grip gets harder and harder as I bring her closer and closer.

She scrapes hard enough to draw blood as she comes. I work her through her orgasm.

Meg screams my name. It's loud enough to wake the fucking neighbors. Loud enough they might call the cops.

It's the best thing I've ever heard.

I push myself up. Look down at her, reveling in her pleasure. I don't know what I want to do to her now. Only that I still need her body close to mine.

My fingers brush her thighs. I motion to the stairs. "Shower?"

She nods *yeah*.

I pull her off the couch, into my arms. She melts into them. Lets me carry her up the stairs.

She looks up at me as I set her down. She looks at me like I'm her balm.

Like this is exactly what she needs.

It is.

And she gets it.

It's just sex. Just the two of us bringing each other comfort. The other shit in my head, in my heart—

That's so much less important than making her come again.

## Chapter Twenty-Two

MILES

I drag her into the shower. Make her come again.

I should let her rest. I really should. But I can't help myself.

After I slip out of the shower, I move into the spare room. Hide her panties.

She arrives a few minutes later. Looks me up and down as she dons her bra, blouse, skirt.

Her gaze shifts to the bed, the floor the dresser.

"Let's go out for lunch." I hold up her underwear. "You can have these when I'm done with you."

## Chapter Twenty-Three

MILES

I hate to complain about inheriting a ten-million-dollar mansion by the beach. Hell, the whole point of a house in Malibu is being just far enough from civilization.

No one to ask for your autograph, gawk at your gaudy display of wealth, shake their head at your trophy wife.

It also means a lack of dining options. Besides a few strip malls and grocery stores, the restaurants here are expensive. Fancy. For rich people who shrug off three-hundred-dollar charges.

I take Meg to the place she'll like the most. A fusion Japanese restaurant on the water.

It's as picture-perfect as everything else around here. A quiet patio with the ocean stretching for miles behind us.

Blue skies, scattered clouds, soft sun. Not too bright. It's pure beach day. The kind of day I used to spend with Damon hiking, sitting by the pool, trying to surf.

He was terrible. He tried to teach me, but he was too far gone to teach a thing.

He loved the water. Loved the ocean.

He didn't care that he fell every time he stood up. He tried anyway.

He was brave. The way she is.

Meg takes a seat. She rubs her shoulders as the breeze ruffles her blouse.

It *is* a sheer thing.

I slip my leather jacket off my shoulders. Sling it over hers.

She nods *thank you* and adjusts the jacket.

It's cute on her. Even though it covers that sheer blouse, I want her wearing it. I love her wearing it.

There's something about her in my clothes—

I like it too much.

In ways I shouldn't.

I push that aside. Focus on the demands of a different body part.

Even though we went twice, I want to have her again.

I want to toss the silverware aside, lay her on the table, fuck her until she's groaning my name.

That desire, I understand.

This feeling in my chest, this need to feed her, clothe her, comfort her?

Uh-uh.

She leans back in her seat. Opens the menu. Gapes at the prices.

Is she really surprised I can afford it? Or just uncomfortable to owe me that much?

Damon always said there were downsides to money. At the time, I thought it was ridiculous. How could there be anything bad about more of something good?

I see what he means now.

Fuck, I should say something soothing. Tell her *don't worry about the money, I have more than I need. Too much. The worst thing an addict can have is money.*

*Better to spend it on you than enough heroin to put me in a coma thirty times over.*

Instead, I tease her. "You're adorable."

Her eyes flit to me. "That's not what you said in the shower."

Fuck, I have no words for how sexy she was. How sexy she is. Right now, daring me to resist her. "Order whatever you want. It's on me."

"I know." She stares at the menu until the waiter arrives. Then she rattles off an order big enough to feed the entire band.

Not that any of them appreciate expensive sashimi.

After the waiter takes her menu, she sits up in her seat. Pulls the edges of my leather jacket over her chest.

It doesn't hide the sheer blouse. I can still see the outline of her bra. I still want to tear off all her clothes.

And talk to her.

Hold her.

Heal her.

It's fucking ridiculous. I *can't* do that. It's simply not possible.

"You all right?" I ask. "You seem a little out of sorts.

Her chest heaves with her inhale. "I'm not cute."

"We'll have to agree to disagree there." I let my eyes linger on her chest. I can barely tell she's blushing, but she is, and it's so fucking sexy. It's ridiculous. "Why don't you want to be cute?"

"It's what you say about your little sister. Someone clueless. Or uncool."

"No."

Her eyes meet mine. "No?"

"It's what I say about a girl who blushes when I tease her. Who tries to prove she's badass by ordering enough sashimi for three. Who drives me out of my fucking mind with her sincere desire to rip my clothes off."

"Oh."

"I love that you're cute, Meg. It makes me fucking crazy. If you don't want me to say it, I won't. But I won't agree that it's not sexy."

"Oh."

"Oh?"

"I'm going to eat all that sashimi."

Of course, that's her response. Fuck, she *is* adorable. So desperate to prove she's a badass. So unaware she's already proven it.

She's standing there, facing her pain, confronting it.

There's nothing more badass.

"I like you the way you are," I say.

"But…" She bites her lip. Doubt flashes in her eyes. She looks at me, studies me, deciding if she believes me. "You're always so collected."

"Not always."

"Almost."

No, I'm just better at pretending. "It's not a competition."

Her eyes bore into mine.

"If it was, you'd be winning."

"I would win the coolness competition?" she asks.

"The sincerity competition."

Her laugh lights up her eyes. "What bullshit."

"It's true."

"You're always collected. Always holding all the cards."

I shake my head.

She nods *yeah*. "You don't tell me what hurts you."

"You already know."

"I know you wrote a song about how you lost someone.

I know you inherited a lot of money. I'm guessing part of that is the giant house."

"Yeah."

"But that's... that's it."

It's not. It's just... she doesn't see it.

I should agree. *Yes, that's it. You're right. I am cool. I am collected. We are casual, so what's it matter?*

*I want to make you come.*

*Then take you home.*

*I'm just being a gentleman here. I'm not sending you home hungry.*

But it's bullshit. I'm trying to impress her. To keep her here all weekend. To make her laugh so hard it fills the big, empty house.

I need sound in that house.

I need her in that house.

"Miles?"

Fuck, I need to say this. I shouldn't, but it's the only way to keep her here. "That's my uncle's house. He died last year."

"Oh. And he's the one with the money?"

"Yeah."

Her expression softens. "I'm sorry you lost him."

"Isn't it weird, how everyone says that?"

"Yeah."

"And the only acceptable response is *thank you*?"

"You care about the acceptable response?"

"Good point." I laugh. "There are times I have to be polite."

"Really?"

"I know. You'd think I'd ace that, every time it came up."

"Of course," she teases.

"I have a lot of latitude. Musicians are expected to be divas."

"Especially beautiful lead singers."

"Face of the band."

"No one can kick you out."

"They could… but it wouldn't go well for them."

"Do you take advantage of that?"

"Maybe." Not on purpose. Not now. When I was using… Fuck. I shouldn't be telling her this stuff. I should be pumping the brakes. "I've told you before. I'm not a good guy."

"Maybe." She turns to the waiter as he drops off our drinks. Green tea. And water. She nods thanks, waits for him to leave. "Or maybe we'll have to agree to disagree there."

"You think I'm a good guy?"

"I can't tell."

"I think you're a badass."

"You do?" Her expression fills with surprise. "Really?"

"Yeah. After Damon died… it took six months to smile. Longer to laugh. It's still this gaping hole in my chest. I still fall asleep thinking—"

"You'll never stop missing him?"

"Yeah. But, here you are after, what, three months? And you're trying. You're figuring it out."

"It doesn't feel like that."

"You are." My gaze shifts to the ocean. This is where I confess everything. Where I explain why this is the last conversation we can have like this.

But I can't.

I'm still selfish. Or a coward. Something that's not fair to her.

I need her too much. Need this too much.

I can't give it up.

Fuck, I'm such an asshole. But it's not like calling myself an asshole changes things.

"It must have hurt, your sister manipulating you. Hiding shit from you," I say.

"Yeah."

"I won't do that." I'm not telling her this, yeah. But I'm not dragging her into addiction bullshit either. If I slip… I'll cut ties. I swear to God, I will.

But I already know that's bullshit.

If I do slip, my word sober won't be worth a cent.

I clear my throat. "I know you want me to explain more. But I can't. You'll have to take my word for it. That it's not something you need to know."

Her eyes meet mine. She stares at me for a long time, deciding if she believes me. She must, because she nods *okay*, and turns her attention to her tea.

I'm telling her the truth.

Or close enough.

My conscience is going to have to accept that.

## Chapter Twenty-Four

MILES

With Meg here, it feels like Damon's place is my place. Our place. I find spare clothes for her. Boxers and a t-shirt that are too big for her slim frame.

She's a beautiful woman. Sexy as fuck. And smaller than she seems. Did she stop eating after her sister died?

Does she eat breakfast, lunch, and dinner now?

Fuck, she eats plenty when she's with me. I shouldn't jump to all these conclusions. Yeah, I was all skin and bones when I was strung out, but I'm a guy aiming at fame. It's not a look that wins points.

After months of workouts, I'm in celebrity shape. It's not something that matters to me, exactly. More that I understand appearances.

I did grow up in Southern California.

I do like the way she stares.

Fuck, I love the way she stares.

And she—

Maybe it doesn't mean anything that she's thin. Lots of women are thin. This is Los Angeles. It's expected.

I lead her to the couch. Take a seat. Pull her into my lap.

She feels right. Soft. Malleable.

She turns enough to rest her head on my shoulder.

I grab the remote. And the PS4 controller. All this technology and Sony can't make a useful remote to save their life. Just the controller that dies after a few hours idling.

Damon used to complain about it. Then shake his head, chide himself for focusing on shit that didn't matter.

For a guy with a ten-million-dollar mansion, he was awfully big on letting shit go.

At the time, I didn't get it. Wasn't I supposed to stand and face my pain, not let it go? He said it didn't work like that. That I had to face it to let it go.

But—

I guess I still don't understand.

I pull her closer. I need to be here. With her. It's easier.

There. I boot up a streaming app. Scroll to *The Lost World*. "This is what you want to watch, right?"

"Clever."

"Clever girl."

"That's from the first movie."

She laughs *you're ridiculous*. "Clever boy."

"I'd love to not watch dinosaurs destroy San Diego, but if you'd rather watch something else, go for it."

"You're going to mock me whatever I pick."

I run my hands along the edge of her t-shirt. "Likely." For fuck's sake, I don't care what we pick. As long as I spend some of the time making her come.

She arches her back, pressing her chest into my hands. "Convince me to pick something."

"Convince you how?" My fingertips skim her skin.

"Like that," she breathes.

"I like the confidence."

"You're stalling."

No. I'm lingering in this perfect moment. I slip my hand into her t-shirt. Brush her nipple with my thumb.

She shudders.

I do it again. "Why would I do that?"

"It's smart, really. You're pressed against me on the couch. You get to mock me and have your way with me at the same time."

"I did go to Stanford."

Her laugh is a struggle. Like she's too wound up to laugh.

I draw a soft circle around her nipple. Then another. A little harder. Harder. Until she groans. "Some part of this you don't like?"

"No." She pushes her chest into my hand. "Keep going."

"After you pick a movie."

Her head nudges the crook of my neck. Then it's her soft hair against my skin. She lets out a needy sigh. "A what?"

"Movie."

"Huh?"

I nip at her ear as I draw another slow circle.

Her groan gets lower.

"Pick first." I bite her a little harder. Harder. Until she yelps.

"What?" Her voice is hazy. Needy. Sexy as fuck.

"Pick a movie."

"Miles…"

I roll her nipple between my thumb and forefinger. "I'm not familiar with a movie by that name."

She responds with a groan.

I drag my lips down her neck. Soft kisses. Then the scrape of my teeth

"Miles… you can't… don't tease me…"

"Me, tease? Never." I bite her a little harder. Bring my hands to the waist of her shorts.

"I don't care about a movie."

"I know." I push the shorts off her hips.

She lifts her ass to help me.

Then the things are at her knees. Her ankles. The floor.

Fuck, she has long legs. I need them wrapped around me again. I run my fingers over her inner thigh as lightly as I can.

Higher and higher and higher, until I'm so close she's panting.

Then to her other leg, from the inside of her knee, to the apex of her thigh.

She pulls her t-shirt over her head.

As much as I like seeing her in my clothes, I like this a lot better.

I'm out of patience. Too fucking out. I need to have my way with her.

I take her hands. Press them into the couch, outside my thighs. Then I bring my mouth to her neck.

Bite her gently.

Then harder.

As hard as she likes.

"Fuck," she breathes.

She's naked in my lap, groaning as she rocks against my cock. I've been in this situation so many times in the last few years. So many naked women offering their bodies to me.

But it's never mattered this much.

It doesn't matter with anyone else.

It was different. A transaction. A way to kill my thoughts.

With her—

It's fucking everything.

Too much. More than it should be.

But that's not an interesting consideration. Not compared to the sound of her groan and the feel of her hair falling over my chest.

I bite her as I tease her.

Again.

Again.

Again.

She lifts her hands. Brings them to my thighs. "Touch me."

"Not yet." I tease her again.

"Please." Her voice drops to a beg. Then to pure need. "Please, Miles."

Hell yes. I sink my teeth into her neck again. Drag my fingers higher, higher, higher.

There—

She groans as my hand skims her cunt.

"Fuck, Meg." I run my thumb over her clit. "How do you get so wet?"

"You."

My balls tighten. I run my fingers over her clit again. Softly. Then hard enough she groans.

Again.

Again.

Then a longer stroke.

Longer.

My fingers skim her cunt.

She gasps as I tease her with one finger.

Then two.

"Fuck." She reaches for something. Gets the fabric of the couch.

But I'm greedy. I want her. "Turn around."

She nods. Turns back to face me.

I watch pleasure spread over her face as I tease her again.

Again.

Again.

There.

Her eyes squeeze shut as I slip both fingers inside her. She arches her back, beckoning me to go deeper.

I do.

She slips her hand under my t-shirt. Claws at my stomach as I drive my fingers into her again and again.

I toy with her until she's panting, then I bring my thumb to her clit, rub her just how she needs me.

It's so fucking beautiful, watching her come. Watching her brow furrow. Her eyelids squeeze tighter. Her teeth sink into her lip.

Her shoulders squeeze together.

Her nails scrape my skin.

Then, all at once, her entire body relaxes. A groan falls from her lips. Then it's my name. Louder and louder, until she's loud enough to wake the neighbors.

It's the greatest thing I've ever heard. It really is. "What did I say about you being sexy?"

She murmurs something incomprehensible.

"Sexiest woman I've ever met."

Her nod is needy. Fuzzy.

I hold her body against mine. "You decide on a movie?"

"Shut up," she murmurs.

"That's no way to thank the man who made you scream so loudly you almost broke the glass."

"Don't be cocky."

"If you promise to stay that loud. I like it." I help her off the couch. "Come on. I have something to show you."

She follows me upstairs. Without her clothes.

Somehow, I have enough restraint to refrain from pinning her to the wall and fucking her senseless.

I lead her to my old bedroom. Turn the light on.

She looks around the room, still hazy. Stops on the navy bedspread. The Nirvana poster on the wall. "Kurt Cobain, huh?"

"Yeah."

"That's a little cliché, isn't it?"

"You this rude to all your friends?" I tease her with my new favorite refrain. "Or only the ones who make you come?"

"I can't say now. Your ego will get too big."

"My ego?"

Her gaze goes straight to my crotch. "Could you, um…"

"Is that an offer?"

"Maybe," she plays coy.

"Maybe I'll pin you to that bed and fuck you right now."

"Is that why…" Her gaze goes to the Nirvana poster. Then the one next to it. For *Empire Strikes Back*. She scans the next wall—it's plain. Then the next.

The one with the shelf full of *Star Wars* books.

Her jaw drops. "No way." She moves to the bookshelf. Picks up a particularly banged up paperback. "You're a nerd."

"Our secret." I stand next to her. Run my fingers over her shoulder. Fuck, the way she murmurs as she fights her desire to close her eyes—I like it way too much. "I have a reputation to maintain."

"Our secret." She smiles. Puts down the paperback. Picks up another. "You care what other people think of you."

"Everyone does."

"But you act like you don't. You act like nothing could ever hurt you."

"You know that isn't true."

She looks me in the eyes. "Tell me another secret."

"Damn, it's hard to turn down a naked woman."

"You did last night."

"You know why I did." And I can't fucking face that right now. "How secret?"

"Very secret."

Okay. This *is* a secret. And it doesn't touch on the shit I can't contemplate at the moment. "I went as Harry Potter for Halloween all throughout middle school."

"You did not."

I did. "I was shorter, smaller. My mom loved making my costume. She loved that kind of thing, the magic, the justice." Fuck. So much for the easy topic. "I was twelve or thirteen. Older kid took my fake glasses, threw them on the ground, stepped on them."

"What did you do?"

"I flipped. Tried to hit him but couldn't. He was bigger, stronger. The rest of the year, I never heard the end of it. Taught me the value of not reacting to things. Then I got bigger, learned how to hit. That was that."

"You stopped showing your emotions and started beating people up because a bully picked on your Harry Potter costume?"

I wish it was that simple. "What is it you always call me?"

"Aloof."

"I'm aloof because I don't want anyone to know my weaknesses. I don't want anyone to know what hurts me."

"But your songs. You're confessing to the whole world."

"Yeah."

"What's the difference?"

"I'm in control. I'm the one on stage, commanding attention, making girls scream." It's terrifying telling her this, but I want her to know. "Most people don't listen closely to the words. They don't see what's right in front of their faces." I run my fingers down her back.

She leans into the touch. "I did. At least, I thought I did. But maybe I just saw what I wanted to see. Saw the person I needed... I listened to that song a thousand times. That guy who was singing. He was my closest friend. He was the only person who knew where I hurt."

"I still know where you hurt."

"But I don't... it's not equal."

"You do." I take a step back. "You know more than anybody else does." I take a seat on the bed. I still want to fuck her senseless here. But not in the same way. In a whole different way.

I've never been with a woman in this bed.

Damon would have killed me.

She moves closer. "This house seems untouched."

"Don't come here by myself. It feels empty without Damon. Feels quiet without his laugh."

She nods with understanding. Looks to the bookshelf. "Do you have a favorite?"

"No."

"Do you like other sci-fi or just *Star Wars*?"

"Mostly *Star Wars*. And *Futurama*."

"Did you ever play *Podracer* or *Rogue Squadron*?"

"Never had the chance."

"You know what this means?"

I can't help but smile. "What?"
"We're watching *Star Wars*."
"Which one?"
"All of them," she says.
"You'll be here until four a.m."
"Do you have something better to do?"
"Yeah." I pat the spot next to me.
"Oh." Her eyes light up. "After that."

## Chapter Twenty-Five

MEGARA

We watch all six *Star Wars* films. Miles knows every line, and he delights in reciting them with me. Well, he delights in mocking me, too—in mocking my very obvious crush on Han Solo. What can I say? Maybe I do have a thing for scoundrels.

It's almost dawn when we go to bed, but this time Miles doesn't put me in the spare room. We sleep together in his bed, in his bedroom. It's not the biggest bed, but it feels so good to be pressed against him. His body fits perfectly with mine. I fall asleep almost instantly, and I wake up in his arms.

Miles stirs when I get out of bed. He drags me to the bathroom, and we take another shower together. It's as amazing as before. We kiss, touch, and help each other with soap and shampoo.

After, he makes me breakfast and coffee. It's like we're playing house, like we're playing pretend at being grown-ups in a grown-up relationship. I know I'm twenty-one, and he must not be more than a few years older, but I've never really felt like an adult. This, though, being in this house alone with him—it feels real.

Miles snickers when we leave for Kara's. "You've been wearing that outfit for almost three days."

"So?"

"Something tells me you don't normally wear low-cut tops and short skirts to hang out with your best friend. Not that I object."

He's right. I never dress up to see Kara. At best, I wear a t-shirt and jeans. I need clean clothes, especially clean underwear. There's no way I'm going commando to hang out with my best friend.

"So, drop me at my place. I'll change."

He shakes his head. "No, I'll take you to a boutique I know."

"I'm not a doll."

"And you won't be on display to anyone but me." He leads me to the front door. "But I'll feel awful about ripping off your panties if I didn't buy them."

"No you won't."

He smirks. "Okay, I won't. But I'm still buying you something to wear today."

"That's not necessary."

He presses his lips into my cheek. "I know. But I still want to make you come in the dressing room."

"Oh."

Oh.

I get in the car without any further objections.

---

THE BOUTIQUE IS BETTER THAN I COULD POSSIBLY imagine. Not the clothes—I couldn't possibly care less about clothes. Miles drags me into the dressing room. One hand under my skirt, one hand over my mouth, he rubs me until I can barely muffle my screams then rubs me some more. I come three times despite my fear that the salesgirl will throw us out.

I pick out a pair of jeans, a tank top, and a set of lacy black lingerie. Everything here is outrageously expensive—more than I make in a month—but he insists.

We, well, I, am right on time to Kara's place. She opens the door and takes in my outfit with curiosity.

"I've never seen that outfit before."

"It's new."

She shakes her head—not buying my version of the story. "Those are expensive jeans."

I nod.

"You wear designer jeans now?"

"I guess."

She raises a brow *okay*. "English Breakfast good?"

"Sure."

She moves to the kitchen and turns on her electric kettle.

I turn over my options as she fixes tea. I trust Kara more than I trust anyone. I should want to tell her about everything with Miles.

She returns to the main room with two mugs of tea. She sets one down on the side table and hands the other to me. There's infinite patience in her eyes, like she could wait eight million years for an explanation.

I sip my tea to buy another ten seconds.

"I was with Miles," I say.

Her eyes light up. "And what were you doing with Miles?"

"We slept together."

"Holy shit, Megara Smart. How the fuck did you not tell me this?"

"It's no big deal."

"Bullshit. Don't act like you don't give a damn. You lost your virginity to Miles. That's huge. Is he huge?"

My cheeks burn.

"He is!" she squeals. "Let's put the issue of your secrecy aside for a moment." Kara leans in close, her eyes wide. "What was it like fucking him?"

"Good."

She stares at me. "Good? You call that a detail. I want a better fucking detail!"

"Is great a better detail?"

"Technically, great is better than good."

"You sound like an English teacher."

"Thank you." She taps her fingers against her jeans. "So…"

"Very, really good. He's good at everything, and he's more tender than you'd expect. But it's just sex. It's really not a big deal."

"Not buying it, sweetie." She shifts to the other side of the couch. "Was it only once or have you been seeing him?"

"A few times. We're… friends with benefits."

"And what, he picked you up last night and dropped you off here with a change of clothes?" She studies me like she's looking for cracks.

Or maybe I'm the one noticing cracks. I don't believe it when I say *it's not a big deal*. It feels like a big deal. Like a huge deal. I say it anyway. "It's really not a big deal. Just a little casual sex."

"Does it really feel casual?"

Damn, is she a mind reader? It doesn't exactly feel casual. But he's been clear about not wanting more. And I don't want more. "I don't want feelings for anyone. What if a medical school in New York is my best option? I don't want anything affecting my decision. Certainly not feelings for a guy."

"But you have feelings for him?"

"We're friends." I think. I hope.

"Hmmm." She nods. "Okay. You're a big girl. I'll drop it if you give me every detail!"

"*Every* detail?"

"Not a blow by blow." She laughs. "Just tell me what's going on. You know, like we're best friends or something."

"That would be something."

"Wouldn't it?" She throws me some serious side-eye.

"Okay." I take a deep breath, and I start at the beginning. I'm vague about the details.

When I'm finished, she throws together a plan. There's a Sinful Serenade show Saturday and the two of us simply must make an impression. She has just the outfit I can borrow. Our height and cup size differences are not an issue.

"You know how we're best friends and we tell each other things?" I ask.

"I don't like where this is going."

"Why are you trying to make an impression if you're set on staying just friends with Drew. You do like him."

"It's not about whether or not I like him. He'll never want me that way. And it's not worth the risk of things changing. When he got back in touch last winter, it felt like I'd found my favorite dress. I didn't realize how much I'd missed him until I heard his voice again. How good it felt just sitting next to him at dinner or during a movie." Her eyes get dreamy. "He's such a good friend. Over-protective, yeah, but he's sweet. And he makes me laugh. I can't lose that. Nothing would be worse than losing that."

"What if he started dating someone else?"

She frowns. "It's going to happen eventually. He's handsome and famous. Girls are always stopping him to ask for his autograph. They're always touching him. Their stupid hands on his arm like they deserve to touch him." She shakes her head. "Is it so wrong that I want him to look at me like he's desperate to rip off my clothes?"

"He does look at you like that."

She shakes her head *no way*.

"He does. Seriously."

"Maybe." She lets out a sigh of pleasure. "I have to read five hundred pages tonight. I can't think about Drew ripping off my clothes or I won't make it through the first sentence." She pulls her knees into her chest. "What would you do if Miles developed feelings for you?"

"He won't."

"But if he did?"

"I have no idea."

---

I'M IN A DAZE THE REST OF BRUNCH. MOSTLY, WE TALK about school. Midterms. Her plans to go home, to San Francisco, for Thanksgiving break. My attempts to avoid going home to see my parents for even a single weekend. The house still hurts too much.

At home, there's something waiting by the door to my apartment—a wrapped box, complete with an aqua-blue bow. The card is simple.

*Good luck studying tonight.*

*- Miles*

I get inside, throw myself onto the bed, and unwrap the box. It's a Nintendo 64 and two faded, grey cartridge games—*Episode One: Podracer* and *Star Wars: Rogue Squadron*.

How the hell did he track down two twenty-year-old

games? I haven't seen either of these, or a Nintendo 64, in ages.

I connect the wires to the TV the same way I did when I was a kid—red to red, white to white, yellow to yellow.

I text Miles.

*Meg: Thank you. I love it.*

*Miles: Always happy to bring you pleasure.*

*Meg: You're very distracting. My grades are going to suffer.*

*Miles: I can take it back if you don't trust yourself.*

*Meg: No! You can't! It's the sweetest gift anyone has ever given me.*

*Miles: You're a nerd.*

*Meg: You are too.*

*Miles: That's our secret.*

We have a secret. We have other secrets. We have a level of intimacy I don't quite understand.

Does Miles have feelings for me? It's possible. Guys don't buy hard to find video games for girls they're apathetic about.

My phone buzzes.

*Miles: Kara tell you about our show Saturday?*

*Meg: She did. I even managed to make plans to go with her. I'm not sure how. I'm not very quick today. Someone kept me up all night then used up all my energy this morning.*

*Miles: You didn't like coming in the dressing room?*

*Meg: I'm not complaining.*

*Miles: It's Saturday. We go on around nine. We're working out some of our new material. Our manager's idea. I'll put you on the list.*

*Meg: Okay.*

*Miles: I'll pick you up. Give her the chance to take Drew home.*

*Meg: I don't think that's happening.*

*Miles: Not yet. But it could. Your friend is hot and Drew isn't fucking anybody. Everybody in the band knows he's not fucking anybody. He's pissy nonstop. Guy needs to get laid bad.*

*Meg: You think Kara is hot?*

*Miles: Not as hot as you, but yeah, she's attractive. And she's a sweet girl. I don't have any interest. Don't have any interest in touching anyone but you.*

*Meg: This is really strange sweet talk.*

*Miles: You can tell me you think Drew is hot if it makes you feel better.*

*Meg: It kinda does. He is hot.*

*Miles: How could you say that? You're destroying my confidence, Meg. I can't believe you even look at other men.*

*Meg: I don't. Not really.*

*Miles: Good.*

*Meg: You really think he's pissy nonstop? That's not a nice thing to say about your friend.*

*Miles: I'd say it to his face. Guy knows he's not all rainbows and sunshine.*

*Meg: Yeah?*

*Miles: Yeah. He has a vision. Only Tom has a different vision. Shit gets heated in the studio.*

*Meg: He punched you in the face once?*

*Miles: Yeah. I was being an ass.*

*Meg: You, an ass? That's shocking.*

*Miles: I know. I'm usually so polite.*

*Meg: And not at all full of yourself.*

*Miles: Not at all.*

*Meg: Do you have a vision too?*

*Miles: Yeah, but I approach songs differently than they do. Tom wants to be popular. Drew wants to make this killer rock music. He thinks he's a guitar legend. And he's right. He's good. But it's not necessarily what will get the most radio play. Then Pete, our bassist, he stays out of the fray so nobody will notice he gets to do whatever he wants with the bass line.*

*Meg: And you?*

*Miles: I own the vocals, the lyrics, the emotional arc of the song. Band knows better than to fuck with that.*

*Meg: It's probably because you're so beautiful. They do whatever they can to appease you so you'll stick around.*

*Miles: Undoubtedly. You must be tired. You're not usually this honest.*

*Meg: I am tired.*

*Miles: Tell your friend that Drew hasn't fucked anyone else in a while.*

*Meg: I'm not sure she wants to know. She insists they need to stay friends.*

*Miles: Trust me. That's not how these things work.*

*Meg: It's terrifying, but I think I do trust you.*

*Miles: Enough to go bareback next time?*

*Meg: Yes.*

*Miles: Fuck. Saturday still six days away?*

*Meg: Last I checked.*

*Miles: I can come over right now.*

*Meg: I have to study. Is it that much better without a condom?*

*Miles: Fuck. Barely remember. Sure you're that busy? You can kick me out of bed when we're done.*

*Meg: But I can't.*

*Miles: Yeah, you'd probably beg me to go again. Okay. Go study. I'll be counting the minutes to Saturday.*

*Meg: Me too.*

## Chapter Twenty-Six

MEGARA

The club is lit in shades of neon and purple. The first floor is already packed. Most of the crowd is casual—jeans, t-shirts, sneakers. A handful of women are dressed to impress.

Kara and I fit into the latter group. Somehow, I don't care that I'm treading the line between classy and trashy. Between the tight, low cut top and the short skirt, I know I'm going to make Miles want me as badly as I want him.

Kara squeezes my hand and drags me up the stairs. She pushes past another set of musician guys all the way to Drew. She finds him like he has a homing beacon.

He does a double take when he sees her outfit. Mission accomplished.

"Who let you out of the house dressed like that?" He raises a brow.

She shrugs like she wears this everywhere. They hug hello. I step aside to give them room. I'm not sure where Kara gets her insecurity. Drew is absolutely looking at her like he wants to fuck her. He's not as obvious about it as Miles is, but he's obvious enough.

He catches me watching him and redirects his stare toward the opposite wall.

I scan the room for Miles. There. He's leaning against the wall talking to a busty woman with long blond hair. Well then.

His eyes find mine, and he immediately excuses himself. Hell, he practically throws the buxom blond out of his way. I nod, but I stay put.

Today, he's coming to me.

A dozen steps and he's next to me. He slides his arm around my waist and leans in to whisper in my ear.

"Let's go out back. Won't be able to think until I'm inside you." He drags his fingertips over the waist of my skirt. "You look fucking amazing."

"I know."

"Damn, I like when you're confident." He nods to the stairs.

"Is there time?" It's eight thirty. He's due on stage in half an hour.

Miles nods. His eyes are heavy. It's like he wants me so badly he can't articulate a single word.

"Hey, Megan," a familiar voice interrupts.

It's the blond drummer. Tom.

"It's Meg," I say.

Miles throws his friend an incredulous look. "Can't this wait?"

"No, it can't." Tom offers me an apologetic smile then he's back to Miles. "Now."

Miles frowns. He's upset. As upset as he was on the beach. More even.

He shakes off his expression, but it's still there in his eyes and his posture. He's unsure of something.

I want to know what it is.

I watch Tom pull Miles aside. There's not a lot of room

up here. They're almost within earshot. I take a seat on the couch and scoot closer. Until they are within earshot.

"You're fucking her?" Tom asks.

"You take issue with casual sex all of a sudden?"

"Does she know?"

"No."

"Fuck, Miles. You trying to give me a headache?" Tom shakes his head. "Are you going to tell her?"

"How the fuck is that your business?" Miles asks.

"If you don't tell her, I will," Tom says.

Miles's voice is low, angry. "Fuck off."

There's a weight shifting on the couch. Someone sits next to me. It's an older man in a bright orange suit. He's balding but he still keeps his hair in a ponytail.

"Meg, right?" He offers his hand. "I'm Aiden. I'm the Sinful Serenade manager."

Okay... I don't see what I could possibly have to say to this guy, but I can be polite. "Yeah, Meg. Nice to meet you."

He looks to Tom and Miles, still in a heated debate. "There's no polite way to say this, Meg, but I need you to go away."

"Excuse me?"

"Miles can't have a girlfriend. He's never written a love song. Girls like that. They like that he's broken, that he's unconquered territory. But now he's writing this song. It's not quite a love song. But it's too close." There's no self-awareness in Aiden's beady eyes. He delivers his suggestion like he's reciting the weather report. "He's going to be the next Adam Levine. Do you want to stand in his way?"

"We're..." Not friends but we're not together. And it's none of his business. "We're not boyfriend and girlfriend. But that's really none of your business."

"Everyone has a price, sweetheart. Don't make me work to find yours."

There's a hand around my arm. It pulls me off the couch and presses me against a hard body. Miles.

"You okay?" he whispers.

I nod.

Miles glares at Aiden. "Don't talk to my friends."

Tom and Miles share a look of understanding. Then Tom is the one on the couch, having harsh words with the manager.

Fame is fucked up.

Miles wraps his arms around me. His voice is soft, sweet. "Did he touch you?"

"No."

"Good… he has a reputation. Stay away from him."

I nod. Miles sounds worried. He's worried about me. He cares about me.

But what was Tom talking about? They have a secret. Miles wrote a new song, a love song? My head is racing. I can't keep up.

"What did your friend want to talk about?" I ask.

He stares at me, not registering my words. Still stuck on the manager. "What did Aiden say to you?"

"It was nothing."

"He didn't touch you?"

"No."

"Or threaten you."

I don't think so. "He just… thinks you shouldn't have a girlfriend."

"And he kindly offered a suggestion that you, what, keep a low profile?"

I should tell him that the guy asked me to go away. But something holds my tongue.

"Meg? What did he say?"

"Something like that."

He pulls back enough to glance at the guy with the ponytail. "You're sure that was it?"

"Yeah, just some PR." I swallow hard. He's so worried. About me. Or is it about me getting too attached? Is he as obsessed with his image? I don't know. "Uh... do we have a profile?"

"Are you selling tips to gossip mags?"

"Do people do that?"

"You didn't read the one about my propensity for handcuffs?"

"Your what?"

He chuckles. "It was one woman. She requested it. Then turned it into... long story. You sure you're okay?"

No. "Do people know about us?"

"That we're fucking?"

"Yeah."

"Just the guys." He keeps staring at his manager.

I want him here. Back with me. I want it more than I should. "Oh. I, uh, I think my parents would flip if they found out I was dating a rock star."

His mood eases. He looks back to me. It's almost all his attention. "Want to bet?"

"Maybe."

His eyes find mine. "Your parents will love me."

"You're cocky." But it's possible he's right. He's a Stanford graduate. He's charming. He's handsome. Except for the tattoos, he looks like a perfectly nice boy.

Miles laughs. "You know they will."

"But how do you know?"

"'Cause I know you." He runs his fingertips over my tank top. "And I know Orange County parents. Where do yours live?"

"Newport Beach."

"Spoiled rich girl." He shakes his head with mock outrage.

"Yeah, and your Malibu mansion is just a place to hang your hat?"

He nods. "When's the last time you saw them?"

"You're trying to make me forget you and Tom were whispering secrets."

"It was nothing. When's the last time you saw your parents?"

It wasn't nothing. There's tension in Miles's face. His brow is furrowed. His shoulders are tight.

He's upset. This is a big secret. Do I trust him enough to let it go?

I'm not sure.

I stare back into his gorgeous blue eyes. "Haven't seen them since the day I left for school."

"They miss you? Beg you to visit."

"All the time."

"Offer to come up for lunch or dinner?"

"They come up all the time. I make excuses."

"Tell me next time. I'll come with you. As your boyfriend."

"You want to meet my parents?"

He traces the neckline of my top. "I'll keep them off your back."

His voice is heavy with need, but I'm not sure if he's desperate for me or for the end of this conversation.

I need to think.

I press my lips to his. Damn, his lips are soft. I can feel the kiss all the way to my toes. It isn't helping me think.

"Excuse me." I take a step backward. "Bathroom."

He nods.

There's something in his eyes, something I can't place. I turn and make my way down the stairs.

## Just a Taste

---

It doesn't occur to me until I'm sitting on one of the black cubes in the VIP section.

Miles wrote a song about me.

I sit next to Kara—it's just us, the band is backstage—and try to make conversation. Gossip about our poetry professor. Nothing all that interesting.

Not when Miles wrote a song about me.

The stage lights go dark. Almost show time. The crowd starts screaming. This is a small space. After all, the band is working on their new material. Miles is singing a song about me. They can't show that off to a large audience. Not when it isn't finished.

How can he be writing a song about me?

The lights go on. The song starts.

It's *In Pieces*.

I can't bring myself to look at the stage. Certainly not to look at Miles. I press my eyelids together.

His voice seeps into my veins.

> Lights out.
> Can't sleep.
> Two weeks now.
> Gaping hole in my chest shows no signs of
>     recovery.
>
> That word, a joke, you laugh.
> "Running away again, kid?"
> A minute here
> and then you're gone.

His pain swirls around me, mixing with mine. It's a

roller coaster. The only thing I can do is hold on and try to survive the ride.

I pry my eyes apart. I can't place the expression on his face. But I know what the song means. I know it means he hurts. And I hurt. But together, we hurt a little less.

Or do I have that all wrong?

His voice cuts clear across the room. "Would you like to hear something off the new album?"

The crowd cheers. Every girl in this club is screaming with glee, including Kara, who's at an ear-bursting volume. I'm sure twenty pairs of panties drop, but who am I to judge?

"It's called *No Way in Hell*. About someone very special." His eyes are on me.

Drew strums his guitar. The song starts. It's something fast and hard, and there's a desperation to the music.

Miles's voice fills the room.

> Three a.m. and I can't sleep.
> A common refrain, I know.
> As a sentiment, it's cheap.
> Someone to call, to hold,
> to love. No way that word-
> She smiles and I drift away—
>
> Oh hell no.
> This can't be.
> No way I, no way she.
> Anyone else, maybe,
> but not me.
> I don't do this kind of thing.

There's no doubt about it. He's singing about me. It's not like before. This song is about me. And he's singing it

Just a Taste

to me. I close my eyes, willing my ears to shut, willing my lungs to breathe, willing my heart to steady.

> Morning now and I can't think
> of anything but her laugh, her cries
> the sound she makes when I sink
> my teeth. Oh wow, those details
> are mine to keep, but she's not
> And suddenly I want-
>
> Oh hell no.
> This can't be.
> No way I, no way she.
> Anyone else, maybe,
> but not me.
> I don't do this kind of thing.

But none of it works. All the emotion in his voice is crashing all over me. He hurts. Somewhere deep inside him, he hurts, and God help me, I want to be the one to take that pain away.

## Chapter Twenty-Seven

MEGARA

After the set, the band reappears in the VIP area. Drew and Kara practically disappear. One second they're here, then they're not quite holding hands on their way out the back door.

And now I'm sitting on my stupid black cube, with the other guys from the band around me. Tom has a pretty redhead on his lap. She giggles, staring at him like he's a prize.

The dark-haired bassist introduces himself. "Meg, right?"

I nod. "Meg Smart."

"Pete Steele." He shakes his head and turns to Tom. "You do have a room."

Tom shrugs. He sips his drink, casually wrapping his arm around the redhead like she's a fancy trophy.

She looks happy. I guess it's not my place to judge.

Miles plops next to me. He spreads his knees wide like he's going to entice me to drop to my knees and blow him in front of his friends.

Not that I'm thinking about taking him back to my place and ripping his clothes off.

I can't do that. I can't touch him until I give him a chance to explain.

"Damn, you're tacky," Pete addresses Tom. "Almost as bad as Drew running off without a goodbye. Must be desperate."

Tom motions to me. "That's her best friend."

Miles smirks, trailing his fingers over my outer thigh.

I bite my tongue to keep from reacting to his touch. "I have a name and it's Meg."

"You know what's up with them, Meg?" Pete asks.

"They're only friends," I say.

Pete nods. "Yeah, I bet. With all due respect to your friend, no way I'd do anything other than drag her to the back seat if I were Drew."

"You mean, if you weren't too busy sexting Cindy?" Tom asks.

"Jealous 'cause your longest relationship was three minutes?" Pete asks.

"It was at three hours," Tom says.

"You assholes are awful gossips," Miles says.

"Should hear what he says about you." Pete taps something into his phone.

"You should try not getting into trouble," Tom says. "Then I wouldn't have to gossip."

Miles narrows his eyes. "Or how about this, Tom? You keep your mouth shut. Then I won't have to use my fist to shut you up."

Tom rolls his eyes.

Pete shakes his head.

Clearly, this is a conversation with history. I'm not part of the history. I'm not in the circle of friends.

Maybe there is something to the concept of asking

nicely. I make eye contact with Tom. "What kind of trouble does Miles get into?"

Tom and Miles share a look of understanding. So much for Tom's claim to tell me if Miles doesn't. It's clear the guys have some kind of code.

It doesn't help my confidence.

Miles pulls me onto his lap. His cock is right under my sex. I'm wearing the lace underwear he bought me at the boutique. It's practically transparent.

I squeeze my knees together. There's no sense in flashing the other guys in the band.

Miles presses his lips against my neck, holding me the way Tom is holding the pretty redhead—like I'm a trophy.

He addresses the other guys. "Don't mention this to the Guitar Prince, okay?"

"You call Drew the Guitar Prince?" I ask.

Pete nods. "Should hear what we call Tom behind his back."

"Fuck you." The drummer pouts.

Pete points to the redhead in Tom's lap. "I'm not one to wait in line." He throws his hand over the side of his mouth, like he's going to whisper. "It's Sticks for Brains. Not the most creative, but it gets the point across."

"Guitar Prince and Miles can coast on talent. What the hell are you offering?" Tom asks.

"Sex appeal." Pete smiles.

"Can it, Sticks," Miles says. "We all know you're not going to fire your brother."

I look from Pete to Tom. Tom has green eyes and dirty blond hair, a mix of young Brad Pitt and Kurt Cobain. Pete has dark eyes and black hair. They're both handsome and well-built, but they look nothing alike.

"Don't worry about me, Meg," Pete says. "I don't share any bloodlines with Sticks. We're foster brothers."

"Adopted," Tom corrects.

I bite my tongue, silently praying for any other conversation topic. Anything besides family.

Tom kisses his pretty lap girl on the cheek and sends her away. Once she's out of earshot, he leans in close and makes eye contact with Miles. "I'm not sure what you two are doing, but Drew will kill you if you fuck things up with that slutty girl, and then I'll be out a guitarist and a singer."

My hands curl into fists. "Hey, asshole, that's my best friend, and she's not slutty. She just has big boobs. And even if she was, she wouldn't appreciate you talking about her like that. So why don't you shut the fuck up?"

"Or you'll ask Miles to shut me up," Tom offers.

Miles presses his lips into my neck. "Please ask. I'd love an excuse."

I shake my head. "I don't want to hear another word about my friend or about Drew. Got it?"

Tom nods. There's annoyance all over his face, but he nods.

Pete laughs. "Damn, you're not even getting pussy and you're whipped. Banging those drum sticks must be frying your brain."

"You play bass in an emo band, asshole. Do you actually do anything?" Tom asks.

"You still doubt that I'm the sexiest member of Sinful Serenade?" Pete asks. "Meg, back me up. I'm way hotter than your boy toy, right?"

Tom butts in before I can even fathom a response. "'Cause that whole girl you know I've got steady rhythm thing is so hot."

Pete winks at me. "Meg knows what I'm talking about."

I blush and squeeze my legs together again. Miles laughs, and he tilts me so my knees are facing away from the guys, so I'm only at risk of flashing the wall.

"Cindy knows what he's talking about," Miles says. "And we've heard what he's talking about in lurid detail."

Pete blushes, but there's a wealth of confidence in his eyes. "You have to admit—I last a long time."

"And he's quite creative, too," Miles says.

I'm lost. I turn to Miles. "You're going to have to explain this to me."

Miles runs his fingertips along my thighs, right under the hem of my skirt. "Pete is a phone sex devotee."

Pete shrugs, playing sheepish but clearly proud as hell. "You'd both understand if you ever tried taking a relationship on the road." He chuckles. "Or if you ever tried a relationship. Period."

I turn ever so slightly, so I'm looking into Miles's eyes. I still can't place his expression.

Feelings well up in my stomach. Is this what relationships feel like? I have affection for him, I do. I'm just not sure where the line stops. We are friends. We do have sex. But is there more to it than that?

"Jesus, now Miles has to prove he has the skilled hands," Tom says.

Pete shakes his head. "Miles convinces girls he's tortured inside, that he needs them to wipe his pain away."

"Right," Tom says.

Pete chuckles. "He has a mouth, and he knows how to use it."

"Is that right, Meg?" Tom asks.

I turn back to them. "My lips are sealed."

Miles whispers in my ear, "Want to get out of here?"

A rush of heat passes through me. I do want to get out of here. I do want Miles to take me home and to drag me to bed. But not like this, not with him guarding all his secrets.

I turn to him the best I can. "Only if you're going to

explain what Tom was talking about. Or should I ask him right now?"

Miles grabs my hips, and he slides me off his lap. We're almost facing each other, and his expression is almost serious. The closest thing to serious I've seen in quite a while.

He nods.

I nod.

And suddenly, this is the most boring conversation I've ever been a part of.

## Chapter Twenty-Eight

MILES

I don't let my friends' *what the hell do you think you're doing* stares linger.

I whisk Meg into a cab.

I keep us exactly where we need to be—in our bodies.

I trail my fingers over her thighs, brush my lips against her neck, whisper dirty promises in her ears.

By the time we get to her place, my body is roaring.

I need to be naked with her.

To be inside her.

To be holding her as she comes.

We park in front of her place. I pay the cab. Walk her up to her apartment.

The elevator takes forever.

The hallway gets smaller and bigger at once. This space is too tiny for how badly I want her.

And for how badly I want to tell her this.

It's usually easy keeping my lips zipped. It's what I've been doing my entire life. But right now...

Fuck, she gets under my skin.

She slides her key into the door. Turns it.

Words rise up in my throat.

I swallow them down. Silence them the way I know best.

I whisk her into the apartment and pin her to the door.

She looks up at me with a needy stare.

Then my eyes are closed and my lips are on hers and I'm kissing her with everything I've got.

I need my thoughts gone.

I need our clothes off.

I need to satisfy her the only way I can.

My hands go to her skirt. I push the garment off her ass. Drag my hand up her thigh.

No teasing.

I stroke her over her panties.

She looks up at me with this mix of confusion and desire in her eyes.

I can't give her what she wants.

But, fuck, I want to give her this. "I need you." I pull her top over her arms.

She arches her back into me.

Lets out a soft gasp.

Kisses me hard.

For a moment, she melts into me. She gives me everything she has.

Then she pulls back. Pushes me away. "Tell me. Please."

"It was nothing. Just Tom running his mouth off." It feels too much like a lie.

"If it's nothing, tell me." Her exhale is shaky. "Please." She stares up at me with those brown eyes. Stares up at me like I'm about to break her heart.

I am.

No matter what I say, I am.

Either I tell her the truth and betray her.

Or I lie and betray her.

"Miles... we agreed. No lies. No secrets."

"It's nothing." My chest tenses. I want to believe it, that it's nothing, that I made the right call earlier.

But even if I think this is what's best for both of us—and I do—I can't deny the weight of this.

I reach for some way to explain it. Something that will soothe her without picking at my wounds. "This is supposed to be casual." But I don't believe that either.

If I tell her, that's it. It's over.

If I don't tell her, that's it. It's over.

It can't be over. This can't be the last time I feel her body melting into mine. It just can't.

"This isn't supposed to be complicated." A whine seeps into my voice. It isn't me. I don't let people affect me like this. I don't let myself need people. But I need her. I need her way too much.

"You're the one making it complicated." She presses her back into the wall. Her eyes find mine. They bore into mine. Demand everything I have.

"Meg." I make my voice firm. "Don't do this. We have a good thing here."

"You're the one doing it."

I swallow hard. "I can't."

"Then you need to leave."

My eyes meet hers. This is a dirty trick, but I don't care about playing fair at the moment. "Wouldn't you rather I leave after?"

Her eyes scream *yes*. Her chest heaves. Her cheeks flush. Still, she presses her palm flat against my chest, ready to push me away. "If you're not going to tell me then leave."

"Meg..."

"Now."

There's nothing else to say. No excuses or please or explanations.

I hold her gaze for a moment. Give her a chance to change her mind.

She doesn't.

## Chapter Twenty-Nine

MILES

I spend the night driving up and down Pacific Coast Highway. The ocean on my left. Then the right. The left.

The stupid fucking radio on high. Playing our song. My moan filling the car.

I turn the stereo off, but it doesn't help. My breath fills the car instead.

My heartbeat fills my head.

The steady *thump-thump* fails to drown the voice flitting through my thoughts.

Fuck, I should have just kept the song on. It's a better way to stay in touch with Damon.

Here I am, running away again.

Failing to face this.

I can admit it. I can see it, plain as day. And I can see the reality of the situation too—

It has to be this way.

It's better this way.

I should have ended it after that night on the beach. I

should have ended it after her first fucking text. I should have ended it a long time ago.

I wrote a fucking song about her.

It's already gone too far.

The fucking thing is dropping in four days. And she's—

It's probably best that she hates me for it.

## Chapter Thirty

MEGARA

Routine washes away any hint of Miles. I go to class. I go to work. I go to Kara's on Sunday and try to avoid any topic related to men or music—especially men who make music.

The goal proves impossible. She turns twenty-one at the end of October, and she's throwing a birthday-slash-Halloween-slash-week-before-midterms party at the Sinful Mansion in Hollywood. I consider calling Drew and begging him to take over my duties as best friend.

The next two weeks are miserable. Sinful Serenade launches their new single *No Way in Hell*—the song about me.

It's an overnight success. It hits number one on the alternative chart, number four on the pop chart. The music video hits ten million downloads by the end of its first week. The thing is gorgeous and stark. It's in black and white. Half is the band playing on the beach, waves crashing around them. The other half is Miles in an empty bedroom, his eyes filled with hurt.

I understood *In Pieces* like the words were written in my

soul. Why can't I figure this song out? I'm sure it's about me. But I'm not sure what it means.

How can he write a song about me in one breath then tell me I don't deserve into his heart in the next?

The song follows me everywhere. It's on every Spotify playlist and Google Play Music station. The damn thing plays every hour on KROQ. I can't go into a store or a restaurant or a coffee shop without hearing it.

The words mock me.

> Three a.m. and I can't sleep.
> A common refrain, I know.
> As a sentiment, it's cheap.
> Someone to call, to hold,
> to love. No way that word-
> She smiles and I drift away—
>
> Oh hell no.
> This can't be.
> No way I, no way she.
> Anyone else, maybe,
> but not me.
> I don't do this kind of thing.

Love. He's using the word love in reference to me. He can share his feelings with the world, but he can't share them with me.

He's not talking to me. Not texting me. He doesn't apologize. He doesn't even ask to cash in on our benefits.

I mean nothing to him.

## Chapter Thirty-One

MEGARA

The Friday before Halloween is particularly busy. I barely have the energy to make it through my shift. Kara's party is tomorrow night. I have no idea how I'm supposed to survive the war my heart and my body are going to wage being in the same room as Miles.

A teenage girl is rushed into the ER. She's unconscious, barely breathing. Her lips are blue. She's thin enough the breeze could break her, and her arms are covered in track marks.

One is fresh.

A few hours old max.

Her mother is at her side. She's clueless. She's lost. Confused. She had no idea her daughter was on drugs.

How could she have no idea? There's no way this girl is any older than sixteen. She's converged in track marks. How the hell did Mom miss that?

The girl is dying.

Doctor Anderson, the doctor I scribe for, pushes me out of the way. "Take five, Meg."

I can't move. I can't pry my eyes away from the girl.

One of the nurses pushes me out of the way. They're rushing to her. But it's too late. It's not going to work.

I know how this goes. The paramedics should've given her Naloxone. It's supposed to counter the opiates in heroin. It's supposed to restart her heart and her breathing.

The sounds around me swirl together until it's this awful mix of air-conditioning, squeaking rubber soles, the erratic beep of the heart rate monitor as the girl's pulse fades away. Nothing they're doing is working. This girl is too far gone. There's nothing anyone can do.

Just like Rosie.

I hide out in one of the single-stall bathrooms, trying, and failing, to will myself to go home. I can't sit in my bed alone. All I'll feel is her absence. We used to live together in a two-bedroom place in the same building. The landlord was understanding when she died—helped me move all my stuff into a studio and offered a discounted rent.

I miss my big sister so much. She was funny and bright and full of life. She understood things that flew right over my head. I thought she had it all figured out, that she knew the secret to balancing school and having a life.

That she really was that effortlessly happy.

I wish she was here. I wish I could tell her how much I miss her, how much worse our parents got after she died. They've always pretended but now they're shells of themselves. They're broken.

She'd know what to do to fix them. She'd know how to cheer me up. She'd definitely know what to do about Miles. She'd take me out, get me drunk, and send me home with the perfect guy to wipe my memory clean. Then, she'd take me to brunch, stuff me with pancakes, and squeal over me finally growing up.

She had me fooled. She seemed okay for so long. She'd look me in the eyes and smile, and I'd feel it in my gut—

everything had to be okay if my sister could smile like that. Even though I knew better, I believed it was okay. She'd never lied to me before, not like that.

I call Kara. I've kept all my grief to myself for so long. I can't do it anymore. I need to be with someone who understands so I can cry my heart out. It's stupid I didn't do it sooner. Her dad died when she was in high school. She knows how this feels, knows enough to drag me out for my own good, knows enough not to press for details.

Damn. Voicemail. I call again. Voicemail again. One more try.

"Hey, Kara, just wanted to say hey… text me tomorrow." I end the call and wrap my fingers around the smooth plastic of my phone.

I need to feel something else, something beyond how much I miss my sister. There's no one else to call. None of my other friends would understand. My parents certainly don't understand. There's no one who knows what this feels like.

No one except Miles.

I dial before my senses can catch up with me.

Damn. The same voicemail.

"Hey, Miles. I thought I wanted to talk to you, but now I'm not sure. I'll see you tomorrow I guess. I…" I hang up before I can tell him I miss him.

---

It's a half an hour walk to the top of the hill where Rosie and I used to hang out. We called our outings hikes, but we spent most of the time talking about school and friends and especially about our parents.

There are houses here, expensive ones. We used to make fun of their blandness. Everything is beige. Everyone drives a black sedan or luxury car. Everyone looks perfect on the outside. Like our parents.

Like she did.

I find an empty patch of grass and take in the view of the city. I can see the entire UCLA campus. To the left is Century City. To the right is the ocean. It's cloudy tonight. I can't see Downtown. I can't see the stars.

I can't see the path to being okay without her.

My phone buzzes. It's Miles. Calling me back.

I stare at the screen. My fingers refuse to move. I'm not sure I can handle hearing his voice. It's already in my head, singing that song again and again.

Again, my phone buzzes. This time, it's a text.

*Miles: Are you okay?*

*Meg: No.*

*Miles: Where are you? I'll pick you up.*

*Meg: Is that a good idea?*

*Miles: I'll take you home. If you want me to leave after that, I will.*

I send him the address of the nearest house. It's pure impulse. I want him here. I want his arms around me.

*Miles: What happened?*

*Meg: There was this girl in the ER… I'm not sure I should discuss this with you.*

*Miles: Let me help you. I want to.*

*Meg: Would you let me help you?*

I stare at the phone for minutes, but there's no response. That's as good as a no.

The world is heavy. I pull my knees to my chest and bring my gaze to the sky. Still no stars but the half-moon is a beautiful shade of silver.

The neighborhood is quiet. No sounds except the moon. Then there's a car. It parks. The door opens. Footsteps come closer.

Someone kneels next to me.

"Hey." Miles slides his arms around me. "Come on. You'll be okay."

I shake my head. But I soak in all the comfort of his arms anyway.

## Chapter Thirty-Two

MILES

I shouldn't be here.

I did what I had to do—I wasn't going to leave her alone, in the cold. Now, she's safe. She's home. She's okay.

Adding me to the equation—

It's only going to make her feel worse.

Meg slips her hoodie off her shoulders. She stares at me, her expression equal parts dare and defiance. It's like she's screaming *I'm taking off my clothes. I know that's going to make you take off your clothes. So let's cut the shit and get to it.*

"You want something to drink?" she asks.

I nod. "Whatever you're having."

"Do you drink?"

"Drink what?" I set her bag on the counter. Shrug my shoulders back. Here it is. Another chance to confess. Or lie. I'm not doing either. How the fuck am I supposed to manage that?

"Alcohol."

"There's never been any alcohol in your fridge."

"There was none at your place in Malibu?"

My brow furrows. Was she really snooping? It doesn't sound like her, but it's not exactly surprising. Not if she knows how full of shit addicts are. "You checked?"

"Am I wrong?"

"No."

She looks up at me again. That same *fuck me, now, I can't stand the sight of your face, so put it between my legs—*

All right, I'm projecting.

So many conversations, so many nights together, so many minutes holding her and I'm still sure of one thing:

I can make her come.

The rest? No fucking idea. But I can do that.

It's the most I can help. If that's really what she wants, if I really do care about making her feel better—

My heart whines. Rare for it. The damn thing is heavy twenty-four seven. Only not around her. It's used to lightness around her.

It wants to connect with her.

My cock doesn't give a fuck about doing the right thing. Or easing the burden in my mind.

Or anything, really.

Fucker wants her long legs, period, end of sentence.

I shake it off as she pours two glasses of grapefruit juice. Hands one to me.

"Thanks." I'm not sure I've had this straight. It tastes strange. Like it's missing vodka. I swallow another sip. Set it on the counter.

Her eyes follow the glass. "Do you drink?"

"No." Not anymore.

"Why not?"

"I don't like the person it makes me." That *is* true. She doesn't want anything to do with me. She ended this.

I'm not obligated to share with her.

No matter how much my heart is begging me to do it.

I move into the kitchen. Move closer to her. "I want to help you, Meg. I know what it's like to lose someone."

"I don't want to talk." She stares back at me with those defiant eyes. "I want to fuck you."

"I'm not your shiny distraction."

"You won't be my distraction. You won't share your secrets. What will you do?"

"Listen to you."

"Listen to me pour my heart out while you stay closed off?"

I swallow hard. I can't tell her she's wrong. She's right too.

My heart screams *tell her, hold her, love her*.

But that's just—

That's how I got into this fucking mess.

She finishes her drink. Turns. Places her cup in the sink. "I'm going to shower first."

"What makes you sure there will be a second?"

"If you're going to leave, lock the door behind you. Okay?"

She turns back to me. Her dark eyes meet mine. She holds my gaze as she strips her panties.

Her cheeks just barley flush as she does away with those.

Fuck. I need to touch her. To pin her to the wall, feel all her skin against all of mine, make her come until she's begging me to stop.

It takes great restraint to stay put.

To stay in the main room instead of joining her in the shower.

She takes an eternity. Or maybe it just feels like that with my body and heart at war. My head—where the fuck is that?

Once upon a time, I knew what the right call was here.

Now?

I force my hands into my pockets as she steps into the main room naked.

I take a towel. Wrap it around her chest.

Her eyes flutter closed as my fingers brush her skin. She wants me, needs me, craves me.

It feels good. Better than it should.

I take a step backward. "You've turned my cock against me."

"Have I?"

Yeah. "It's agony doing anything besides tearing that towel off your body."

She drops the towel. Pushes her hair over her shoulder.

"You're killing me here," she groans.

I take a seat on her bed. "You're killing yourself."

"I'm not doing this. Not with you so miserable."

"Then don't. But you're the one turning your cock against you. He and I have the same idea for how this should go."

I can't deny the argument.

Hell, I don't know why there's some voice in my head screaming *this is what she needs*.

But there is.

And it's too fucking annoying to ignore.

I slide into bed next to her. Kick off my shoes, peel off my socks, do away with my jeans and t-shirt.

She watches with rapt attention. Then she catches me staring and she blushes, embarrassed.

She still doesn't see what she does to me. It's ridiculous.

Meg turns her back to me.

I move closer. Rest my head in the crook of her neck. Run my fingers over her shoulders. "Lie with me."

She nods *okay*. Melts into my body as I draw circles over her arm.

I need to tell her something. I need to make her understand why things are the way they are.

Why I can't be the person she needs.

I want to be that guy. I want to live in a world where love is beautiful and shit comes easily.

But I don't.

"My uncle. He had cancer. In his pancreas. I didn't take it well. I ran off. Got into fights. Drank too much. Fucked a bunch of women without exchanging first names." I pull the blanket over us. "I spun out of control. Worse than I ever had before."

"What do you mean?"

"I fucked up. I wasn't there for him. The guy was dying and I was stewing in self-pity over it. Same problems I'd refused to deal with for years."

I pull her closer. Until I can feel her heartbeat.

My fingers trace the line of her arm, all the way from her shoulder to her pinkie. Then back up, down to her ring finger, again and again.

A sigh falls off her lips. One I recognize. One that means *I need you*.

But it's different now. More than *I need you inside me*. Not quite *I need you to save me*. Something in between.

"I know it hurts. I know you miss her. I know it feels like it will never stop hurting. But you need to realize it's not your fault," I say.

"How do you know?"

"'Cause I know." I swallow hard. "Trust me."

"How? Tell me how. I want to trust you, Miles. I really do. Tell me what it is you're hiding and I will."

"I can't." I wish I could, really.

I press my lips to her neck. Pull her closer. Let my hand slip lower. Draw shapes over her hip.

Her body responds to mine, but her heart stays locked.

"You sure you don't want to talk about it?" I ask.

She shakes her head.

"You might as well," I say. "Since you're not going to get laid."

Meg responds with a growl.

It's adorable. And so her. I laugh. Pull her closer. "You'll feel better."

"I'll feel better with your cock inside me."

Me too. Fuck, two months ago, I would have fucked her twice by now. I don't know where I found this concern. Only that I can't shake it.

She arches her hips, rubbing her ass against my crotch. "That's how I need your help. I don't care how you do it, but I need to stop thinking."

"You need to get this off your chest."

She nods *maybe*, but she still grinds against me. "If I do and I still feel like shit, will you admit I'm right?"

Fuck. That feels too good. It's destroying my resolve. "Yeah. But I'm still not gonna be your shiny distraction."

She takes a deep breath. Lets out a slow exhale. Her posture changes. Stiffens. She's drifting away. Into something ugly. "There was this patient today. She was young, a teenager. Her mom was with her, screaming, but completely clueless. She had no idea her daughter was a drug addict. There were track marks all over the girl's arms and legs, but Mom had no idea."

"I'm sorry."

"Rosie was the most important person in my life. She was my best friend, and we never lied to each other. That's what our parents did to us. They would lie right to our faces. When my cousin ran off and joined the army, they pretended it wasn't because of a fight with his parents. When my mom lost her job at the hospital, they told me she decided to quit. She was miserable every day she was unemployed, but she said it was fine. Every time anything went wrong, they pretended like it was nothing, like everything was fine. Rosie was older. She'd dealt with it longer, and she saw through it before I did. So she made me swear that we'd never bullshit each other like that. "

"Yeah?"

"Yeah. And it worked. We got into so many fights over our honesty, but we always made up. When she graduated, everything started going wrong. She said she wanted to take a gap year. It was a lie. An obvious lie I should've called her on. She bombed her MCATS. It was the first time she failed at anything, and she was miserable about it. Miserable with this big, happy, *everything is okay* face. I'm sure she thought she was helping me—all I did that semester was go to class and study for my MCATS—but it didn't help. It was just the first lie to drive us apart."

"It's not your fault, Meg. That's what drugs do to people. They get them wrapped up in all this bullshit. Drug addicts are great liars. There's nothing you could have done."

"But that's the thing. It wasn't drugs at first. It was a test. Then it was her future. She gave up," she says.

Fuck.

"It broke my heart when she died."

"I know." What can I say? *Stay the fuck away from me or it will happen again?* I open my mouth. Try to find the words. Fail completely. "I'm sorry."

She swallows hard. "That's why I can't do this with you. Not if you're going to hide something from me."

She's right. I'm right. We're both right. And it means one thing: This can't happen.

I should leave. Say *I'm sorry, you're right, I can't help you. I'm gonna go. Feel better.*

But I can't. I can't leave her like this.

And I can't let her go either. Proof I'm a selfish asshole. Not that it helps my point.

I struggle through my exhale. "If you knew the whole story, you'd kick me out again."

"Do you really trust me that little?"

"I trust you more than I trust anyone."

"Then why won't you tell me?"

"I can't talk about it yet." I drag my fingertips back up her arm. "I've never been disappointed over a relationship ending before."

"This is a relationship?"

"Us, being friends with benefits. I won't tell you my secret. I'm breaking the terms." I should just say *it's over*. "It's up to you. I don't want to leave. But I will."

"I don't want to stop. I want to be able to trust you."

"If you can't have that?"

"I want to stop thinking." She leans into my touch. "I want to feel good." She arches her hips again. "Have you been with someone else?"

"No."

"It's been weeks."

"I don't want anyone else." I study Meg. The hurt in her eyes. The heave of her chest. The scrape of her fingernails. This is what she needs. It's not the only thing she needs—she needs a guy who can share his heart with her, who can make her feel whole and loved—but I don't have the latter. I can only offer her the former. "You sure?"

"Yes."

"This isn't going to change. I'm not going to spill my guts to you."

"I know."

My body whines. My hands go to her hips of their own accord. "You still want to go bareback?"

"Yes." She turns. Meets my gaze. Stares at me like she's staring into my soul.

It's too much.

I can't take it.

I can't let her believe I have more to offer than this.

My fingertips brush her neck. Her collarbone. Her chest.

I cup her breast with my hand. "I've been going crazy thinking about you."

"You think about me?"

"All the time." I bring my lips to her neck. "I miss the way you taste."

"You've been thinking about fucking me."

"About you. I miss your moans. I miss your laugh. I miss the way your body fits into mine."

She shudders as she moans. It's fucking gorgeous. Music. Poetry. Art.

Better than I remembered.

Meg's eyes meet mine. "This is on my terms, Miles. It's just sex. You do what I want. You come when I call."

"I like the sound of that."

Her laugh is soft. "I mean come over."

My fingers trace the outline of her smile. "I love your laugh."

"No. You don't say things like that. This is sex. That's it. You don't get to say you miss me, that you love my laugh, that you want to tape my heart back together. Not if you're going to keep everything to yourself."

"Okay."

"Okay?"

"Yeah." I bring my hands to her hips. Push her onto her back. Bring my body over hers.

She looks up at me with those defiant brown eyes. She looks at me like I'm going to save her.

Then her eyes close. Her hands find my hair. Her lips find my lips.

Her kiss is electric.

All her need pours into me. It makes sense. Right now, it makes sense.

I'm what she needs.

I'm bringing her pleasure.

The world is a beautiful place.

I don't wait. I run my fingers over her nipples. Bring one hand to her legs. Wrap them around my hips as I grind against her.

"Fuck, you feel good," I breathe.

She responds with a groan.

I grind against her until I can't take it anymore. Then I toy with her nipples. Fuck, the way she groans as I flick my tongue against the perky bud—

This is heaven.

I toy with her until she's panting, then I press my lips to her stomach.

She shudders as I move lower, lower.

"Miles—" Her hand knots in my hair.

"I've been dreaming about this." Which isn't me. I'm not a selfish fuck. But I don't go down on random women.

It's too intimate. Too personal.

With Meg—

Fuck, I need to taste her.

I pin her thighs to the bed. Bring my mouth to her. Tease her just enough to get her panting.

I still know exactly what she needs. My body still remembers every inch of her body.

I keep her pinned as I lick her up and down.

My fingertips dig into her thighs.

She groans with pleasure at the hint of pain. Tugs

harder at my hair. The kind of tug that means *for God's sake, don't stop*.

I tease her until her breath hitches. Then I go right where she needs me. Lick her just how she needs me.

She comes fast, groaning and shaking as she bucks against my mouth.

I pull back enough to kiss her stomach. Then her breasts. Fuck, I love the sound she makes when I suck on her nipples. "You're sexier than I remembered."

She groans as I flick my tongue against her.

Then it's the soft scrape of my teeth and her groan is louder, lower, enough for the neighbors to complain.

Maybe they do.

I can't hear anything but her.

She rocks her hips against mine. Rakes her nails over my back.

My balls tighten. "I missed you."

"You missed this."

"No." I scrape my teeth against her nipple until she groans. "I missed you."

"Fuck me." She rocks her hips again. Her eyes meet mine. It's there, in those soulful browns. She believes me. She needs me. She needs me as much as I need her.

"Fuck yes." I cup her hips, shift her into position.

She wraps her arms around me.

My eyes meet hers. I hold her gaze as I lower my body onto hers.

Almost—

Fuck.

She's wet and soft. Without a condom, it's so much. Overwhelming.

I push deeper.

Deeper.

There—

She sighs as I enter her.

It's exactly what's in my head.

This moment is perfection.

Maybe I can't connect with our clothes on. Maybe neither one of us can share our heart. Maybe she's gonna kick me out of bed when this is over.

It doesn't matter.

This is what matters.

This is everything.

I kiss her deeply as I thrust into her.

The kiss she returns is aggressive. She bucks her hips to meet me. She digs her nails into my back, spurring me on.

I move at that same steady pace.

It's different than normal. I'm in my body and my heart. I'm feeling her heart too.

I can't explain it.

I don't understand it.

But I still need it.

I really fucking need it.

She scrapes her nails harder. Kisses me deeper. Spurs me on.

I move a little faster, a little harder—

There.

She groans as I hit exactly the right spot.

She rocks her hips to meet me. Squeezes me with her soft thighs. Tortures me with her hard nails.

She's mine.

Right now, she's mine. And there isn't a single part of me that wants it another way.

I stay locked with her until she has to pull back to groan. Her breath hitches. My name falls off her lips.

Then she's there, clawing at my back as she comes on my cock.

Her cunt pulses, pulling me closer. Closer.

## Just a Taste

Fuck.

Bliss overtakes me. With my next thrust, I come. I thrust through my orgasm, groaning her name as I spill inside her.

Slowly, I untangle our bodies. Shift off her. Behind her. She nestles into my chest.

I wrap my arm around her waist. "Better than I remembered."

"You have a terrible memory." She lets out a soft laugh.

"Or maybe it's like that song. I love fucking you more today than yesterday, but not as much as tomorrow."

She murmurs something that sounds like a yes then falls asleep in my arms.

## Chapter Thirty-Three

MILES

It's torture leaving Meg. It always is. But for once, it's crystal clear it's necessary.

These are her terms.

Sex. Period. The end.

All friends, no benefits.

I get home early, but Tom is already up, already setting up his party. I fix breakfast and coffee. Head to my room. Stay there as long as possible.

Through half a book, another attempt at a song, two episodes of a sci-fi TV show.

Until the hum of conversation raises to a low roar.

Then music.

Cars arriving.

I give up, head downstairs, watch Tom flirt with a cute goth chick. She's slim and tattooed. Not his usual type. I guess he's bored with usual.

Hard to blame him.

He nods *hey*. Kisses his hook up goodbye—on the cheek, of course—and tosses me a water bottle. "She's coming?"

"Why are you so obsessed with my love life?"

"You're the only person who isn't replaceable."

I can't help but chuckle. Takes balls to say that. I hold up my bottle to toast.

He holds up his plastic cup. "I'm proud of you."

"Uh-huh."

"You did the right thing."

"Kept Drew from threatening to quit?"

"It's more than that."

At the moment, I don't know what to believe. Tom *is* a fame whore. And this band is his family. Sure, his brother is always going to be his brother.

But any conflict reverberates up that.

Of course, he wants shit less chaotic. We all do. We're just… no one's willing to compromise enough to make that happen.

"Drew said she's coming," he says.

"Okay." What the hell does he want from me?

"You're gonna be here?"

"Did someone else take my room?"

He raises a brow. Moves closer. Close enough to whisper. "Are you okay?"

"You care now?"

"Lay off it, dude. We both know the truth."

"What's that?"

"You're one stitch away from falling apart."

Fuck him for noticing. "Whatever." I shrug like I don't care.

He shakes his head. "You're not fooling anyone."

"Fuck off."

"Proving my point."

"You don't have a say in what I do."

"Why'd you dump the honors student then?"

I didn't. Not exactly. And those details are none of his business. "Stay the fuck away from her."

"Right back at you."

I shrug, but it's even less convincing. I don't really have the moral high ground here. When she called, I came.

When she insisted I fuck her, I caved.

Now that I know she's going to be here—

My body is already buzzing. My cock is already whining. My heart is already—

I don't know anymore.

I told her a lot. Too much.

But it felt good. Right. And she didn't run.

Maybe this is possible.

Or maybe I fucked up miserably.

---

She's there. On the terrace, lying on a lounge chair, staring at the orange sky.

My cock whines *fuck her now. Fuck the implications. Make her come.*

It's a very persuasive argument. "How come, every time I see you, you look like you're begging to be mounted?"

She turns to me. Looks up at me with all this hurt in her brown eyes.

She's been through so much. And she's still holding strong.

She still expects something of me. Wants something from me.

I want to be there. To be that guy. But I don't know how.

I can't offer it.

"You were gone this morning," she says.

"I had to take care of something."

"What?"

Tom threatening to cut a track. Nothing important. Nothing that demanded immediate attention.

I had to leave. To get away from how badly I wanted to stay.

It's too hard to think around her.

My heart *and* my cock start arguing with my head. Right now, with those brown eyes trained on me, with that proud chest pointed in my direction—

Like she knows I have more to give and she'll take it by any means necessary.

I want it way too much.

"Band stuff." I move closer. Rub her shoulder. "That's what you want, isn't it? Just sex."

"Yeah, right." She clears her throat. "I just…" She looks up at me. Tries to make her expression playful. Gets most of the way there. "I guess I'll… fuck you later."

"Until then."

## Chapter Thirty-Four

MILES

Fuck me.

This girl isn't going easy on me. That's for sure.

She's by the couch, with Drew (of course he went as a cop. I wonder if his friend is picturing those handcuffs around her wrists).

In a gold bikini.

A Princess Leia bikini.

My teenage fantasies come to life.

I guess we're finally on even ground for the first time. Since I'm basically her fantasy come to life.

Fuck, I sound like an asshole. Even though it's true. Even though it's been true of half the women I've fucked.

They don't even notice that it's *Miles Webb, rock star.* Just *hot tortured rock star.*

They turn toward something. Meg's friend, Kara. She's dressed as a mermaid. It's just as sexy as Meg's costume. Her shell bikini top barely covers her tits.

God, those things are huge.

I bet Drew is dreaming about coming on them. Dirty bastard isn't gonna share that shit either.

He's the only guy in the band that keeps his, ahem, conquests to himself. Not that there have been any conquests recently. He never was the one and done type, but since he got back in touch with Kara—

Let's just say I'm surprised he can still play guitar with how much he's wearing out his hand.

Fuck, he'll punch me in the face if I say that.

Tom would laugh though. Tom's a bigger asshole than I am. An accomplishment, really.

"Hey." The drummer pats my shoulder. Like he read my fucking mind. "Nice outfit."

"Your fantasies come to life?" I tap my vest. My blaster. "I have all sorts of phallic implications."

"Uh-huh." His eyes flit to Meg—now alone on the couch. "You did end things?"

"What about *fuck off* was confusing to you?"

"Miles—"

"I know."

"Seriously. Are you gonna tell her?"

"Again, the whole *fuck off* thing."

"Lay off it, asshole. We both know the truth here."

I shrug like I don't care.

"You should tell her."

"It's just sex."

"She know that?"

"She asked for it."

Tom chuckles. "Your personality is that obnoxious, huh?"

"Something like that."

His laugh gets louder. Higher. It's the funniest thing he's ever heard. "You know you have to dance with her."

"Do I?"

"Yeah. Couples costumes."

"Where's yours?"

"Saving it for later." His grin widens. The guy loves occasions, including Halloween. It's weird he's not in a costume yet, honestly.

As weird as me wearing one.

He shakes his head *fuck, you are doomed*, but he still escorts me to the middle of the room. Amongst all sorts of people in themed pairs.

Buttercup and the Dread Pirate Roberts.

Jack and Sally.

Sid and Nancy.

Kurt and Courtney.

Will I be a costume if Tom's right? Maybe in a few years. If I adopt a signature style.

At the moment—

My thoughts disappear as her eyes meet mine.

She blushes as I look her up and down. Fuck, that girl is playing to win.

If she keeps this up, I don't have a chance.

I try my best poker face. Offer her my hand. "Princess."

Her lips curl into a smile. "Scoundrel."

"It suits me."

"It does."

I bring my hands to her waist. Pull her closer.

The music shifts. Some pop song with a ridiculously fast beat. Good for running, but this—

I move at half time. Guide her through an easy sway.

She wraps her arms around my neck. Rests her head on my shoulder. In her wedges, she's as tall as I am.

We fit together perfectly.

It makes my thoughts cloudy. It makes my heart full. In some way it hasn't been full in a very long time.

When the song finishes, I lead her toward the backyard.

A friend stops her in the kitchen, asks if she wants to play some drinking game.

I step in. "Sorry, but I need Meg desperately."

The girl looks at me with wide eyes. She nearly blurts out *what, you have a rock star boyfriend?*

I pull Meg away before the girl has a chance. I lead her to the patio table outside.

It's cold. She pulls her arms over her chest. Rubs her triceps.

"Come here." I sit. Pull her into my lap. Wrap my arm around her.

"You're sober, aren't you?" she asks.

"Yeah."

"I think we're the only two sober people at this party."

"You looking for a ride home?" I lower my voice, so she knows *exactly* what I'm offering.

"No." She bites her lip. "I don't know. Were you looking to get out of here?"

Now, I am. I press my lips to her neck.

She lets out the world's softest groan.

My cock whines. "Soon. What about your friend?"

"She's fine. Drew cleared his room for her."

"His room or his bed?"

"You can't tell by his mood?"

I laugh. "I can, actually. He's not."

"Is he that obvious?"

I nod. "Is she?"

"Sort of. We haven't talked about guys in a while. I've been trying hard not to think about anything but midterms and medical school."

"Have you made any decisions about where you're applying?"

"Not yet." She stares into my eyes. Brushes a stray hair

behind my ear. Her touch is sweet. Tender. "But I don't want to think about it tonight."

"Princess, I think you might be taking advantage of me."

She smiles.

"Just because you're royalty, that doesn't mean you can use me for my body. Even if I am a scoundrel."

"No?" She takes my hand. Places it on her hip, right at the waist of her skirt. "You're not desperate for me to take this off?"

I shake my head.

"So you're desperate for me to leave it on?" Her smile widens. "You have a fantasy of screwing the princess."

"You sure this is what you want?" I don't know why I ask. Our terms are clear. It should be obvious. But it's not.

She nods.

"Then let's go."

"Where?"

"My place in Malibu."

"Now?"

I help her to her feet. Offer my hand. "Hey, Princess, I've got the fastest ship in the galaxy. I can get you wherever you want to go in the blink of an eye."

"You mean the death bike, don't you?"

I chuckle. "You'll hurt her feelings."

## Chapter Thirty-Five

MILES

She changes into normal clothes for the ride. I feign insult, like it's the world's greatest tragedy she's no longer wearing a gold bikini.

Truth be told, I would have insisted. I don't want her freezing her ass off.

It's the decent thing to do.

I'd insist if it was Tom in a gold swimsuit. Now, there's a disturbing thought.

I push it out of my head as we ride. I always love my bike. Another cliché, I know, trading one rush for another. But fuck it is a thrill.

And having her chest pressed against my back, her arms around my waist, her fingers digging into my jacket—

It makes the damn thing even better.

I park in the driveway. Help her off the bike.

She pulls her arms over her chest. Rubs away her goose bumps. "It's freezing." Her eyes shift to the seat. They light up in a way I recognize. A way that usually means *I want to mount you*.

I guess it still does. "You like it."

"No."

"You do."

She tries to deny her smile. "A little."

"You want to try driving her?"

"God no." She steps away from the bike. Brings her body next to mine.

Fuck, she still smells good. Like that same strawberry shampoo. Like Meg. "We can go up and down PCH. Miles of coast."

"And giant cliffs if I steer wrong."

"I know you can swim." I motion to the pool in the backyard.

"Yeah, that's going to save me."

"Of course. It's just like jumping off the high dive," I say.

"At fifty miles an hour."

I take her hand. Lead her into the house. "Plus the time in free fall."

"Yes, very safe." She pushes the door closed behind her. "You know, at the hospital, we call them donor cycles."

"I've heard that."

"I really shouldn't ride one."

"You could have asked me to take the car."

"I know." She shrugs my jacket off her shoulders.

I take it. Drape it over the chair in the dining room. "I can always bring the car if you'd prefer."

Her eyes shift from me to the bike—it's visible through the window next to the door—then back to me. "You're asking me to take personal responsibility?"

"Admit you want to feel that power between your legs," I tease.

"I do." She motions to me. "So take off your pants."

"Right now?"

"Well..." Her eyes go to the stairs. "I guess we could use a bed."

"Could we?"

"If you insist."

I take her hand. "If *I* insist?"

"Uh-huh." She stares into my eyes, looking for something, finding it. "If you insist."

"If you're going to keep looking at me like that, I'm going to have to insist."

---

AFTER, WE SHOWER TOGETHER. I FIX A MIDNIGHT SNACK. It's simple. Eggs, green onions, sriracha, but it still fills me with all this pride, watching her eat the food I made her.

Taking care of her.

It's not our terms. It's way beyond our terms. But I can't stop myself.

We hang out on the couch, not really watching TV, kissing, touching, whispering dirty promises.

She falls asleep in my arms. I carry her upstairs. To my bed. Then I get in next to her.

For once, I sleep soundly.

I still wake up before her—the girl is under slept. Still fix coffee. Bring it to the backyard. Stare out at the horizon as I dip my feet in the pool.

There's no clarity in the blue sky or the warm water, but they're soothing all the same. Familiar.

Damon loved hanging out here.

Damon would have loved her. How brave she is. How much shit she gives me. How she won't take shit from me.

He'd had it hard, really fucking hard. Lost his sister. Stuck with her irritating kid. Dealing with the same damage my mom had from their fucked-up parents.

But he never showed it. He didn't hold on to shit that hurt him. He faced it and let it go. Then he opened himself to all the beauty and joy in the world.

I didn't get it then.

Now...

I'm starting to see more, but it's fuzzy, like an out of focus picture.

I hang out until Meg wakes, then I fix her breakfast, put on *The Matrix*.

We don't look at the screen much.

It's as perfect as our other weekend here. Like the world is ours. Like this place is ours. Like it's a place for joy and laughter and orgasmic shrieks.

The kind of place Damon would have wanted it to be.

Well, maybe not the screaming orgasms. Though I'm pretty sure he'd insist on generosity. He didn't talk about sex much, but when he did, he always focused on respect, communication, safety.

The usual parental shit. Plus some stuff I really didn't want to hear. Not from my uncle. Who wants to picture their family members eating out strangers?

Disturbing.

I break to piss. Return to Meg on the couch with her phone pressed to her ear, her eyes wide with concern.

"You okay?" I mouth.

She holds her hand over the receiver. Mouths, "parents."

"You know you can mute your side."

She smiles as she flips me off.

I move closer. Motion to the spot next to her. Then to the speaker. Mouth, "can I?"

She nods *sure*.

Her mom's voice flows through the speaker. It's mostly

matter-of-fact. A little hurt. Like she's upset she doesn't see Meg more.

I know the feeling.

"I've been busy." Meg fails to sell that.

"Tell them you're busy because you're seeing someone," I say.

She stares at me like I'm crazy.

"Trust me. It will give you something to talk about besides med school." I know enough now to know her parents still live in Orange County. They can't be happy she's trying to move across the county. Or that she fails to make the one hour drive to visit them. Sure, she doesn't have a car, and it's fucking impossible to get anywhere without one here. The train would be a four-hour affair.

But I'm also sure they offer to visit. Or pick her up.

How could they not?

She considers it for a moment then she brings her attention to her phone.

Her mom says something about Thanksgiving.

"I'll come with you." The words fly out of my mouth. I don't think about it. I just say it.

Meg looks at me like I'm crazy.

It is crazy. Meeting parents over the holidays is the ultimate boyfriend task. And I want to do it. But—"I'll pretend I'm your boyfriend."

She just stares at me.

"They're coming to LA today?" That's what I've gleaned so far.

She nods *yeah*.

"Invite them to meet us at Nobu. I'll pay. You'll eat enough sashimi to dull the pain."

She half-smiles.

"It will impress them."

"Maybe."

"You have to admit I'm charming." I brush her hair from her eyes. "For a scoundrel."

"I don't *have* to admit that, no."

"You know it's true."

"Megara." Her mom's voice flows through the speaker. "Are you there?"

"Tell her," I mouth.

She nods. "I'm sorry, Mom. That's just… that's Miles. My boyfriend." Her exhale is shaky. "We've been dating a few months now. And it's kept me busy."

"You're seeing someone?" Her mom's voice perks up.

"Yeah. He's great. Really, really great. Smart." She looks to me for help.

"Tell her I went to Stanford," I whisper.

"He's a little older. Graduated from Stanford a few years ago."

"Oh, that's great, sweetie. Miles was it?" her mom asks.

"Yes. Miles. You'd like him." She tries to come up with a reason, but she can't.

I'm good with parents. I know what matters to them. I know how to impress them. But my chest is getting light anyway. I'm actually nervous about impressing Meg's parents. It's ridiculous. "What's your mom like to do for fun?"

"She doesn't have time for fun. She's a surgeon." Her brow scrunches with concentration. "She likes mythology. And foreign films."

Fuck, I've got nothing. "Skip that part. Invite me over for Thanksgiving."

Incredulity streaks her expression.

"Trust me. She'll be excited that you want to introduce me."

She shoots me a *really* look.

I nod *really*.

She nods *okay, your funeral*. "Sorry, Mom. He's a little distracting. He really wants to meet you guys. Do you think he could come with me for Thanksgiving?"

"You're coming home?" Her mom's voice perks. "Of course, honey. We were hoping you'd come home. You don't have work?"

"No. My supervisor gave me the entire week off." She bites her lip. "Miles, he doesn't have a lot of family around here. I know he'll appreciate this."

"Yes. It will be nice having company since we don't…" Her mom's voice breaks. "You two can stay the weekend. Or just Thursday. Your father is working Friday but it's the early shift. Then the weekend—well, you know the drill."

Meg's brow furrow again, but it's more frustration than concentration.

I shift back. Give her some space.

She tries to avoid a question about med school. Talks about her job at the hospital. Asks about her parents' work. I don't get most of the particulars, but I can see medicine is the family tradition.

She stays focused for a while, then her cheeks flame red. Redder than I've seen them in a long time.

"Yes, Mom, we're being safe." Her voice gets high-pitched, like she's reverting to teenage girl form.

It's adorable. I full-on belly laugh.

"Not funny!" she whispers.

Very funny. I should torture her. Make her endure an entire conversation about safe sex.

But I want to rescue her. In every way I can.

"Let me talk to her," I say.

She looks at me funny. "What are you going to say?"

"A bunch of stuff about how great you are."

"Okay…"

"I know how to charm."

"And how to annoy," she whispers.

"But also how to charm."

She motions *kinda* but she does hand me the phone.

I swallow hard as I bring the phone to my ear. "Is that you Mrs. Smart? I've heard so much about you."

"Have you?"

"Yes. Meg talks about you and Mr. Smart a lot."

"Please, it's Susan."

"I'm Miles."

"It's nice to meet you."

I turn up the charm. Say all sorts of stuff about how much I adore Meg, how smart and sure she is, how much I wish I could apologize for stealing her time, but I'm just not sorry. Because I need it all.

It should feel like I'm hamming it up.

But it doesn't.

## Chapter Thirty-Six

MILES

I take Meg to lunch then I drive her home. I know I have to go. Have to leave her to her fucking life.

All benefits, no friends.

That's the deal.

I need to do better.

I kiss her goodbye. Get on my bike. Drive back to the place in the Hills.

Pete is in the backyard, his jeans rolled to his knees, his feet in the pool, his eyes on his Kindle.

He's concentrating.

On his book.

Or on something else. Another fight with the girlfriend maybe. I swear, they fight more every fucking day.

Usually, I want to roll my eyes when I hear about it. Right now, I'm sympathetic. I want to pat him on the shoulder. Tell him it will be okay.

Not that he needs my advice. Dude usually lets shit roll off his back. Anything, really. Anything except her.

I guess I get that too.

"Hey." I sit next to him. Dip my feet. "Place got clean fast."

"You know Tom." He shrugs. *Tom is Tom.*

The drummer can work miracles. I'll give him that much. "How'd you grow up with him without killing him?"

"Who says I didn't try?"

"If you tried, you'd succeed."

His chuckle is low. "True."

"I guess you're above all that shit."

"He means well."

"Maybe." I lie back. Look up at the sky. It's still blue and bright. Clear too. No clouds. "You been here the whole time?"

"Went out."

"Where?"

"Jazz club."

"You left a party to go to a jazz club?"

"Is that a question?" He taps his Kindle. Sets it down next to him. Turns to me.

I shake my head. "How do you do it?"

"Do what?"

"Survive."

"You're still here."

"Yeah, but it's fucking easy for you."

"Yeah. Easy for me. Easy for Tom and Drew. Easy for every person in the world besides you." He raises a brow, that classic *why are you doing this* look of his.

"You know what I mean."

"Do I?"

"It seems easier. For you." I push myself up. Look into his dark eyes. Usually, I can read him like a book—the guy is honest to a fault. Right now, I can't.

"You think you're the only person in the world with problems?" He arches a brow.

"No. More that… look at you."

"Can't see me."

"You've never fucked up in your life."

"Well, I wouldn't want to get on your turf." He chuckles.

I laugh too. "How do you do it?"

"I know what matters to me. Do you?"

I thought I did, but now… "When's our next show?"

"You and I both know that isn't an answer to that question."

"Uh-huh."

"You can fool me. But you won't fool yourself."

"Thanks, Dr. Phil."

"Dr. Phil?" He chuckles. "You should update your references."

"Do you know?"

"You think I keep track?"

"Fair enough." I kick my feet. Feel the water move past them. "You and Cindy on?"

"Why? You gonna invite me to a threesome?" He holds a poker face. It's an epic poker face, truth be told.

"No. I don't want to share this girl."

He laughs, even as he shakes his head. "You know that's bullshit, right?"

"I know you like to watch, but don't be greedy."

He chuckles. "No deal. I'm always greedy." His smile gets wicked.

I know where this goes—heard it enough times from the other room. I can't say I'm opposed to hearing it again. The guy really is a walking erotica factory.

Or whatever the fuck you call an audio version.

Usually, I'd say *go on*. Right now, I'm not there.

I'm still thinking about Meg.

"It is bullshit," Pete says. "That I don't fuck up. The last time with Cindy..." He shakes his head *not going there*. "Everybody feels like shit sometimes, Miles. It's just some of us try to cope in ways beyond drinking or fucking everything that moves."

"You, yeah. We?" I raise a brow *you sure about that*.

His chuckle is low. Hearty. "It will get old to Tom. And since Drew starting hanging with—"

"He can't admit he's into her."

"Pot's calling the kettle black there."

"Maybe."

"Maybe? Fuck." He shakes his head. "You're admitting that to yourself?"

"Yeah."

He picks up his Kindle. Taps the screen a few times.

"What?"

"Just checking the news."

"Why?"

"Want to see if pigs are flying."

I flip him off.

He just laughs. "Maybe it will be good for you. Caring about someone. Having a reason to try beyond—"

"Not getting a lecture from Tom?"

"He does mean well."

"He's your brother. You have to say that."

He shakes his head *hell no*. "I'll tell him when he's being an asshole."

He would, yeah. "Could you tell him today?"

"I'll be on alert."

"Thanks." But I already know my problem isn't with the bossy drummer. It's with myself.

---

FOR THE FIRST TIME IN FOREVER, I'M NOT BLOCKED. I

stay busy writing lyrics. Composing songs with the guys. Practicing.

I text Meg here and there, but only here and there. She's studying for midterms. No time for a booty call.

I try to satisfy myself, but it's just not the same. I need to hear her come.

Late one night, I give in to my craving.

*Miles: Midterms start tomorrow?*

*Meg: Yes. No time for distracting rock stars with very distracting mouths.*

*Miles: And hands.*

*Meg: And cocks.*

*Miles: Only have the one. Is that not enough for you?*

*Meg: You know what I mean!*

*Miles: I'll get a sex toy.*

*Meg: Don't start. I have to go to bed. First midterm is at nine a.m.*

*Miles: Studying all night tomorrow?*

*Meg: All night every night.*

*Miles: Been thinking. Sure would be a nice benefit if you could take a relaxing study break at home.*

*Meg: Yeah?*

*Miles: Without ever leaving your bed.*

*Meg: I'm listening. Well, reading.*

*Miles: Text me tomorrow when you're done studying. For your reward.*

*Meg: I'm not a puppy.*

*Miles: You'll like it.*

*Meg: I'll consider it. Good night.*

*Miles: Dream about me.*

I give her a few minutes to reply. When she doesn't, I figure she fell asleep.

*Miles: Guess that's failure. Don't worry. You can collect your reward tomorrow.*

*Miles: I had a dream about you.*
*Miles: Tell you about it later.*
But she didn't. She texts me an hour later.
*Meg: I'm awake and I'm all studied up.*
*Miles: You are a good girl.*
*Meg: And you're a very bad boy.*
*Miles: That's such a stereotype, Megara. I expected better.*
Okay. Go time.
I call her.
"Who is this?" she plays dumb.
"Just a young man who is very good with his mouth."
Her laugh is hearty. Her voice is teasing. "Is that right?"
"Mm-hmm. You swear you're done studying."
"On my love of *Jurassic Park*."
"And you're awake?"
"Wide awake," she says.
"Put your phone on speaker."
I do.
"What are you wearing?"
"Shorts and a tank top."
"Mm-hmm." Fuck. I'm already hard. Way too fucking hard. "Take off the shorts."
Her breath gets heavy, but she doesn't say anything.
"Do you want to hear me come or do you want to go to bed alone?"

## Chapter Thirty-Seven

MEGARA

I'm hot everywhere. Not just my cheeks but my chest, stomach, and back too. I open the window. The cool air does nothing to lessen the heat building in my body.

Miles wants to listen to me come? The guy makes sexy sounds for a living, and he wants to hear mine over the phone.

I'm back at that night again, only this time, I'm at the club, listening to Miles and Tom mock Pete for his constant phone sex. The night flies by, and I'm here, half-naked and about to cry because Miles can't bring himself to explain.

All the heat in my body pools between my legs. The damn thing can't be helped. It has an addiction to Miles. There's no other explanation.

My head is failing to pull back, failing to protect me. I guess the studying really tired it out.

Miles's exhale flows through the speakers. He's waiting, and he's not doing it patiently. Technically speaking, the ball is in my court. I can say yes or say no.

Technically speaking, this arrangement is entirely on

my terms.

My eyes flutter closed. The breeze sends a shiver up my legs and thighs. No underwear tonight. No bra. Just this tiny tank top and shorts, like when I was on the couch with Miles.

No, I can't go there. If I'm going to do this, I need to be in this moment. And, damn, I want to enjoy this moment.

"You swear you're not fucking with me?" I ask.

"I'll prove it."

He's quiet for a minute. Then my phone buzzes with a picture message. It's Miles, in his bed, alone. His hand is tugging at the waistband of his boxers.

God, he's so freaking yummy it's ridiculous.

His voice flows through my speakers. "You want more?"

A blush spreads across my cheeks. It's not like I'm used to guys offering to send me nude pictures.

Okay. He sent me a picture in his underwear. It's only fair I do the same. Even if I'm not wearing any underwear. I pull my tank top to my bellybutton so my breasts are on display.

I've never taken a sexy picture of myself before. I know all the ways it's a bad idea, all the ways it could hurt me, but I don't care.

This feels too good for me to care.

I snap a picture of my chest and neck and send it to Miles.

He lets out a groan. "Fuck, Meg, you're killing me."

Yes. Perfect. I'm going to be the one in control here. "How so?"

"I miss your tits."

"You saw them last week."

"I want to see them every day. To see that look on your

face when I suck on your nipples."

So much for control. I'm melting. Heat rushes through my body. Whatever it is we're doing, I can't stop until I get what he promised me, until he's groaning in my ear.

"What else?" I ask.

"Take off your shorts," he says.

I do. "Take off your boxers."

There's a low groan and then silence. A moment later, my phone buzzes. He took off his boxers and sent me a picture. That must be…

I look at my new picture message. It's Miles. All of him. He's naked and hard, his hand wrapped around his cock. I always thought it was strange when women wanted these pictures, but now I understand. That's Miles, hard and desperate and out of his mind because of me.

"I've never done this before," I say.

"Me either."

"Really?"

"Really."

I pull my tank top over my head and toss it aside. I'm naked on my bed. If I close my eyes, I almost feel like he's here, like he's watching me. I run my fingertips over my chest. "I don't know what to say."

"I don't care what you say. I just want to hear you come."

Dammit, I'm on fire. This is perfect.

I don't want to hear anything except his breath and his moans. Maybe my name rolling off his tongue like he's so desperate he can't find another word to explain his pleasure.

I set the phone on the bed next to me, between my mouth and my ear. My hand trails over my chest, teasing my nipples the way Miles does.

It's good already. Not as good as him, but close. I play

with my nipples until his breath is as heavy and strained as mine is. Then I trail my hand down my stomach, below my belly button, between my legs.

My breath hitches in my throat. "You have to do it, too."

His voice is heavy. "After. I want to hear you first."

My eyes flutter closed. It's not as if I've never touched myself before. I made it to twenty-one without ever having sex. I touched myself plenty. But never with an audience.

My breath goes all the way to my core. He's never done this before either. No reason to be self-conscious.

I slide my hand between my legs with a soft touch. It's a tease, at first, the kind of thing Miles would do. I work my way to my clit then back off again. Slowly. Until I can't take it anymore.

Through the speakers, his breath is heavy. Desperate. It stirs something in me. Makes me just as desperate.

No more waiting. No more gentleness. I rub myself hard.

It's not as good as when Miles touches me. It's lacking a certain patience, a certain heat. But it's still damn good.

The pressure inside me builds at a record speed. I lose control of my breath. Of the sounds escaping my lips. I let out a soft moan. Then a louder one. My hand moves faster, drawing circles over my clit. I make the circles smaller and tighter until they're in just the right spot.

"Oh." My voice picks up. I'm almost screaming.

No room for shyness now. His voice is louder, heavier, more desperate. I'm affecting him, and that feels so damn good.

I rub myself until I'm at the brink. Deep down, I know this won't be enough to satisfy my craving. I need more than Miles's breath in my ear. I need his hands and his mouth and his cock.

The ache between my legs is so intense. Almost more than I can take. The pleasure in my arms and legs and chest spins inward, pooling in my core until it's a deep, desperate pressure.

A groan flows through the speakers. It sends me right over the edge. That pleasure drives a little deeper, squeezing me until I can't breathe. One more brush of my fingers and I come. My orgasm is pulses of ecstasy. The pressure releases bit by bit, spilling into the purest, deepest bliss.

Miles lets out a low moan. "Don't know how I can follow that."

My cheeks flush. "You moan more than that on one Sinful Serenade track."

"Depends on the track," he growls. "You sound so fucking sexy. Can't remember the last time I was this hard."

"I want to hear you, too." No awkwardness. I have to say it. "I want to hear you come."

No snappy comeback. There's some shifting, sheets moving, a body planting on the bed. He must be getting into position.

His breath gets heavier and heavier. He must not have control of it any longer. It's strained and desperate. I relax into my bed, letting the sounds of his pleasure wash over me. He moans, low and deep, and purely animal. They get louder and lower. It's so much better than anything on any song—and I've paid very close attention.

"Mm-hmm."

He's not wasting time either. Everything that flows through my speakers is desperate and needy, like he wants this as much as I did. His groans run together. Louder. Higher. Like he can't control them at all.

There. He's coming. I'm not sure how I can tell, but I

can. His voice strains. His breath gets choppy. He lets out one last moan, louder than I've ever heard before. Then, he's sighing in pleasure. His breath steadies. Still strained, but not completely out of control.

"Relaxed?" he asks.

"More like keyed up and wishing you were here."

"Happy to listen to you go again."

"I should get to bed."

"When's your last midterm?"

"Friday night. Why?"

"No reason." He exhales slowly. "Good night, Meg. And good luck."

"Good night."

I hang up the phone, pull the sheets over my head, and try desperately to fill the craving I have for Miles.

I fail.

---

THE WEEK IS A BLUR OF TEXTBOOKS AND TESTS. BY Friday afternoon, the only thing I want is the sweet embrace of my sheets. I need a million hours of sleep.

The elevator is all the way on the top floor, so I take the stairs to my apartment. Every step is pure agony.

And there he is, the only thing better than those million hours of sleep. Miles is leaning against my door, his hands in the pockets of his leather jacket, his lips pursed like there's something right on the tip of his tongue.

"You survived." He smiles.

I nod.

"I bet you'd like to celebrate that."

"Okay."

"If that's not a problem for you."

"I can clear my schedule." I fish my keys out of my

backpack, open the apartment, and pull Miles inside with me.

The room is a verifiable mess. Paper everywhere, clothes strewn over the floor, dishes piled in the sink.

Miles shakes his head. "I like what you've done with the place."

"Thank you. I'm trying something new with the dishes. And the laundry. And the shower."

"Dirty girl."

My lips curl into a smile. "Not quite yet." I toss my backpack on the ground. "How long were you waiting?"

"Not long." He runs his fingertips over my chin, tilting my head so he's peering right into my eyes. "But it would've been worth waiting longer."

"And what is it you're waiting for?"

He presses his lips into mine. His hands slide into my hair as his tongue swirls around mine. The kiss breaks and he pulls back. "That."

My heart thumps against my chest. I've ignored my body for days. It's time to give it a little attention.

His fingers skim my wrists. "I've been thinking about you all week."

Okay, it's time to have some fun. I tease him. "I've been thinking about midterms all week."

He pulls his shirt over his head. "What are you thinking about now?"

"There was this angular velocity question."

"Are you only in science classes?"

I trace the lines of his chest. "Who's thinking about midterms now?"

He pulls me onto the bed, pulling my body on top of his. It's messy. I slip and land on my side. He shakes his head like he's going to punish me.

"You think you're clever?" he asks.

"Absolutely."

He unzips my hoodie. Then his hands are on my stomach. My skin burns at his touch. Midterms seem so irrelevant now, but I'm not done teasing him yet. It's too much fun.

"And molecular biology," I say. "That was impossible."

He tugs at my t-shirt. I lift my arms to help him get it off.

His eyes pass over me slowly. Then it's his fingers skimming my sides. "You should have said hard."

My cheeks flush. "I, um…"

He unhooks my bra and pulls it off my arms. "Um…?"

I plant my hands on his chest and press my crotch into his. Hard. Yes, he is absolutely hard.

Deep breath. I want him desperately, but I want his smile as much as I want his cock. "And my Roman Poetry elective."

He unzips my jeans and pulls them off my ass. "That's a shit choice for an elective."

He runs his fingertips over the waist of my panties. A gasp escapes my lips. Midterms. Electives. They're so quaint, so far away, so much less important than this.

I rub my crotch against his. "It's better than you'd expect."

He shakes his head. "You're making this hard."

"I can tell."

He smirks. "But I'm going to beat midterms."

"You really can't." I press my lips to his. Damn, he tastes good. And I feel good. Light. Like I can float.

"That so?"

I nod. "It's all biology."

He laughs.

Then he makes me forget what year it is.

## Chapter Thirty-Eight

MILES

For a few days, things are easy. We text all day. Flirt all night. Fuck all weekend.

It's beautiful, like the world is ours, like nothing else matters.

I ignore Tom's *if you don't tell her I will* warnings.

I ignore Aiden's bullshit.

I walk out of practice, meetings, photoshoots on a cloud. Life is good. Easy.

It's possible for shit to just be good.

Uncomplicated.

Even this thing with her parents over Thanksgiving. I'm helping her out. Fucking her when she needs it.

That little voice in my head, the one that's saying *it's more than that*—

That voice is wrong.

I know where we stand.

And so does she.

I let Meg sleep in, but she still drags her heels about getting ready. When she finally finishes packing, she changes into an incredibly sweet and innocent polka dot cardigan.

It does things to me. Makes me want to tear the buttons off her sweater and wrap my arms around her.

Innocent Meg is corruptible. But the girl dressing to impress her parents, terrified to face the reminder of everything she's lost—she's something else entirely.

I understand her better than she thinks I do.

Better than I want to.

I step into my sneakers. "You look nice."

"Thank you." Those nerves creep into her voice.

She has to face home eventually. But not yet.

I bring my gaze to the v of her sweater. Drop my voice to that low, demanding tone. "Are you wearing anything under that?"

"Yes." Her laugh is soft. "My parents will not be cool with us making out in front of them."

"I'm not sure," I tease. "Your mom was asking if you're having safe sex."

"I will leave!" She fights a smile. "I swear I will."

I laugh. "And go where?"

"Anyplace I don't have to die of embarrassment."

I pull her into a hug and press my lips to hers. "You won't die. I promise."

She melts into my touch. "I don't know if I can do this."

"You can."

She stares back at me, apprehensive.

"Come on." I offer my hand.

She takes it. I grab her suitcase and lead her to the garage. Place her stuff in the trunk with mine.

It's been a long time since I've packed for a trip for two.

## Just a Taste

A million years ago, Tom and I used to drive up and down California for no reason at all. And there were a bunch of weekend trips at Stanford. But since we really took a swing at this, it's been overstuffed vans and too many familiar faces.

Meg is quiet as we get into the car. Even as I pull onto the 405.

"You hungry?" I ask.

She shakes her head.

Insisting she eats something is pure boyfriend. I shouldn't go there, but I can't let her stew. "Want coffee?"

"Later."

Sooner. But we'll get there.

She leans in to the center console. Turns on the radio. Finds the preset for KROQ.

A familiar riff fills the car.

Fuck.

She has uncanny timing. She really does.

There I am, pouring my heart out for anyone who wants to listen.

And there she is, the reason why I was so fucked up I had to spin my thoughts into a song.

And she's picking me apart.

She's always picking me apart.

I hate it.

And I need it.

*Three a.m. and I can't sleep.*
*A common refrain, I know.*
*As a sentiment, it's cheap.*
*Someone to call, to hold,*
*to love, no way, that word—*
*She smiles and I drift away—*

Her cheeks flush.

She stammers something that sounds a lot like why the fuck did you write a song about me. But then I'm probably projecting.

She's bright red.

I'm… well, I'm still good at playing cool. "You know, most girls feel flattered when someone writes a song about them."

Her lips curl into a frown. "You've never said that it's about me."

My fingers curl into the steering wheel. "It is."

"Oh." Her voice drips with surprise.

But how? How can she not see the way she gets under my skin? How hard I try to keep her away? "You're cute when you're nervous."

She just stops herself from rolling her eyes. Turns to the window. Watches strip malls and matching houses blur together. "Why did you write a song about me?"

I wish I could explain it to her. Honestly, I do. But I can't. "Something came over me, an itch, and the song was the only way to scratch it."

"That isn't an answer."

"Yes, it is." My eyes find hers for a moment, then they're back on the road. I know what she wants to hear. Hell, I wish I could tell her that it was because I'm madly in love with her. Because I wanted to profess it to the whole fucking world. But that isn't true. "It's just not the answer you want."

The radio station goes to commercial. Thank fuck. I've had enough of hearing myself groan.

Don't get me wrong. I love singing. I love singing like

## Just a Taste

I'm coming. But I don't want to be stuck in the headspace that got me to write that song.

Meg asked me to share the truth with her.

I couldn't.

I can't take more from her now.

But, somehow, I can't bring myself to push her away either.

No. It's worse than that. I'm magnetically attracted to her.

But this shit isn't getting worse.

I'm here to help her. That's all.

She leans back in her seat. Taps her fingers against the passenger seat. "Is this your car?"

"Yeah."

"Then why do you always ride the death bike?"

"I like having something powerful between my legs."

"Besides your cock?"

I chuckle. That response is so like her. "You're not supposed to spell out the joke."

"Yeah, but I like thinking about your cock." There's a smile in her voice for a moment. Then it's gone. Her breath gets shallow. Irritated. She's not sticking in the joke. She's still thinking about the song, about what it means.

"If I could explain it, I wouldn't have to write the song." I keep my voice steady. "I felt something. I wrote the song. The end."

"Thanks. You really cleared things up."

"You're cranky today."

"Fuck off."

"Let's stop for breakfast."

"I'm not hungry."

Yeah. She is.

Fuck it being too much a boyfriend thing.

I'm not letting her go hungry.

I pull off the freeway. Find a Starbucks. Park. "Come on. I'll buy you coffee, green tea, whatever your heart desires."

She frowns, but she does follow me into the shop.

I slip my arm around her waist. Pull her closer. But getting into character—I'm here to play her loving boyfriend, after all—isn't helping with drawing a line between us.

Too much of me doesn't want that line.

Too much of me wants to tell her everything.

But that's selfish. And I've taken enough from her for one lifetime.

The girl behind the counter looks at me the way a dog looks at a bone. Her eyes light up with recognition. Her hands clap together. Her tongue slides over her lips. "Welcome!"

I pull Meg closer reflexively. Uh-uh. That's no good.

I break our touch and step aside. "You want to grab a seat?"

"So you can flirt with the employee?"

My fingers trail over the edge of her cardigan. Fucking hands moving of their own accord. They're good to me most of the time. Right now, they aren't respecting my wishes. "I only flirt with you." I press my palm against her lower back, nudge her toward the table in the corner. I'd rather not piss her off more, but whatever works. "I just don't want to subject anyone else to your hunger-induced mood."

"Maybe my mood is bullshit induced."

"Only one way to find out." I step up to the register. She stays next to me. Moves closer to me. Like she's marking her territory. "Black coffee for me. Large. And for my friend—"

"Large latte. Extra shot."

## Just a Taste

"And." She's eating something.

"One of the egg sandwiches. The one with spinach."

The girl nods at me. She barely acknowledges Meg's existence. "I love Sinful Serenade."

I shoot the barista my best wink. "Thanks, honey."

"Would you sign something?" Her eyes go wide. She reaches under the counter and hands me a marker.

This really isn't the most opportune moment, but I know how to play my part. I shoot her my best smile as I sign a napkin.

She gushes for a minute, goes on and on about how much she loves *No Way in Hell* and how cruel her manager is for not letting her play it.

It's sweet, but it's not what I want.

I can't have what I want.

I can't...

God, this is fucked.

I wait for our food and drinks then join Meg at one of the cushy armchairs. She's staring at her cell, lost in her thoughts.

She nods thanks as I place her sandwich and coffee on the table. Then she's pushing herself up. Moving to the fixings like they hold the secrets to the universe.

I sip my drink.

It's good. Warm. Comforting. Unhelpful in this situation.

Meg is all tense and awkward.

But she's also opening herself up. Inviting me in. Asking for me.

She slides back into her seat. Stares into my eyes. "Why did you really invite yourself home with me?"

"The answer to that question is self-evident."

"Jesus, I forgot you were going to be a lawyer." She takes another sip. Lets out a heavy sigh.

I have to answer her. "I want to help you. With your parents."

"Wouldn't you rather see your family?"

"I don't talk about my family."

She presses her lips together. "I'm not going to push you."

My eyes go to the ground. This is it. There's nothing else left to say. I have to dive back into that ugly memory if I want to get through to her. "Here's the thing, Meg. I'm only telling you this so you understand why I'll never fall in love with you."

"I know."

I stare into her eyes, trying to find her intentions. "And you're sure you're okay with that?"

"Absolutely." She presses her palm into her thigh. Taps her toe against the tile. "This relationship is just sex."

I want to believe her, but I don't.

Fuck.

I hate going here.

But it's time.

Deep breath. "My dad left when I was in middle school. Bored of the whole suburban thing. I was angry. I did nothing but play my guitar and get into trouble. But my mom… she fell apart. She couldn't get out of bed, couldn't even bother to get herself to the shower. It broke her heart. That's what love does, it breaks your heart."

"But she… now…" Her voice gets shaky.

I can't look at her. Can't look at anything but the clouds forming in the sky outside the window. "She killed herself."

"Oh." She shifts.

Then there's a splat. Her coffee cup hits the ground. Spills everywhere.

"Shit. I better get that." She jumps from her seat. Rushes to the counter for napkins. Fumbles over them.

She's all thumbs.

She can barely walk straight.

The fangirl cuts her off. "I can get that."

"No, it's okay." Meg rushes to the spilled coffee. She drops to her knees and mops it up one napkin at a time.

But there's no getting this back in the box.

It's out there, infecting the air.

The perky barista wheels over a mop. She nudges Meg *I've got it*.

Meg leans back on her heels, her eyes fixed on mine.

She's looking for something.

Asking some question I can't answer.

The barista promised to make Meg another drink.

Meg nods and slides into her seat. "Sorry."

I wait until we're alone. Fuck, there's so much I want to say. But none of it is right.

There's only one thing left to do now.

What I've been avoiding for way too long.

"That's about what I expected." My tone isn't curt enough. It isn't *go the fuck away* enough. I need to do better. I need to make it clear that I'm never going to love her. "You're clumsy when you're hungry."

She ignores my attempt to push her away. "I'm sorry you went through all that."

"I survived."

Her eyes fill with sympathy. "You're alone."

Yeah. But I'm used to that. "I've been alone a long time. It's easier that way."

"Oh."

She stares at me like I'm breaking her heart.

Maybe I am.

But better now than later.

Better now than after she falls in love with me.

## Chapter Thirty-Nine

MEGARA

We park in the driveway of my parents' Newport Beach house. Miles grabs our suitcases from the trunk. When I go to grab one, he shifts his arms so it's out of my reach.

Okay. I guess my mom will appreciate him acting like a gentleman.

The oak door is locked. I knock instead of fishing for my keys. Mom will also appreciate the chance to make an entrance.

Nerves rise up in my stomach. The last time I was here, I felt like I was suffocating. Everything was off and wrong, and Rosie's absence was haunting me.

Then Miles's arm is around my waist and I'm sure it's going to be okay.

Mom answers the door. "Honey, I missed you." She takes a long look at Miles and nods a hello. "I'm Susan Smart."

"Miles Webb. Nice to finally meet you." He shakes her hand. "I can see where Meg gets her looks."

Mom blushes. "Thank you. Come in." She pushes the door open. "How was the drive?"

"Good. Not too much traffic." I step inside and scan the room. It's as gorgeous and pristine as I remember. But something is missing. There used to be trophies on the mantle—Rosie's volleyball trophies. They're gone. One more piece of her is gone.

"Can I get you anything? Coffee? Tea? A snack, maybe?"

I bite my tongue. "How about we put away our bags first?"

She nods of course and leads us up the stairs. There used to be half a dozen framed pictures on this wall—family photos, the cheesy ones sent as Christmas cards—but they're all gone.

Mom smiles. "Did you kids want to stay in Meg's room or would you like to stay in the spare room, Miles?"

We don't have a spare room. We have Rosie's room.

I know we have to move on eventually. I know people grieve in different ways. And maybe it hurts Mom too much to have Rosie's stuff here…

But how can she call that the spare room?

How can she take down all those pictures and hide all those trophies?

Miles steps in. It's like he can tell I'm about to snap.

"Thank you so much, Mrs. Smart." Miles looks to me. "What do you think? Want me to stay with you?"

I nod.

He turns to Mom. "You sure it's all right?"

She nods. "Yes, it's good for you, sleeping next to someone you love. The touch produces oxytocin. That's the love hormone. It's what makes you feel all warm and fuzzy." She offers a half-smile. "Dopamine too."

"I know dopamine. The pleasure hormone." Miles offers her a very full smile.

"Yes." Mom turns to me. "I'm glad you found someone smart."

"He did go to Stanford, the show off." I try my best *I'm having such effortless fun joking about my boyfriend* smile. It's horrible.

He places our suitcases in my room then slides his arm around me. He leans in to whisper. "Should I tell her I have a motorcycle?"

I laugh. I'm tempted to tell her myself. I have no idea how Mom will act toward the bad boy version of Miles. Ever since Rosie died, she's been unpredictable.

Mom leads us downstairs. "How did you two meet? Meg doesn't talk about guys very often."

"She's studious." Miles plays with my hair. "She's quite the nerd, really."

Mom smiles. "She went for Princess Leia for Halloween five years in a row."

"This year too," he says. "I'm a friend of Kara's. Well, a friend of a friend."

She nods. "What do you do, Miles? Meg didn't mention it."

"I work in the entertainment industry." He winks at me. "Not that interesting."

"Do you need any help with dinner?" I ask.

"No, it's all prepared except the turkey, and that's in the oven." She motions to the table, directing us to sit. "Coffee or tea, you two?"

"Green tea." Miles smiles. "If it's not too much trouble."

I'm not sure if he's teasing me or taking care of me. Both maybe. Whatever it is, I like it.

I lean in to whisper. "Thank you."

"You want me to tell her about Sinful Serenade?"

"Up to you."

"Most parents don't react well to the knowledge their favorite daughter is having a torrid love affair with a rock star."

"Because you've met so many girls' parents?"

"Seen it happen."

"To who?"

He shrugs.

Mom steps into the room. She sets out a teapot and three mugs. "I haven't used this thing in forever." She looks at Miles. "Meg is busy. Can't get home much."

"I'm sure that's partly my fault." He smiles wide, charm turned to a thousand.

"You look familiar, Miles. Are you from around here?"

"I lived in Irvine for a while. But that's probably not it. I'm in this band. Sinful Serenade. We have this song that plays a hundred times a day on KROQ."

Mom smiles. "I haven't listened to KROQ since high school."

"It's about the same. Foo Fighters, Red Hot Chili Peppers, and Nirvana around the clock."

Mom blushes, totally charmed. "You're sweet, but those bands came long after I finished high school."

"I can't believe that."

She turns to us, friendly but maternal, too. "Do you do well?"

He nods. "Well enough." Under the table, he slides his hand over my thigh. "I write songs on the side. It's go big or go home, but I've had a few hits."

Mom's eyes light up. "Really?"

Miles names a few songs that put the popular in pop. Mom's demeanor changes. It's not that she's horribly superficial. More that, around here, money talks. It takes a lot to impress a family of doctors. Apparently, millionaire songwriter with gorgeous blue eyes is enough to do it.

I zone out as Mom grills Miles. He's perfect and charming—the picture of a sweet, supportive boyfriend. He leans his head against my shoulder and praises my wit, my beauty, my excellent work ethic. He speculates wildly about some future we'll never see—where he tours based on my school schedule and settles down in the city where I do my residence.

For a guy who doesn't do boyfriend, he sure is good at playing one.

———

We have a late dinner. The table in the dining room is covered with the good linens, the good china, the good silverware. It's the kind of meal royalty eats.

Dad sits next to Mom, scooping potatoes absentmindedly. He's not really all here, doesn't seem to have much to say. He hasn't had much to say since Rosie died, and he's on the same, let's just never discuss it again, wavelength as my mom.

He pays careful attention to Miles, but there's no sign that Dad objects to my so-called boyfriend. Dad isn't even bothered by the tattoos that peek out from Miles's t-shirt.

This is what I wanted, the attention on Miles instead of me. But it feels wrong for them to so easily accept him. Shouldn't they be prying about his intentions? Shouldn't they be worried about their little girl?

Miles is too charming, too good at convincing them he adores me.

She clears her throat. "You know, I'm so thankful to have my daughter and her friend here. And she's healthy, and she's going to medical school next year." She holds up her glass of wine like she's toasting me. "You're going to do great anywhere."

"Thank you." I hold my water to my chest, avoiding anything close to a toast. "It'll be nice to finally get out of Southern California. Spread my wings and see the world." And get away from this house and the way it tears open a hole in my gut.

"If that's what you want." Mom sips her wine slowly. She sets the glass down, folds her hands, and looks directly at me. "Megara, honey, what are you thankful for?"

I bite my lip, fighting my temptation to call out the bullshit. This is supposed to be a nice family dinner. I'm not going to ruin it by pointing out how much we're pretending that Rosie isn't here.

"For honesty," I say.

Mom frowns, not sure what to make of that. "It is important." She pats Dad's hand. "Especially in a relationship."

The mood shifts, her desperate hold on pretending like my sister never existed gone. Her expression is misery. The memory must be hitting her like a ton of bricks.

I know that feeling. It's a horrible feeling. Half of me wants to rush to comfort her. But the other half can't forgive her for erasing Rosie from the house.

I know it isn't fair. She's coping the only way she knows how.

But it's still wrong that there's no sign Rosie every existed.

Mom shakes her head and that hurt is gone. Back to an everything is okay smile. "I miss Rosie, too. I wish she was here. But she's not. She's gone, and keeping her stuff around isn't going to bring her back."

I offer my best smile. This conversation won't go anywhere unless we're honest, and I can tell she's not ready to admit how much it hurts. I'm not sure I'm ready either.

Miles cuts in. "I'm thankful for your hospitality." He smiles, all charm.

"My pleasure," Mom says. She turns to me. "You've really found a nice young man."

I make eye contact with Miles. "He's the perfect boyfriend."

He raises an eyebrow.

"He bought me an N64," I say. "You remember how Rosie and I used to play with ours? The one cousin Jimmy gave us. For a while, she loved racing games."

Mom frowns but makes nothing of it. "Yes, I remember. I remember a lot about your sister. More than I want to remember." A tear forms in her eyes.

I pull together some kind of an apology, some way to connect over how much this hurts.

Nothing comes together. I have no idea what I should say here.

Mom pushes out from the table. "Excuse me, Megara, Miles. I'm developing a headache. I'm going to lie down."

Dad looks at her with concern. She waves like it's fine and makes her way up the stairs. Her steps are calm and even, but I'm pretty sure her hands are shaking.

---

MILES MAKES EFFORTLESS CONVERSATION WITH MY father. Sports, movies, requests for embarrassing stories about me. After dinner, they take to the TV. Dad flips around channels, eventually settling on a rerun of some kind.

I creep upstairs. If my mom really wants to talk about Rosie, I want to be there with her.

The door to her room is open a sliver. She's sitting on the bed, in the dark, her hands wrapped around a silver frame.

That frame used to be on the wall. One of the family pictures. An old one, when we were kids, before everything went wrong.

There are tears running down her cheeks. They're silent, like she doesn't want anyone to know it hurts.

I grab onto the doorknob, but I can't bring myself to push the door open.

What would I say?

I don't have the answers. I don't have a clue how to handle this.

My grip on the knob releases. Better to go to my room, alone. Better to cry, alone, where I won't hurt anyone else.

A few hours pass. I pull my comforter over my head and read one of my Star Wars books. The words don't make an impact. Everything about this house is suffocating.

My dad goes to sleep. The lights go out. Miles joins me on the bed and wraps his hands around me. He goes right for the gold. His hands slide under my cardigan, tracing the outline of my bra.

"We can get this off now," he says.

The heat rushing through my body is the first pleasant thing I've felt all day, but my parents are three doors down. "Not here."

His lips skim my neck. "You're right." He sinks his teeth into my skin. "No way you can stay quiet."

"I can."

"Don't dare me, princess."

The pet name makes my sex clench. "Or?"

He runs his fingers over my inner thighs. "There's someplace I want to take you."

"Yeah?"

"You'll like it." He pulls me off the bed. "Of course, you'll be coming so hard you'll barely be aware of your surroundings."

I like it already.

## Chapter Forty

MEGARA

We take Pacific Coast Highway south to a long, empty street that cuts through the hills. Everything is dark except for the stars and the moon.

I rest my eyes. It's late, and this day stretched on forever. Miles has my head spinning. I don't know which way is up or down. That's enough to drive me mad, but the house, my parents… it's like my sister never existed.

The car slows to a stop. We're at a red light. Miles has that same determined expression. He knows where we're going. He knows what he's doing. He knows exactly what he's getting out of this relationship.

He turns onto a steep, winding road. There's some kind of lab at the top of the hill. We stop just short of it to pull onto a large patch of dirt. It's a makeshift vista point.

Miles turns off the car. "Take a look."

We make our way to the edge of the hill. The quiet suburbs go on forever, this mass of twinkling lights. The black sky is dotted with stars I've never seen before.

"This was the closest thing we had to a make out spot in high school," he says.

I clear my throat. "Did you… come here a lot?"

"Yeah. But I was always alone."

My tense muscles relax. "Always?"

"Unless someone changed the definition of always."

I don't bother with a comeback. There's too much to take in. This place is beautiful, and I'm the first girl Miles has ever brought here. I try not to let it mean anything. My heart thuds against my chest.

I pull my arms over it to keep all the warmth in my body.

Miles slides his arm around my shoulders. "Cold?"

"Yeah."

"Come here." He slides into the back seat, pulling me with him.

His body is close to mine. Inches away. There's just enough light to make out the expression on his face. He looks sad. But I don't know what that means.

He's warm, and he smells good. I need that, need him comforting me.

His fingers skim my chin. He guides me into a kiss. It's soft and sweet, the kind of kiss that should mean *I love you*. But this one can't.

That's not possible.

I tug at his leather jacket. I need him closer. I need it to mean *I love you*.

When the kiss breaks, Miles stares into my eyes. "Are you okay?"

I shake my head. He shouldn't ask things like that. He shouldn't act so damn sweet.

"What is it?"

My lungs fail me. My vocal cords fail me. My mouth is sticky and confused. There's no easy way to explain this, but I want to try. "My parents... they erased my sister's existence from the house. It's not right."

"They're trying to cope."

"I know. But that doesn't make it easier."

He runs his hand through my hair. "They care about you. Let them."

I close my eyes. His touch is delicate. His voice is soft. But he's never going to love me and he's better off alone.

I pull back. "Who the hell do you think you are to tell me to let someone care about me?"

He doesn't falter. "Fair enough."

It doesn't bother him. I hate that it doesn't bother him.

His lips skim my neck. Heat surges through me. All I need to do is close my eyes and surrender. It doesn't matter if he'll break my heart later. It doesn't matter that my parents are erasing my sister's existence.

I lean into his lips. He moves faster, scraping his teeth against my skin, tugging at my cardigan.

"This is all I can offer you," he says.

Every place he touches is on fire, desperate for more of him, whatever he can offer. "I know."

He pulls my sweater over my head. "You've hurt so much. I can't bring myself to add to that."

His eyes find mine. They're dead serious, and there's such a sweetness to his gaze. He does care about me, even if it's only enough not to completely discard me.

I turn away, staring at the perfect view outside. "Then stop saying things like that. If you care about me, don't act like you're going to fall in love with me."

His voice is even. "Fair enough."

"And that. Stop with that. You have all the cards in this relationship. Stop bragging about how fucking collected you are."

He runs his hands over my shoulders, pulling my bra

straps down. "I'm not collected." He unclasps my bra and rubs my nipples. "It's just that all my attention is already focused somewhere else." He takes my hand and slides it over the bulge in his jeans.

My breath catches in my throat. "That's not the same thing."

He pinches my nipples, sending pangs of desire all the way to my toes. My body screams with want. It won't forgive me if I do anything besides touch him.

"I do care about you." He pulls my jeans and panties to my feet in one fell swoop. "But this is the only way I can show you."

"I know."

His fingertips skim my thighs. "Are sure you're okay with that?"

I let my eyes flutter closed. "I have to take it or leave it."

Miles runs his hand over my calf, the inside of my knee, my thighs. "You can leave it."

"I'd believe you if you weren't about to fuck me."

He grabs my knees and arranges me so I'm on top of him. "I can stop. I'd rather not, but I can."

"Don't. I want you to show me how you care about me." I squeeze my eyelids together.

If this really is all Miles can offer, then it has to be enough. I need him to show me how he cares, even if it's with his cock inside me.

He rubs my shoulders, bringing my body onto his. The back seat is too small for two tall people. One of my legs is squeezed between his knee and the seat. The other is skimming the floor.

Miles is three inches from me. He brushes a hair behind my ear. His fingers slide over the curve of my chin. It's soft and sweet, like he loves me.

"You okay?" he asks.

"Show me."

He presses his palm flat against my back. "Look at me."

I pry my eyes open. He's staring at me, staring through me. It's like he can see inside me, see how close I am to crumbling.

"You don't look okay." His voice is just as soft and sweet as his touch.

"Don't pretend it matters to you."

"It does." He wraps his arms around me and holds me close. "Meg…"

I press myself up, so we're eye to eye. "Show me, whatever that means, or drive me home."

He holds my gaze. It feels like forever passes, but it can't be more than a minute. Then, his eyes flutter closed, and his lips find mine.

It's the same kiss as before. One that normally means *I love you*. His hands slide to my ass, his touch soft and delicate.

We're inches apart. His cock is just under my sex.

He takes my hips and guides me onto him. It's slow and gentle, and then he's all the way inside me.

I plant my hands around his head and bring my body closer. We're face-to-face. Staring into each other's eyes. He keeps his grip on my hips, guiding my movements to drive his cock deeper inside me.

He stares at me like he loves me.

I close my eyes and press my lips into his. Soft. Sweet. Perfect. Or, it would be, if this whole situation weren't so hopelessly fucked.

He holds me close, shifting into me with a steady rhythm. His lips stay on mine. His tongue explores my mouth. It's gentle and delicate, like he wants more of me.

I kiss him back. I swirl my tongue around his. I rub my

body against his. The pleasure builds in that same soft, slow way, until it's too much to take.

Miles breaks the kiss. He stares into my eyes, runs his hand through my hair. His pupils dilate. His fingers dig into my skin.

"Meg..." It's a soft groan, but it's filled with desire.

He keeps things slow. My sex clenches. It's a slow burn. More. More. More. It feels like it's going on forever, like it's never going to stop.

I press my lips into his, kissing him harder. But, still, he stays slow. He rocks into me. He holds me close.

The pressure inside me builds. More. More. More. It's so much. It's too much. An orgasm wells up in me. I moan into his mouth. More. I still need more. I kiss him harder, hold him closer.

Pleasure rocks through me, all the way to my fingers and toes. But I'm greedy, and I still want more.

I dig my hands into his hair. I squeeze my thighs against his. I rock my hips to meet him.

Miles groans into my mouth. His fingers dig into my skin. He thrusts ever so slightly harder. Pleasure wells up in me again. It's faster this time, more intense.

He breaks the kiss. Stares into my eyes. Nervous energy passes through me. He's inside me. I'm about to come. But the way he's staring at me... I've got no clue what it means.

I stare back. I dig my nails into his shoulders.

Pleasure floods my body. I can't fight it anymore. I cry out as an orgasm spills through me, mixing up all the feelings inside me, so I'm half in ecstasy, half in hell.

He holds me tightly, thrusting into me with that same perfect rhythm. I hold his gaze, groaning as another orgasm builds.

He moans, still holding me tightly, still thrusting into

me. His pupils dilate. A shudder runs through his body. Almost. His teeth sink into his lip.

Still, he moves with that same rhythm, slow and steady. He shakes, harder, harder.

His eyes stay glued to mine. I watch his face contorting. His breath gets heavier. His groans get lower, louder. He squeezes my hips. There. His eyes roll back as he comes.

He rocks into me one last time, and he fills me.

It sends me over the edge again. For a few moments, everything else fades away. I only feel the pleasure coursing through my fingers and toes. I only feel good.

My resolve fades. I collapse my body onto his, trying hard to hold on to everything that feels good.

Miles relaxes into the seat. He squeezes me tighter, holds my body against his.

His heart is pounding against his chest, against my chest. His breath is in my hair. This means something, I'm sure of it. But I've got no clue what that something is.

## Chapter Forty-One

MEGARA

I wake up alone. No one is home. Dad is at work. No telling where Mom is. She's as uncomfortable in this house as I am.

There isn't a peep on my phone. No telling where Miles is either.

I eat breakfast with the TV. Even with two hundred channels, there's nothing that can tear my attention away from him. Wherever he is. Whatever he's doing.

I fix a cup of coffee. A second. A third. My mouth goes dry. My fingers shake. It's a lot of caffeine, but it's a nice enough buzz—probably the most pleasant thing I'll feel all day.

I still remember last Thanksgiving. Shit was already bad with Rosie. She was already pretending, already on drugs. But the four-day weekend was a perfect respite. It was the four of us, but really the two of us. We watched movies all night, plowing through the pumpkin pie, the pecan pie, the chocolate pie. There was a lot of pie. We spent the entire day shopping, emptying our checking accounts. And, for the first time since she started dating that awful Jared, it felt like she was my sister and not my enemy. It felt like we were being honest.

She was probably high the whole time.

I push off the couch and inspect the mantle. There are tiny dents in the plaster in all the spots that used to house Rosie's trophies. I was so jealous of those trophies. Rosie had everything—perfect grades, perfect friends, perfect boyfriend. She was athletic, smart, fun.

But with the drugs, she was nothing anymore. All those parts of her disappeared.

The backyard door slides open.

"Can I skip breakfast and have you instead?" He shuts the door. He stands in front of the sleek glass windows, shirtless and dripping with sweat. His eyes meet mine. "You okay?"

"No. I hate it here. I hate everything about this house."

"It will get better."

"How?"

He says nothing. Just moves closer. "You want to join me in the shower?"

I shake my head. I can't handle that right now.

"Talk to me, Meg. I'm here because I want to help you."

"Which is it—do you want to help me or do you want to be alone? Do you care about me or is this strictly sexual?"

His brow furrows. "Suit yourself."

He storms up the stairs and slams the door behind him.

I want so badly to join him. I want so badly to have my body pressed against his, nothing between us but the running water.

I want to be his plaything. But I need to be his everything.

## Chapter Forty-Two

MILES

She's right. I'm not being fair. I'm not playing by her rules.

I'm not listening to mine.

I try to wash those thoughts away, but they're not on my skin. They're somewhere deeper.

She stays in my head as I shower, change, send out the mandatory check-in texts. Apparently, Tom and Pete had yet another Thanksgiving fight. Happens every fucking year. It's excellent proof of the drummer's caustic attitude. He can engage blow up fights with even the most down-to-earth guy in existence.

Yeah, Tom claims it's some shit about how his mom is bringing over her girlfriend and she wants him out of the house. But I know that's bullshit.

Ophelia *would* warn Tom and Pete about loud sex she's about to have with her girlfriend. Or fuck buddy. She's not *really* the commitment type.

But it's not like Orange County lacks bars. Or women who he wants to fuck again. If he's back in Hollywood, it's because he's done for the weekend.

Which means another fight about Pete's girlfriend.

I want to blame Tom, but, once again, he's right. The girl's bad news. Not because there's something wrong with her. She seems like a perfectly reasonable person.

No, it's more that they just don't work as a couple. Maybe they did once. But not anymore.

Fuck, what am I doing thinking this shit? Couples don't work. Love doesn't work. It's more pain.

I don't care how wrong the words feel. They're true.

And Tom is an asshole. Regardless of how right he is.

I head downstairs. Try to pour my thoughts into lyrics. A verse comes. A snippet of a chorus. But it's not what I want to hear.

It's all wrong.

This is all wrong.

"Hey." Meg sits next to me. She's no longer frustrated. At least, she's no longer looking at me like she wants to slap me more than she wants to fuck me.

No, nor is it more like she wants to hold me more than she wants to slap me.

Which is probably worse.

I…

Fuck, I keep making excuses, but they're all bullshit. I know where this leads. I need to do it fast. Like a Band-Aid.

I turn to her. Look into her big, brown eyes. Try to find the right words.

They won't come. They'll never come.

I can't do it.

I can't hurt her.

Damon's voice echoes in my head. *If you run, you'll be running forever*. He's right. He's always right.

But then—

Maybe this is what he means. Maybe I'm holding my ground here. Maybe—

Fuck, my head hurts.

"You want to do something?" she asks.

My eyes flit to her chest for a second. Then they go right to her eyes. "Like?" I raise a brow, but I don't sell the flirtiness.

"It is Black Friday."

"So you want to go shopping?"

"We can see the koi."

Fuck, I remember the koi. Tom and I used to go to Fashion Island—the most expensive mall in the area, and that's saying something—and marvel at the excess. The place screams of money. The kind of money that's showy.

My mom was comfortable. But she wasn't like Damon. It wasn't like now. I couldn't blow five grand on a watch.

Now that I can, I don't give a fuck.

Back then it seemed like something that mattered. Like I'd be happier if I had a luxury car instead of a second-hand sedan. Like that would somehow fix my fucked-up life.

"Miles?" She rests her head on my shoulder. "Can we not fight?"

That's fair. "You eat breakfast?"

"Yeah."

"Coffee?"

She nods.

"So you won't be cranky."

She flips me off, but it's playful. Ish. "I'm going to the car."

"You're going to my car?"

"Yeah."

"What makes you think I'm coming?"

"If you don't want to come, don't come." She shrugs like she couldn't possibly care less about my presence, then she picks up her bag, slides into her shoes, and moves to the door.

And I must be as fucked up as it gets, because her apathy soothes the storm brewing in my gut.

---

We window shop for a while. Make small talk about the crowds, the designer brands, the way everyone in Orange County has that Orange County look.

Coiffed hair, designer purse, trendy shoes.

She stays close. It feels right. Like we're a normal couple, strolling the mall on a day dedicated to the excesses of capitalism.

It's a beautiful day. Classic California. The morning was grey and cloudy—we are close to the beach—but now the sky is a brilliant blue. High sixties and sunny. Comfortable. Easy.

Meg stops in front of a shop. It's something local, not a chain that spans the country.

She stares at a pink dress on display. I can't say I pay much attention to fashion, but fuck, that thing is short and low cut. I can already imagine her in it.

Out of it.

Half-out of it.

The two of us outside some club, me pressing her against the wall, fucking her senseless.

That's where we need to be. A place where I can give her everything she needs. A place where the entire world makes sense.

I pull her closer. This isn't the place. Or the time. I have to help her. It's what I promised. I just... Every time I try some other way of helping her, I make shit worse. "You're thinking something."

She steps forward, breaking our touch. "Nothing important. Just thinking that if my sister were here, she would've made me buy that dress."

"It would look good on you."

"No. I can't wear bright colors."

"Why not?" I wrap my arm around her waist. Pull her body into mine.

She purrs as my lips brush her neck. For a moment, she's mine, then she shakes it off. "I'll stand out."

"You stand out now. You're gorgeous."

"That's sweet of you to say, but it's not true. I'm too tall, too skinny, too flat-chested."

Does she actually mean that? Since when do women from Southern California feel insecure about being tall and thin?

Yeah, Meg isn't the curviest woman on the planet. But she is fucking gorgeous. And her tits are perfect. God, that sound she makes when I bite her nipple—

My voice drops. "One more negative word about your boobs, and I'm dragging you into that dressing room and forcing you to appreciate them."

"Oh."

I consider dragging her to the car. It's in the garage. Dark. But crowded. Someone will see. "Try on the dress."

"You want me to go shopping?" Her voice gets incredulous.

"I want to think about you naked in that tiny dressing room. Go." I press my palm into her lower back to lead her into the store.

She follows me. Goes to the rack with the dress.

I sit in the cozy chair in the middle of the room. A boyfriend chair. Or maybe a kid chair.

Mom used to sit me in them when she went shopping. But that was a long, long time ago.

Now—

Fuck, I can't remember the last time I was with someone in a women's clothing store. The guys and I have needed to pick up clothes, fast many times. Sometimes we're just out and there's no time for laundry. Sometimes we have a sudden need for formal wear.

Other times we're just fucking bored.

But this...

This is different. Something much more boyfriend. Something I really shouldn't—

"Oh my God." A salesgirl approaches me. She leans in, her voice a stage whisper. "Are you Miles Webb?"

"Depends on what you're about to say." I take off my sunglasses. No sense in hiding now.

She laughs. "You're so funny."

If she says so. I nod *thanks*.

"Oh my God, I loved that song so much. What was it called?" She hums the chorus on *In Pieces*.

I let her go on for a minute, then I nod, take her through the lyrics of the chorus.

Her eyes get bigger. Brighter. "Yeah. That one! It's so... real, you know? And that new song... *No Way in Hell*. Is it true it's about falling in love?"

I have a canned answer. It's practiced too. I shrug like I couldn't possibly tell her. "My lips are sealed."

Her eyes turn down. "Really?"

"Really." My gaze goes to the flash of pink by the dressing room. Meg's standing by the mirror, staring at me and the salesgirl. She must have heard everything, because what she's feeling is written all over her face.

Not. Discussing. That.

I nod goodbye to the salesgirl. Turn to Meg. "I'm

buying you that dress." Sending my thoughts to places that make sense.

"That's not necessary." Her frustration fades to shyness.

Fuck, I love when she's shy. Why is it so fucking sexy? "Already picked out some stuff to go under it." I motion to the table of lacy lingerie next to the boyfriend chair.

Meg flushes.

The salesgirl blushes even more. "Excuse me. I can ring you up. Would you like to wear it out?" She smiles, the picture of customer service.

I nod *hell yeah*.

Meg bites her lip. "Sure, yeah." She follows the salesgirl to the register.

I grab a set of lacy lingerie. It's the least I could do.

'Cause buying her underwear and a dress really makes up for the other shit I'm pulling.

I can't even convince myself of that.

Fuck. This is—

I'll figure it out when we get back to LA. I can't leave the girl alone with her parents. She'll implode.

Maybe I'm hurting her with this. But that will hurt her worse.

I swipe my credit card.

Meg takes the bag. Once we're outside the store, she turns to me. "Is it about falling in love?"

If I knew, I wouldn't have to write the song. I try to find my canned expression, but it won't come. So I settle on something close. "It's about whatever you want it to be about."

"That's not an answer."

"It's the only one you're going to get."

## Chapter Forty-Three

MILES

Thankfully, it's hard thinking anything besides *I need to fuck her* with Meg in that dress. The doubts in my head drift away. To a place just out of reach.

My shoulders relax. My stomach eases.

But my fucking heart? It still knows. I need to handle this. I need to stop hurting her.

"Can we leave tonight?" She tugs at my t-shirt in a way that screams *I need your distraction*. "I don't know what I'll say."

"I'll tell them."

"Thanks." She stops in front of the restaurant.

It's some place that charges a lot for small portions of healthy foods. Not that it's bad. It's pretty good, actually.

They even have a poke bowl. Though I know better than to suggest Meg order sashimi in sauce. She considers that sacrilege.

I pull her close. Tell myself I'm stepping into my role. That it's only because I'm stepping into my role.

By the time we're at her parents' table—the hostess

seems to recognize me, but she doesn't say anything about it—I believe it. I'm a doting boyfriend. For the next hour or so.

Meg's mom takes in her dress. There's something there. Something I don't quite see.

Her sister. Was she the type to wear bright colors? To do things at one hundred percent?

It's how she sounds when Meg describes her, but I have a hard time imaging the vivacious pre-med student. I have a hard time seeing anything but the empty eyes and the greasy hair and the desperate need for another fix.

She must have been really fucking high functioning to hide it for so long.

But, hey, I've been there, done that. People see what they want to see.

Like I—

Not going there yet. After this, sure. Right now, I have to hold on to my promise to help her survive the weekend.

"Your dress is lovely," her mom says. "New?"

"I'm afraid I insisted." I step in. Cut off the family conflict. Whatever the specifics are. Meg wants to remember her sister. I get that. But it's clear her mom isn't there yet. And I get that too. I also know, from experience, that they aren't going to find a way to compromise until they've worked through shit on their own. "It's stunning on her, isn't it?"

"Yes." Her mom forces a smile. "You do look beautiful."

"Thanks." Meg smooths her dress. She searches my eyes for something, but I'm not sure what it is.

I glance at the menu. At the moment, I really don't give a fuck about food. But I do need to eat something. And I need to make sure she eats. "I'm afraid Meg and I need to leave after this."

"Oh?" Her mom asks.

"I have a deadline."

"What do you do, son?" Her dad asks.

"I'm a songwriter." I add some detail to my usual answer. "Pop, mostly. The rules are strict, but I have fun with it."

"Anything I would know?" her dad asks.

I name a few recent hits. It seems to impress her mom. Which is kinda nice. I haven't impressed anyone in a long time.

Damon would be proud I made something of myself. Not so much the other shit, but that, yeah.

No one in the band really gives a shit about my dabbling in songwriting. If anything, they find it irritating. Shouldn't I be focusing all my attention on Sinful Serenade, not a side project that adds to my considerable wealth?

They have a point.

But they don't see things for what they are. They don't see that those are two different things. The pop music is fine, but it's a confection. I don't pour myself into it. That's why I need it.

I need the empty calories to fill the space in my head.

Maybe that's my issue. I'm not all that proud of those songs, either. Sure, they do well and they make people happy. But they don't make people feel anything.

They don't share any deeper meaning.

They don't take some ugly thing in my head and turn it into something beautiful.

They sure as fuck don't make me feel understood—

Not that my Sinful Serenade songs do much for that lately. No, there's only one thing that makes me feel understood lately, and she's sitting next to me.

But then maybe Tom is right and I have my head up

my ass and I'll always want more. Maybe Drew is right and I should focus more on kick-ass chord progressions and less on the emptiness in my heart. Maybe Pete is right and I know, deep down, that I won't ever feel acceptance from outside myself.

Fucker is too God damn perceptive.

At least Drew and I can agree on needing epic chord progressions.

Hell, at least Tom and I can agree on achieving more.

Or going out and fucking some pair of hotties.

At least, we used to.

Now...

I move the conversation to pop music. New stuff, at first, then older and older, until I find the genre that speaks to Meg's parents. Her mom lights up at my mention of new wave, but her dad stays far away.

We order. Eat. Drink—her parents order wine. I insist I'm declining because I'm driving. Meg gives me this *really* look but she doesn't say anything. She just sips her expensive green tea.

After we finish and linger over dessert and coffee (at least that cheers Meg up), I insist on paying, escort Meg to the car, drive home in silence.

It takes a few minutes to pack. I bring our stuff downstairs. Meg lingers in her sister's room. It's not her sister's room anymore. Just a room with a bed, a dresser, a window overlooking the tiny backyard.

I get it. Why her parents changed things. Why she hates it.

But she's too raw. Too hurt. Her heart is too full of pain. There's no room for extra compassion for her parents.

There's no room for my bullshit.

I know what this means. I do. I just—

## Just a Taste

The hurt in her eyes steals every thought in my brain. She moves down the stairs. Comes straight to me.

Stares at me like she's going to devour me.

Because she's hurt.

Because she wants me.

Because she wants me to make her feel something else.

I should say no, insist I won't be her distraction, but I don't want to.

I want to be her distraction.

I want to make her feel good.

If only for fifteen fucking minutes.

She rests her hand on my thigh. Leans in to bring her lips to mine.

I pull her into my lap. Into a slow, deep kiss.

Her hands go to my hair.

Mine go to her hips. She struggles to keep her balance —I am on the edge of the couch—so I move. Bring the two of us to the wall.

She groans as I pin her to it. "Fuck me. Please."

"Tell me it's because you want me."

"Miles—"

"And not because you're miserable."

Her eyes find mine. "I want you." Need drips into her voice. It mixes with the hurt. Then she pulls her dress to her waist and I stop seeing the hurt. "I want you inside me."

Just need.

Pure, deep need.

I let her down so she can do away with her panties. "What if your parents come home?" That's not going to make shit easier on either of us.

"They won't. They hate it here as much as I do."

Fuck, there's so much she's dealing with. So much I'm forcing her to deal with.

I ask myself one more time: is this the best thing for her?

The thought slips away as she reaches for my jeans. Again, the hurt in her eyes fades. Becomes pure need.

Maybe it isn't what's best for her long term. But it's what she needs right now.

And it's the only fucking thing I can offer her.

"Say it again." I press my lips to her neck. A soft scrape of my teeth. Then harder. Harder. Hard enough she yelps.

"I want you inside me."

Fuck. I push her dress aside. Then her bra.

She groans as I cup her breast. I should be patient. Take my time warming her up.

But I need her as much as she needs me.

I need her.

Period.

I rock my hips against hers. Take her hands and slide them around my neck. "Careful. I've never done this before." I shift my hips, pinning her harder.

"You say that to all the girls you pin against the wall?"

"No." I sink my teeth into her neck until she murmurs my name. "Only you."

Meg digs her fingers into my neck. She slides her other hand down my torso. Slips it under my t-shirt.

Her palm goes flat against my stomach. Then it goes, lower, lower—

She unzips my jeans. Cups me over my boxers.

Her eyelids flutter closed. "Fuck me." Her head falls back. Just barely. She's against the wall. She's pressed against me.

It feels so right.

Too right.

But then, this *is* what she needs. It's the first time she's looked at peace all fucking day.

## Just a Taste

I push my jeans and boxers off my hips.

She rocks against me.

She's already wet.

Already desperate for me.

Fuck, she feels good.

I shift my hips, teasing her. But it drives *me* out of my fucking mind.

I need to be inside her.

I need to feel her come on my cock

I need to hear her groan my name.

"Mmmm." She groans as I tease her again and again.

I bring my lips to hers as I slide inside her.

She groans against my mouth. Then her lips part. Her tongue slides into my mouth. Swirls around mine.

She kisses aggressively.

Like she's claiming everything I have to give her.

Right now, I feel like that's possible. Like I can give her everything she needs. Like I can be everything she needs.

I shift a little deeper.

She kisses me harder.

We rock together, both of us going deeper and harder, until her groans are vibrating down my throat.

She claws at my neck.

She's close.

I need her there.

I need to feel that.

I shift her hips, so her clit is rubbing against my pubic bone. I move a little slower to start.

Then faster.

Until my name rolls off her lips.

I move exactly how she needs me.

Her eyes flutter open. For a moment, she stares at me like I'm her everything.

For a moment, I want to be her everything.

I want her to be my everything.

Then her eyes close and mine follow and I drive into her.

Again and again.

Until she pulses against me.

Meg groans my name as she comes. I work her through her orgasm, then I pin her harder.

Move faster.

She tugs at my t-shirt. My hair. My back.

Her nails sink into my skin. Hard and harder. Until it hurts. But I love the way it hurts.

Like she's in so much bliss she can't help but claim me.

I rock into her again and again. Until she pulls back to groan my name.

She comes faster this time. Pulses harder.

It pulls me over the edge.

I rock through my orgasm. Groan her name as I come inside her.

Once I'm finished, I set her down. Help her into her dress.

She looks up at me with hazy eyes. Like she doesn't know where we stand.

I don't know what to tell her.

We're two broken people trying to fuck our pain away.

But we're more than that too.

We're something we're not supposed to be.

## Chapter Forty-Four

MILES

Meg asks me to stop at the cemetery. I let her guide me. Park in the lot.

Follow her along the grass.

It's dry. No recent sprinklers. I guess even cemeteries understand there's a constant state of drought in California.

It's not like especially green grass helps the dead.

They're gone.

They're not coming back.

It doesn't matter how many flowers we pile on a grave.

Nothing changes that.

Maybe I should be more sentimental—I have my moments, really—but I can't buy into this bullshit.

Yeah, I get it. I visit Damon sometimes. But I know he's not there. I know he's not anywhere.

That's why it's so fucking hard.

My shoulders tense. I try to shake it off. Fail. I can't let this be about me.

It's for her.

I'm here for her. Being what she needs.

I can do that for another two fucking hours.

She moves with steady steps. A few rows down, then a few more columns.

She stops in front of a simple headstone. Sits cross-legged.

"You want a minute?" I offer.

She shakes her head. "No. I like your company." Her smile is sad. "Even when you drive me out of my mind."

"Am I doing that now?"

She motions *a little* but she smiles. Just barely. "It's nice, having you here… knowing you know how it feels."

"Yeah."

"It hurts for such a long time. Then one day you wake up and it doesn't hurt quite as much, and you're not sure how you're supposed to deal with that." She looks up at me. "Do you know what I should do?"

"No." My voice is a whisper. I barely know what I should do. It's getting clearer, but I don't fucking like it.

"I wonder if anyone does." This time, her smile only lasts a second. It's not for me though. Her attention isn't for me right now.

It's for her sister.

She turns to the tombstone. Runs her fingers over her sister's name.

Tries so, so hard to feel some sign of life.

But there isn't any.

I know that as well as anyone.

It still hurts, when she doesn't find it. She still shrinks back, lips in a frown, eyes turned to the ground.

Her heart still breaks a little more.

I want to hold her.

I want to tear her clothes off and fuck her pain away.

I want to promise her it gets easier.

But I can't fucking lie to her. I really can't. As it is—

I've done enough to the poor girl.

She settles into her seat. Folds her hands in her lap.

Meg stares at the stone for a long time. Slowly, she speaks. "I'm sorry." She plucks a blade of grass. Traces its edges. "I wish I'd stopped running sooner. I should never have let you get away with lying to me. But I understand now, how it starts. It's one lie, one temptation. Then it snowballs into something you can't control." She drops the grass. Watches it flutter to the ground. "I'm sorry. I love you, and I miss you, and mostly, I forgive you."

I swallow hard.

It's not for me, but it's what I need to hear. It's what she needs to say.

Which means I—

Fuck, I don't like this. But this is way past what I like.

I sit next to her. Hold her close.

She melts into my arms, but it's not because it's me and her. It's because she needs someone, anyone, and I'm better than nothing.

When she's ready, I help her up, lead her to the car, open the door for her.

I need to do this gently.

If that's even possible.

I brush her hair behind her ear. Run my fingers down her neck. Over her collarbone.

Her eyes still flutter closed. Her lips still part with a soft murmur. Her head still falls to one side.

She still responds to me.

But now, I—

I have to stop being selfish. "Hey."

"Hey."

"Look at me."

She does.

"We still have those same terms—no lies?"

"Yeah."

I force the words from my lips. "I have to ask you something."

"Okay."

"Do you have feelings for me?"

## Chapter Forty-Five

MILES

Her eyes streak with confusion.

She sucks in a deep breath. Exhales slowly. "Frustration comes to mind."

"You know what I'm asking."

"You know enough about my feelings."

Probably. This isn't exactly fair to her.

"I know where we stand, Miles." Her voice stays calm. Even. "We're friends who have sex. That's all." She says it with conviction. Like she believes every fucking word.

I want to believe it too. To believe that this doesn't have to change.

But I don't.

I help her into the car. "We should go."

"What does that mean?" Her eyes bore into mine. They ask for an explanation. For comfort. For love.

I can only give her one of those things.

I study her expression, trying to find what she needs the most.

Fuck, is this right or am I listening to my cock?

I try to channel Damon. To hear his voice. But it's just that mantra again.

Be brave, live.

He's not here to explain. To tell me if living is fucking her all weekend or cutting her loose.

To tell me if I'm doing the right thing or hurting her worse.

He should have explained this shit better.

Fuck.

She reaches for me. Rests her hand on my thigh. It's part *fuck me*. Part *stay with me*. All *I need is you.*

I want to be the person she needs.

But that's like wanting Damon to still be alive.

It's impossible.

Wanting it doesn't change shit.

"I want to beat the traffic." I dodge the question. Turn on the car.

Thankfully, the radio is in the middle of a Foo Fighters song. Thank God for KROQ. It never changes.

Meg leans back in her seat. She plays with her dress. Pulls it up her legs—just barely.

I'm not sure she realizes it.

It's subconscious. Like her body knows how to convince mine.

That's what she wants.

And I—

I can give her that. "I'm falling behind on breaking my orgasm records."

Her shoulders relax. Her expression softens. "Are you trying to kill me?"

"Are you complaining?"

Her lips curl into a smile. "My place or yours?"

"Mine."

# Just a Taste

Habit takes me to our place in Hollywood. I don't know why. I'm usually in Malibu with Meg.

Yeah, it would be nice to fuck her on the couch here. And I've been thinking, hard, about laying her on one of those lounge chairs outside.

Or maybe against that kitchen table.

In the pool.

On the balcony.

Anywhere, really.

Of course, there's no luck today.

Tom's car is out front.

Fuck me. I need to pay more attention.

I help Meg inside. Cross my fingers, hoping Tom is upstairs with a chick.

Or downstairs with a chick.

Anywhere, really, as long as he's in party boy mode, not *I'm somehow the fucking parent in this band and I'm going to tell you what to do.*

He's not.

He's sitting on the couch, light from the TV dancing off his face. A zombie movie from the sound of it.

Doesn't that shit get old?

"Your fuck already kick you out?" I try to keep it light.

He doesn't bite. "Been here awhile."

"Why do you pick fights with your brother?"

"You're asking *me* why *I* pick fights?" Tom chuckles *okay, right.* "Hey, Meg."

"Hey." She forces a smile.

"You mind if I borrow Miles?" he asks.

"Later," I say.

"No. Now." He offers her an apologetic glance. "We

need a little privacy." Tom's voice gets serious. "It's important."

"Don't ask my guest to acquiesce to your bullshit," I say.

"You don't want to have this conversation in front of her," Tom says.

Shit. Why is he still going on about this?

It's my life.

Maybe I don't have it under control. But who the fuck does Tom think he is, trying to give me advice much less orders?

"Give me a minute." I bring my lips to Meg's ear. "I'll make it up to you. Promise."

She looks at me like she doesn't believe me, but she still nods an *okay*.

Tom motions to the stairs. Turns to Meg. "We have cable. Any channel you want. Even the dirty ones."

"I'm good, thanks." Her cheeks flush.

It's adorable. Reminds me this isn't a totally fucked scenario.

God, the thought of Meg watching porn on our couch—

That's gonna be interesting later.

I shrug, like this doesn't matter. Follow Tom to my room.

He opens the door for me. Motions *after you* like he's a parent who found a joint hiding in my shit.

Or more accurately, like he's the bandmate who's knows there's heroin in my suitcase and wants me to admit it.

Like facing it is going to change shit.

Get real.

"I thought we talked about this," Tom says.

"We did."

He stares at me, not accepting that answer. "You can't do this."

"Are you worried about me or her?"

"Seriously, asshole, get off your fucking high horse."

I shrug.

"Do you have any idea how much all of us worry about you."

"You worry about losing the face of the band."

"Yeah. And I worry about you. I guess I'm an idiot, 'cause some part of me actually gives a fuck. Jesus." He shakes his head, sending his sandy hair in every direction. "That makes one of us, I guess."

"Whatever lecture you have, can we get it over with?"

"Does she know?"

"Does she know what?"

"Your favorite ride at Disneyland." He shoots me a *get real*. "What the fuck do you think?"

"Space Mountain."

"Miles."

Whatever. "She knows what she needs to know." My voice is more defensive than usual. Yeah, Tom's bullshit is bullshit. But so is mine. It's not true. She doesn't know what she needs to know.

"So she knows you're a drug addict?"

"Fuck off."

He rolls his eyes. "Seriously, you're twenty-six. Stop acting like a teenager."

"Stop acting like my mom."

"You first." His laugh is more frustrated than anything. "You think I like this?"

"Yeah."

He rolls his eyes *whatever*.

"We're casual. She gets that."

"You spent Thanksgiving with her."

"So?"

"So either you're full of shit or you don't know what casual means." His eyes meet mine. "You really think you don't care about her?"

"It's just—"

"'Cause no one else believes that."

"What the fuck do you want, Tom? I've got shit under control. I haven't used. I haven't spun out. I haven't touched a bottle since—"

"I found you face down in an empty hotel room."

"That girl threatened to kill herself. That's a sensitive issue."

"And you were twenty fucking minutes away from an obituary. What if I'd been out a little later?"

"Whatever."

"Yeah, that solves it." He shakes his head *what the fuck am I going to do with you.* "You remember what happened last time you lost someone you cared about."

"That was my uncle. Not some girl."

"You really believe that?" he asks.

I'm not dignifying him with a response. Fucking asshole. Who does he think he is, on his high horse?

Like this is for me.

And not for his ego.

For his need to boss people around.

Get rich.

Stay famous.

Fuck him.

"You keep running off, spending weekends by yourself. Or with her. I don't fucking know." Tom's voice is heavy. "She deserves to know what she's dealing with."

"There's no dealing. I've been fine for the last fucking year."

"And Detroit?"

"Fuck you."

"Are you fucking blind? Even I see it. That girl is crazy about you. What happens when you fuck things up. What if she threatens to kill herself because she can't live without you?"

"She's not like that."

"Right."

"She doesn't even drink." It's a weak excuse. Flimsy as all hell. But fuck Tom.

He's an asshole.

He's not better than I am.

He's not doing this because he cares.

This is bullshit.

He's full of shit.

And I—

"Fuck you. Seriously." I push toward the door.

"You need to tell her you're a drug addict," he says.

"Fuck. You."

"I'm not watching you relapse, Miles. I'm not going to spend my nights wondering if you're in some hotel room choking on your own vomit. I'm not going on tour with you in that self-destructive bullshit state."

"Then don't."

Fuck him.

He can kiss my fucking ass.

I take another step toward the door.

But there's a sound in the hall. Footsteps. Moving away. Down the stairs.

Fuck.

I push him out of the way. Storm down the stairs.

After Meg.

She's already halfway to the door. "I'm leaving."

"Meg—"

"What? I'm 'some girl' and this is all casual. What does it matter to you if I leave?"

"Don't." I run after her, but I'm too slow.

She pulls the door open. "Fuck you." She slams the door behind her.

## Chapter Forty-Six

MILES

Thank fuck for this bike. I swerve around sedans and luxury cars. Drive way faster than the speed limit. Beat Meg home.

Where is she?

How is she getting home?

Fuck, I get that's she's pissed, but she can't do this. She needs to be safe.

I suck a breath through my teeth. Try to think of what I'm going to say. It's not like I can deny the truth.

I knew I needed to tell her. I tried to talk myself into it a thousand times.

It just—

It wasn't possible.

Now that the cat's out of the bag—

No, I'm full of shit. She's right.

Yeah, I couldn't tell her. I wasn't ready. But I knew what that meant. I knew I had to let her go.

I just… didn't.

My shoulders tense. My jaw cricks. I still don't know what to say. I still can't offer her what she needs.

What she deserves.

What if I could? If I could be that guy? Be her everything?

Fuck, I don't even know where to start.

The elevator dings. But it's not her. It's a handsy couple, making out on their way to the door. Or maybe they're strangers. That's the thing to do on a Holiday like today.

Forget your lack of family. Drown your sorrows. Fuck a stranger.

If it weren't for Meg, I'd be there. Fucking a woman I'd forget tomorrow.

Would I be sober?

I'd like to think so, but—

The randy couple disappears into their apartment. They don't notice me. Which is good. I'm as ostentatious as it gets.

A bad boyfriend or a crook.

An occasion to call the cops.

I pull out my cell. Send another frantic text.

*Miles: You don't have to forgive me. But tell me you're safe.*

It's not helping my case. It's not helping her. I'm playing boyfriend again.

Breaking my promise to her.

Breaking my promise to myself.

She shouldn't give me the time of day. She should throw me out of her fucking building. She should tell me to fuck off.

We both know that.

I can't play fair here. I just can't.

I slide my cell into my back pocket. Leave it for as long as humanly possible—probably thirty seconds. Check again.

Still nothing.

## Just a Taste

I go like that forever.

Until the door to the staircase swings open and Meg steps into the hallway.

Her eyes go straight to me.

To mine.

Fuck, she looks so hurt. I did that.

I broke her heart.

Where do I get off, standing here, asking her to consider offering it to me again?

Is that what I'm asking?

I don't fucking know. I don't know how the hell this works. Or what I say.

Only that I have to make this right.

Somehow.

She moves closer. Stays a few feet away. "Get out of my way."

I step in front of the door. "I'm going to explain."

"Fuck off." She turns, pressing her shoulder into my chest as she slides her key into the door.

I stop her from turning the knob. "Listen."

"No."

I should let her go. It's the decent thing to do. But I don't. I hold her in place.

Run my thumb over space between her thumb and forefinger.

Her eyelids flutter closed. For a second, her desire takes over. Then she blinks and her expression is back to white-hot rage.

"I'm not leaving until I explain." I make my touch softer. So soft she lets out a low murmur. "You can slam the door in my face or tell me to fuck off. But I am going to stay here until I explain. And we both know the walls are thin."

She almost smiles. Snaps back into frustration. "Miles—"

"Here." I release her. Turn the key. Push the door open. Step inside.

She stares at me, dumbstruck. "That's my apartment."

"Are you coming in?"

"What if I don't?"

"I'll have to chase you wherever you go."

Her brow furrows. Then just barely softens. "That sounds annoying."

I motion *come inside*. Take another step backward. "You could save yourself some time here."

She shakes her head. Stares *what the hell is wrong with you*. "If I ask you to leave, you will."

I'll make her ask a few times, but I will. She knows I respect her.

Or maybe she doesn't.

Fuck, I don't know what I'd think if I were her. Only that it's not good.

She steps inside.

I press the door closed behind her.

She shrinks against it. Looks up at me like she's not sure if she wants to slap me or tear my clothes off.

Both maybe.

"You want to sit down?" I ask.

"You're pinning me to the wall." Her eyelids flutter closed. For a second, her expression is pure need. Then I step backward, and her eyes fill with that same anger.

I take a seat on her bed.

She moves around me. To her desk. "Make this good. I have to study."

Fuck. It's harder to think with her here, not easier. "I was afraid this would happen."

"That lying would blow up in your face? How did you think of that one?"

"That you'd overreact to my recovery."

"Fuck you."

I'm not making this better. I need to make this better. But I can't lie to her again either.

This needs to be the entire truth.

No matter how much it hurts.

"I almost told you that night in Malibu." I don't have a good excuse. "But you were so hurt. I couldn't add to that."

Her eyes shift to the window behind me. "You didn't tell me because you wanted to fuck me."

"I could have fucked you right there, in my car. You were begging me."

"Okay, because you wanted to keep fucking me. Same difference."

That's not fair and she knows it. "Meg—"

"No lies, no secrets. That was our deal." Her voice breaks. "But you still kept this a secret."

"I didn't want to upset you."

"Bullshit."

I swallow hard.

She tugs at her jeans. "You don't even respect me enough to admit you lied."

"It's not like that."

"Then look me in the eyes and apologize for keeping this from me."

"You would've ended things."

"That's not an apology." Her eyes flare with hurt. She turns away. Turns her entire body away from mine. "You should go."

"Meg—"

"You don't trust me. I don't trust you." Her voice

wavers, but she presses on. "What the hell are we doing this for?"

I try to find her gaze. "I couldn't tell you. It still hurt too much."

"I'm sorry, Miles, but you were so clear yesterday. Today, too. I'm 'some girl' to you. And you want to deal with everything alone. Where the hell is there room for me in that?"

She's right.

I don't know how to change things.

No, it's worse. I'm not capable.

It's so clear. I'm fucking this up worse. Hurting her worse.

All the honesty I'm offering—

It's too little, too late.

Everything I have to offer her is too little.

"I guess you're right." I stand. Run my hand through my hair. Try to find some way to ease the unease in my gut. "We should have ended this earlier. Now, feelings are getting involved."

"Excuse you?"

"Tom was right. The way you're looking at me—"

"Fuck off." Her eyes bore into mine. "Feelings are getting involved? Feelings have been involved. What the hell do you call holding me all night? Or promising I can tell you anything? You met my parents. You promised you cared about me. You stared into my eyes and kissed me like you loved me. What the hell do you call that?"

"I didn't mean to lead you on."

"Yes, you did," she says. "You get off on me caring about you."

"Meg."

"Do you love me?"

I don't know. A month ago, I would have said *fuck no*.

Six months ago, I would have said *that's not possible*. Right now? What the fuck is love, anyway? "I told you when this started—I don't do relationships."

"No, you just treat me like your girlfriend and act like my boyfriend and expect me to know the fucking difference!"

"Meg—"

"It doesn't matter. You don't respect me. You throw away my feelings. You lie right to my face. You're nothing to me."

My stomach drops.

"I'm not putting up with it anymore. Go. Away. Now."

"Is that really what you want?"

She holds my gaze for a moment, then she lets out a choppy breath. Nods. "Yes." Her voice is heavy with a mix of hurt and anger.

I try to find the need in her eyes, but there's nothing but anger.

So I nod. "Fine."

I leave.

I think about her the entire drive home.

I stare at my cell all night, waiting for her to change her mind.

She doesn't.

## Chapter Forty-Seven

MILES

"Are you ever leaving your room?" Tom taps the thin door. Of course, he doesn't add *I know I contributed to this mess and I'm sorry*. No, it's pure *I know better*.

I want to be pissed at Tom.

I want to blame him for all this.

I want to scream *fuck you, asshole*.

But this isn't his fault. It's mine.

Hell, he did what I couldn't. He told Meg what she needed to know.

And she did need to know. I get that. I get how everything wasn't fair to her. How I've been a fucking asshole.

I just don't get how to fix it.

"Really?" Pete chuckles. I guess he's in the hall with his brother. "Even for you, Tom."

"What?" Tom's voice gets indignant.

"You should see his face," Pete says to me. "Might be worth opening the door."

"Dunno. You gonna punch him," I say.

"Some of us need our hands," he says.

353

"Fuck, you better be talking about the bass." Tom's shudder of disgust is in his voice.

I'm not sure why he doesn't want to hear about his brother's sex life. It's not like they're blood relatives.

Besides, I've heard rumors about the two of them sharing.

Not that I believe the rumors. Pete will watch, yeah. He'd participate too—even if he claims he wouldn't, and he does.

But it would be more as a… visitor.

He's not the sharing type.

Not that Tom is. If I hadn't—

Fuck, I need to burn that image from my brain.

"I'm actually proud of you," Pete says to his brother. "For respecting his privacy."

"He's still in there?" Drew joins the fray.

"Is this a fucking band meeting?" I ask.

Drew raps on the door. "You're gonna want to see this."

"Did *you* hit Tom?" I ask.

"Better," he says.

"Hey!" Tom whines.

"What could be better than that?" Fine. I will open the door. But not because of shit Tom said.

Tom can kiss my ass.

Even if this is my fault. And I'm mad at myself.

He's still a dickhead.

Said dickhead shoots me a look of pity. "When's the last time you took a shower?"

Drew nods *it's not good*. He holds up his cell. "You're gonna want to hustle."

"What?" I ask.

He motions *look at the fucking screen*.

It's a text from Kara.

She and Meg are heading to a club in Hollywood.

*Kara: I'm not saying you should come with Miles. But I'm not saying you shouldn't come with Miles.*

*Kara: This message never happened.*

"Yeah?" I play cool. "You gonna go? Make sure someone else doesn't come on her tits?"

Drew doesn't bait. At all. He just chuckles. "Take a fucking shower and get dressed. I'm leaving in ten minutes."

"Told you," Tom says.

"Seriously." Pete steps back. "If he hits you, it's on you."

Tom looks at me like he's daring me. "If you'd rather hit me than figure some shit out."

I think the guy lives to drive me insane. That, or I'm more pitiful than I feel. 'Cause sometime yesterday, he changed his tune. Came to me with some bullshit about how *maybe, it's actually best if I make things up with her. 'Cause I really am a miserable asshole sober. Sober and without Meg... no one wants that.*

"She does deserve better," Tom says. "So... If you want to throw down." He mimes pushing up his sleeves.

Pete chuckles.

Drew too. "Seriously, Miles." He slides his cell into his back pocket. "Ten minutes."

"Yeah."

Drew shoots me a look that means *this is real business*. "And don't fuck it up or I'll be the one hitting you."

## Chapter Forty-Eight

MEGARA

Miles and I are over. Period. End of sentence.

I shouldn't be thinking about him.

I let Kara drag me to this club—she convinced me somewhere between "it will be fun, promise" and "it really would make him jealous, even though that's not worth a damn. Living well is the best revenge"—and now I'm here. In a tight dress, teetering heels, enough makeup to make Rosie proud.

And, hey, maybe Kara is right. It's not like ignoring the radio and trying to bury myself in school has helped.

My brain still goes to him.

It's bullshit. He doesn't deserve space in my brain. Not anymore.

I'm here. Having fun. Channeling Rosie.

This place is her scene. Packed.

There must be two hundred people on the dance floor. It's some mix of tourists and locals, celebrities and ordinary people, the barely legal and the pushing forty.

The crowd has one thing in common—amazing style.

The guys are in suits. The women are in tight cocktail dresses and shiny heels.

Kara locks arms with me. "Let's start with a drink. If you want."

My shoulders tense. I roll them back, but it does nothing to relax them. Deep breath. I'm twenty-one. Drinking is normal. Fun. Maybe the only way I'll actually allow myself to dance with a stranger. "Yeah. I do."

"You sure?"

"Positive."

Kara leans over the bar, squeezing her arms together to highlight her cleavage. The bartender notices instantly.

"What are you drinking?" He stares at her chest.

"A Paloma for my friend. Actually, two Palomas." She turns to me. "It's like a grapefruit margarita. You'll adore it."

My heart flutters. "Okay."

I scan the room. There's a VIP area in one corner. I can just make out a few famous faces—a singer known for her outlandish costumes and the stars of this awful teen soap I totally never, ever watched.

"Here you go, ladies." The bartender offers up our drinks.

Kara pays and she drags me to a velvet booth. It's plush and soft and there's a curtain in front. I pull the curtain closed, and suddenly we're hidden from view. It goes to just past our knees and it blocks out the rest of the club.

They're sex curtains.

Kara pulls the curtain wide open. "Don't get any ideas." She sips her frothy pink drink. "Shit, you really are going to love this."

I take a sip. It's amazing—tart and sweet with the faint

taste of alcohol. My face flushes. I already feel more relaxed.

"I want fifty of these," I say.

"Going from zero to drunk pretty fast there." She slides her arm around my shoulder. "But I get it. You don't want to think about that asshole, but not all your brain cells are cooperating."

"They can either assimilate or be destroyed."

Kara laughs. "I missed this Meg."

"Me too."

She downs half her drink. She looks at me like she's reading a gauge. "I see a few hot guys, and they look lonely. Want to fix that?"

I polish off my drink, stand, and smooth my dress. "Well, we can't have lonely, hot guys."

We move to the dance floor.

There's barely any wiggle room. I've never been a big dancer, but there's something intoxicating about the thumping music and the soft blue-purple lighting. I throw my arms over my head and sway my hips in time with the beat.

Kara laughs. She drags me farther into the fray. We dance like we're the only two people here. I look around the club. It's built just like the place where Sinful Serenade had their secret show, only with a smaller stage and more room to sit.

The music fades into the next song. I circle my hips and roll my shoulders. Usually, I feel so insecure about my dancing. But tonight, anything goes.

A cute guy comes up to me. He's wearing a grey suit, and he's a little stiff. A total Business Guy. He motions as if to ask me to dance. I look back to Kara. She mouths *go for it*. So I do.

I press my back against his chest. He grabs my hips,

holding my body against his. I close my eyes, trying to inhale the sensation, but there's nothing there. It doesn't hold a candle to Miles.

I turn around so I'm facing Business Guy. He's cute. Nice eyes, clean haircut. I slide my arms around his shoulders. He moves his hands to my waist.

He really is handsome. And he smells good. His body is hard. Not his cock—I'm not that close—but his arms and his chest.

He's safe, comfortable. I'm not going to fall in love with him. It could be one easy night.

He leans closer, his mouth a few inches below my ear. He's quite a bit shorter than I am, and I'm wearing three-inch heels.

"Can I buy you a drink?" he asks.

"Yeah." I wave goodbye to Kara—she's already dancing with a jock—and follow Business Guy to the bar.

He slides his hand around my waist and over my hip. It's a little much so soon, but there's something nice about his touch. Not electrifying. Just nice.

"I'm Johnathan," he says.

"Meg."

"What are you drinking, Meg?"

"Paloma."

He signals the bartender and orders our drinks. Whiskey on the rocks for him. Paloma for me. Figures I'm drinking something girly and pink.

I take another look at Business Guy. Johnathan. He is cute. And he seems nice enough. He probably owns his own house. Not a mansion in Malibu, but a modest house somewhere nice. He'd probably take me to breakfast in the morning then never call me again.

The bartender arrives. Drinks are ready. Johnathan hands the pink one to me and raises his glass to toast.

## Just a Taste

Whatever. I'll toast. To all the lonely people in the club.

He scans my body. It's sexy when Miles looks me over, but this is awkward. I pull my arm over my chest. I don't want Johnathan picturing me naked.

"Do you go to school around here?" he asks.

"UCLA."

"Let me guess your major."

Oh, lord. I take a long sip of my drink and nod politely. He bought me this amazing grapefruit concoction. I'll entertain his guessing game.

"Sure," I say.

He scratches his chin. "There's something intellectual about you."

Yeah, I look really intellectual in this tight silver dress. Does he use this line on every girl he meets, or just the ones who strike him as gullible?

I take another sip. It's perfection. I guess I can entertain him for another thirty seconds. "Is there?"

"Yeah... I can see you curled up in bed with a good book."

"What kind of book?"

He smiles. "History."

My drink is empty, but the good news is that my head is spinning. There's something amusing about Johnathan. It's been a while since I've been tipsy, but I'm sure it's the alcohol talking.

"Excuse me." A familiar voice cuts through the room.

Miles.

## Chapter Forty-Nine

MEGARA

Miles steps in between me and Business Guy.

What the hell does he think he's doing here?

"You mind, buddy?" Johnathan says.

"I do, actually." Miles plants his hand on my hip. "Since when do you drink?"

"Since tonight." I swat him away like my body isn't humming from his touch. "I'm having a conversation."

"You don't seem interested," Miles says.

"None of your business what I seem anymore. Excuse me." I step away from Miles and lean over the bar the same way Kara did. "Another Paloma please!"

"How many have you had?" Miles asks.

"Oh, let me check. Hmmm. That's also not your business."

"I'm talking to the lady," Johnathan says.

Miles turns and glares like he's going to deck Johnathan right in the mouth. It works.

Johnathan steps back. He mutters something under his breath and disappears into the crowd.

Miles brings his attention back to me. "What the hell are you doing?"

"You're the one who followed me here. What, did Kara rat me out to you?"

"Drew."

"Asshole acted like he could keep a secret." I shake my head. "Did he at least tell you to apologize?"

Miles nods. "Threatened to break my jaw if I broke your heart."

"I knew there was something I liked about him."

Miles reaches for my hand.

I take a step back. "Last time I checked, we're nothing. So what the hell are you doing following me to clubs?"

"I wanted to see you."

"To what—screw with me one last time? Leave me alone."

He leans closer, until his chest is pressed against my back. "I can't."

"Sure you can. It's called self-control. You made yourself clear a hundred times. You don't do boyfriend. You don't fall in love. Hell, you want to be alone. You don't have any right to scare that guy off."

"You'd rather he be the one pressed against you?"

I bite my tongue. "Doesn't matter. We're nothing."

His mouth hovers over my ear. "I miss you."

"You miss fucking me."

"No, I miss you." He digs his fingers into my hips and pulls my body closer. "Let's talk somewhere private."

"You want to talk now that you can't have me." I press my palms against the hard muscles of his chest. I mean to push him away, but my hands like his chest so much they linger there. "You had a million chances to talk. I'm not interested in talking to you anymore."

"But you'd fuck me."

I stare into Miles's eyes. As usual, he's unflinching. Staring through me like he's untouchable.

Heat surges inside me. I'd certainly like to fuck him. His body already feels so damn good.

"Yes," I say. "Right here."

"Are you drunk?"

"Not yet."

Right on cue, the bartender drops off my drink. Miles pulls a twenty from his wallet, slams it on the bar, and waves the bartender away.

I grab my drink and make a move for the booths. Miles follows, but I ignore him.

I take a seat and wrap my lips around the straw. It's just as sweet and tart as my first drink, but this time I'm more desperate for the release from my inhibitions. There's this nasty bit of politeness in my brain keeping me from telling Miles exactly what an asshole he is.

Miles sits next to me. He's wearing converse, jeans, and a t-shirt. Even his clothes are cool and casual.

I down half my drink. "Can I help you somehow?"

"I should have told you about my recovery."

"Hmm, so close to an apology, yet something is missing."

His eyes find mine. "I'm sorry I kept that from you."

I finish my drink and slam it on the table. "Thank you. But that's not enough."

"Meg." His voice is low, desperate. He pulls the curtain closed so we're hidden from view.

"You're playing a game, but nothing has changed. You don't respect me. You don't love me. You don't trust me."

He pushes a stray hair behind my ear. "I respect you."

"And the other two?"

"I don't know." He traces the outline of my collarbone. "I've never done the other two before."

His fingertips skim the neckline of my dress. My body buzzes with want. He feels so much better than Business Guy. He feels so much better than anything.

"Let me take you somewhere quiet," he whispers.

I squeeze my thighs together. "I don't want to talk."

He pulls my dress aside and slips his hand into my bra. "I do."

I bite my lip. "I'd believe you if you weren't feeling me up."

He rubs my nipple. "Is this really all you want from me?"

His eyes meet mine. There's a desperation in his expression. He means this. He wants more from me, more than sex.

But I'm not so sure.

His hand works its magic on my breast. Damn, he's good at this. Want builds in my core.

I need Miles. Now.

His eyes light up. He knows he's driving me out of my fucking mind.

"Will someone see?" I ask.

"No." He rubs me with his thumb. "Would you care if they did?"

Right now, I don't care about anything but him touching me. I only barely manage to shake my head.

Miles leans closer. "Answer me. Please. Is this really all you want from me?"

His lips are inches from mine. I close my eyes and kiss him. He's soft and warm, and he tastes like Miles. Like going home.

"No," I breathe. "But I'm never going to get what I want from you."

"What makes you so sure?"

I copy his words, the ones he used to explain why he was so sure he'd never fall in love. "I just know."

He drags his thumb over my nipple, sending pangs of lust to ever corner of my body.

My breath hitches in my throat. "There must be two hundred people here."

"I know." He drags his fingertips over my thighs. "But I still want to hear you come."

"Miles." A groan escapes my lips.

"That's a start." He unhooks my bra.

Then his hands are on my panties. He doesn't waste any time. He pulls them to my knees and runs his fingertips over my clit.

I bite my lip to keep from screaming. God, I missed this. I missed him. I missed everything.

I press my lips into Miles's. He kisses back hard like he's claiming me as his. My head is swimming. This is wrong, this is dangerous, but this is so fucking good.

He pulls me onto his lap. I plant my knees on the bench, straddling him.

I sink into his body. He's hard. I need that.

With the curtain closed, we're out of view. Still, it feels naughty and dangerous, undressing in public.

It's exciting.

All those awful you shouldn't do this thoughts swirl around my brain, but in my inebriated state, they simply fly away. This is far from my best idea. Someone might see. Miles might think I forgive him. That this means I'm his.

I still don't know if I can be his for the long haul. But for tonight, it's perfect.

His touch is gentle as he strokes me. I kiss him hard, digging my nails into his shoulders.

The noise around us fades. I'm on top of the fucking world.

This is easy.

Life is easy.

Being with him is easy.

My body fills with pleasure. It spreads from my core all the way to my fingers and toes.

He strokes me with an even rhythm. Again, and again, and again. An orgasm wells up inside me. It's so tight, so tense, so fucking amazing.

I bring my mouth to his ear and moan his name again and again. A wave of pleasure washes over me. Every bit of tension in my body releases.

It feels so fucking good.

He kisses me. I sink into him, my chest against him, my thighs against his. I can still feel him—hard through his jeans.

I grind my crotch against his. "Please."

His eyes are heavy with desire. "I fucking missed you." He tugs at my dress, exposing my breasts. He flings my bra aside. "I've been going out of my mind thinking about you."

"Like this?"

He pulls my dress lower. "Like everything." He grabs my hips and lifts me. "This is going to be quicker than I'd like."

"I don't care." I shift closer to him. "As long as you're inside me."

"Mm-hmm." He unzips his jeans, shoves his boxers aside, and wraps his hand around his cock.

Yes, please. I shift my hips so I'm hovering over him. He grabs me, bringing me down hard.

I gasp as Miles enters me. It's like coming home, like I'm exactly where I need to be. I grab his shoulders and shift over him, pushing him deeper.

He sinks his nails into my ass, guiding me. His eyes find

mine. He's staring at me, through me. Before, it was too much. But it feels right. I see him, everything inside him. He's not honest yet, not mine yet, but maybe we can get there.

He presses his palm against my back, bringing my breasts to his mouth. His lips close around my nipple.

Pleasure floods my body. He's so much better than I remembered. He's perfect.

He sucks on me as he fucks me. I squeeze my thighs, pressing my hands against his shoulders for leverage. My body screams. I never want this to end. Never.

I dig my hands into his hair, holding him close. Everything else about this relationship is a mess, but this is perfect.

Here, we're perfect.

I groan, arching my back to push him deeper. My heart thuds. My breath is strained. Pleasure wells up inside me again. It's so tense, so tight, so much.

Miles sinks his teeth into my nipple, a tiny hint of pain. Then his eyes are on mine. He's looking at me like he loves me. I almost believe him.

I arch until he's deeper, until he's as deep as he'll go. One more thrust, one more tug at the knot inside me, and an orgasm washes over me. It's harder, more intense, and it takes everything I have to resist screaming his name.

Miles claws at my back. He holds my body against his as he thrusts into me.

He lets out a heavy moan.

He groans and shakes and scrapes his nails against my skin.

He's about to come. I can feel it in his body, hear it in his voice. Pressure wells up in me again. I'm making him come. I'm bringing him all this pleasure.

"Mm-hmm."

He holds me against him as he fucks me. It's hard and fast. I have to squeeze his shoulders to stay upright.

Then he's there. His cock pulses, filling me.

He collapses, sinking into the bench seat.

His eyes find mine. His lips part like he's going to speak, but he says nothing.

I shift off him, find my underwear, and pull it on. There's no way to clean up. This will have to do.

There's no sign of my bra. Oh well. It was nothing special.

He reaches for my wrist. "Come home with me."

"That's not a good idea."

"Then tell me what this was."

"I don't know." I find my purse and slide it over my shoulder. "But I enjoyed it."

"Go somewhere with me."

My heart flutters. "Where?"

"It's a surprise." He runs his fingertips over my wrist. "I'll fuck you there. If you're still in the mood."

"That's not a good idea, either."

He stares right into my eyes. "There has to be some way I can convince you."

That look cuts straight to my soul. No matter what I do, I can't fight it. I still want to take all his pain away.

I swallow hard. "Okay. I'll go."

## Chapter Fifty

MILES

Meg wraps her arms around her chest. She rubs her triceps as she shivers.

She's wearing nothing—that sexy as sin scrap of a silver dress and fuck me heels. Of course, she's freezing.

I slide my leather jacket off my shoulders and drape it around hers. "I guess your buzz is wearing off."

Her nod is apprehensive. She isn't taking it as a joke. She isn't taking it at all.

But she's here with me.

She got what she wanted and she's still here with me.

Even without the jacket, I'm burning up. My stomach is in knots. My limbs are light as feathers.

She has all the cards.

She has the power to tear me in half.

And, this time, I'm pretty sure she realizes it.

I press my palm against her lower back to lead her across the grass. She takes cautious steps. Stops to dig her heels from the mud.

Then she doesn't. She nearly trips over her shoes.

But I catch her in time.

It feels good. Holding her. Saving her. Keeping her close.

She looks up at me with curiosity. She wants to know why we're at a cemetery across the street from a mall.

I'm going to explain the best I can.

I just hope that's good enough.

I hope I'm good enough.

I kneel between her legs. Slowly, I unhook her right shoe and peel it off her foot. Then the left.

She lets out a soft murmur as my fingers trail over her ankles, but she keeps her eyes on the dark sky.

I look up at her. Try to find her gaze. "You okay?"

Her lips press together. Slowly, she nods. "Not really dressed for mourning."

"I disagree." I push myself up. Hold her shoes with one hand. Hold her with the other. "You're celebrating life." Damon would love her shiny dress. He'd love that we came here after fucking in a club. He'd love her, period. "You know that tattoo on my chest?"

"I'd love to be reminded." Her voice lifts to a bouncy tone. She's teasing me. She still likes me enough for that.

I can do this.

I pull my t-shirt down my chest to show off my ink.

*Be brave, live.*

Fuck. It's been a long time since I've needed to be this brave. It's harder than I remembered.

"I always thought it was a little new age for you," she says.

I can't help but laugh. She really does have me pegged. "It's a recovery thing. A reminder to experience life instead of trying to numb myself to anything that might hurt."

She stares back at me, those brown eyes full of confusion and hurt.

## Just a Taste

I did that to her.

I tore her heart out.

I have to put it back together. Even if it means backing off.

I run my fingertips over her cheeks, down to her chin, and tilt her head toward me.

It brings us eye to eye.

Some of that hurt softens.

She wants more from me.

She wants to trust me.

I want to be worthy of that trust. Whatever it takes. "I know you hate when people are cryptic."

"Accurate."

"But give me a minute." I need to do this there.

I press my palm into her lower back and lead her to the spot.

There. The plain grey tombstone is the same as it was before. *Damon Webb. Father, Uncle, Friend.*

"He adopted me legally after my mom died. I took his name instead of my dad's." I set her shoes on the grass so I can hold her hands with both of mine. "The quote. It's cheesy. But it was something my uncle always said when I started causing trouble. He saw right through my bullshit. When I got suspended for getting into a fight, he'd sit me down on that leather couch and toss a bag of frozen peas in my hands. Then he'd kneel next to me, stare into my eyes, and he'd tell me that if I wanted to run, I'd be running forever."

"Yeah?"

"Yeah, he was a smart guy. Self-made fortune, knew all the business stuff that bored me to tears. He knew how I felt losing my mom, especially to suicide. It hurt him too. He was angry too. But I got into fights every week. I got suspended fifteen times. I broke all my guitars."

She stares back, attentive, curious.

I squeeze her hands. "After my twentieth fight, we made a deal. He'd buy me one more guitar if I agreed to be brave and confront how much it hurt to lose my mom. I could wail on that guitar all day. I could scream my lungs out, write a song that was nothing but 'Fuck Simon.' That was my father's name. But if I got in trouble, even one more time, that was it. I was going to boarding school."

"And?"

"And that was it. I wrote a song about it. I felt a little better. Every time I wanted to hit someone, I wrote a song instead."

"How did you start doing drugs?"

"It wasn't a problem at first. At least I didn't think it was. I liked the way it relaxed me. Made me calm. Made me feel like I didn't have to take on the world. But it became a habit. Tom confronted me. I slowed down enough that I could hide it. But when Damon got cancer… I freaked. Ran from it. I couldn't go five minutes sober. Couldn't deal with those thoughts." I rub her shoulders. Force myself to push through this. I've never told this to anyone who mattered. It's terrifying, laying my heart bare, but I want her to know. I want her to know all of me. "That's how I know you're strong, Meg. You confront your pain headfirst. You never come close to buckling."

"I can't say that anyone has ever complimented me for not doing drugs before." She laughs.

It warms me everywhere. "I really do love your laugh."

"I love yours too."

I wish I could linger on that. I wish we could stand here laughing all night. But I need to get the truth out. Every ugly inch of it. "I only stopped because Tom threatened to kick me out of the band, and I didn't want my uncle to die thinking I was that same stupid kid who kept running away." My voice drops to a whisper. "I was in rehab when he died. That was the part that hurt the most, that he was alone because I was stewing in self-pity."

"But you weren't stewing anymore. You were confronting it head-on."

"Yeah. Maybe." I slide my hand through my hair. "I'm sorry I didn't tell you about my recovery. At first, I didn't think this would be serious enough it would matter. By the time I realized how much you hurt, how much you've been through… I told myself I couldn't hurt you more. And that was true. But it was bullshit too. I was scared. Scared I'd lose you if I told you."

She hugs herself a little tighter. "Okay."

"It's not a good excuse. I was wrong. And I really am sorry."

"Thank you."

"I like you, Meg. I really do. And I'm pretty sure you like me too." If I could offer her more, I would. But I still don't understand that four-letter word.

"I do, but—"

"No but." I pull her closer. Try my best to soak up every inch of her. "That's all we need to know." She feels good. Like she's everything I need.

And she's holding me like I'm everything she needs.

But it must not be enough, because she's breaking our touch.

She takes a step backward. "I'm sorry. I understand why you lied, but I'm not sure I'm ready to trust you yet. I want to. But I'm not there right now."

"Could you get there?"

"I don't know. But, Miles, I want to be with someone who loves me, who wants to share himself with me because he loves me. Not because it's the only card he has left to play."

That's fair. "I can do that."

"Maybe. But I... I'll believe it when I see it." She pulls the jacket tighter. "Can you take me home?"

"Yeah." I suck a breath through my teeth. Press my palm into her lower back to push her forward. "I really am sorry."

"Me too."

---

I drop her off, bring her suitcase up to her apartment door.

She stares back at me like she's not sure what she should do with me.

Like she doesn't know what I want.

I can offer that. "I'd like to come in." I want to linger in her bed all night. I want to hold her close. To promise her I can fix this.

"I'm not up for... that right now." She plays with her key. "Finals start Monday. I've got to turn everything off so I can study."

"When are you done?"

"The twelfth."

"I'll see you on the twelfth."

I pull her close and press my lips to hers.

It feels right, kissing her. Soft. Sweet. Intimate.

For once, I want that. I want to see everything in her heart and share everything in mine.

I can't do anything about the former.

But the latter...

I can make that happen.

Hell, there's only one way I can make that happen.

And I've only got a week to do it.

## Chapter Fifty-One

MEGARA

Finals fly by in a sticky mess of anxiety. After our last test, Kara and I crash on her couch and take turns picking movies to marathon. Sometime around midnight, I turn my phone on.

It's been a week since I've seen anything but my school email.

The screen flashes on. Those little bars appear next to the connection icon. Notifications pop up—a dozen mixed text messages and one voicemail.

I check the texts. Mostly little things—one from my mom about vacation, one from Kara, a bunch from the people in my study group.

The voicemail is from Miles.

Kara can read the look on my face. "Put it on speaker?"

"Okay." I'm going to need someone to talk me down.

I tap the play button. There's a burst of static, then it's Miles.

"Hey, Meg. I know you asked me, well screamed at me as you were rushing out of the house, not to write any more songs about you. But I couldn't abide by those terms. This might not make it on the album, but the single is going live Tuesday. It will be everywhere. This is the acoustic version. Drew would cringe if he heard my attempt at his guitar solo, but you'll get the idea."

My heart collects in my throat. A song. He wrote another song about me.

It's what he does when he doesn't want to run away from his feelings.

There's the strum of a guitar. It's a pleasant melody, but it stirs up something inside of me. Something uncomfortable. I go to delete the message, but Kara grabs the phone.

"No chance in hell." She climbs on top of the couch to hold the phone over my head.

> It's all over.
> I'm gaga out of my head,
> one of those idiots
> I always made fun of.
>
> Everyone said, "boy can't you see
> that girl is crazy about you."
> Just shook my head.
> "No way, not her, she's even
> as the number two."

His voice is heavy, but there's something sweet about it, too.

> It's all over.
> That flutter in my chest.
> Love, funny word,
> what the hell does it mean?

> Everyone said, "boy can't you see
> that girl is crazy about you."
> Just shook my head
> "No way, not her, she's even
> as the number two."

Air escapes my lungs. It's perfect.

> It's all over.
> I surrender.
> First time I ever have.

"Holy shit." Kara's jaw drops. "I was waiting to show you this." She jumps to her computer and pulls up a gossip site. "In case you never wanted to hear another word about him."

She turns the screen so it's facing me. *Sinful Serenade Singer Gets Hot New Tattoo*. There's a picture of Miles beneath it, shirtless, of course, and right above his chest, opposite *Be Brave, Live*, reads *Megara*.

Holy shit.

I try a deep breath. Nothing is happening. My stomach flip-flops. I'm queasy. He got my name as a tattoo. He got my name as a tattoo. My name. Tattoo.

"There's more." Kara points to the middle of the article.

*When reached for comment, Miles Webb had one of his trademarked cheeky replies.*

*"I made a deal with this friend of mine, that if I ever fell in love with someone, I'd get her name tattooed on my chest. What can I say? I'm a man of my word."*

*We asked how he felt this would affect his reputation for extracur-*

*ricular activities (let's face it—the man is a slut!) he laughed right in our faces, well, right into our cell phones.*

*"I doubt it will be any harder to take home women. I mean, look at me. But I don't care about other women. The only woman I want is Meg. If she won't have me, then I'll be alone. No one else could ever compare to her."*

Kara grabs my shoulders, turning me so we're face-to-face. "You okay? You want me to beat him up and smash every computer that ever saw a fragment of the MP3?"

I shake my head.

"Talk to me, sweetie."

"He loves me."

"Yeah, I'm pretty sure he does," she says.

"He's so… how the hell do I respond to this?"

She smiles. "I have an idea."

## Chapter Fifty-Two

MEGARA

Kara presses her phone to her ear. She paces around the apartment shaking her head. She's totally frantic.

"How are you not freaking out?" she asks.

"It's a lot to take in. I'm not sure how I feel."

She shakes her head and throws her phone onto the couch. "Drew isn't picking up. But they're probably at the house."

"It's almost one a.m."

"And the guy you love sent you a declaration. This is no time to wait!" She grabs her backpack and nearly tears it apart in search of her keys and wallet. "You okay wearing that?"

I look at my finals outfit. It's jeans and a t-shirt, not the thing of romantic declarations. I should throw on a princess dress and heels, something that would look as dramatic as this feels.

"Fuck it, wear that or I'm dressing you. You have five seconds to decide," she says.

"Will it be slutty?"

"Three seconds."

"Okay, dress me. No. It doesn't matter. Let's just go."

"Good thinking." She lunges for her phone, wraps her hand around my wrist, and nearly drags me outside. "I wish you could drive stick. I'm so nervous for you."

My heart thuds against my chest. My head is still swimming. Miles loves me. He trusts me. He respects me. This is everything I want.

"I'm so nervous for me," I say.

She fumbles with the lock. Checks the door twice. Then she drags me to her car.

Kara drives like a maniac. She breezes through yellow lights on her way to the freeway. She's at seventy, eighty, almost ninety.

"I'd rather get there alive," I say.

She slows down, but her fingers are tight around the wheel. She's almost more nervous than I am, but I don't think that's technically possible.

My stomach is tied up in knots. My heart is thumping against my chest like it's the freaking Jaws theme. And my breath—it's technically impossible, but I'm pretty sure I haven't taken a breath since I heard the song.

Kara pulls off the freeway. The Sinful mansion is way up in the Hollywood Hills. It's still another ten minutes to their place. Breathing would go a long way toward arriving alive.

I force myself to inhale, but it only heightens the tingling sensation in my body. The song might not mean he wants me. It might be an apology or an admission that ends in *sorry, but it's over*.

I close my eyes and force myself to exhale. Kara is here. Whatever happens, I'll survive.

But I'd much rather survive with Miles.

We turn onto one of the local streets, and we drive up,

up, up the winding roads into the hills. The lights are on in the house, and Miles's car is in the driveway. His bike is there, too.

He must be here.

Kara parks and jumps out of the car. She's back to bouncing around, ready to knock down anything in her way. She's on my side this time. Thank God. I need the ally.

I climb out of the car. My feet feel wobbly. I'm in sneakers, but I can barely stand. Jelly. My legs are jelly. I press my palm against the car to stay upright.

What if he asks me to get lost? What if I misinterpreted everything?

"Come on." Kara grabs my hand and pulls me up the stone steps.

Somehow, I don't slip. I make it all the way to the oversized front door. Knock. I need to knock. I curl my fingers into a fist and tap it against the door. It barely makes a sound.

"I think I'm going to faint," I whisper.

Kara shakes her head. "You've got this." She presses the doorbell.

*Ding. Dong.* It really does make that sound, like the game we played when we were kids where we'd press the neighbor's doorbell, run away, and watch to see if they came out.

Ding Dong Ditch. And it sounds like a fantastic idea. Run away, never face Miles, never get the crushing news that he doesn't love me.

The door opens. Damn. That means we lose the game. It's Tom, and he's halfway undressed. Jeans. No t-shirt, no shoes. There's giggling in the background. Ah, there's a half-naked woman in the kitchen. His conquest of the day.

Or Miles's conquest of the day.

My heart thuds. If it keeps beating this fast and hard, it's going to burst right out of my chest.

"Jesus, what did he do now?" Tom asks.

Kara sticks her tongue out. She presses the door open. Tom stumbles back. He almost falls on his ass, but somehow manages to recover.

"Come in, please." He rolls his eyes. "Should I call him? I don't even know where to start."

Kara rolls her eyes. "I'm more than happy to storm up to Miles's room and drag him down here."

"Give me a minute," Tom says. He makes some kind of signal to the half-naked woman then turns back to us. His lips purse and he exhales in a dramatic sigh. "He's fucking devastated, you know."

"Just get him," I say.

"You want to tell me what this is about?"

"Meg needs to speak with Miles. Get him or I will," Kara says.

"What do they need to speak about?" Tom folds his arms.

She glares at him like he's the source of all evil in the universe. "They're in love."

Tom raises an eyebrow. He looks at me as if to ask *is this shit true?*

I nod. As far as I know.

He finally drops the pout. "I hope you're right. But, I'm going to do this the old-fashioned way." He pulls out his phone and dials Miles.

There's the faint sound of a ring. A door opens. Footsteps

Miles appears at the top of the stairs. "You can't walk one fucking flight, Tom?" His eyes find mine, and the irritated scowl drops off his face.

He looks nervous. Miles, the rock star sex god, is nervous because of me.

"Meg. Hey." He clutches the banister on his way down the stairs. "Everything okay?"

I open my mouth, but no sounds come out. It's too sticky. Deep breath. "I heard your song."

His lips curl into the tiniest smile. "Yeah?"

"Yeah." I press my fingers against my hips. "That one about me, too?"

He reaches the bottom of the stairs. "I haven't fallen in love with any other girls this year."

My breath catches in my throat. He said... he must mean... he must...

I'm dizzy. My legs are wobbly. "You, um, did you mean what you said?"

"Every word." He takes a step toward me. "Though, technically, I sang them."

"Technically."

Miles sends Tom the evil eye. "A little privacy, maybe?"

"Hell no." He raises his voice. "Drew, Pete, you fuckers here to see this?"

"It's okay," I say. "They can stay."

Miles is five feet away. "I usually write songs to avoid these kinds of declarations."

"You're screwed now. You have an audience and expectations."

He smirks. "If there's anything I know how to do, it's put on a show."

"All I want is the truth."

One more step. He's six inches from me. He brushes my hair behind my ear. "I love you, Meg. I had something perfect right under my nose, and it took me forever to realize it. But I realize it now."

Tom's jaw drops. "YOU FUCKERS ARE MISSING OUT!"

A bedroom door slams and Pete appears at the top of the stairs. He spots Miles. "He's out of his room?"

Miles shakes his head. "They're really ruining the moment."

"No, it's perfect."

He slides his hand around my waist. "I'm not good at this relationship thing, but I want to do it with you."

"You sure?"

"Positive." He pulls me closer. "If you're willing to forgive me for being an utter idiot."

"Yeah." I lean into him. "The biggest idiot."

"I'll take that as a yes." He presses his lips into mine.

All of our other kisses were amazing. All of our other kisses set my body on fire. But this one is on another level. It's like every bit of need in him is pouring into me, like he's prying himself open for me and showing me all the ways he hurts.

The kiss breaks, and I pull back. I stare into his gorgeous eyes. "I love you, too."

And, I swear to God, he melts.

The world is spinning around me. There's clapping. It's Tom, I think. Then it's Kara, and Pete. I look around the room, and Drew is there, too.

They're clapping, but it's not like this is silly. It's like they mean it.

Miles leans a little closer. "Assholes were convinced I'd die miserable and alone."

"Utter assholes."

"I'd say let's give them a free show, but I want you all to myself."

He presses his lips against mine again. It's as sweet as

the first kiss, but it's hotter. It's so hot, I'm pretty sure I'm going to ignite.

"Okay, I think that's my cue," Kara says. "You're taking her home tomorrow."

"Stay," Pete calls out. "We're going to have to blast a movie if we want to hear anything besides Miles screaming in ecstasy." He laughs. "Though, Meg, you're free to make as much noise as you want."

"That's my girlfriend, asshole," Miles says. "If that's okay with you."

My body fills with warmth. "Absolutely."

"You're lucky I'm preoccupied, or I'd kick your ass." Miles leads me up the stairs. "Tom, berate Pete about the loud phone sex."

"Anytime." Tom sends us a salute.

We pass Drew and Pete. My cheeks burn. I mouth thank you, though I'm not sure who I'm thanking. Everyone, I guess.

They're all happy for us.

Pete winks at me. I'm pretty sure Miles sees it, but I don't think he cares.

We're going to be preoccupied for the rest of the night.

# Epilogue

## Megara

That can't be him. It must be a mirage. There's no way Miles is standing in front of the bio building, his hands in the pockets of his leather jacket, his lips curled into a smile.

I must be imagining things.

He's supposed to be in Tokyo. Or was it Osaka? It's hard to remember your boyfriend's schedule when he's a globe-jetting rock star.

His blue eyes fix on me.

That's him.

That's really him.

"You survived your first semester of medical school." Miles slides his arms around me.

His arms are heaven. I grab onto his waist as tightly as I would if I was on the back of his bike. Miles is here. My boyfriend is here. We have the next four weeks to be together before I'm due back for spring semester.

His hand curls around my cheek. "I missed you."

"I missed you more."

He presses his lips to mine.

He tastes so fucking good.

I dig my hands into his leather jacket. It's too slick for me to get a grip so I tug at his soft t-shirt. He's here. He's not in Asia. He's at UCI Medical School, with his arms around me, with his lips against mine.

I slide my hands under his t-shirt and soak in the warmth of his skin. "You're supposed to be in Japan. Didn't you have a show?"

"In Osaka." He pulls me closer. "Encore was fourteen hours ago."

"You flew straight here?"

He slides his hand around my neck. His voice is light, teasing. "You catch on fast."

I flip him off. It only makes my smile wider. At the moment, it doesn't feel like I'm ever going to stop smiling. "Give me a break. I've only slept ten hours in the last week."

He smiles back. "Good thing I'm planning on spending the next two weeks in bed."

I nod and look up at him. I'm nearly six feet tall but Miles is still two inches taller. "I can't believe you're here."

I haven't seen him in a month. Twenty-nine days to be exact. His band, Sinful Serenade, has been on an international tour. This was the first tour where neither one of us could visit.

It's the longest we've been apart.

It's been awful.

Miles spends four or five months a year on the road. I should be used to it by now, but I'm not. Every time he's away, I miss him more than the time before. Every time, he feels farther away.

Every time, the separation is sweeter.

I missed him so much.

## Epilogue

My knees falter as I sink into his body. I'm too tired to move. But it's okay. He's got me.

He pulls me closer. His lips hover over my ear. "How is it none of your classmates recognize me?"

I nestle into his chest. "Do you want me to scream 'Oh My God, are you really Miles Webb? I love that one song you do, *No Way in Hell*.'" I offer my best schoolgirl giggle. "Is it really about falling in love?"

"I want you to scream—" He sucks on my earlobe. "But only the Miles part only once we're alone." His hands go to mine. "You have any energy left?"

"Enough for a proper reunion."

He laughs. "I'm not sure you do." He squeezes me one more time then he steps back. He nods *follow me*.

I take a shaky step. Miles has a point. I can barely walk. I'm not sure I have the energy to fuck his brains out the way I want to.

His expression is a mix of amused and concerned. "I'm taking you somewhere. We can go to bed after that."

"Which kind of to bed?"

Miles laughs. His piercing blue eyes shine in the sunlight. "The kind where you come until you can't take it anymore."

---

I ASPIRE TO MAKE CONVERSATION BUT MY LIDS ARE heavy. I close my eyes, rest my head against the window, and drift in and out of sleep.

Miles squeezes my hand. "You're exhausted, aren't you?"

I nod.

"Was thinking about taking you to a hotel in Beverly Hills and fucking you against the wall."

"You were not. You're teasing."

"I was *thinking* about it." He smiles. "Wasn't a plan yet, but it occupied a lot of space in my thoughts."

"It's been twenty-nine days."

"I've been counting."

"I think you're as responsible for my hand cramps as finals are."

He laughs. "For once, I beat school."

"Miles, it's been twenty-nine days."

"It has."

"And we aren't having sex right now."

"Better change that soon." He squeezes my hand.

I squeeze back. He rubs the space between my thumb and my pointer finger with his thumb. It's sweet, intimate. He's really here. We're really in the same space together.

And I'm really exhausted.

My hands go to the zipper of my hoodie. I have a surprise for him, but I'm terrified to reveal it. This is serious, forever, the next level of commitment.

It's been a year, but we haven't talked much about forever. A while back, he asked about getting married. I said I wanted to wait until I was done with my first year of medical school, and that was it. We haven't talked about anything since.

We haven't even discussed getting a place together. I stay with my parents during the week—they live twenty minutes from campus—and with Miles on the weekends—his place is nearly two hours from school, depending on the traffic.

The zipper is cool against my skin. I pull it down an inch but I can't will myself to pull it down anymore.

Soon. I need to do it the first chance I get. Before the sex. I don't want him getting derailed when we finally get out of our clothes.

# Epilogue

It's been way too long.

Miles changes lanes and exits the freeway. He pulls onto a familiar street. We've been here before. Together.

Oh.

There's a cemetery on our left—the cemetery where his uncle is buried.

It's a strange choice for a celebration, but it's perfect.

Miles parks and helps me out of the car. He slides one arm around my waist.

His eyes go to the ground. Is he actually bashful? I'm not sure I've ever seen him bashful before.

"You don't have to explain," I say.

"Sure you don't want a celebration with champagne on the beach?" He leads me through the wrought iron gates.

"Neither one of us drinks."

"Sparkling apple cider."

"I don't like sparkling apple cider."

"What if I'm licking it off your tits?"

"Then you're the one drinking it."

He laughs and squeezes my hand.

The shining sun casts a glow over the vivid green grass. The world is alive today. Except for the mild chill in the air, there're no signs of winter here. The sky is bright blue and free of clouds. The air is somewhere between crisp and warm.

I follow Miles to his uncle's grave. *Damon Webb. Father. Uncle. Friend.*

Miles's eyes fix on mine. "You remember what I said about Damon?"

"How he'd sit you down and tell you to stop running from your feelings?"

"Yeah. I always have a lot of time to think when we're on the road. That's how it started, me taking drugs. I needed a way to shut out my thoughts." He runs his fingers through my hair.

"I know." I lean into his touch. "Everyone runs sometimes."

"You don't. You never did."

"Yes, I did. Just used school instead of drugs." I stare into his clear blue eyes. I don't want to run from my feelings either. I'm scared of the constant separation, but I love Miles more than anything. I want forever with him.

I want him to see the evidence of our forever.

Here goes nothing. I press my lips together. "I have to show you something."

"Let me go first." He presses his palm into my lower back. "Okay?"

I nod.

"This tour, it felt like we were traveling twenty hours a day. I had a lot of time to myself. Mostly, I thought about you. About us having a life together. About how much brighter my life is than it was before I met you. Used to be the only thing that soothed me was writing a song or stepping on stage. But you…" He stares back at me. "I know I promised to wait until you finished your first year of med school, but I have to do this now. I have to do it here." Miles lowers himself onto his knee.

He… he's really doing this.

He pulls a ring box from his jeans and flips it open. "Megara Smart, will you marry me?"

## Miles

Meg's brown eyes go wide. Her fingers go to her soft, pink lips. She stares at me like she's in shock.

Usually, I know how to work an audience, but right now I'm too nervous to have a clue.

Is that *oh my God yes* or *oh hell no*? I know she loves me, but she's young. School comes first. It should. I love how ambitious she is.

None of that makes waiting easier. I've done a lot in my life, had just about everything a guy could want. Nothing—not platinum albums, or Grammys, or ten thousand fans screaming my name—compares to Meg.

Her eyes soften. Surprise fades to joy. Her lip corners turn upward. "You're asking in front of your uncle."

I swallow hard. Fuck. I can't remember the last time I was speechless. A nod is all I can manage.

"That's sweet." Her smile spreads to her ears.

"He would have loved you."

"Really?"

"Really." He would have adored her. Especially the way

she gives me shit. And the way she doesn't take my shit. And those gorgeous brown eyes of hers. That vibrant smile. The way she laughs with her entire body.

"Why?" she asks.

Where the hell do I start? "You make me better. Stronger."

"You have it backward. You make *me* better. You make *me* stronger."

My smile widens. Still, my stomach and chest are floating. Fucking nerves. Stage fright has nothing on marriage proposals.

"You're supposed to answer," I tease. "But I am willing to kneel here all afternoon."

"You can't kneel here all afternoon. I need you on your knees later."

I melt. I'm asking her to marry me and she's replying with a sex joke.

She's perfect.

Her voice drops to a whisper. "Yes. Of course."

She's smiling. Her brown eyes are bright.

She's not just happy. She's ecstatic.

My entire body goes light I slide the ring onto her finger.

"Is this really happening?" She stares at the ring. Her eyes fill with wonder then they're back on me. "It's huge."

"We both know you can take huge."

She laughs as she traces the outline of the stone.

I want to feel every ounce of her joy. I wrap my arms around her and pull her into a deep kiss.

"Miles," she murmurs. "Your Uncle will see…"

Her hands go to my hair. She pulls me closer. Her lips part to make way for my tongue.

I know her body, know how to make her needy. I drag my fingertips up her thigh until she's groaning into

## Epilogue

my mouth. She arches her body into mine, spurring me on.

She sighs as she pulls back. "Not in front of Damon."

"Why not?"

"Miles!" she squeals. "I don't want him to think I'm a tramp."

"He wasn't eighty-five, princess. He didn't think anybody was a tramp."

She flips me off playfully then looks at the tombstone. "I love your nephew—"

"He adopted me."

She nods. "I love your son more than anything. I'm sorry we couldn't meet. I'll try to take good care of him."

I push myself to my feet and slide my arms around her.

Relief floods my limbs. I fucking missed her.

Meg presses her lips against mine with a hungry kiss. We have a lot of time to make up for, but she's clearly exhausted. I can't fuck her the way she deserves to be fucked. Hell, it's not just what she wants. I haven't gone twenty-nine days without sex since I started having sex.

I need to be deep inside her. I need her nails raking across my back, her limbs shaking as she comes.

I need her coming again and again.

My lips press together. I fucking miss the taste of her. Especially the way her thighs press against my cheeks as she comes on my tongue.

Now to find a spot private enough I can peel her jeans to her feet, slide between her legs, and lick her until she's screaming my name.

"I have to show you something," she murmurs. Her fingers dig into my shoulders.

She's close to falling asleep in my arms. This will have to wait until we're in a proper bed. I'm not about to go easy on her. Not for anything.

"Miles." Her fingers find the bare skin of my chest. She pulls my t-shirt aside and traces the lines of my tattoo.

Her lips part with a sigh of desire. A lot of women have ogled me, but none do it the way Meg does, with this mix of need, lust, love, and appreciation.

No one knows me the way she does. Damon is the only other person who ever saw me, all of me.

She takes a half-step backward.

Her eyes fill with vulnerability. Even now, after a year, it's rare she has her guard this low.

Slowly, she pulls the zipper of her hoodie to her waist. Her hands go to her chest, covering her cleavage.

Huh? Meg isn't shy about her breasts. She knows how much I appreciate them. In fact… there's no one in the parking lot. Should take her there and suck on her nipples until she's purring my name.

Her eyes turn down. Her cheeks flush.

She's nervous.

"I… I did this last weekend." Her cheeks turn even more red. "Damn. This is scary. How do you strip on stage every night?"

"I know my strong suit."

She smiles, but it's quickly replaced by a nervous look. Slowly, she peels one hand off her chest. The other goes to the strap of her tank top and pulls it aside.

My exhale sucks up every drop of breath in my body.

There's ink on her chest. Three little words: *Be Brave, Love*.

The song I wrote for her, to tell her I loved her.

The song she begged me not to write.

A mirror of the tattoo I got for my uncle. Same place on her chest. Same font.

"I don't know that I've ever seen you speechless." Her voice lifts until it's confident. "I should get more tattoos."

## Epilogue

My hand goes to her skin. I trace the lines with my fingers. My words are on her body. This connection between us is on her body.

It's forever.

The ink curves over the swell of her breast. It's outside her bra. It will be on display whenever she wears something low-cut.

I'll see it every time I get her naked.

I need her naked immediately.

"Let's go." I slide my hands to her waist. Again, I pull her body into mine. "I need to be inside you."

She laughs. "I'm holding the cards."

"You're always holding the cards."

She shakes her head. "No. I'm not. But right now, I have you exactly where I want you." She slides her hand over the neck-line of my t-shirt. "It's intoxicating. Is this why you're obnoxious twenty-four seven?"

Blood is quickly fleeing my brain. Her hands on my skin do nothing to help the situation.

We're teasing. God knows I love teasing her. "You don't find me charming?"

"You are charming." She smiles. "You're charming and you're at my mercy."

"I'll rip off your clothes right here."

"Not in front of your uncle!"

"In the car."

"Let me see yours again." She tugs at my t-shirt.

I pull the garment low enough she can see every tattoo on my chest. Her fingers go to her name—*Megara* in thick black letters—then they're on the quote on my other pec. *Be Brave, Live.*

"People are going to think you're the world's biggest Sinful Serenade fan," I tease.

"I am." She looks up at me. "There's no one in the world who appreciates your mouth more than I do."

Damn, she's reveling in having the upper hand. Can't complain. She looks just as adorable drunk with power as she does blushing.

This is going to be a miserable drive. But it will be worth it. My place is forty minutes without traffic. Drew and Kara's place is closer. Twenty minutes. But it's only useful if they're out.

Damn, it's hard to concentrate with all my blood rushing to my cock. I could swear Drew said something about flying straight to San Francisco to visit with her family. But maybe that was Pete flying to New York to see Jess's family.

Meg laughs with glee. "You're at my mercy."

I stare into her brown eyes. "Was it the marriage proposal that gave it away?"

She bites her lip. "That helped."

Okay. Need enough blood in my brain to think of where I'm going to rip off her panties.

I take her hand and change the subject. "You get that ink by yourself?"

She smiles. "You won't believe me."

"Try me."

"Mom came with me."

"Susan went with you?"

"You have to call her Mom if we're getting married. She'll die of happiness." Meg bites her lip. Her eyes bore into mine. "Do you like it?"

"I fucking love it." I plant a hard kiss on her lips. I'm tempted to pin her to the car right here. I need to show her how much I love the tattoo. How much I love every inch of her. "Now get in the car so I can have my way with you."

# Epilogue

---

Three minutes on the road and I give up on getting to a house. Any house.

I need Meg naked immediately. I need her screaming my name as she comes.

I pull into the nearest hotel. It's a budget chain. Not as high class as the night of our engagement deserves, but I can't say I give a fuck about the setting at the moment.

Meg clears her throat. She's attempting confident and aloof, but with the way she's pressing her knees together and biting her lip, I know she's as desperate as I am.

Fuck, I bet she's wet.

She's always fucking wet.

It takes much too long to check in. Meg perks up as we take the stairs to our room. Her hand slides under my leather jacket. Then under my t-shirt.

Damn, I love the way her hand feels against my skin.

I unlock the door and push it open. Might as well make a gesture. I scoop her into my arms and carry her over the threshold.

She laughs with glee. "Miles! If you break my back, I'm not marrying you."

"Fair enough." I kick the door closed and set her on the bed.

"You know I'm keeping my name," she says.

I smile. "You know I'm about to rip off your jeans and panties and lick you until you're screaming *my* name."

Her lips part with a sigh of pleasure. She still attempts to stay in control. "I did know that."

"Good. Unbutton your jeans." I sit between her legs and take off her socks and shoes.

She relaxes into the bed, squeezing her toes and arching her back.

Fuck, I almost forgot how responsive she is. It's been a while but there's no excuse forgetting anything about the woman I love.

I roll her jeans to her knees. "You should keep your name."

"Really?"

"Yeah. It will mean the world to your mom."

"Oh." She shifts her legs to help me. "Carry on then."

"Take off the top and the bra."

She does. I pull her jeans to her ankles.

I soak in the sight of her body—her long legs, the gentle curves of her hips, waist, chest.

It's still there.

*Be Brave, Love.*

I can't wait any longer. I pin her to the bed.

She squirms, arching her back and rubbing her crotch against mine.

"Too many clothes," she murmurs.

Way too many.

I pull my t-shirt over my head and toss it aside.

I kiss her hard.

She groans into my mouth as she squirms. My focus shifts lower. My cock will get what it wants soon.

This first.

I kiss my way down her neck. Then I'm at her chest. I take one of her nipples into my mouth and suck gently.

"Miles," she groans. Her hands go to my hair. She tugs at it as she rocks her hips against me.

I suck harder. Until her groans get low and desperate. When I'm convinced she can't take it anymore, I do the same to her other nipple.

My hand slides down her torso. It finds her panties and pushes them aside.

I place my palm against her.

## Epilogue

Fuck. She's wet.

I trace the lines of her tattoo with my tongue then kiss my way down her stomach.

She squirms with anticipation. Her sighs get louder. Her hands go the comforter. She squeezes it so tightly her knuckles go white.

"Miles," she breathes. "Please."

The need in her voice sends the last available hint of blood to my cock.

I pull her panties to her feet. Under normal circumstances, I'd tease her a little longer. Right now, I need her taste on my tongue and her moans in my ears.

I press my lips against her inner thigh. She gasps, her back arching.

I kiss my way up her thigh.

She smells fucking good. I pin her legs to the bed. She sighs, impatient and needy.

She's exactly where I want her.

Slowly, I slide my tongue over her clit. She tastes like home. And she's already filling the room with her groans, already digging her fingers into the back of my head, already bucking against my lips.

Fuck, I love being between her legs. Best place in the whole fucking world.

I lick her up and down, taking my time tasting and teasing every inch.

Her knees fight my hands. Her hips buck. Her groans fill the room.

My fingers dig into her soft skin as I make my way back to her clit. I play with my speed and pressure until her thighs are shaking with pleasure.

I hold her in place so I can work my magic.

She bucks against me, moving her cunt against my lips like I'm her personal sex toy.

My tongue works harder, faster. I lick her until her knees are pressed against my ears. Until she's screaming my name.

There.

Her hands dig into my shoulders as she comes. She shakes, all the muscles in her body tensing. Then everything goes slack.

Her legs fall open. Her back relaxes as she collapses into the bed. One arm falls at her side. The other stays on me.

Her touch is soft as she drags her fingertips to the back of my neck.

She looks down at me with pleading eyes.

She doesn't have to ask. I need inside her. Need her soft folds enveloping my cock.

I shimmy out of my jeans and boxers and reposition our bodies so I'm on top of her.

She tattooed her body for me.

She's going to be my wife.

The intimacy of it overwhelms me.

My hands go to her hips. I pull her body onto mine. My cock strains against her cunt. Already, she feels fucking good.

I need to watch the pleasure spread over her expression as I fill her.

I need our eyes locked as our bodies join.

For a moment, I take in the gorgeous mix of desire and satisfaction in her expression. Her cheeks are flushed. Her lips are pursed.

Her hands slide around my neck. They settle on the back of my head.

She pulls me into a deep kiss.

Need and affection pour from her lips to mine.

# Epilogue

I dig my fingertips into her hips as I slide inside her. One delicious inch at a time, I fill her.

Damn, she feels good. Wet, warm, silky smooth.

I lower my body onto hers, pulling her closer as I thrust deeper. Meg keeps her hands pressed against the back of my head. She pulls me into another kiss. It's still deep. Still hungry.

Thoughts slip away. I'm only aware of the sensations in my body. Her soft lips. Her aggressive tongue. Her hips shifting to push me deeper.

My body takes over. It needs more. Needs harder. Needs every inch of her.

She rocks her hips as I thrust into her. We're working together to bring our bodies closer. To bring each other to orgasm.

"Mm-hmm," I groan. My nails dig into her skin.

She breaks free of our kiss to groan. Her eyes fix on mine for a moment then her lids press together.

Her lips part with a sigh. She's almost there. I know how to get her there.

I guide her hips so I can drive deeper. She groans.

Then it's her hands on my chest. Her nails digging into my skin. Her hips arching.

She groans. "Miles."

Her thighs squeeze against my hips.

And she's there. Her cunt pulses around my cock, pulling me closer, inviting me deeper.

I shift my hips to drive into her.

Fuck. She feels good.

My lips go to her neck. Her shoulder. I sink my teeth into her skin as an orgasm takes over.

With my next thrust, I come. She groans. One hand goes to my ass, holding me close as I fill her.

I linger inside her for a moment. Then I shift onto my side and pull her body into mine.

"Promise we'll never be apart that long again," she murmurs.

"I can't promise that." I pull her closer. "But I promise I'll do whatever it takes to make this work. Always."

---

**Want More Sinful Serenade?**

Sign up for the Crystal Kaswell mailing list to get a bonus scene from Just a Taste. You'll also get exclusive teasers and news on new releases and sales.

Turn the page for an excerpt from *Strum Your Heart Out*, Drew and Kara's story, available now.

### *Sinful Serenade*
*Sing Your Heart Out* - Miles
*Strum Your Heart Out* - Drew
*Rock Your Heart Out* - Tom
*Play Your Heart Out* - Pete
*Sinful Ever After* – series sequel

## Strum Your Heart Out

SPECIAL PREVIEW

[Buy *Strum Your Heart Out* Now](#)

A buxom fan saunters in my direction. But she's not interested in me. I am invisible to her.

Her eyes are on Drew. She smiles. She shoves her hand in his face like I'm not here. "Oh my gosh. You must be Drew Denton. I'm such a big fan."

He shakes her hand, no signs of interest on his face. "I am."

She drags her fake red fingernails over Drew's forearm and thrusts her chest at him. "I love Sinful Serenade," she slurs. "You're sooooo good with your hands."

The worst thing about having a rock star guitarist for a best friend is hearing that line over and over and over.

Drew's lips curl into a smile. A smug expression creeps onto his face. "That's what I'm told."

And there's the second worst thing—hearing him give that same flirty response to every fan who is too rude to acknowledge the girl sitting next to him. Is it that obvious we're just friends or is she too desperate to care?

"Do you think... oh, gosh. Could you sign my, um..." She giggles. "My chest?"

His eyes dart to said chest. It's hard to blame him when her top is cut down to her belly button. No judgment. I've worn far sluttier things. Hell, my current getup could go toe to toe with this girl's in a *who is showing the most boob* competition.

A girl has to do what she can to get what she wants.

Apparently, this girl wants Drew's attention on her cans.

It's working. His eyes are wide. His mouth is open. He's staring like he's thinking about burying his face between her boobs.

Not that it bothers me or anything. Not like I want him to look at me that way. Not anything like that.

I adjust my bustier top for maximum cleavage potential and push myself up from my seat. Drew looks at me for a second, then his attention goes right back to the fangirl.

She drags those red fingernails up his biceps. "How do you stay so... fit on tour?"

He smiles. "On the floor."

She gasps like she's not at all familiar with the concept of push-ups. He smiles, all cocky and smug and totally cool.

He never flirts like this.

Never.

It shouldn't bother me. He's my friend and he can flirt with anyone he wants.

Doesn't mean I have to watch it.

I make my way to the dance floor, through the horde of twenty-something beautiful people here for the scene and not the music.

It's a pulsating, throbbing, electronic thing. Perfect. I step onto the vinyl. Eyes closed. Arms over my head. I shift my hips back and forth. No fancy moves. Just instinct.

The fangirl's hyena laugh cuts through the room. I must be imagining things. There's no way she's louder than the music.

Drew is still talking to her. Not so much flirting but certainly staring at her cans.

This tension builds in between my shoulder blades. It's all wrong. My body is loose and free when I dance. Tension is not part of the equation. And Drew is my friend. He's flirting with a floozy. So what? He's a rock star. He probably flirts with lots of floozies.

He probably fucks them too.

My nostrils flare. I shake my head and press my eyelids together. No. I refuse to feel this right now. I refuse to feel anything except the music.

I throw myself into dancing. The world melts away, one piece at a time. The rest of the club. The hyena laugh. Drew's wide-eyed, lust-filled smile as the fangirl mauls him.

It's not even on my mind.

I move closer to the speakers. They drown out every other thought inside my brain. I'm only a vessel for the music. My hips move of their own accord. My chest shifts. My arms sway.

I'm free.

And then there are hands on my hips. Strong hands. A guy's hands. It's a normal part of clubbing. Usually one I enjoy.

But this feels off. I take a step forward to break free of the hands, so it's nothing but *me* and the music. Better. That tension between my shoulder blades relaxes. I drift into bliss...

The damn hands are back! I turn to face this guy. He's

tall. Broad. He looks like a TV actor—handsome but not out-of-this-world hot. Any other night, I'd welcome him as a dance partner.

I throw my arms above my head and match his movements. He's a good dancer—perfectly in time with the rhythm. It's not all together awful.

He takes a step toward me, so he's pressed up against me. Those hands go to my hips again. No more bliss. I'm utterly on edge, tense and strained in all the wrong places.

"Excuse me." I make my way to the bar, some area free of guys with too few manners to ask permission.

The guy follows me. "Can I buy you a drink?"

"No thank you."

"Come on. It will be fun." He grabs my wrist. The left. Right above my silver watch.

I pull my hand into my chest. Manners be damned, next time he does that, I'm slapping him.

I offer my most polite smile and shake my head. "No thank you. I'm here with someone."

"Who?"

Fine. I hate using this line, but it's the only thing that works on guys like this. "My boyfriend."

The guy takes a long, hard look at me. At my cleavage, mostly. That awkward, awful tension builds between my shoulder blades again.

What the hell? This is supposed to feel good. A hot guy is checking me out. A hot guy wants to press his body up against mine in time with the music.

"Your boyfriend lets you go out like that?" he asks.

"Believe it or not, I have this funny thing called free will." I step backward. "And I don't let guys tell me what to wear."

"Your boyfriend sounds like a pussy."

"I'll let him know your feelings." Okay. The bar thing

isn't working. Time for the nuclear option. I make my way to the women's restroom.

The guy follows. "I only want to talk."

"And I don't."

I take a quick step, but, even with my heels, I've got short legs and this guy is all kinds of tall. He's faster than I am.

He grabs my wrist. The right. I shake it off. No slapping necessary. Yet.

"You don't have to be so rude," he says.

Obviously, I do, because he's not taking the hint. I turn so I'm facing the asshole. Anger flares in my gut. I manage to hold my tongue. There are merits to telling this guy what he can do with that grabby hand, but it seems silly to cause a scene. It's easier to slip away with a careful excuse. No conflict necessary.

"Excuse me, ladies' room," I say.

He reaches for me again. Left wrist this time. Okay, that's it. I pull my hand free and go to slap him.

Someone stops me. His hand closes around my tricep. There's something right about it. Something magical.

It's Drew. Drew's hand is tight around my arm. Drew is touching me.

He looks at the asshole guy. "Can I help you?"

The guy looks at me with disbelief. "This is your boyfriend?"

I throw Drew a *please play along* look. "Yes. And we're very busy tonight."

"Is this guy bothering you?" Drew asks.

"It's fine."

"It doesn't look fine." Drew's eyes narrow. He stares down the guy. "You followed her across the dance floor."

He was watching me?

"We were having a conversation," the guy says.

"You grabbed her. Do it again and it will be the last time you ever touch anyone or anything beautiful," Drew says.

The guy holds Drew's stare. Trying out some kind of intimidation and failing miserably. I almost feel bad for him. Idiot has no clue what he's in for.

The guy takes a step back. He mutters under his breath. "She's not even that hot."

"We both know that's not true." Drew slides his hand around my waist.

But the guy is still staring at us.

I turn to Drew. I slide my arm around his neck to sell the whole *we're clearly a couple* thing.

But the guy is still staring at me.

Drew stares back at him. "Either you leave in the next thirty seconds or we take this outside."

It does nothing to scare the guy off.

I grab Drew's arm and squeeze as hard as I can. No way I'm going to be responsible for the kind of fight that will get all three of us kicked out of the club.

Drew turns back to me. He takes my arm and places it around his shoulders. It's like he's promising this won't get out of hand.

His eyes find mine. He mouths, *You trust me?*

I nod. Yes. Of course.

His palm pressed into my lower back, pushing my body into his. He leans closer. His eyes close.

Mine do the same. Pure reflex. I rise to my tiptoes.

His lips brush against mine. A quick kiss to start. Then it's more. He sucks on my lower lip. He digs his other hand into my hair.

My heart picks up until it's going so fast I can't keep track. I'm aware of every inch of my body. The light feeling in my chest and stomach. The strain of my calves. The flutter building between my legs.

This is why I dance.

Drew releases me. He steps back and looks as if to check that the coast is clear. His demeanor shifts. No longer my fake boyfriend. Just my best friend. "You okay, Kara?"

"Yeah."

His arms goes back to his sides. His body moves away from mine. My heart is still racing. My chest is still light. I'm still acutely aware of every place that stretches, of every flutter or rush or buzz of electricity.

Drew kissed me.

For show, but still.

Drew kissed me and my entire body is still in overdrive.

Drew. Kissed. Me.

And, God I want him to kiss me again.

[Buy *Strum Your Heart Out* Now](#)

## Stay In Touch

Thank you for reading *Just a Taste*. I hope you loved Miles and Megara's story as much as I did.

If you enjoyed this novel, please help other readers find it by leaving an honest review on Amazon or Goodreads.

Want news about new releases and sales before anyone else? How about exclusive sneak peeks and bonus scenes? Sign up for the Crystal Kaswell mailing list.

Want to talk books? I love hearing from my readers. You can find me on Facebook or join my Facebook group. You can also follow me on Instagram and Twitter.

You can find more of my books here.

## Author's Note

Working on Miles's book has been bittersweet. I was expecting a fun foray into my favorite book. After all, *Sing Your Heart Out* was the first book I loved that other people loved too (I actually wrote it before *Dirty Deal/The Billionaire's Deal*, if you've been with me long enough to remember that TBD came out before SYHO did).

Don't get me wrong, I love *Dirty Deal*--a lot--but I was thinking strategically with it. With Miles, I put some genre stuff in place (he's a bad boy, so he should have a motorcycle, right?), but I mostly followed my heart... and my obsession with a lyricist who shall not be named. Okay, he's been named before and will be named again. But, much like Miles, I prefer to keep an air of mystery. Cheeky answers leave more to the imagination. And isn't reading all about the power of imagination?

Miles isn't based on the lyricist I loved madly back in high school (and still kinda love today, much to my chagrin), but Meg's relationship with him was. The whole push/pull, cheeky one-liners/confessions of deep hurt, pushing me away then letting me in... totally based on my relationship with the guy. Why did he act like such a dick then spill his guts in songs? Why wouldn't he let me in!?!?!?!

I hate to admit it, but I'm not sure I'd have a career without the guy. I don't think I'd understand romance heroes without him. I certainly wouldn't get the whole "book boyfriend" thing. (I don't really want romance heroes to be *my* boyfriend. I want them to get with the heroine! But this guy... oh yeah... I wanted everything in his heart) I wouldn't understand the appeal of the hot and cold, the broken bad boy, the desperate desire to be the stitches that hold someone together.

It's been wild, stepping into Miles's head, actually getting the chance to be my crush. Yes, I always wanted him, but I wanted his respect as an artist as much as I wanted his admiration as a lover. I wanted to be him as much as I wanted to be with him. When I wrote all those songs for *Sing Your Heart Out*, I felt like I had that. I was the beautiful broken boy with the beautiful broken heart.

And now... that's basically my job. To craft beautiful broken boys with beautiful broken hearts and make everyone fall in love with me. Sure, it's not the way I envisioned it back then. (It was supposed to be *my* beautiful broken heart, not some fictional guy's). And I could say A LOT about the gender roles in romance and how men are allowed to be effed up in ways women are not. I push back against that as much as I can, but the reception is not always what I hoped.

But, I'm not 17 anymore. I don't want the kind of turmoil that inspires powerful lyrics. I still want people to understand me, respect me, admire me, love my broken parts---

But I no longer want that to happen publicly.

This guy... he's still there, writing songs. But they aren't really the same. They're more careful, more crafted, more

## Author's Note

loud pop music. Don't get me wrong. I like pop music from time to time, but it's not the same. And as much as I wish he'd write another versions of THAT ALBUM, the one that convinced me someone out there understood my pain, I get it. I get how hard it is to put pieces of yourself in your work, to watch people miss the point or reject it. It doesn't always feel worth it.

And, sometimes, even when you mean the world to someone... you have no way of knowing. This guy certainly doesn't know the impact he's had on my life. I owe my career to him. And several of my adult friendships. My high school BFF is the one who introduced me to obsessing over musicians, including this one in particular. But that relationship ended in flames, the way many young relationships do. We were both struggling to adjust to college, 3,000 miles apart, asking too much of each other. It was the kind of thing that happens a lot when you're 18 and overwhelmed.

We got back in touch a few years ago, but our lives had gone in different directions. Predictable directions (she was a bio maven back in high school; now she's a doctor. I was, well, like this--as in a music and sex obsessed writer who wanted to show people how beautiful and fragile relationships are-- but younger back in high school. Now I write romance novels where broken people help each other heal), but different ones still. We didn't have anything in common anymore. She didn't even listen to that band anymore (or at least that's what she told me).

A few years ago, I made a really close friend who shared my obsession. But, recently, that relationship fell apart too. It was less dramatic end, two adults saying "I guess this won't work out," not two teenagers screaming I hate you into their phones. But that didn't make it hurt

## Author's Note

less. That did make it easier to see all these silly thoughts I expected to share and keep them to myself.

I wish I had a twist for this letter, a happy ending where everything was better than ever, but I don't. There's a loss in my life. It's not a big loss compared to what Meg or Miles went through, but it's there, and it sucks. Writing helps. And it hurts sometimes too.

But it's still been amazing amazing diving into Miles's book. Even though it comes with a little more baggage than I expected. In a way, that works, since Miles is all baggage. It's been especially amazing writing scenes with the whole band together. I love all my guys, but the men of Sinful Serenade will always be my favorite. *Sing Your Heart Out* will always be my favorite book.

There's nothing like the first time something clicks. And these guys were my first. By the time I finished this series, I knew I wanted to write stuff like this for my entire career. Or at least a really long time.

It was amazing revisiting. I hope you enjoy it as much as I did.

If you loved getting into Miles's head and you want more, please let me know (in a review, on social media, in an email), then let all your friends know. Let's get the entire world talking about and falling in love with Miles. And I want an excuse to write books for Drew, Tom, and Pete too.

If you're new to this series, please check out [Drew](), [Tom](), and [Pete's]() stories in the rest of the Sinful Serenade books.

## Acknowledgements

My first thanks goes to my husband, for his support when I'm lost in bookland and when I desperately need a tech issue fixed, yesterday.

The second goes to my father, for insisting I go to the best film school in the country, everything else be damned.

A big shout out to all my beta readers, especially Imma and Tina. I cannot count the number of ledges you talked me down from.

Thanks so much to my ARC team, my street team, the amazing women in Crystal Kaswell's Groupies and to the awesome team who made this book possible, my assistant Gemma, my editor Marla, the amazing cover designer Najla Qamber, and equally amazing teaser designer Gel at Tempting Illustrations.

As always, my biggest thanks goes to my readers. Thank you for picking up *Just a Taste*. I hope you'll be back for the next one.

## Also by Crystal Kaswell

### *Sinful Serenade*

*Sing Your Heart Out* - Miles

*Strum Your Heart Out* - Drew

*Rock Your Heart Out* - Tom

*Play Your Heart Out* - Pete

*Sinful Ever After* – series sequel

### *Dangerous Noise*

*Dangerous Kiss* - Ethan

*Dangerous Crush* – Kit

*Dangerous Rock* – Joel

*Dangerous Fling* – Mal

*Dangerous Encore* - series sequel

### *Inked Hearts*

*Tempting* - Brendon

*Hooking Up* - Walker

*Pretend You're Mine* - Ryan

*Hating You, Loving You* - Dean

*Breaking the Rules* - Hunter

*Losing It* - Wes

*Accidental Husband* - Griffin

*The Baby Bargain* - Chase

### *Inked Love*

*The Best Friend Bargain* - Forest — coming in 2019

---

### *Standalones*

*Broken* - Trent & Delilah

*Come Undone* - A Love Triangle

### *Dirty Rich*

*Dirty Deal* - Blake

*Dirty Boss* - Nick

Sign up for the Crystal Kaswell mailing list

Made in the USA
Monee, IL
14 August 2022